THE
AFTERTHOUGHTS

Rene Fenner

ISBN: 978-1-7364262-0-3
ISBN: 978-1-7364262-1-0

Cover design by: Nisbey
Printed in the United States of America

For Mom and Dad. I would be nothing without you.
Sorry for cussing.

CONTENTS

THE AFTERTHOUGHTS

CHAPTER 1

The Wolves choose when we die. Our city is well aware of this fact, but the rest of the country is struggling to accept it.

"The government brainwashed civilians to become terrorists!"

I scoff at the latest conspiracy theory to dominate social media, viewing the short news clip as I stroll down the hallway at Parkhill Hospital.

"Saw it with my own eyes," the video continues. "People with electrodes on their heads, chanting gibberish!"

There's a shrill cry as I approach the ER. Then, a crash. I turn off my phone, run toward the noise. Nurse's instinct tells me this is more commotion than the usual patient high on crack.

The automatic doors open to the unit's back entrance. Five surgeons dash through a hallway toward the exit in a distinct formation. One surgeon holds a blood-soaked instrument—a three-sided knife, hollow in the middle, with edges inside and out sharp enough to slice through metal. I've never seen one up close: A Triangle Blade.

It's the terrorists.

"Wolves!" I yell. A 'surgeon' spins around. Hidden under the scrubs, surgical cap, and face shield is the infamous black mask with white lines around the eyes and mouth, resembling a wolf—the uniform that earned the terrorists their name.

A paramedic in a Houston Fire Department t-shirt darts in front of me. I recognize Brandon from the Day of the Dead tattoo sleeve on his left arm.

"No!" I grab the back of his shirt and use all my weight to stop him. "Do you have a death wish? They'll kill you if you get in their way, Brandon. You know that."

Breathing hard, we watch security guards cower and scramble out of the Wolves' way, clearing a path for their escape. They vanish through the door. Once the Wolves are in the clear after killing their target, they scatter and disappear.

Brandon notices something behind me. "The patient."

A man is hoisted from an EMS gurney to an ER stretcher. The stab wound to his abdomen is deep enough to have severed his aorta. The blood dripping from a forehead laceration is reminiscent of the one on my dad when they pulled him out of the debris after the first attack by the Wolves.

My co-workers prepare for a massive blood transfusion. It's clear, though, the victim has lost more blood than can be replaced. He won't survive. Doctors and nurses hover around him, their shoes soaked in crimson.

"Any suggestions?" the attending physician asks. No one answers. "Time of death 14:02."

Brandon runs a hand through his hair, pulling at it in frustration. He shoots a deadly scowl at me, then storms out the door and into the ambulance bay. He knows I'm right behind him because when he's far enough away from the doors, he whips around to yell without anyone else hearing. We've perfected this method of fighting over the years.

"Why'd you stop me, Resi? I could have caught up to them."

"And what? Take them on, five against one with nothing but your *manly* fists? Who do you think you are, B?"

He presses his lips into a thin line. He has no retort, so there's a clear opening to lay the guilt-trip on thick.

"What am I supposed to tell Sarah if you get yourself killed? She doesn't deserve to lose another parent."

Brandon's features soften. He gives me a *that's not fair* glare, but I refuse to give into it. I step toward him. "And I don't deserve to lose someone else either."

Got him. He flops onto the curb, head hanging between his broad shoulders. Anger still radiates from him, and his skin seems darker than usual, like he's been in the sun.

I sit next to him. My shoe grates a pebble against concrete. I kick it and watch it land on a red line reserving the area for ambulance parking. "Did you know he was the Wolves' target?"

Brandon bobs his head up and down. "Yeah. No one else around him was injured. We called ahead. The hospital had plenty of notice to call for military reinforcement and get security set up. *Security*," he spits. "They're a joke. What's the point if they won't protect the victims? They didn't even *try* to stop them."

No one has ever killed, or even incapacitated, a Wolf. They seem indestructible. We don't know who they are, where they came from, or why they attack.

But we've noticed that, as long as someone else is their target, you'll stay alive if you keep your distance. *That's* why the security guards didn't interfere. Soldiers are stationed everywhere in anticipation of attacks, but their presence hasn't made much of a difference. Brandon knows that and still went after the Wolves unarmed.

Brandon's partners roll their gurney out to their ambulance. Kyle is a stocky, bald man in his early forties with square shoulders and a short neck. He's quiet, but intimidating, with a badass-factor as thick as his dark mustache. Firemen and women are required to have their EMT or paramedic license. Kyle trained Brandon and they've been partners for as long as I've known him. He was there for me the day everything went to hell, so although we're not particularly close, I have a special appreciation for him.

Travis is new to the truck, and I have yet to spend much time with him. He's young, energetic, and seems talkative. I'm sure he annoys Kyle. Still, I can't help but think they'll be good for each other.

"You know, Kyle and Travis don't run after psychopaths." I nudge Brandon's shoulder with mine.

He gives a short laugh. "Travis might once he figures out what the hell he's doing. Kyle's too old—would probably break a hip."

There's a wry smile in Brandon's sideways glance. He has cooled down enough to move on. He scrubs his hand down his face, then turns toward me, eyes soft. "You okay? The injuries on that guy were similar to your dad's."

"I'm fine," I answer too quickly. It's a lie, of course, but it's one he knew I would tell. I'm not sure why he even asked. I haven't been fine since the Wolves left me without parents. But if I don't dwell on it, I can fake it enough to feel somewhat close to being fine. I'm fine-ish.

"Of course, you are," he says with a disbelieving smirk.

"Come on." I use Brandon's shoulder to lever myself off the ground. "The rest of these patients aren't going to heal themselves." As we walk, I playfully punch his arm. "You ruined what I thought would be a slow day."

"There was an attack at the hospital? Are you okay?"

We've only been dating a few months, but I can tell by the panic in Cole's voice that he cares about me.

"Completely unharmed," I say. "How's the conference?"

I hear a *hmf!* and a heavy sigh. I imagine him falling onto a fluffy hotel bed.

"Weird," he says. "Miami is just now getting their first Wolf attacks, so they're in the hunker-down-and-hide phase. Hardly anyone showed up."

We responded the same way in Houston until we realized the Wolves would find their targets anyway. During the hiding months, the killings continued in victims' homes. The city eventually reopened, but we stay in small groups so fewer people were hurt during attacks. Although we have warned the rest of the country about the Wolves, it's hard to understand until you experience it up close. Many think it's a hoax until it happens to someone they know.

"They'll figure it out soon," I say.

"I miss you."

I smile warmly and run my hand over the sweater Cole left in the front seat of my car. Even before we started dating, he had been a huge support since losing my parents. Missing him this early in our relationship is unexpected, but it's there. "You too. I'm at Joey's Market now."

I pull into the parking lot and turn off the engine. A black van is parked two spots away. The windows are tinted. I can't see inside.

My heart beats faster.

"Be safe," Cole says.

I bring my key back to the ignition. I know they'll get me if I'm their target, but I can entertain them with a car chase first.

"Resi? Everything okay?"

The van reverses out of the parking spot and drives away.

I release a breath. "Yeah. Everything is good." I recall a popular internet meme from earlier this month: *Is it a Wolf or is my neighbor just taking the trash out in the dark?* We're always on alert, but it's usually nothing.

Cole and I say goodbye and I head into the market, stopping to glance over the growing number of flyers for missing persons spanning the wall outside; countless adults and nine children. I continue into the market when I don't recognize anyone on the new posts.

Joey's is the closest convenience store to my house. The owner knows me well enough to save a bottle of my favorite wine when they run low. But tonight, they're fully stocked. I grab a Pinot Noir before heading to the checkout counter, digging in my purse for cash.

Suddenly, I crash into the counter in front of me, dropping the change I had fished from my wallet. The bottle of wine shatters on the floor. I can't catch my breath. A ringing in my ears grows louder each second. I see double.

I desperately hold myself up on the counter. Shadows run around. Muffled yelling. I focus on the surveillance mirror above me: Black uniforms with gray sleeves. Black and white masks. They carry strange guns, Triangle Blades—*Wolves.*

I reach back and touch my head where it throbs, but I fail to hold myself up with one arm. My shoulder lands on the glass shards of the wine bottle. I groan. My skin is slick as red wine seeps through my scrubs. I try to raise my hand to my eyes to see if my head is bleeding where I touched it, but my arm is too heavy and drops to my stomach. The fluorescent lights above me fade, and now, all I see is darkness.

I blink. I recline on a soft sofa in a bright living room with red and gold accents. I feel safe. Relaxed. But I shouldn't. I don't know where I am.

I spot a cup of coffee on a table beside me and reach for it.

A man's hand picks it up and lifts it to my mouth.

There is no man. That is not my hand.

I peek through the French doors. Giggling and the stomping of young feet run in my direction. Children I somehow know are coming to greet me.

The doors burst open. A girl slides on the wood floor in her white tights with no shoes. The boy with her looks younger. His Spiderman tennis shoes light up every time he steps.

"Papa! Papa! You're home." They jump into my lap, wrap their arms around my neck.

"Papa?" I ask.

Did I ask? I try again. "I'm not your Papa."

I'm speaking, but the words won't leave my body. "What's happening?" I wonder aloud, but my voice echoes back to me like I'm in a cave.

One more time. This is ridiculous.

Vibrations in my chest and movement of my jaw tell me that my voice is working this time. "I'm home. I missed you."

My own gasp echoes back after a deep, male voice resonates from my chest. I think I am dreaming, but this all feels so real.

"Nico?" A woman calls from another room.

Nico. That's me.

"Yes?" My booming voice replies.

"Dinner will be ready soon."

I gently squeeze the child embracing my neck on the right. The girl, maybe six-years-old, beams at me with a proud grin displaying two missing teeth. "Amore, clean up your hands and help Mama set the table."

"Okay, Papa." She pecks my cheek, then runs toward the voice preparing dinner.

"You too, Patatino."

I am killing this Italian, I think, after effortlessly using two Italian terms of endearment I didn't even know I knew.

The boy's arms tighten around me. His head burrows into my neck. "No, Papa. Hold me for one more minute."

I chuckle, my chest rumbling. "You know, Pata-tino, to be a good Papa one day, you must learn to cook and clean and provide for your family. That starts with learning to set the table."

He pulls back to look at me. Sky blue glasses frame his winsome brown eyes. His cheeks are rosy and have some baby fat that makes my heart swell.

He holds his head high. "I'm going to be a Papa just like you when I'm big."

"Well then, you better get going and help your sister."

"Not without you." He throws himself back around my neck.

"Okay, okay." I stand, holding him close, and he wraps his legs around my waist. My hand—the one that isn't my hand, but a man's—reaches into my slacks to empty the pocket. I set its contents on the side table: a wallet, keys, business cards, and two Tylenol pills. I reach for the coffee, finish it before heading to the kitchen.

My body jolts as I carry the boy across the living room, like someone is moving me, but no one is there. I feel hands on my skin, turning and positioning me, but it's only the boy and me. I want to hunt for the cause of the disturbance, but my head only allows me to face forward.

Another jolt and my vision blurs. I blink to clear my eyes, but the room around me and the boy in my embrace fade. My arms weaken when I try to hold him tighter. The smell of spices reaches my nose and is swept away just as quickly.

I dart my eyes around the room when I awake. I'm back at work in the ER at Parkhill Hospital. "What the f—"

"Resi," Edda says. She scoots forward in the chair next to my bed. No, a stretcher. I'm on a stretcher. "I'm so glad you're awake." She takes my hand.

My brain is still trying to catch up to my circumstances. I'm confused, but having my best friend here is comforting. Her jet-black hair is tied into a messy bun, and the bronze skin of her face is stained with tears.

Brandon is asleep in a chair with his long legs stretched out in front of him. His eight-year-old daughter, Sarah, is sound asleep on his chest. Edda isn't wearing her scrubs, and Brandon changed out of his paramedic uniform. I assess my own attire—a hospital gown. That confirms it. I'm not here because I'm on the clock.

The back of my head throbs. I reach back.

"Leave it alone. Stitches," Edda tells me. "No brain bleed, so you'll live. They got some glass out of your shoulder too."

Right. I stopped to get a bottle of Pino. Leave it to me to drop the wine and commit a party foul in the middle of a terrorist attack.

"What happened?" I ask. "I know I was at the market, but that's it." All I remember after that is a living room of red and gold. Such a strange dream.

"You know those weapons the Wolves use that look like paintball guns?" Edda begins.

"Yeah."

"You got paintballed. Except the paintballs are golf ball-sized bullets that are shot at a speed that could crack a head open and have a bounce to them. A man and a woman died at the scene. The impact probably killed them instantly. We assume the one that hit you bounced a few times first, so you weren't hit quite as hard. The store owner, Joey, gave the paramedics the bullet." Edda reaches into her purse and pulls out a round, silver bullet, about one and a half inches in diameter. "I thought you could sift through your parents' research to see if you can find anything on this type of metal."

I examine the ball, taking it from Edda's hand. "Why didn't Joey give it to the police or military?"

Edda shrugs. "Said he recognized you from the store and didn't want evidence in the wrong hands. It's hard to know who to trust these days."

I offer the bullet back to her. "Hold onto it for me?"

My parents might indeed have research on metal that bounces. My dad, Astor, was a world-renowned neurosurgeon and neuroscientist. My mom, June, was an infectious disease physician and pharmaceutical scientist. They owned the Kepler Research Laboratory in the basement of the building next to Parkhill Hospital where they researched everything in their fields, as well as anything that interested them at a given time. Before their attack, Dad studied ways to digitally project thoughts, and mom was developing a new cure for pain. They always dabbled in side projects too. Mom was particularly interested in special materials, so bouncing metal would have piqued her curiosity.

But I haven't stepped foot into the research lab since they were attacked ten months ago, and curious or not, I'll be damned if I go now. There's too much *them* there. The Kepler lab holds their life's work, and about eighty percent of my childhood memories. Being there without them, knowing all that was left undone, it's too painful. I don't do that kind of pain anymore.

Brandon stirs, letting out a gravelly hum as he takes in his surroundings. His tired brown eyes crinkle at the corners. He keeps his voice low so as not to wake Sarah. "Hey, Rez," he says. "And you thought it was going to be a slow day."

I smile.

"Papa? Papa, no!"

I straighten my back. "Who was that?" The voice is young, familiar.

Brandon kisses Sarah's head and repositions her on the chair before moving over to the stretcher. "The other victims who died on the scene were brought in. It sounds like one of their families arrived."

I shake my head, like jostling my brain around my skull will help put the jumbled pieces back into place. It doesn't. It just reminds me that my head hurts. I force myself to take deep, long breaths. It was only a dream.

"Rez? You okay?" Brandon places a hand on my knee, and it refocuses my attention. I release the sheets I had unknowingly seized into my fists.

"Yeah," I rasp. I clear my throat. "Déjà vu or something. I had a weird dream before I woke up."

Another voice sounds through the hall. "Nico? Oh, Nico. Please, no!"

"*Nico.*" I swing my feet off the bed. I ignore the friends calling my name and I'm out of my room in seconds. My legs shake, but I keep moving forward. I grab a door panel to fling myself into a room where several people gather. A woman weeps over the chest of a man lying lifelessly on the stretcher. Her hands cling to his blood-soaked button-up shirt.

Children whimper. I creep toward them. My hand trembles as I raise it to the shoulder of a boy. He turns around at my touch, tears streaming out of his eyes framed by sky-blue glasses.

I stumble backward, grasping at my chest. "How..." I barely get one word out. I can't breathe. I struggle to inhale, but the more I try, the dizzier and more panicked I become. A large figure steps in front of me. My body leaves the ground, moving further away from the boy.

"Wait!" I reach for him, but my erratic breathing chokes down any more words. Even if I could speak, my brain has lost the ability to form anything into logical sentences.

Tile cools my legs when I land on the floor and lean against the wall. A paper bag covers my nose and mouth. Brandon kneels in front of me. I realize he's the one who carried me out of Nico's room. *Paper bag, I'm hyperventilating.* I close my eyes and take deeper breaths through the bag.

"Four seconds in, four seconds out," Brandon says.

He counts to four. I swear he's taking too long to get there.

"One, two, three, four."

I follow his advice, inhaling against my spasming lungs. *One, two, three, four.* The dizziness starts to subside. My breathing regulates. *One, two, three, four.* I drop the bag.

"Resi, what just happened?"

Edda sits next to me, but I can't take my eyes off

Nico's room, the curtain now hiding the grieving family behind the closed glass door.

"I have no idea," I say, racking my brain for an explanation.

I'm a nurse. I'm used to dead people. But inhabiting their bodies in my sleep?

Oh, hell no.

CHAPTER 2

"Dr. Locke, I'm fine."

There's a low, steady beep from the cardiac monitor to which I'm attached. I lean over and press the *Silence* button.

"It's silly for you to keep me here. You know me. I can take care of myself."

"You're like a niece to me, Resi," Dr. Locke says. "I want to make sure we're not missing anything. Stay for a few more hours. I'm doing what your father would have done."

I squint, debating whether I'm touched or annoyed by his protectiveness.

Definitely both.

Many of the older doctors at Parkhill watched me grow up. It's a small medical world, and my parents never met a stranger. Locke is good at addressing their absence without specifically focusing on their deaths, which I appreciate. I don't always handle it well when people talk about them.

The monitor beeps again. It's a noise I hear every day at work but it is much more irritating right now.

Locke presses his stethoscope to my chest. "Edda said you had a panic attack."

My face heats. I'm embarrassed to have lost control like that. I can't believe Edda told him. But then again, it wasn't subtle. "Oh, I don't know that it was a panic attack. I just..." I usually think quickly on my feet, but I'm flustered at the moment. "...felt like it was a good time for a dramatic scene?"

Locke pinches the edge of his glasses and slides them into his hair, which used to be jet black, but isn't quite gray yet. "You're a lot more difficult than your parents were. Do you know that?"

I was seven when I found a book my parents were reading called *How to Raise a Strong-Willed Child*.

"Yeah, I know," I say. "Look, I must have seen this guy at the store before I was hit. Then, I had this crazy dream about him, and he turned out to be dead. It freaked me out. That's it. I swear."

Locke stares, unimpressed. I've lost the battle. "You know the protocol for injured Wolf bystanders. If any unusual symptoms arise..."

"You'll be the first to know." I give reassuring finger guns and immediately wonder why I'm so awkward right now.

Locke leaves, walking past the two soldiers standing outside my hospital room. Part of our city-wide protocol is to have military protection for injured bystanders for twelve hours after an attack. It's really a protocol to make people feel better. We all know that if I had been a target, the Wolves would have come back to finish the job by now.

The beeping grows louder because I'm moving, and the cardiac monitor thinks my heart rate is higher than it is. I groan at the soreness in my muscles as I turn the monitor off before ripping the cords from my body.

I'm the worst patient.

There are six missed messages from Cole on my phone. Calling him back would be the appropriate thing to do, but I don't feel like talking about my night. I ignore the messages for now. I'll be a better girlfriendy-type later. I'm not sure what to call us. We haven't labeled our relationship yet.

"Where are you going?" Neil, one of the soldiers, asks as I walk out of the room. Neil's partner for the night is Joanne. Both are dressed in camouflage combat uniforms.

"C'mon," I say. "I'm taking a lap around the ER."

Neil crosses his arms in front of his chest. "Is that allowed?"

"It's fine, I work here." And I'm not waiting for his blessing. They have no choice but to follow.

There's a room blocked off with yellow *Caution* tape. Nico's room has already been processed and cleared out by the Terrorism Unit.

"Tanner, is this the other victim who died in the attack tonight?"

Tanner never looks up from his computer at the nurses' station. "Yep. Young woman. Cops are still trying to identify her."

I lift the tape.

"You can't do that, it's a crime scene," Neil says.

"Like I said, I work here." Neil's totally right. I shouldn't be doing this, but I know how to handle a crime scene and won't tamper with any evidence. "And you're here to protect me, not annoy me."

"We could report you."

I glance at Joanne, who looks like she could not care less about what I'm doing, then back to Neil. "You must be really popular back at the base." I duck under the tape. The soldiers stay outside the door.

I approach the covered body with a strange need

to see who else was in the attack with me. Slowly, I lower the sheet to reveal her face.

My throat tightens. She can barely be called a "young woman." She's a girl. I can't imagine she is any older than a teen. I graze the back of my fingers against the smooth, brown skin of her cheek, paled by the lack of blood flowing to her face. I hate that she's alone. I wonder when her parents will notice she's gone.

The chair scrapes the floor as I drag it next to the bed. I disregard the mutter from Neil and sink into the chair, tuck myself into a ball. My arms lay across my knees and chin on my arms. The comfort of the position makes my eyes blink slower.

The bright lights are blinding. I want to squint, but I can't. A roar of applause fills me with exhilaration. I try to shield the light to see in front of me, but both my hands are restrained.

Not restrained. Held. Someone is holding my hands.

My arms lift above my head in a swinging motion, then fall back down as my body bends at the waist, and my head flies forward in a quick bow.

I take a few steps back with the hand-holders. A curtain drops in front of me, blocking the lights.

I recognize the same sensation of the dream I had earlier tonight—the sense of being confined to someone else's body. I must be dreaming again. But I feel different than I did as Nico.

I'm the girl.

But that's ridiculous. It was a nightmare. You can't fall into dead people's bodies.

The line of handholding breaks. Young men and women surround me. They look college-aged and have excessive amounts of makeup on. "Good show!" I say to a boy in a dirty tank top and oil-stained slacks. Suspenders hang from his waist. I have a fond affinity toward him, and feel a sense of pride in his performance.

But I've never met the guy before. I didn't even *see* his performance.

"You too," the boy says. We walk through a dark backstage area. "It went well tonight."

"The audience was fantastic. They were electric and reactive!" The voice coming out of my throat is female, but it's deeper and smoother than mine. There's a breathy flirtatiousness to it.

We walk through a set of double doors which displays a poster with huge block letters advertising a play:

TENNESSEE WILLIAMS' STREETCAR NAMED DESIRE
AT THE UNIVERSITY OF HOUSTON
PLAYING NOW!

The boy with the oily clothes and I part ways. I enter through a door that says LADIES in block letters.

Three other girls occupy a dressing room. A long mirror with lustrous, round lightbulbs dominates the space. The girls are in various stages of undressing, pulling bobby pins out of their hair and wiping thick layers of makeup off their faces. I walk toward an empty seat and open a drawer, flipping open the lid of a blue box to retrieve a face wipe. I take the moist cloth in my hand, feel the cold sensation against my cheek, and observe myself in the mirror.

My eyes fix onto the reflection staring back at me. I swipe my face with the cloth and remove an assortment of colors from the soft, dark skin with pink tones that make me question the girl's need for blush. I'm her—the dead girl.

The dead girl I fell asleep next to.

Asleep. I'm asleep. It *is* another dream.

"Wake up," I say aloud, but my demand echoes right back to me. "Wake! Up! Resi!" Nothing. I groan. "Stop. Please, make this stop!"

If I were in my own body, my heart would be racing with anxiety, but it's not. Instead, I finish removing my makeup, my desire to panic overridden by the need to change out of my costume so I can eat. My stomach growls.

A green, floral dress, knee-length, with a classy V-neck, hugs my body. It is 1940s style; fitted at the waist and pleated below the hips. I step out of beige heels and reach awkwardly over my head to find the zipper at the top of my back.

"Are you guys going to dinner with the rest of the cast?" I—no, the dead girl—asks, struggling to keep the zipper tab between my—her—fingers.

A girl nearby appears behind her to help. She unzips the dress and goes back to her section of the mirror. "I am," the girl says. Her short blonde hair is curled forward to frame her face. "I'm starving. Is your back feeling better?"

"Actually, yes," says the dead girl. "It's way better today. But I'm going to steer clear of Pilates for a while."

A hand lands on the girl's shoulder. "Resi?" a voice says.

I want to respond, but I'm busy stepping into the dead girl's jeans.

"Resi?" the voice says again. The girl is swaying back and forth. Someone is nudging her shoulder.

No. *My* shoulder.

I open my eyes.

Dr. Locke hovers, nudging me lightly. "What are you doing here?"

I turn to the corpse. A thousand needles dance their way across my stomach when my eyes land on her face. The girl I studied in a dressing room mirror lays before me, vibrant pink color and sultry voice stifled by a heart that refuses to beat.

I breathe, remembering Brandon's advice: *four seconds in, four seconds out.* I can't let Locke know what's going on. He will admit me to the psych facility. Act normal. I need to answer his question, but I can't remember what it was. Thoughts swirl through my mind; So many thoughts that somehow, I have none. I search for words.

A word?

Any word.

I only find one. "Whoa."

CHAPTER 3

I twist my body into a gawky position so I can use my phone while it charges. The power cord doesn't quite reach the stretcher, so my arms are hanging off the side. It's uncomfortable, and the shoulder that had glass removed from it is scratching against the material of my gown, but I'm too lazy to get up and sit on the floor next to the outlet.

I glance at the guards outside my door to make sure they're not watching me, just in case they have laser-sharp eyesight to see what I'm typing into a Google Search:

> ABILITY TO SEE INTO DEAD PEOPLE'S MEMORIES
> WHY AM I ABLE TO GET INTO DEAD PEOPLE'S BODIES
> SUDDEN ABILITY TO TAKE OVER BODIES OF THE DEAD
> HIT HEAD AND NOW I SEE DEAD PEOPLE.

Every search ends with weblinks for palm readers, mediums who summon the dead, websites that interpret dreams of deceased loved ones, and the IMDB page for The Sixth Sense.

Good movie. But not what I'm looking for.

I pat the sore, itchy sutures on my scalp. I can't help but wonder:

> EFFECTS OF BRAIN DAMAGE TO THE OCCIPITAL LOBE.

I tap on the first article listed. Within the opening paragraph, I read, "Damage to the occipital lobe may cause vision loss, misidentification of colors, and visual hallucinations."

That's it. I'm hallucinating.

But the experiences are so real. They are not only visual. I feel, hear, and smell them. I fully experience every step, every emotion. I tasted Nico's coffee, melted into his affection for his children, smelled the spices from the kitchen. I wanted to squint as the bright spotlights on stage blinded my eyes, and I felt the cool cloth against the girl's cheek. Everything was tangible. It doesn't make sense.

But maybe I *am* mentally unstable. It's only a matter of time, right?

Frustrated, I roll onto my back and let my phone fall to the floor.

It's fine. OtterBox.

There's an image of Joey's Market on the hospital room TV. I grab the remote, unmute it.

"Two dead and one injured tonight in what appears to be another Wolf attack," a woman reports, "bringing the death toll by the Wolves to 521 in Houston, and 1,302 nationwide over ten months. This number does not include those gone missing."

"Ready to go, Resi?"

I sit up as Locke enters the room. "Ready."

"No other signs or symptoms have come up over the past few hours?"

Other than hallucinating about dead people? "Nope. Nothing."

Only five of the twelve mandatory hours of military protection were spent at the hospital. I have a front and back door, so I tell Neil and Joanne to situate themselves like a reverse mullet—Joanne being the party in the front, Neil the annoying business in the back.

They don't think I'm funny.

I throw my keys onto the coffee table with a loud clack, and I plop onto the couch. I immediately regret the loud noise and hard landing. My head throbs, reminding me that it is still on the mend.

I could tidy the pillows thrown haphazardly around me or dispose of the paper plates left on the kitchen table, but that would be way too adult. Maybe in my thirties, I'll use real plates and even clean them after. But probably not. Instead, I go to my desk to commence my nightly routine of dead-Mom-searching.

I take the key from under the desk, held in place by a magnet, and unlock the bottom drawer. I hide everything this way, so when people come over, I don't look quite as insane as I probably am.

I should get a therapist.

The drawer holds a single file, which I place open-faced in front of me.

A worn, fragile map of Houston with four red dots on various locations in the city is the first item I carefully remove from the file. Each dot represents places I swear I saw my mother in the months following her attack. I pin the map to the wall using the same hole I use every night.

Next is a news article. The title reads, WORLD RENOWN SCIENTIST FOUND DEAD IN HOUSTON BOMBING. Highlighted in the article is the phrase: "DNA found at the scene identifies the victim as June Kepler, MD, PhD, PharmD."

They also found limbs and confirmed her identity through her fingerprints.

The next two items I tack to the wall are notes

from the police report after the bombing and a list of Mom's contacts, which I compiled from her cloud.

Once the items are in place, I click the SURVEILLANCE icon on my desktop. A video monitoring system pops up. Kyle, Brandon's paramedic partner, is also a hacker in his spare time, though not many people know it. He helped me gain access to the neighborhood's cameras. I click on yesterday's date and press Play, then Fast-Forward. The surveillance shows Harvard Street in the Houston Heights, the street I lived on as a child —the one my parents lived on until the day they were bombed. It's being rebuilt now.

I sit back and watch the sped-up video surveillance while scanning my eyes over the map, photos, and articles I've seen every night for ten months, hoping something new will catch my attention. I glance over the names on Mom's contact list, then back to the surveillance video.

When I first started this, it was an obsession. I would stay up all night looking for clues that didn't exist, making connections I fabricated in my mind. I waited for my mother to show up at our old home as I watched the screen intently. I spent every ounce of energy and emotion on this project.

Now, it's like a superstition. I stare at each item, watch the surveillance of the previous day, but I purposely detach from it with no emotion left to spend. I don't believe that Mom is alive anymore, but stopping makes me feel guilty.

My search tonight feels different, though. My animosity toward the Wolves is more palpable. I feel more than I want to feel, and my mind is all over the place, sorting through my dreams. Seeing dead victims at the hospital usually doesn't faze me, but it's like I know tonight's victims. They had full, satisfying lives that were ripped away so abruptly. How could these have been hallucinations if I knew how they felt? How could I have known about Nico's children and wife before I saw them at the hospital? I stare at the grainy black and white photo of my mom included in the article about her death. I wish I could talk to her, ask for her advice, listen to her assure me that I'm not crazy.

But I can't. *She* can't. She's dead.

And I'm pissed.

I shake my head to get out of my daze. I never allow myself to go to that place emotionally. Staying home alone tomorrow with these thoughts won't help. I need a distraction.

Are we short on nurses tomorrow? I text Devon, the charge nurse on duty in the morning. *Can I pick up a shift?*

The reply comes back a few minutes later. *You sure you don't need to rest?*

I'm sure.

The texting bubbles come and go a few times, teasing me. He's debating the answer.

Let's compromise, he says. *Pick up half a shift and come in tomorrow afternoon after you've had a good night of sleep.*

I'll take what I can get and reply with a thumbs-up emoji.

I lean forward at the desk and rest my head in my hands as cars drive by on the screen. My eyelids are heavy. I'm sure I won't miss much if I close them for a few seconds.

A book lands in front of me. "It's s-so good to meet you. I—I've been a fan since you ran for mayor." A nervous voice stumbles through her greeting. I recognize the old man on the cover of the book. I open it to sign a blank page in the front. A pale, loose-skinned hand scribbles the name *Roy Maxwell.*

Roy Maxwell. That's the guy on the cover.

That's *me.*

I'm in another dream—another memory. *Damn it.* I fell asleep. "Wake up!" I try to yell, but my voice is confined to this body. I want to be panicking, doing something about this, but I'm calm, maybe even bored.

I close the book and hand it to the woman. "Thank you for your support all these years." The deep voice is soft and gentle. Kind.

I don't follow politics much, but I do remember Roy Maxwell making an appearance on the Houston Morning Show recently. He retired from the senate or something and decided to write a tell-all memoir. That was just a few days ago.

Roy Maxwell is alive.

Why am I dreaming about an old, retired politician?

"Gah!" I groan, the noise refusing to leave Roy's chest. My—his—hand throbs as he signs another book. I want him to let go of the pen, drop it, rub the ache out, but Roy only pauses for a moment, loosens his grip, and continues through the pain.

Note to self: research ways to avoid arthritis.

A blaring horn startles me awake. I'm disoriented, but I recover quickly. My cheek is hot and sore where I was laying on my arm. I take in my surroundings to be sure that I'm at my house. The surveillance on my laptop is now a live feed, and the time in the corner says 9:00 AM.

I finally recognize the obnoxious ringtone as the one Brandon set for himself because he thinks it's funny to make me jump. His name appears on the screen.

"Hey," I answer, my voice hoarse.

"Did I wake you?"

I rub my eye. "Mm. It's fine."

"How you feeling?"

"I'm okay." I haven't had time to assess how I'm feeling, but that's the answer I would give anyway. "What's up?"

"My captain needs me to go into the station and get some paperwork done, but I have Sarah. Would you mind—"

"Not at all." I walk to the front window and peek through the blinds. Joanne, the party in the front, is gone. They must have fulfilled their twelve dutiful hours.

"You sure?"

"Yeah. I'm working this afternoon, though. Drop her off here, and we can meet you for lunch at the hospital."

"Thanks, Rez."

I end the call and get ready for the day, happy to be distracted from all the weird dreams for the morning.

Old, retired politicians are not the usual characters to invade my thoughts at night, but regardless, dreams about *living* people I can deal with.

"Former State Representative Roy Maxwell was

found dead in his Houston home this morning. Cause of death, exsanguination after his throat was reportedly sliced. Home security footage shows a Wolf striking the video camera with a Triangle Blade. That's the seventh attack in Houston and the fourteenth in the nation this week. The total death count since the Wolves first attacked ten months ago is now 1,304."

I gawk at the television screen. Roy Maxwell *was* dead when I had that dream. This is really happening. I didn't know Maxwell or that he was killed, yet his memories invaded my dreams.

"Will surveillance footage be released? Can anyone confirm that the Wolves are of human origin and not alien descent?"

I know that high-pitched, pressured voice all too well. Mischa Linelli, the leading lady of the conspiracy theorists, graces the TV screen in her signature red square glasses and purple beanie, hair tied back in a braid.

I learned the hard way that Mischa's cell phone is always recording. One of her earliest videos theorized that my father was not actually attacked, but was operating the Wolves from the White House. She questioned me on the subject. A few of my choice words went viral.

"Resi? Will you check my answers?"

Sarah's voice snaps me out of my thoughts like a door-jam finally pushed open. I mute the TV, lean into the girl next to me on the hospital room couch to analyze her third-grade math homework.

"Numbers eleven through fifteen are wrong," I say. "How many cents are in a dime?"

"Ten."

"Right. You know how to do this." I remove one of her earbuds. "Maybe you'd be more focused if Taylor Swift wasn't shaking it off in your ear while you're counting." I nudge her with my elbow as she giggles. She removes the other earbud. "I thought you liked doing your homework up here with Dad and me because it's *quiet*."

"I know," Sarah replies. "But I hate counting money."

"Grown-ups don't like it very much either."

"None?"

"Well, only these weirdos called accountants. I dated one once, and he asked if we could do my taxes *for fun*."

She crinkles her nose. "Huh?"

"Trust me. It's weird."

Sarah's eyes wander to the unconscious man on the hospital bed, whose room we have commandeered. Tubes and wires are connected to him from head to toe, but he breathes on his own. In fact, breathing is about all he can do on his own. If I chopped off my dirty-blonde hair, grew six inches, and aged thirty years, I could pass as his twin. Astor Kepler, my father, lies in a coma going on ten months.

His skin is pale, sunken, and he's been doomed to don an ugly hospital gown, but otherwise, he looks exactly the same as he did ten months ago. All he's lacking is the money clip he fidgeted with. His name was engraved incorrectly, ASTRO KEPLER, PhD, MD. He loved that it was misspelled as his favorite baseball team. The clip never once held money. He played with it, letting his fingers dig into the clamp, then releasing it with a snap. He said it helped him think because he had ADHD and needed to do something with his hands.

"What were you thinking about before I asked you to check my homework?" Sarah asks.

"Nothing in particular." I can't be positive, but I'm willing to bet it's inappropriate to confide in an eight-year-old about dead-people dreams. "Go back and try number eleven again."

Sarah drops her shoulders in a pout. "Why do you like to be up here if you won't ever talk about him? Daddy and Edda tell me stories, but you don't, and you're the best at telling stories!"

Ah, she assumes I was thinking about my Dad. It's another sore subject, but talking about Dad with Sarah isn't as grueling as it is with adults for some reason. Plus, it's easier to explain than 'I see dead people.'

Really, it was such a good movie.

I've been silent for too long because Sarah starts to whine. "Come oooonnn. I like to hear about your mom and dad. I only got to see them on holidays which isn't even fair because they were so fun!"

"You know, you're just as persistent and annoying as *your* dad sometimes," I point out.

"Pleeeaaase?"

"Okay, okay," I say, to Sarah's delight. "I'll tell you *one* thing, then homework. Deal?"

Sarah scoots back into my arm to get comfortable. "Deal."

I glance around the dim room, mulling over what to say. In ten months, the room has been decorated with pictures of people meeting my dad, letters of admiration, and "get well soon" cards, none of which he will ever read. I spot Sarah's iPod and headphones resting in her hands.

"You know," I begin, "Dad loved music, like you."

"Really?"

"Oh, yeah. We had music in our house all the time when I was growing up. And he was famous for his dance parties. He loved to talk about how music affected the brain."

"What do you mean?"

"Well, when you listen to Taylor Swift, do her songs make you happy or sad?"

Sarah contemplates her music library. "Some songs make me happy, and some make me sad. And sometimes they make me excited or angry."

"Exactly. All of those emotions are happening in your brain." I point to Sarah's temple. "Music is special because it can make you feel all sorts of things and connect to what you're already feeling. It can also make you remember certain events or times in your life. When I hear a song from N'SYNC or Spice Girls, it's like I'm right back in elementary school."

"Spice Girls?"

"Spice up your life? One of the best and tackiest eras of human history?" I frown when Sarah shows no signs of recognition. "Girl Power!" I exclaim in an English accent, holding up my index and middle fingers in a peace sign. Still no reaction. I sigh. "You have so much to learn."

I pick up the money-counting homework from Sarah's lap. "Music actually makes you smarter, too. And some types of music can help you concentrate. Dad taught me that different things like talking, reading, or running activate certain parts of your brain, but music activates your *entire* brain. It's like it gives your brain a workout. He would say 'music is your mind's yoga,' which he would follow with some embarrassing yoga pose in public."

Sarah fixes her eyes on Dad and chews the inside of her cheek. "Didn't you say that he's sleeping so his brain can heal?"

My heart sinks. Technically, she's right. Short comas serve to help the brain heal, in a way. But the length of my father's coma gives me minimal hope of salvaging his unique mind. "Yes," I say, deciding the truth is too complicated and sad. "So his brain can heal."

Sarah stands, walks over to Dad. She sets her iPod gently on his chest, then pinches the earbuds into her fingers, and carefully places them in his ears. She returns to her iPod and presses Play. "Here, Mr. Astor," she whispers. "Maybe this will help."

Stab me in the liver. I shouldn't be surprised by her compassion. This is the same eight-year-old girl who saw a homeless man on the street a few months ago and stopped to give him her shoes that were ten sizes too small for him. Then, she demanded to Brandon that they start donating their belongings to the Salvation Army. Sarah is always considering other people more than herself. Still, I'm moved by the sweet gesture.

The buzz of my phone alerts me to a text message from Brandon. *Cafeteria.*

"Your dad is back," I tell Sarah. "We're going to meet him downstairs for lunch."

Sarah gathers her things and heads toward the door.

"Don't you want your iPod?" I ask.

"He needs it more than me."

I withhold from gushing like an obnoxious aunt who wants to pinch a baby's cheek. Instead, I play it cool, simply throwing my arm over Sarah's shoulder when I catch up to her.

"Resi?" Sarah says. She doesn't press the button when we get to the elevator, a favorite pastime, so I wonder if she's about to change her mind about the iPod.

"Yeah?"

"Do you think a song from when I was a baby will help me remember my parents better?"

I turn to her, a smile forming on my lips even through sadness. I think of the day Brandon brought Sarah home, almost two weeks after pulling her out of the house fire that killed her parents when she was four. She was shy and withdrawn back then, and it took a while for her to bond with and trust us. By the time Brandon officially adopted her two years later, she had become my best tiny friend, the kid I'd do anything for.

"I don't know, Sarah. Maybe." I sweep a strand of her curly hair away from her eyes. "It never hurts to try."

CHAPTER 4

I buy lunch for Sarah and myself. We meet Brandon and Edda at a round table in the center of the hospital cafeteria. I catch sight of Charlotte, my parents' former research assistant, across the room, taking a shortcut to the lab. She still uses it for her Ph.D. work in genetics. It's next door to the hospital, so I see Charlie occasionally in passing, but we haven't spoken much since Mom's funeral.

"Mind if I join you?"

I perk up at the sound of the cheery voice. "Cole?" I stand and tug him into my embrace, almost knocking the tray of food out of his hands.

"Hey, Cole," Edda says. "Welcome back."

"What are you doing here?" I ask. "You're not supposed to be back for another week."

"It's hard to pay attention in a conference and listen to old men lecture about Smallpox when your girlfriend was hurt in a Wolf attack," he says. He kisses the top of my head. "Being away sucked. Happy to see you in one piece."

This is the first time either of us has referred to me as his girlfriend out loud. It's odd, but not wrong. The dimple on his right cheek pops out as he grins and takes a seat next to me.

"Uh oh," Edda says. Her face tightens, observing something behind me.

"What?"

"Sympathetic white-coats are pointing at you and walking in this direction. Brace yourself."

Damn. I shut my eyes and exhale forcefully. I'm already in a weird mood today, and this is not what I need right now. Between a blow to the head yesterday and my new-found ability, going to work may not have been the best idea.

I never said I wasn't stubborn.

"Yep," Brandon says. "They look like Kepler-sympathizers. Want us to field it, or are you good?"

They know I don't always handle these conversations well, but I can't avoid them all. Hopefully, this will be short, sweet, and we can move on quickly. "I've got it. Thanks, though." I twist around and see three men and one woman walking toward me. I force an agreeable demeanor, standing when the woman waves.

"Resi Kepler?" Man One initiates the conversation. Flat-ish nose with freckles. He's familiar, but I can't quite place him.

"Yes, hi. Nice to see you," I say.

"You've grown into such a beautiful young lady." The woman: kind smile, light blonde hair, bright yellow plastic shoes under her navy-blue scrubs, a cute and quirky style. She was a regular at my parent's big parties.

"You have. You're a mirror image of Astor."

"Definitely. But those green eyes are your mother's."

"That's what I'm told." My fake small-talk banter is spot-on, so far. Mom and I really did have the same eyes. *"If I could smell your eyes, they'd be spearmint; you're the Spearmint Twins,"* my dad would tell us.

"And you always had their same love for research, as memory serves. We thought you would follow in their shoes. They are such decorated scientists and physicians," Man Two points out. He's the least recognizable of the quartet and clearly an admirer more than a friend if he's more impressed with my parents' accomplishments than personalities. He's older, his skin translucent and wrinkled. What little hair he has is white, hugging his bald head like a wreath.

Man Three hasn't spoken yet, but I recognize him as a doctor from one of the admitting teams. I see him when he comes to the ER to assess patients who will be staying at the hospital for a while. It wouldn't surprise me if he knew my parents, but he might just be tagging along. Either way, he has at least heard of them. If there are celebrities in the medical field, my parents were it. They both held multiple doctoral degrees and won awards for some of the most advanced medical discoveries. So, when remnants of my mother's body were found along with my comatose father in the explosions of the first Wolf attack, medical professionals from around the world mourned.

"Oh, you have no idea," says Man One. "This little one *loved* to tell us all about her parent's newest projects."

Ah. We've moved into the phase of these conversations where the mourners reminisce about me in front of me. I stuff my hands into my pockets because my extremities feel awkward.

"But I remember this stubborn little lady at a young age announcing to the Kepler Christmas party that she wanted to 'take care of people by *applying* the research,'" the woman says.

My nose involuntarily twitches. Why does this woman suddenly come off as condescending? I had high hopes for her and her quirky yellow shoes.

"Little Resi stood up on her chair that night and declared, 'I'm not going to be a scientist. I'm going to be a *nurse*.'"

All four doctors howl with laughter.

"A nurse!" I guffaw pretentiously. "How ridiculous." I hear Brandon snort behind me. "Can you *believe* someone would want to be a nurse more than a researcher?"

They clearly don't catch on to my facetiousness. I provoke their amusement for a few more moments before their joy dies down, leaving an opening for the comments I anticipate are coming. I want to turn around to my friends and bet someone twenty bucks that the next question will have to do with how I'm "holding up."

The woman takes a cautious step toward me, her head low, but her eyes focused. "How are you holding up, Sweetie?"

Damn. I should have hypothetically bet fifty. "Oh, I'm fine. I'm holding up just fine. Thanks for asking." The doctors tilt their heads and nod almost cartoon-like, in perfect, sympathetic sync. "You know, taking it one day at a time," I add, and I'm sure my tone is sarcastic enough that they'll notice, but maybe they don't know that *niceness* is not something I inherited from my parents.

"We miss your folks tremendously," Man One says.

Me too. My mother's eyes enter my mind. So clear and close. I remember standing in front of the packed church. *"She was driven and compassionate, determined to end the pain of those she loved,"* I said in her eulogy.

Man One continues, "Their absence leaves a huge hole in our community. A hole that no one could possibly fill."

Even though Dad described them as a scent, to me, Mom's eyes were like the rainforest, bringing depth and life to anyone who saw them. A warm, rich green that used to give me hope.

"They are irreplaceable scientists."

A hope that's dead.

"And friends!"

A warmth gone cold.

"And entertainers!"

Explosions. Fire. My childhood home blowing into flames. The news playing it on a loop. Wondering which parts of the debris are pieces of my mother.

Ten-month-old memories that feel new every time they assault my thoughts.

Push it aside. Breathe, I tell myself. I take a long, deep breath and thrust my emotions to the back of my mind, hoping my parents' friends will wrap this up soon. I can't think about them anymore. Once the sadness bursts through the Hoover Dam I've built around my emotions, I won't be able to stop the resulting flood.

"Yes. What memorable parties they threw," the woman says.

"Some of the best," Man One agrees.

Man Two leans in and places his wrinkly hand on my shoulder. "Of course, we don't mean to speak of your father as though he is gone. We know that he will pull through," he says in a low, quiet tone.

My polite smile fades, and I still the leg I didn't realize I had been bouncing. My cheeks simmer.

"Uh oh," one of my friends says behind me.

Pull through? This guy is a medical professional, and he's telling me that Dad will 'pull through?' Does he think I'm a moron?

"Yes." The woman shifts on her dumb, yellow-clad duck feet. "We have no doubt that he will, um, wake up one day soon and get right back to work."

Apparently, they *all* think I'm a moron. I glower at her, fuming, remembering the last test the neurologist did to measure his brain function.

Nothing.

Idiot Man Two continues. "I'm sure you pray every day for that moment to come. We do too, Sweetie. We do too."

I'm done.

I pinch the man's wrinkly skin and remove his hand from my shoulder like it's a dirty diaper. "Okay... Well, thanks for the condescending bullshit."

"Aaaand we lost her," Brandon says. A chair scrapes against the tile floor. My friends are about to try and stop me, but I've already snapped. There's no going back. I'm locked and friggin' loaded, ready to fire a verbal massacre.

"Let's just take a step back into reality where arguably the most brilliant neurosurgeon and scientist in the world is laying in a coma. A man who success-fully treated brain tumors thought to be inoperable; discovered how to digitally project peoples' thoughts; created prosthetics that could be wired to and per-fectly controlled by the mind; and—oh!—figured out how to use stem cells to grow a human eyeball in his spare time. *That* man is now paying thousands of dollars a month to lay around this hospital in a persistent vegetative state." I stop, hold a palm out for dramatic effect. "Oh, I'm sorry. Let me say that a little slower: per-sis-tent ve-ge-ta-tive state. Since you clearly have zero understanding of it, I suggest a quick Google search."

My volume increases with each sentence. I'm overreacting, I know I am, but it's flowing out of me now, and I can't stop it. I ignore Edda's attempt to grab my attention and pull my elbow out of her grip. "The man's entire life was the brain! He didn't just study them and work on them and fix them, but he *had* the most incredible, imaginative, genius brain I've ever witnessed. That man's brain is now a past-tense mythical story that will go down in history books and never be added to. It's a pile of gyral mush. Do not for *one minute* think this irony is lost on me. You and I, and every educated person here know that Astor Kepler will not open his eyes and 'get back to work.' You think I *pray* for him to wake up?"

Edda's hand is back on my arm now. "Resi, calm down."

My voice hitches, and I curse my quivering chin for giving my emotions away. "I would *never* pray for that man to live in the hell of a less-than-astonishing mind." My pitch rises with my narrowing throat. I hone in on the anger, refuse to be sad. "So, take your memories and your pity and your pathetic lies about believing my dad will 'pull through' and shove them up your—"

"*Resi!*" Cole stands and seizes me by the shoulders, jogging me out of my fit. The entire cafeteria has quieted behind four shocked physicians.

41

"Ah, damn it," I say, spinning back around to my friends. My blood is still pumping, and the need to resume a venting session bubbles inside me.

I'm not sure what it is that comes over me, but I throw my arms into the air. "I'm having dreams about dead people!"

◆ ◆ ◆

Multiple hands usher me to the nearest empty space: a conference room around the corner from the cafeteria. Brandon and Edda push me inside.

"Cole. Hey Bud," Brandon says. "Stay out here with Sarah, would ya? Glad to have you back."

Cole peers into the room, his brows ruffled as Brandon closes the door and leans up against it. "Oh yeah, you're holding up just fine," he mocks.

"You can't kick Cole out!" I yell.

"He offered to watch Sarah," Brandon says.

I ignore the barely-there smirk on his mouth. "He *just* got back, Brandon. I haven't seen him in—"

"Resi, what's going on?" Edda interrupts, concerned and impatient. "You can usually handle those kinds of comments about your dad. Is it the concussion that's making you this crabby?"

"It's not the concussion." I cross my arms, walk down a row of chairs around a long, rectangular conference table. "I told you. I'm having these dreams."

"Resi, a lot of nurses have dreams about death. It comes with the territory."

"No, this is different!" I'm too defensive. I take a moment to compose myself. "There's something really strange going on."

"Zombies," Brandon states.

I brush past his idiocy and try to explain as best as I can, starting with last night's Wolf attack.

"So, you're dreaming about people who are dead, but the dreams are from when they were alive?" Edda clarifies. Brandon and Edda now sit across the table from me.

"Yes. But they're more like memories than dreams. I can see, feel, taste, touch. I *become* the dead person. Like, I inhabit their bodies."

"But you have crazy dreams all the time," Edda points out.

"Falling through a mansion of Jell-O with Willy Wonka is a *tad* less realistic than what I'm describing here."

"Rez," Brandon says, hands clasped, forearms leaning against the edge of the table, "are you sure you haven't seen these people before and you're recalling something in your dreams?"

"No." I'm back on my feet, pacing. "I wondered about that with the first one, but that's not it. I have never met these people. They aren't even *my* memories. They're the dead people's memories. Why would I only dream of the memories of dead people I've never met? And I'm not even there. Well, I'm there, but I'm in the person's body. I don't even have control of my own thoughts and emotions because I'm feeling what they're feeling."

They share a look I've seen before: the silent, gentle concern of family members when patients are brought to the ER for new-onset psychosis. My friends think I'm crazy. I should have kept my mouth shut.

Edda stands, ties her hair into a ponytail, ambles toward me. "I know you don't like to talk about it, but maybe this has something to do with how your parents were attacked. You never really dealt with that."

I swallow the outburst of rage that threatens to surface. I hate it when she tries to psychoanalyze me. She thinks she's qualified because she minored in counseling.

"I shouldn't have said anything," I say. "I know it sounds crazy. I wouldn't have told you if I wasn't so hot-headed out there." I push a chair under the table because it feels final, and I'm ready to end this useless chit-chat.

"Resi..."

"Lunch is over," I say. "We have to get to work."

Edda blocks my path to the door. "Resi, are you sure you should be working today? Maybe you should rest for a while."

The insinuation that I'm not mentally fit for work makes me even more tense. I know she's not trying to piss me off, but... she's pissing me off. "I'll manage, Edda." My eyes flit between her and Brandon. "Can this stay between the three of us, please?"

They agree.

I walk out of the room. "I'm sorry," I mouth to Cole, then make my way over to him as Sarah moves toward Brandon.

"What the hell was that about?" Cole murmurs. His arms are crossed, but he doesn't look too angry or defensive. He knows that Edda, Brandon, and I have years of friendship established, but sometimes I wonder if Cole still feels like an outsider.

Sometimes *I* still feel like he's an outsider. That's not how I want things to be, though. At least, I don't think so.

"I'll explain later. I picked up a shift." I tilt my head in the direction of the ER, indicating that I should go.

He nods. "Explain tonight at the symphony?"

I look up at him questioningly.

"I know you have a lot going on, but I bought tickets hoping I could take you out."

His thoughtfulness overcomes the fact that he already bought tickets and didn't really give me a choice. We make plans for him to pick me up after work, then he walks in the direction of his office.

"Ready, Resi?" Edda asks.

Frustration causes my jaw to clench as I observe her worried face again, even if it is hidden behind a light smile. I know I shouldn't, but I feel a need to prove myself—prove that I'm not completely insane. If I could get inside the morgue and somehow guarantee that I could fall asleep...

"I have to make a quick phone call," I say. "I'll see you in the ER in a minute."

When she disappears, I scan through the contacts on my phone. I hesitate, my finger hovering over the name *Charlotte Clay*. I haven't spoken to her in months. She must be angry with me for not staying in touch. But she's the only one working in my parent's lab now, and she has access to what I need.

I tap her name and imagine my nursing license falling down a gutter.

"Charlie, hi. Yeah, I saw you too... It *has* been forever, I know... Um, listen, I want to catch up, but I need you to do something for me. You know I wouldn't ask if it wasn't important, and I know it's a lot but I'm going to request that you don't ask questions."

CHAPTER 5

"Everyone gather at the charge desk!" a voice yells as soon as I step into my first patient's room.

It's an unusual request in the middle of the day.

I make my way to the charge desk where a swarm of nurses and physicians gather. I join in the back of the crowd and watch Devon's bald head as he conducts the meeting.

"There was an attack at an event in Hermann Park. Several bystanders stepped up to fight against the Wolves, and many were injured," Devon says. A murmur spreads through the group. People never fight the Wolves.

"That's, like, six attacks this week," a tech, Kennan, says.

"Eight," I correct.

"We shouldn't be here. We should go home, stay there, and stay safe," someone suggests.

"Yeah," Kennan says. "The Wolves are escalating."

Another murmur throughout the crowd.

"It doesn't matter," I say loudly enough to be heard over the chatter. Once the volume lessens, "We still don't let these bastards dictate our lives. We know they'll still find us if we run or hide, so there's no point. For all we know, this is an anomaly. Maybe there will be fewer attacks next week."

Many in the crowd nod in agreement, some whisper to one another.

"Look," Edda says. "Other people can backtrack to the start of this war, run and hide if they want, but not us. We're here to save lives, right?"

"Exactly," Devon says. "We're adrenaline junkies. We live for this shit."

That earns a chuckle from the crowd.

"How many were targets?" someone yells.

"We don't know how many of them were actual targets," Devon answers, "so assume everyone is at risk for the Wolves to come finish them off. Don't leave patients alone, but stay safe. It's great that people are fighting back, but I don't want those people to be you. You can't save anyone's life if you're dead."

Devon rubs his head and looks at a sheet of paper in his hand. "This might not be the right time to mention this," he says, "but Julia, a nurse who has been with Parkhill for six years, has not shown up to work in two days. We called her family, checked her house, but it seems she's gone missing, assumed to be a Wolf disappearance. She was supposed to be in today, so we're short, but three more nurses have called to say they are coming in to help. More will probably come without notice."

Many people have gone missing since the Wolves started attacking, but I'm still shocked to hear about Julia. We aren't best friends, but I enjoy her company. She sneaks protein bars to me to make sure I get food on days I'm too busy to take a lunch break, and she always has gum.

Devon explains the assignments, none of which involve Edda or me. Everyone disperses, but he holds up his index finger to tell us to wait.

"Are you feeling okay, Resi?" Devon asks, his tone hushed.

I lean in instinctively because he's acting like he's going to share a secret. "Uh, yeah. I feel fine. What's going on?"

"Good, I need two people I trust upstairs. Come on." He starts power-walking out of the ER toward the elevators.

Edda and I share a look of confusion as we follow.

"Want to expand on that?" Edda asks. We file into the elevator.

Devon swipes his badge and presses the button for the roof. "Wish I could," he says. "Life Flight is transporting a patient here. They told me to recruit my best and make sure they're trustworthy. That's all. It's probably the governor or someone important."

I would be flattered to be chosen for such a top-secret mission if it wasn't for the unyielding concern I'm receiving from Edda. A look that oozes 'are you sure you're okay? Because I'm worried you might be clinically insane.' Crazy or not, I'm still a damn good nurse, and I'll prove to Edda that I'm just as competent as I was two days ago.

The helicopter lands, and I shield the wind it generates with my arm, ducking as we run to help the flight nurses with the gurney. Ducking honestly has no purpose, but I do it because it makes me feel safer, like it will protect me from the spinning blades of the helicopter if they loosen and fly toward my head.

Each of us halts suddenly when the gurney from the chopper hits the ground. My legs grow heavy and my head dizzies. An unconscious man with blood-stained light blonde hair is tied down with restraints, a Triangle Blade protruding from his clavicle. A flight nurse holds his black and white mask, which ripples in the wind, dangling between her palm and the metal of the gurney she's pushing. The Triangle Blade penetrates a black and grey uniform.

No one in the ten months of this terror has captured a Wolf.

Edda turns to me, and after a few unsure seconds, she blinks hard and shakes her head once to reset her focus. "Non-maleficence. Do no harm," she yells over the powerful pulsations of the helicopter. "We treat him like we treat everyone."

We come to our senses and roll the gurney inside. The heart monitor to which the Wolf is attached and a bag of supplies rests between his legs. The Triangle Blade almost spans the width of my shoulders and stands a foot above the man's chest.

"If it didn't hit his lung, he's one lucky bastard," a flight nurse says. "He's breathing fine so far but lost quite a bit of blood."

"Blood bank has already been called," Devon says. The elevator door opens as soon as he presses the button.

"Holy…" Dr. Locke stands in the elevator. We pull the gurney in and join him, then I press the button for the ground floor, back to the ER. "I was called to meet you. I had no idea it was—I thought their uniforms were impenetrable."

The Wolf on the gurney suddenly thrashes and bucks, his eyes wild.

"He's awake!" a flight nurse yells.

"No shit," I reply, eyeing his movements for the best way to keep him restrained.

"Do you have Ativan? Versed? Any kind of sedative?" Devon asks the flight nurse.

"Give me that bag," the nurse says to me.

I grab it from between the Wolf's legs, barely missing a knee to the chin when I pull back and toss the bag to the nurse. She and Devon crouch and sort through the supplies. Edda throws herself onto the man's legs to hold him down further, but his knee plows her chest, causing her to clutch it and stumble back. She winces as she leans against the elevator wall.

"I'm okay," she says when she sees me start toward her. "Just knocked the wind out of me."

When I turn my attention back to the Wolf, his left wrist restraint comes loose, his hand slipping through the knot holding it down. I'm on his right side near his feet, and the space between the elevator door and the gurney is too tight for me to run to the other side. The only other people left standing are the second flight nurse and Dr. Locke, who are on the patient's right side near his head, trying to stabilize the area where he was stabbed. Devon is closest to the loosening restraint. He is drawing up medication on the floor, but he's my best bet.

"Devon!" I point to the Wolf's wrist. "His restraint." But it's too late. The Wolf frees his arm, reaches for the Triangle Blade, and pulls it swiftly out of his chest with a howl.

"NO." Our protests resound in unison. He holds the blade high as everyone steps back—a visceral reaction to a weapon we've seen kill hundreds of innocent people. But the Wolf is distracted when he notices the blood flowing out of his wound, which pulsates in time with the beating of his heart. He hit an artery.

"Idiot!" I yell. "You just killed yourself faster."

The chime of the elevator alerts us to our arrival back to the ER. Devon takes advantage of the diversion of the door opening and grabs the man's wrist. His grip loosens immediately, and the blade falls to the floor.

"That was easier than I thought it would be," Devon says.

"He's getting weaker," a flight nurse replies.

I step out of the elevator and grab the first blanket I see, then hold it to the Wolf's wound at his shoulder, leaning with all my weight as the others wheel him to the room.

"You," the Wolf says, his eyes almost accusatory as they lock onto mine.

I don't know what to do. I browse my co-workers' reactions, but they're as taken aback as I am by his exclamation.

"What *about* me?"

He gasps for air; that sound made when too much water goes down the wrong pipe. He starts to panic and grasps at the rails beside him. He can't breathe.

"Tracheal deviation," Edda says, pointing to his neck where his trachea curves to the left. "He has a pneumothorax. I'll set up for a chest tube."

"You made your lung collapse with that stunt you pulled," I bark as I continue holding pressure. I search the room for someone standing around doing nothing, and instead opt for a shout to anyone listening. "Somebody grab the emergent blood and call the OR."

I want to ask again. I want to know what it was that made him pause at the sight of my face. But it will have to be later. The Wolf's eyes roll back, and he passes out.

CHAPTER 6

"We did everything we could, but between his lung collapsing and the blood loss, we couldn't get him stable fast enough," I explain to Cole as we walk hand in hand toward the theater. I'm wearing my favorite black dress with blue and grey jeweled accents, and my feet already throb in high heels, but I have a whole symphony to lounge through, so I don't let it bother me.

"Any idea why he thought he knew you?" Cole asks.

"No idea. It was so bizarre."

"Did they figure out what the uniform was made of? I thought it was impenetrable."

I shrug. "No idea. But I guess the Triangle Blade cuts through it."

We walk into the lobby. It's busier than expected. More and more civilians have decided to try and get back to everyday life. Maybe people were inspired by the civilians fighting back and hearing that a Wolf was caught. Whatever the case, it warms me to see so many people happy, dressed up, and carefree. The city has been through so much. We all deserve a night out.

"Did they identify the Wolf?"

"That's the strangest thing." We show our tickets to the usher, and he leads us to our seats. "His name was *Bert*. Can you believe that? Bert. Like a neighbor down the street you borrowed a shovel from. He was a husband and father of two kids, but he went missing from San Antonio a few months ago. He was a football coach, just a normal guy. Until he wasn't."

Cole steps aside so I can shuffle to my seat. We're six rows back in the orchestra section.

"So many people were injured," Cole says when we sit. "I heard there was a similar situation in Los Angeles yesterday where more civilians than usual were hurt in an attack."

"At least people are finally fighting back, you know?" I whisper energetically. "We've been so scared of the Wolves. It was refreshing to see that all those people jumped into action. They outnumbered the Wolves and teamed up trying to take the weapons, put them in choke holds, jumping all over them. A lot of people were injured, but only two died, who bystanders say the Wolves originally aimed for and seemed to be the targets. So, maybe fighting back didn't quite work, but at least they tried. It's about time."

"But the Wolves still got away."

"All but one."

Cole leans in, steals a kiss. Then he admires me with a half-smile. "I don't know if it's because I haven't seen you for a while or because I love listening to you get all medical, but I couldn't resist. You're beautiful."

I shimmy my shoulders. "It's got to be the dress. You should see me in something other than scrubs more often."

Cole laughs, displaying that damn dimple. "No, I mean it. It's not just the dress." He pauses, then tucks a loose piece of hair behind my ear. "It's you. Sometimes I'm so drawn to you it's disarming."

And then I'm speechless—major points for the dimpled doc.

The house lights dim, and the orchestra takes their seats on stage. One instrument sounds a long note, prompting the rest of the instruments to tune themselves to its pitch. The music of strings and horns quiets the chatter of the theater. I've always thought this was one of the most important parts of a symphony, if not the most important. One note sets off a flurry of chaotic sharps and flats, some runs and scales, filling the room with the uncomfortable tension of dissonance until each instrument finds its pitch, and they land in perfect unison. It gives me a rush of excitement and anticipation.

The audience applauds as the conductor walks onto the stage and bows.

The opening melody of Sibelius No. 2 resonates through the room. Music allows me to feel. Joy and sadness, pain and healing, love, and fullness; it all overwhelms me. I lose myself as I listen and watch as the bows of the stringed instruments dance, and the conductor waves his hands fluidly to the rhythm.

I'm no less entranced half-way through the third movement of the symphony. I close my eyes during a softer section of the music and let it move my imagination. The sweet sounds dissolve until one instrument sounds a long note prompting the rest of the instruments to tune themselves to its pitch. The music of strings and horns quiets the chatter of the theater. This is one of the most important parts of the symphony, if not the most important. One note sets off a flurry of chaotic sharps and flats, some runs and scales, filling the room with the uncomfortable tension of dissonance until—

Wait. I've already heard this tonight.

I open my eyes.

Did we move? Am I further back than I was before?

An uncomfortable sensation in my lungs forces a cough, and I cover my mouth with my hand.

No, not my hand, I observe—a man's. Again.

Shit. I fell asleep. I'm in a memory.

Shit. Shit. Shit! That means someone is dead. At the symphony!

I attempt to identify who I'm sitting next to, but the body I inhabit faces forward and listens to the music, refusing my desire to twist his neck to the right or left.

Why does this keep happening? What am I supposed to do with this? Why can't I just see who you are? I remember how simple it was to identify the girl in the mirror of the dressing room, and in my frustration, I start to speak aloud in this new person's body.

"This would be a whole lot easier if you were in front of a mirror, dude."

Before I can lament any further, I'm ripped from the symphony and standing in front of a mirror staring at the reflection of a short Indian man in a black suit, washing his hands in the theater bathroom.

"What in the…"

The man in the reflection dries his hands with paper towels and walks to the lobby to meet a woman dressed in a dazzling purple Indian sari. I sense his elation at the sight of her. He loves her. The woman hands him a glass. He sips. Whiskey. I hate whisky, but this time it tastes smooth, and the man's body relaxes.

He reaches into his pocket and retrieves their symphony tickets.

"Look at the tickets, look at the tickets." Maybe I'll at least figure out where they're sitting.

But his movements are too quick as he hands the woman one of the tickets.

"Damn it. Wait. Stop!" I panic.

The body in which I reside and the entire world around me pauses. The crowded lobby of the theater glitters with frozen, smiling faces. Three women pose for a picture behind the woman in the purple sari. A young girl joyously stands mid-twirl next to them with the skirt of her dress fanning out. A man to the left laughs with someone outside of my view, his hand in the air like he's about to buckle over and slap his knee. The bartender in the right of the dead man's distant vision is pouring red wine into a glass. The wine is frozen in mid-air like he's pouring it in zero-gravity. Directly in front of me, what the man's eyes are focused on, is the woman in the purple sari happily accepting the ticket, her hair pinned in a loose bun.

My own breathing is all I hear inside this body, steady but harsh.

I'm controlling it. I wanted him to stop... Why did I want him to stop?

Tickets, I remember.

I can't force the man's eyes to move, so I focus on his peripheral vision, peering as much as possible onto the ticket he's handing to the woman.

THE HOUSTON SYMPHONY PRESENTS:
SYMPHONY NO. 2 IN D MAJOR OP. 43 BY JEAN SIBELIUS
ADULT PRICE: $62
SEC: ORCHESTRA, ROW:...

The patter of applause after the third movement

startles me awake. Then the fourth begins. I'm flummoxed for a moment and glance around. I'm back in my original seat. I examine my hands to make sure they're my own, then lean over to Cole.

"Someone died here," I say with quiet urgency.

The dimple taunts me. "Really? Who?" he asks, as if he's playing along in some game I'm initiating.

"No, I mean, there's someone here right now who is dead."

"What? Resi, you were dreaming," he whispers, still smiling. "I saw you nod off."

"No. Trust me. This orchestra has to stop."

"Resi, they're almost done. I'm sure everything is fine."

"Advik? Advik? Somebody help, please!" a woman cries from the back of the orchestra seating. I leap to my feet and hurdle myself over the people in my row to get to the aisle. The orchestra's melody fades quickly. The house of the theater is too dark to find the purple sari.

"Turn up the house lights," Cole yells as if he's reading my mind. He appears beside me seconds later.

"He's not breathing. Please help!"

We whip our heads in the direction of the voice and run toward a group gathering. The victim has been pulled into the aisle, and a woman is pounding compressions into his chest. Her heels are discarded behind her and her hair is falling from what was once a neat updo. Her compressions are deep and quick. She's trained in CPR.

"You look like you know what you're doing," I say. I kneel opposite her beside the man.

"Medic in the army. You?"

"ER nurse."

"Good." She stops and places two fingers on the man's neck. "Take over. No pulse. I'll call an ambulance."

I know he's dead. I know it. But my instincts kick in, and I can't stop myself from doing CPR anyway. I also know that, sometimes, half the reason for CPR, even when there is no hope of revival, is to show the family that we did everything we could to save their loved one. So, I continue compressions for the man's wife, for the woman in the radiant purple sari, the woman he loved.

"Help! Up here! Help! She's not breathing!" a voice screams from the Mezzanine above us. I turn to tell Cole to go, but he is already moving.

"I've got it," he says.

The quiet concern of the audience shifts into a panic when they realize this must be an attack.

White foam oozes from the man's mouth. I recall the discomfort in his chest when he needed to cough.

"Ambulance is on the way," the army woman says.

"Have you heard of the Wolves using poison?" I ask.

She looks at the man under my tired arms, then back at me, and shakes her head.

Exhaustion weighs on us when Cole walks me to my door hours later.

Cole breaks the silence. "So, you knew that—"

"Yep," I reply, my tone flat.

"Because you had a dream of—"

"Yep."

"Both of them?"

"No. Just the first one."

"Wow." He rubs the back of his neck. "Do you want to talk about it?"

He believes me. That's refreshing. And a part of me does want to talk about it. I still have so many questions and unknowns about this *thing*, but he can't answer those questions, and talking about it feels vulnerable. I'm not quite there with Cole yet. I find myself wishing Edda or Brandon was with me tonight. The thought makes me sad that my best friends still think I'm psychotic. But I don't need them. I've been doing things on my own for a while now, and I can deal with this myself. There is nothing Cole, Edda, or anyone else can do about these dreams. I just have to get used to them.

"I'd rather not, if that's okay with you."

He nods. "Okay."

I appreciate that he doesn't push me. I reach my hand to his cheek, then lean in and place a small kiss to his lips.

"Thanks for taking me to the symphony," I say, feeling my lips bend just slightly. The smile grows when Cole's mouth twitches, and his shoulders start to vibrate. I join his howl of laughter when it echoes through the street, doubling over with a hand over my face. With the dramatic turn the night took, thanking him for the symphony reminds us that there was a symphony at all. I don't know if it's our exhaustion or the ridiculousness of the situation that makes us laugh so hard, but either way, it's good to laugh.

"Can I come in?" Cole asks, stepping in closer, placing his hands on my shoulders.

I pull my bottom lip between my teeth. I'm sure his company would be nice, but it would cut into my important nightly routine of searching for my mom, and I have a lot to process tonight.

"Not tonight. A lot has happened, and..."

He squeezes my shoulders. "I get it."

We say our goodbyes and I walk into the house. My mind jostles back and forth between the images in Advik's memory and seeing his lifeless body in my own.

The laptop powers on as I sit at my desk and pin the map to the wall.

I was in the same room as Niko and the actress when they died. Same with Advik. Maybe that's how I was able to get their memories.

Surveillance shows the same street as always. Nothing new or exciting. I click Fast-Forward.

I controlled it. I stopped the memory when I told it to stop. I was able to move to a memory that helped me figure out who he was.

How?

I open Google Chrome, type into the search engine, ASTOR KEPLER RESEARCH ON MEMORY. And in another window, ASTOR KEPLER RESEARCH ON DREAMS.

I scroll through the myriad of articles and case studies my dad has published about the brain. None mention people's memories after they die.

But he didn't publish all his work, and he wasn't finished with his research on digitally projecting thoughts before his attack. There's so much more he studied; file cabinets full of unpublished brilliance in his office.

The office in the Kepler Lab.

I remember the fake brain Dad would use to teach me any number of things involving the mind.

"Oh, my gorgeous girl," Dad would say to me. I was eight or nine years old. Mom and Dad were rushing to finish their work at the lab to get home for another of their epic parties, but I didn't want to go. I loved spending time at the lab and I had been having fun painting the filing cabinets. So, I asked why he loved dance parties so much. He placed me in Mom's lap. She wrapped her arms snugly around me while Dad pointed to an intricate rubber model of the brain. "What a wonderful question."

I asked because I didn't want to go, not because I wanted to learn something new, but everything had an explanation with Dad. "Dancing involves the motor cortex." He pointed to a ganglion on the top left of the brain, then moved to another. "The somatosensory cortex, basal ganglia, and the cerebellum. It strengthens memory and neuronal connections, exercises your body, and most importantly..." He threw the rubber brain over his shoulder. I watched it bounce on the floor. "It's fun!"

Hector, the resident lab skeleton dressed in Dad's baby blue prom jacket and matching top hat was the supporting character in many of dad's anecdotes. "May I have this dance, dear Hector?" Dad asked as he bowed toward the skeleton with his hand outstretched. After a pause, he looked up. "What's that, Hector?" He stood and placed his ear next to Hector's head like he was listening to him whisper. "Ah, you're absolutely right." He turned to me. "Excuse me, Miss, would you mind if I borrowed your beautiful mother for a dance?"

"What do you think?" Mom whispered in my ear.

"He's kind of cute, right?"

I nodded with a giggle and let my mom get up. She took the top hat from Hector's skull and placed it on my dad's head. Then, I watched as my two favorite loons spun around their laboratory in each other's arms.

I click out of the Google search, then walk to the kitchen for a glass of water to soothe the ache in my throat.

She loved my father mightily, I said to the attendees at Mom's funeral. *Embraced every quirk with her entire heart, never turned him away when he asked for a dance.*

There are no happy memories once they're polluted by terror. I push it aside. Try to forget.

Screw the lab. I can't do it. I don't *want* to do it. Why put myself through that?

I can hear Edda analyzing me in the back of my mind. "You're coping through avoidance, but you need to grieve."

I know grief, Edda. It sucks. No thanks.

It's only as I set the water glass down that I notice the manilla envelope on other side of the kitchen. It's the thick kind with bubble wrap lining the inside. My name is printed in large letters on the front of it, my family emblem stamped on the top left corner: a compass with an anchor in place of the arrow. The delivery came from the lab. I fiddle with the necklace on my chest—a charm of our emblem.

I know exactly what it is when I see the stamp. I forgot that in my heated frustration and need to prove myself to my friends, I called Charlie and made an absurd request. I open the envelope and pull out a note:

Hope you don't mind, I let myself in.
Oh, and if I get arrested for this, I'm taking
you down with me!
Love,
Charlie

I'm surprised Charlie followed through. She's not one to break the law willfully. She probably did it to avoid any awkwardness since we don't speak much anymore.

I reach in again and pull out the contents. Two glass vials containing the same substance: Propofol.

Horrible idea, Resi, I say to myself as I place them in my purse. *I'll give them back to Charlie tomorrow.*

I don't need to prove myself to anyone. Instead, I'll ignore it. There's nothing I can do about dead people's memories, anyway. From now on, these dreams don't exist.

CHAPTER 7

"Hey. Happy day off," I say to Brandon when he walks into my house the next day.

"Thanks." He flails himself onto the couch, his feet hanging over the arm. He reaches for the remote on the coffee table and turns on the TV. "Same to you."

I enjoy seeing Brandon so relaxed and vulnerable. He is on guard when on duty, ready to save lives in a moment's notice, ready to defend himself if injuries are from domestic violence or gang-related. He never knows what he is going to walk into on a call as a paramedic and fireman. His demeanor is similar with Sarah, constantly checking on her, making sure she has everything she needs, never relaxed. So, when his days off fall on the days Sarah is at school, he can truly rest and enjoy himself.

I clear dishes from the table and set them in the sink. "I'm going to finish cleaning the kitchen, then we can go." He finally agreed to go to the flea market with me after badgering him for weeks.

"Cincinnati had their first Wolf attack this morning." Brandon is watching the news. I'm not even sure he heard me. "Only one target, but some others were hurt too."

Water from the sink splashes over the dirty dishes, so I raise my voice a bit. "That's horrible, but maybe people will stop thinking it's a hoax. How many states is that now?"

"Twenty." He crosses one leg over the other at his ankles. "Attacks in new cities always make me wonder why they started in Houston."

"And why we have so many more attacks than other cities," I add. "It's happening more and more. I think there have been ten killings nationwide just this week. That's twice as many as usual. I'm kind of hesitant to go out."

Brandon keeps his eyes on the TV but points the remote at me.

"What are you doing?"

"Changing your mind."

My eyes roll. "You're mastering the dad-jokes, I see."

"You're easier to find and kill when you're in your own home, Resi."

"I know, but—"

"It *feels* safer. But it's been proven that it's not. We all agreed to live our lives, and you've been bugging me about going to the flea market for months." Dramatic. It's only been a couple weeks, but I get his point. "We can't let the Wolves dictate how we live our lives."

"Yeah, yeah. I know. That's my line," I say. He's right, but I can't shake the anxiety pinching my stomach; the image of Advik under my hands as I compressed his chest. I slide a coffee mug onto the dishrack, deciding I won't let it get to me. "Oh, and do you mind if we swing by the hospital on the way home from the flea market? I need to meet up with Charlie for a minute."

Brandon perks up on the couch. "Sure," he says. "Charlie Clay? Your parents' research assistant?"

"Yep."

"I haven't seen her in a long time," he says. "You two still keep in touch?"

"No, not really. I see her around the hospital, but I haven't talked to her much since Mom's funeral."

"So why the sudden meeting? I thought Charlie was one of those things you avoid because of your parents."

I stop what I'm doing and stare at him blankly. He knows we have an unspoken rule about not mentioning my maladaptive coping mechanisms. Plus, he's wrong. I don't avoid her. I just don't have reasons to interact with her anymore since I'm not at the lab.

I avoid the lab. Not Charlie.

I think.

"I called her and said I wanted to meet," I say, returning my attention to the dishes. "I have something to return to her."

Brandon stands and strides over to the bar stool on the opposite side of the kitchen counter. "*You* called *her*?"

Obviously, I don't want to get into it, so his third-degree questioning is annoying. "Yeah. I called her. We don't have to make it a huge thing."

"What are you returning?"

"None of your business." I expected that question and decided on the answer before the conversation.

"Why the hospital? Why not meet her at the lab?"

"You *know* why." I shoot him a glare, then focus on the frying pan under the faucet. He already said it, I avoid the lab because it reminds me of my parents. He's intentionally pushing me.

"When?" He ignores my hints to drop it and continues the interrogation.

"I told you. After the flea market."

"No. When did you call her?"

"The other day, Brandon. It's not that big a deal."

Brandon examines me, his eyes narrow. "You told Edda that you were making a phone call after you told us about your dreams. I heard you say that when Sarah and I were walking out," he recalls, stepping on my hope of evading the dream topic. I'd rather not have someone make me feel crazy today. "Is that when you contacted her? Did you tell her about your dreams? Did you ask her for your parents' research on dreams? Because that's a great idea."

"I don't even know if they ever studied dreams."

They probably did. They studied so many different things I could never keep track. I was occupied with my own interests, and some of their research was done before I was even born. I only kept tabs on the projects they wanted to publish. But my dad was a neuroscientist. I'm *sure* he studied dreams.

For argument's sake, however, "This has nothing to do with my parents. And I said I don't want to talk about it." I scrub a plate that has nothing on it while I think about the fact that it would be smart for me to ask Charlie to investigate any research they have on dreams. But their work is so unorganized, it would take her ages to find anything useful.

"Well, it *should* have something to do with your parents," Brandon says. "Maybe their research could help you figure out why you're having these dreams. Especially since your dad did research on the brain. I'm sure he knows a lot about dreams with grief and Post

Traumatic Stress Disor—"

"You know what?" I drop the plate in the sink and place my wet hand on my hip. "Cole asked me last night if I wanted to talk about something and I said 'no.' You know what he did? He dropped it."

Brandon's head rears back at the abrupt shift. "The hell does that mean? What does Cole have to do with this?"

"*He* respected my answer and didn't push me." I point a finger at him.

Brandon lets out an exasperated 'ha!' and gets up from his seat.

"This is funny?" I ask.

"Cole doesn't push because he doesn't know you and because he's a pansy."

I scoff. "Cole knows me plenty."

"If he knew you, he'd know that you *need* to be pushed sometimes, Rez." He moves around the counter and into my side of the kitchen. "You think you're made of steel, *so* independent, but you shouldn't be handling this on your own."

"Why can't I handle this on my own? Because I'm a woman?" Brandon isn't misogynistic, but it's the only button I can think to press at the moment.

"Oh, please, Resi." He's a foot away from me now, his large frame standing rigidly over me. I cross my arms and turn my head away, his intensity too vexing to look at. "Don't give me that bullshit. This has nothing to do with you being a woman. You shouldn't do this by yourself because you're *human*. No one should have to deal with this on their own. It's too much. We all see horrifying shit every day, and *you* lost both your parents when it started. And now, you're having

weird dreams about dead people after months of trying to hide the fact that you're still searching for your
mother."

My eyes go wide and drift to my desk, empty but
for my laptop which is shut down.

"Yeah. I know about that," he says. "So, no. I'm
not going to be a pushover and let you shut me up. I'm
going to force you to let me in and never let you be
alone in this. Ever. So, *you* shut up and get used to it."

I have no response. I'm not even sure what
we're talking about anymore, but there's something
strangely soothing about the danger of Brandon's stare.
It tells me that I'm known and loved; that he demands
to be a part of my life even if it's painful.

"You like Cole because he's safe," Brandon spits.
His volume drops, but his disgust of Cole is sharp. It
pulls me away from his glower. "But the dude is boring
and soft."

I slam my hand down on the faucet handle to
turn off the water. "There's nothing wrong with safe."
I'm done arguing, so I go to grab my purse from the
countertop. "Are you coming with me or not?"

"I already told you I would go." He grips my
elbow to stop me before I reach for the doorknob. He
sighs, and his body relaxes. "I didn't mean to start a
fight."

I release the tension in my shoulders too. "It's
okay." I gesture with my head toward the door. "Let's
go."

We're quiet as I drive. I'm embarrassed that he
knows I've been hunting for a dead person. I can't blame

him if he thinks I'm crazy—that *is* crazy.

I tap my thumb on the steering wheel. "How'd you know?"

I see him turn toward me in my periphery, and he takes a few seconds before he answers, maybe trying to remember what I'm talking about.

He looks back out the window. "I dropped Sarah off at your place one morning before work, and I guess you forgot to clean it up. I saw how worn the map and articles were. Figured you'd been doing it for a while."

I nod. "And you still left your kid with me?" My voice is quiet—hesitant. "Even though that's kind of crazy?"

The small laugh through his nose is barely perceptible. "Who better to relate to my kid who misses her mom than my best friend who misses her mom?"

A smile slowly dances across my lips. My love for Sarah and gratefulness for Brandon's trust makes me feel things. He is sweet enough that I've almost forgiven him for his comments about Cole.

But my smile reverses when the thought occurs to me. "Does Edda know?"

He sputters. "You think she'd find that out and not say something to you about it?"

"Good point."

"Oh, god." Brandon leans forward in his seat. His hand reaches for the handle of the door. "Park the car and get down."

"What?" He opens the door before I have time to come to a complete stop. "What are you doing?" I reach for his arm to stop him, but he steps out of the car and rushes toward the market. I park and turn off the ignition.

As soon as I see it, I shuffle and reach for my phone. My fingers shake when they press 9-1-1.

"We need police and an ambulance at the Bargain Bucket Flea Market immediately." I step out of the car, drop my phone on the driver's seat without hanging up so they can locate us, then crouch while walking warily to the scene.

Four Wolves slink away from the flea market in a circle carrying Triangle Blades as they make their escape. This is one of the Wolves' strengths: even when they only target one person, they attack as a group; they have each other's backs. Wolves always outnumber their targets. They are strategic and skilled in everything they do.

About three feet away from the Wolf pack lays the target. She is motionless on the ground and bloodied around her chest. Seven or eight people stand at a distance around them, watching the scene play out behind cars and outdoor furniture displays. A four or five-year-old boy screams and weeps alone from a shopping cart full of table chairs as the Wolves pass by him. A pit forms in my stomach, discerning that the boy has just been left motherless. I feel for him, wanting nothing more than to hold him and tell him that he will be okay.

The same lie everyone told me.

Three bystanders point guns toward Wolves, which I recognize as a defensive habit, but everyone knows guns will be fruitless. Police and military tried all sorts of ammunition when the Wolves first appeared, but stopped when they realized it didn't work.

Someone fires a shot to prove it. The bullet hits the thigh of a Wolf, then it falls to the floor next to him like a coin thrown against rubber. Not one Wolf flinches. As usual, they continue moving away from the crime. I imagine they laugh at the public's pathetic attempts to stop them.

I have no idea what comes over me, but it's happening. I'm yelling, "The Triangle Blade! It pierces through their uniforms!"

My voice startles the crowd, and in a moment of weakness, two Wolves rotate their heads in my direction. The boy, still weeping, stands and balances himself in the seat of his shopping cart, reaches for the head of one of the Wolves as he passes. He latches onto the mask and pulls the Wolf's head back with a yelp. Brandon and two other people nearby—a man and a woman —jump into action. I think they are military. They're dressed in regular clothes, but I can tell by the way they're built and move, upright and systematic.

Brandon swings at someone. I wonder if I should jump in and help him fight, but I can't keep my eyes off the boy. The Wolf he is latched onto holds his blade away, as if he is trying to keep the boy from harm. The Wolf reaches back with his opposite arm and takes a fistful of the boy's shirt to throw him off, but the boy's grip is stronger than the Wolf expects.

"Get him off!" the Wolf yells.

A Wolf fighting the military woman sees the struggle and mocks him. "Schooled by an infant?"

The woman stumbles to her right when he elbows her cheek. She steadies herself and swings her arm, but the Wolf stops her fist with one hand and uses the other to drive his blade through the flesh of her abdomen. My breath becomes ragged in my throat at the woman's guttural roar.

Without warning, the Wolf jabs the blade further into her, then jerks it back. The horrifying sounds of gurgling replaces her screams as she sinks to the ground.

Sirens ring out in the distance.

The Wolf flings his wrist once to whip blood off his weapon, then turns to his accomplice struggling with the boy. He reaches up, takes the boy by the arm, and uses all his power to unlatch him from his teammates back, catapulting him into the air toward a large armoire. The boy's body crashes into it, but his head is further out than the edge of the furniture, and it snaps to the side. "No!" I dart forward as the armoire falls over opposite him, and he slumps to the ground.

"Not his spine. Please, not his spine," I pray, running around the chaos behind furniture displays to get to him.

I fall to my knees and place my fingers to the kid's neck. He has a steady pulse, but he isn't breathing. I open his jaw, careful not to move his head, and breathe into his lungs twice, watching his chest to make sure it rises with each puff of borrowed air. I wait, but he still isn't breathing. I check his pulse again, then give two more breaths.

The next breath comes on its own. Then another. And the boy opens his eyes. I lean back on my legs in relief.

"Hey, bud. I'm Resi," I say, placing myself in his view and assessing his head. "Can you tell me what hurts?"

Pupils are even and normal in size. Eyes track my movements. No bleeding from his nose or mouth.

He blinks slowly. "My neck. And my head."

I nod, assess his ears. No blood or cerebrospinal

fluid. I glance over his body. No obvious deformities. He winces, raises his arm like he's going to hold his head, but I grab his hand instead. "Can you raise your other arm?"

He does. Good. I take his other hand in mine. "Now, squeeze my hands."

"Okay," he says. Nothing happens.

There's a shift in the movement of the fighting crowd a few meters away from us. I glance up and see the Wolves moving away from everyone else.

"Squeeze *really* hard," I encourage, returning my focus to the boy.

His eyes water as he glances from his hand to my face. "I can't do it."

"It's okay, you're doing a great job," I say.

Arm function, but not hands. C5, maybe a C6 injury? Or is it C7? I can't remember. I shake my head, try not to draw any conclusions yet, and place his arms down gently. "Can you wiggle your feet?"

"Like this?" he asks. I try to keep my face from showing my fear while I watch his feet lay limply on the concrete.

He's paralyzed.

I force a soft smile. "Okay, buddy. It's important that you stay very, very still." I position myself to hold his head steady, so he doesn't cause further damage to his spine. "Do not move your head at all. Can you do that for me?"

"Yes." His voice quivers.

The crescendo of the sirens indicates that the police or ambulance has arrived, but as I lift my head to see them, my view is blocked by a Wolf hovering over me.

I should be screaming, but my brain shuts my larynx down. Email advertisements for boxing classes flash through my mind, and I silently curse myself for deleting them. Instead of drop-kicking the Wolf, like I'm sure I could have if I'd paid $59.99 a month for a membership, I continue stabilizing the boy's neck and helplessly wait for the Wolf's move.

But he just stands there, moves his head to the boy, then back to me. I might be reading too far into this, but I get the feeling that the Wolf is concerned about him.

"He—he's okay," I stutter.

The Wolf bobs his head once, then flees. The other Wolves have already disappeared.

My eyes land on Brandon, still in the spot where he was fighting, a few feet from the woman who was stabbed minutes ago. He's on his hands and knees, catching his breath, his arm bleeding from a gash.

"Brandon!" I call out.

He holds his hand up. "I'm fine. Just a cut." He rolls over to lay on the concrete, and a young woman runs to him with a piece of cloth and pats his arm where it bleeds. I scowl as she tends to him.

"Hold some pressure on it," I say under my breath. "She obviously has no idea what she's doing." I glance down to smile at the boy.

He's not breathing.

CHAPTER 8

"Brandon, get over here *now*."

The ambulance pulls in. I breathe twice into the boy's little lungs.

"What happened?" Brandon lands on his knees on the other side of the boy and presses his fingers to his throat.

I give two more rescue breaths. "He has a pulse," I confirm, "but he snapped his neck and keeps losing his respiratory drive. Legs and hands paralyzed."

"Shit," Brandon says before giving the next two breaths.

"Ambulance is here. Think they can intubate on a kid this small with a c-spine injury?"

Two more breaths, then he looks the boy up and down. "They'll have to. He needs an airway."

Two more breaths. I nod. "We need to bag him before we lose his pulse." My chest tightens. I know how quickly these things can go downhill.

"We're not too far from the hospital," Brandon says. "If we get him there fast, he has a better chance." He twists his back to address the paramedics who are climbing out of their vehicle. "Backboard, c-collar, and bag-mask for a pediatric patient," he yells before they can get too far from the ambulance.

Two more breaths. "Do you know them?" I ask.

He nods. "They're good."

The medics run to us with the supplies. We place the collar around the boy's neck and log-roll him onto the backboard. A paramedic places the mask over his face and squeezes the bag, giving more consistent and effective breaths than Brandon and I could have maintained alone.

"We're riding with you," I say as they carry him to the truck.

I run to my car, a few paces away from the entire scene, grab my purse and phone, and lock everything up before meeting them again. I jump onto the back of the ambulance, start dialing the hospital while digging in the paramedic's supplies. "Go to Parkhill Hospital," I tell the driver.

"Emergency Room, this is Devon."

I hug the phone between my ear and shoulder. "Devon, it's Resi." I tape a probe on the boy's finger, connect it to the monitor to see if he's getting enough oxygen.

"Hey, you calling in for tomorrow?" Devon asks.

"No, I'm bringing a patient to the ER with Ambulance 313." The monitor starts reading the boy's vitals when the EKG leads are placed on his chest. Pulse 110, normal sinus rhythm, oxygen saturation 91%, and rising. "Pediatric Trauma Code 1, four or five-year-old boy." A paramedic places an oropharyngeal airway into his mouth—a small tube that will keep his tongue out of the way while they deliver air through the bag and prepare for intubation. I reach for a needle and tourniquet, take the boy's arm to find a vein. "Call surgery and get the CT scanner ready."

An arm lands across my chest and pushes me away from the boy. "Let the paramedics do their job,

Rez," Brandon says.

He's right. They're doing everything that needs to be done, I'm just getting in the way. I sit next to Brandon and go back to my call. "He was thrown maybe ten feet or more by a Wolf into a piece of furniture and snapped his neck. He's paralyzed and unable to breathe on his own. They're bagging him now but preparing to intubate." I recheck the monitor. His oxygen saturation is climbing. Good. "Pulses are present at 110, BP and O2 sats are stable." I look out the front window, seeing that we're closer to the hospital than I thought. "ETA five minutes at most."

"Got it," Devon says. "We'll see you when you get here."

I hang up and my eyes are drawn to the gash on Brandon's arm. "Damnit, B." I grab a rag from a shelf nearby, hold his arm steady with one hand, and put pressure on the wound with the other. "You're still bleeding." And it's deep. "You need stitches."

My eyes sting as they focus on his arm, the blood soaking through the material under my hand. He was hurt because I made him come to the flea market with me. A kid might be paralyzed. These attacks are becoming more frequent—I'm witnessing them in person more often. The Wolves keep escalating.

Tension grows in my chest. Thoughts run chaotically through my mind.

"Brandon, I..." My voice is shaky.

He reaches over, and places his hand on my shoulder. "Stop," he says, his voice soft and soothing. "Whatever you're thinking, stop." His hand moves from my shoulder to my chin. He nudges it. "Look at me."

Technically, I *am* looking at him, but I lift my

eyes anyway from his arm to his face.

"Breathe."

I do, inhaling slowly. *Four seconds in, four seconds out.*

"We're okay," he says. "I wanted to be here with you. This isn't your fault." Sometimes I'm baffled by how well he can read me. "We live our lives and save other lives when they need saving. We take this day by day, take whatever precautions we can. Right? This still would have happened if you stayed home but the kid wouldn't have had a fighting chance without you there."

Suddenly, reality surfaces, and I'm embarrassed by how much I was letting my anxiety show. It's something I usually suppress and hide. *Push it away,* I tell myself. I nod, straighten my back as the ambulance comes to a stop, and the doors open. "You're right." I set the rag down. The bleeding has stopped. "Thank you."

He smiles and jumps out of the ambulance, helps unload the gurney as gently as possible.

"I've heard of a few kidnappings but never an actual Wolf attack on a child," says Edda as I get out of the ambulance. The paramedics wheel the boy in before us, and I notice that they intubated while Brandon and I were talking.

"They didn't attack him. *He* attacked the Wolf," I explain. "His mother was the target."

"Resi Kepler!"

I turn toward the voice calling my name and see Mischa Linelli running down the sidewalk with her phone in one hand and a mic in the other. "Are you serious? Now is not the time, Mischa. Go away."

How did she know to find me here? I don't have

time for this.

"Who is that? Is it a child?" Mischa asks. "What happened?" She's getting too close now and I don't want her to get a good view of him. "Resi, I have questions about you and your—"

I whip around and invade her space. It startles her enough that she steps back. "What is wrong with you?" I say. I don't care if she gets this on video. She can manipulate whatever footage of me she wants, but I'm worried that she recorded the kid. That story won't be safe in her hands.

Her phone is easy to snatch away.

"Hey!" she protests.

I stop the video she's recording, then delete it. "You have no right to be back here, Mischa." I shove the phone into her hand. "No one has time for you and your conspiracies today. *Leave.*"

I don't give her a moment to respond before I walk into the ER and stand back. Edda and the rest of our ER team has taken over.

The CT confirms my fear that his spine is fractured too high. Brandon and I follow him to surgery, but I'm afraid that even if they can save him, he'll be paralyzed for life.

But there isn't a chance to fix his spine in surgery before his blood pressure spikes and heart rate drops, then eventually it stops pumping.

They compress his chest for an hour, circulating the boy's blood for him. They push epinephrine, hoping it will stimulate his heart to start beating again. The ventilator blows air into his lungs. But the flat line of his asystole heart pierces through the room.

"I'm calling it," the surgeon, Dr. Chen, says. The

nurses stop what they are doing and step back. One man flings his gloves from his hands and throws them on the ground as he pivots away from the boy with his thumb and finger pinching the bridge of his nose. Dr. Chen's voice wavers. These words are never easy with children. "Time of death, 11:43."

I stare at the boy who was so brave that he took on a Wolf to avenge his mother. How strong and full of life he was as he held onto the mask, refusing to let go. The Wolves didn't think him a threat, so they passed by closely enough for him to latch himself to them. Whether the Wolves got away or not, this boy is a hero.

I go over it in my head. We stabilized his neck, maintained his airway, identified the problem, and rushed him to surgery to fix it as soon as possible.

We did everything right, but I still feel defeated.

What would that Wolf have done if I told him the boy would not be okay; that he was going to die? What would the Wolf have done if I told him they killed him?

Anger stirs, heats my entire body like magma filling me, starting at the toes and working its way up to my chest.

"Did he tell you his name?" Brandon asks. I almost forgot he was standing next to me. "Those medics said his mother didn't have any ID on her, so we can't identify either of them. He's Unknown in the system for now."

"No," I answer shortly. "He didn't tell me." And I hate it. I hate that I didn't ask for his name. I should have asked for his name.

I grab my purse from the windowsill where I had set it when we got there, and I slide it over my shoulder. The two vials I placed inside it last night hit against one another with a *clink.* The noise reminds me of why I wanted it in the first place. Suddenly, I know what to do.

"But I can find out."

"How?" Brandon asks, but I'm already heading back to the emergency room, leaving him at the OR.

I text Charlie on my way there. *Can't meet today. Sorry. Maybe another time.*

The memories of the dead might come to me because they died when I was in the same building. At least that was true for Nico and the actress. Maybe it will work with the boy.

It's worth a shot. The boy deserves for his name to be known.

The supplies are readily available back in the ER, and even though I'm not in scrubs, no one questions me when I gather what I need for an IV.

I slap a sign on the door of an empty room so no one will come in: PROCEDURE IN PROCESS.

The tourniquet slaps my flesh when I fumble and fail to tie it around my arm. I'm successful on the second try, then finding a vein to start the IV is easy. I feel a bit like a meth-addict when I stick myself, but I do it anyway, flush the IV with saline and secure it with tape.

A few slow breaths help calm my trembling hands before I take a vial from my purse: *Propofol.*

The label confirms that I have exactly what I need: a potent and fast-acting anesthetic used to put people to sleep for surgeries and intubations. There are risks, and probably safer options, but those options either take longer or don't guarantee sleep. Propofol has a strong chance of unconsciousness and wears off quickly, so I won't be groggy for too long when I wake up.

I stare at the medication and bite my lip. Propofol *could* cause my blood pressure to drop or make me stop breathing.

It killed Michael Jackson.

But he was on tons of benzos. It was a combination of drugs that ultimately led to his demise. Right?

Plus, Propofol's half-life is so short, it will wear off in minutes along with the side effects.

It will be fine.

To be safe, I'll text Edda before I knock myself out.

The milky liquid fills the syringe as I draw up the lowest effective dose and attach it to the IV. I place the vial on the countertop, so Edda will be able to see it when she comes. Before I push the drug, I write a message to her: *Room 17. Come ASAP. Just you. No one else. Bring bag mask in case something goes wrong.*

I press *Send*.

"I'm so getting fired," I say before pushing the Propofol through my IV. It burns. I count out loud as I continue to push, feeling weaker and sleepier already. "Ten, nine, eight, seven... sih..."

"GO TIGERS," I shout to the team of tiny soccer players on the field. A searing headache pounds at my temples, but I power through it to cheer and clap as the players stumble over one another. The woman next to me almost spews her bottled water when we see three children in a row miss the stagnant ball.

A memory. I did it, I realize. But this isn't right. I'm not the boy like I expected.

Someone's hand is on my shoulder, pointing to the field. "Elisa, Jack has the ball."

My eyes follow the finger until they land on Jack. And there he is—the boy from the flea market. But he is slightly smaller and younger.

I'm the mom. I think of the woman's body in the flea market. Maybe she didn't die until we got there, so I got her memories before the boy, I speculate.

Pride surges through me—her—when Jack dribbles the ball towards the goal. *Phillips* is written on the back of his jersey, along with the number 8. He kicks the ball as hard as he can, falls backward, and misses the goal by at least ten feet. Elisa places her hand to her heart and laughs.

Stabbing pain shoots through her head. She squeezes her eyes shut and rubs her temples with the pads of her fingers.

"Good Lord, this headache," I say in Elisa's body. The echo of my words bouncing back to me reminds me of the memories I've seen before.

Since I have the name, but I'm still asleep, I suppose I'll play around with this. I'll try to control it like I did in the last one. Jack runs toward Elisa and she kneels down with her arms open, squinting as the sun shines through her sunglasses, aggravating the headache more.

"Momma," he says as he hugs her. "Did you see me?"

"I did. You were the *best*. I'm so proud of you."

I melt into the boy's triumphant smile. "Go get your snack," Elisa says, and Jack skips to a crowd of children receiving their snacks and juice boxes.

Control. I can control it, I remind myself, finding

my own mind again. I remember the two things I commanded in the memory at the symphony—location and freezing the moment.

I ponder my destination. "Go to your home," I command.

But nothing happens. Elisa stands on the same field watching Jack giggle with his friends while he eats his Rice Crispy Treat.

"Okay. Uh, everything stop," I say. "Freeze."

Jack runs back over to her. The other children disperse to find their parents.

"Seriously? What the hell? Pause. Stop. Quit!"

Nothing works.

Her hand folds over Jack's, and she reaches into her pocket to get the car key. A Honda CRV beeps, its lights flashing twice in the parking lot at the press of a button.

"Elisa!" The woman she was standing next to earlier jogs toward her. "I wanted to double-check and see if you and Jason would be coming over for our date night tomorrow."

"Elisa, Jason, Jack," I note. "The Phillips."

"Absolutely," Elisa says, forcing enthusiasm through the increased pain in her head caused by speaking with any kind of energy. "We'll be there."

The headache starts to subside, and a layer of film covers her eyes. Her surroundings blur. The friend's voice is muffled as she replies, and I don't quite catch what she says after that.

I blink a few times and notice the fluorescent lights of the hospital room. I rub my face and groan. I need to wake up and act alert, so no one notices something is off.

WHACK!

"That'll help." I pop up on the hospital bed after a hand smacks my cheek. I'm attached to a blood pressure cuff and an oxygen saturation monitor.

"WHAT THE HELL WERE YOU THINKING?" Edda shouts. In the four years we've been best friends, I've never seen her so angry. "Propofol? Were you trying to pull a Michael Jackson? Do you not remember what happened to him all those years ago? I should kill you myself."

I massage my stinging cheek. "Did I stop breathing?"

"No, but that's not the point. You're an idiot, Resi," she answers. "Damn it!" An anxious fury thickens the tension in the room as she paces, then doubles back to lean with her hands on the counter next to the sink.

Her intensity startles me. She's an emotional person, but anger usually isn't one that prevails. "I'm sorry, I must have scared you," I say. "I needed to find out what the boy's name was, and since he died while I was with him, I thought I might dream his memories."

Edda shakes her head, sighs. "And did you?" She turns around to face me, her arms crossed in front of her.

"No," I say. "It was his mom."

Edda's expression changes from disbelief to something a little softer. "His mom?"

"Elisa Phillips," I say, refusing to lose eye contact. Edda's arms uncross and fall to her sides. "Or at least Phillips was the name on the back of Jack's jersey. Jack—the kid's name was Jack. He played soccer. Horribly, but he loved it. Elisa drove a Honda CRV and had awful migraines."

Edda slumps onto the stretcher next to me. Her mouth is open, but nothing comes out. A few beats later, she finds her words. "His mom was brought in. A pointless attempt to revive her. She's a couple rooms down from here."

My eyes widen. She didn't seem revivable at all, so I wasn't expecting her to be brought to the ER.

"Her husband was on the phone with her when she was attacked, so it didn't take him long to find her," Edda says. "His name is—"

"Jason." I finish her sentence.

"Yeah, Jason Phillips. He identified both Jack and Elisa," she says, dumbfounded. She pauses for a beat. "So, you're having dreams about dead people."

CHAPTER 9

"This is stupid. I don't want to sit here and explain myself to everyone," I grumble. I'm just short of pouting in a lawn chair on the backyard porch of Brandon's house with Cole, Brandon, Edda, and Edda's husband, Coen, the next night. Signs stick up from the ground in the yard with the names of different vegetables written in Sarah's handwriting. There is enough room for tomatoes, carrots, and celery, but nothing has sprouted yet. A hand-built, wooden swing set with chipped pink paint occupies the rest of the space.

"Resi, chill. We believe you," says Edda. "Between my story and Cole's, who could doubt it? We just want to talk about this."

Brandon nods. "We wanted to believe it before, too, but it doesn't make sense. How is this possible?"

"You think I know the answer to that?" I snap. Cole reaches for my arm as some sort of lame comfort, but I pull away and point a finger at him. "Don't be sweet with me. I'm still mad at you for making me come here."

Cole picked me up for a date, but unbeknownst to me, everyone else had planned an intervention to make me talk.

I don't know why I'm so defensive. I'm happy that my friends believe me, but now they're trying to dig into this ability I don't understand and I'm uncomfortable making it the center of attention. These dreams make me strangely insecure, like something is wrong with me. I'm a circus freak.

"It's barely been three days since these dreams started," I say. "I already told you everything I know. There's nothing else to say."

Edda turns to Coen. "Any ideas for how this is happening?"

Coen is a genius, but this is beyond any prodigy's knowledge. It's weird and creepy and no one will understand it. Can't we leave it at that?

"I don't have an explanation, my love," he says to Edda. "I've considered every logical possibility, even that of Resi being the murderer, which would be the simplest answer. But the theory is impossible given the retelling of her dreams and the events that occurred on Friday."

My jaw drops at the suggestion. I shouldn't be offended by his comments. It's just Coen. He's a brilliant man who tends to spout off his thoughts and facts without consideration of anyone's feelings. He and Edda have been married a year, and Edda finds his habits "adoooorable".

Tonight, they aren't.

"The same goes for the night of the symphony," Coen continues, sweeping his dark hair back, which always falls in front of his eyes. "Since Dr. Walton accompanied you to the theater, there wouldn't have been time for you to set up a plan and target two victims by contaminating their drinks. Plus, from what my sensational wife explained, it seems it was evident the night you were hospitalized that you were startled by the name 'Nico' and the sight of his children. These occurrences give me confidence that your chronicles are factual and that you had nothing to do with these deaths. But there is still no scientific explanation."

"We don't think you killed anybody," Edda assures me when she sees my eyes begging him to stop talking. "Resi, I know you don't want to, but maybe you should consider—"

"No," I say. The thought has entered my mind dozens of times, but the answer is no.

"But they probably have a lot of research on—"

"I said no!" I raise my voice.

I remember the last time I was in the lab. I was sick with the flu, lying on a couch in the office. The lights were dim, and Dad was trying to make me laugh by playing Peggy Lee's *Fever* on his antique record player. Mom came in, sat down next to me on the couch, offered me tea and a grilled cheese sandwich.

"Still making those grilled cheeses over a Bunsen burner?" I asked, chills making my body shiver.

Mom laughed. "Of course. My sick-day specialty."

I sipped the tea, then set it on the table in front of the couch. Mom moved so I could lay my head in her lap.

"Did you ever think you'd still be taking care of your kid after she was a fully grown adult?" I asked.

She brushed her fingers through my hair with just enough pressure against my scalp to make me want to fall asleep. "I love taking care of you no matter how old you are, Honey."

Dad walked to the couch, sat by my knees. "Your mom is right. You cause more buildup of dopamine in our synapses than cocaine ever could."

I felt the feverish heat behind my eyelids when I rolled my eyes. "You're so weird, Dad."

"Even so," he said. "We'll love and take care of you till our dying days."

That would be weeks later.

"My parents' lab and all their research are off-limits," I say to my friends. If anyone has an explanation for what is going on in my head, it's Astor and June Kepler. But I can't convince myself to set foot in the lab. Not if they aren't in it. Not if they aren't making grilled cheese sandwiches and playing classics on the turntable. I can't do it. It's too much.

"Okay, okay." Edda holds her hands up in surrender. "We can figure this out on our own."

"Maybe there's nothing *to* figure out," I say. "I have these dreams. They're not hurting anyone. It's just something I have to deal with. I don't think there's anything you or I can do about it. Let's drop it."

Movement in the corner of my eye catches my attention. Sarah is out of bed, hiding at the edge of the sliding door where she thinks no one can see her, but I spot her mischievous eyes and wink at her. Sarah loves to listen in on our conversations and will sneak right back out if we send her to bed. I'll give her a few minutes, then point her out to Brandon.

"It's not what you can do about it, but what you can do *with* it," Cole suggests.

"What does that even mean?" I ask.

Edda jumps in. "I think what Cole means is, maybe you were given this gift to—"

"*Gift?*" I bark. "How is this a gift?"

"Well," Edda says. She places her hand in mine. "I mean, it's scary and strange, but it's also unique and maybe even powerful."

"Yeah, you're like one of the X-Men," Brandon says.

"So now it's a superpower," I say.

"Actually," says Coen, "the X-Men were mutants, a subspecies of humans born with superhuman abilities. It's a fictional concept. The likelihood of a mutant being—"

"Will all the men on this porch please shut up for a minute?" I interrupt.

Brandon holds a fist to his mouth to hide his laughter.

"Sorry," Coen says.

"I know it's a burden," Edda says softly. "I can't imagine. It must be weighty. But maybe you're having these dreams so you can help in some way. You know, if you do it safely and legally. Not with Propofol."

"These people are already dead when I have the dreams, Edda. I can't help them. I can't bring them back to life." My tone is sharper than I mean for it to be.

"But maybe you can help find the Wolves or figure out who they are," Brandon suggests. He leans against the rails of the porch. "All of the people you're dreaming about are Wolf victims, right? You have insight that no one else does. This could lead you to help stop the war."

The porch is quiet while everyone waits for me to respond. I think about Nico's children in the first dream: the love and affection Nico felt for them, which I experienced so palpably in his memory; their hugs and kisses; his son's chubby cheeks, and his longing to be just like his father. I think about the cruelty of having that man torn away from his kids. I would do anything to replace their mourning with the sweet giggles I heard as they ran to greet Nico in the safety of their home.

But there's nothing my dreams can do about it.

"I'm not sure what you guys want from me," I say. "I'm not a superhero. I hardly ever work out. I can't save people. This isn't my fight."

"Then whose fight is it?" Edda asks. "Nothing is working. No one has figured out who these terrorists are, and there are more attacks every day. We should all own it if there's something we can do, right?"

"You told me the other night," Cole adds, "that you thought it was great that so many people stepped up to fight against the Wolves at the Hermann Park attack. There's no reason you can't fight too."

"You don't understand," I say. "The memories have nothing to do with the Wolves or how the victims were killed."

"As far as you know. Maybe you're missing something," Edda suggests. "What about that Wolf at the ER who recognized you?"

"No. That guy was crazy. He lost a ton of blood, was about to die, and was delusional," I argue. "And the memories are random. Unrelated to the attacks. Plus, I wouldn't be able to do anything because I'm completely enslaved to that person's body. I feel and say and do whatever that person is doing in their memory. I can't even hold onto my own emotions or thoughts for long because I become so much a part of that person."

The symphony tickets flash into my mind.

"Except the night of the symphony," I say. "That memory was different. I had control over it, somehow."

"What do you mean?" Edda asks.

"When I was in the memory, I knew that the man had been to the bathroom before the show started. I knew the memory was there, but I hadn't seen it yet. When I said it out loud, I went to that memory, and the victim was in front of the bathroom mirror. And when I said 'stop' during the memory, everything froze. I've said things like that in other dreams, but it didn't follow my commands. I deliberately tried it last time, and it didn't work."

"What was different?" Brandon asks. "Did you do anything different that might have given you more control?"

"No. Nothing."

"It was the music!" All five of us turn toward Sarah's muffled voice. I forgot she was there. She leans her body backward to pull the sliding door open.

"You know, Brandon," Coen says, "children Sarah's age need ten to eleven hours of sleep every night. Sleep deprivation could alter her mood, behavior, and cognitive abilities."

Brandon raises a brow toward Sarah. "See? I've tried to tell you that not sleeping makes you dumber."

Sarah laughs and shakes her head. "Resi, it was the music. The music gave you the control," she says.

"Come on, Jellybean," Brandon says. He holds his hand out to Sarah. "Back to bed. Don't want to thwart your cognitive abilities."

"Wait," I say, holding a palm up to stop Brandon. "What do you mean, Sarah?"

"You were at the symphony," she says. "You told me that music activates your whole brain. That's why you had more control. Your whole brain was working because the symphony was playing."

I hash through her theory. "That's a good idea, Sarah. But dreaming activates the whole brain too."

"But does it make you smarter like music does?" Sarah asks.

"No, I guess not," I say. Dreaming works differently from music to influence brain function and memory.

"Maybe the music activated your brain in a different way than the dreaming did."

I remember all the ways my father used to rave about music and its effect on the brain; the way he would change a song during different subjects that I would study for school when I was younger so that I would better recall information. I think about the images he showed me of the brain listening to music; how every area would light up to show that it's activated. There's an upward draw to my lips, remembering his stupid yoga pose to show that music was yoga for the brain.

The music *could* have activated my brain during those memories in a way that gave me more control.

I yank Sarah, wise beyond her years, into my lap and tickle her in a bear hug. "You're brilliant, you little spy."

"You think I'm right?" Sarah asks.

I shrug. "Who knows? But it's the best theory we've got."

"Maybe we can test it somehow," Edda says. "We can spend a night at a cemetery, and you can fall asleep with music on. Then, we'll see what happens."

"Yeah, let's see just how creepy we can make this *gift*," I say.

"You have a better idea?" Edda asks.

My original plan to test this out involved the morgue and Propofol. "Maybe. But you won't like it." I debate telling her, knowing she won't approve based on her reaction the last time I sedated myself. If I do suggest it, it will be a fight—one I'm not too keen on having tonight. "Why don't we sleep on it?" I say. I pull Sarah in tighter. "And we'll start by tucking this girl back into bed."

Sarah takes my hand and we walk to her room. I perch myself on the edge of the bed as she shimmies under the covers. I tuck the comforter in on each side, effectively transforming her into a bedtime burrito. "There. Now you're stuck forever."

Sarah wiggles to test the snugness. "Thanks, Resi." She forces her heavy eyelids to stay open.

"You're my favorite. You know that, right?"

She giggles. "Mhm!"

"Don't tell the others."

"Resi?"

She catches my attention just before I stand. "Yeah?"

"My dad is a firefighter."

I squint my eyes. The statement is too obvious for her to be finished. "Yes, he is."

"Well, my first parents died in a fire," she says. "If my dad dies too, where will I go?"

My esophagus plummets into my intestines. My instincts beg me to tell her that Brandon won't die, that everything will be okay. But I can't lie to her, not one orphan to another. Brandon's job *is* dangerous sometimes. He and I haven't talked about it, but there's no debate in my mind about the answer. I lean over, propping myself up with my arm on the other side of the

Sarah burrito, and I make sure her hair is out of her eyes, so I can lock mine onto them.

"You'll go with me," I promise. "As long as I'm around, you'll never be without a family. Deal?"

Sarah nods, and her eyes flutter to a close. "Deal. Night, Resi."

"Night, babe."

The next morning, I awake refreshed. I find unexpected relief in the fact that all my friends understand what is going on with my dreams. It's less lonely. I didn't realize how lonely I'd been feeling until now. I slip into my scrubs to get ready for work and walk into the kitchen to make breakfast.

A knock at the door.

I glance at the clock on the microwave. 6:03 AM.

Strange. Concerned about who could be knocking at my door so early in the morning, I go to my phone to see if anyone texted about picking me up for work.

Twenty-six missed calls.

My heart speeds up.

I scroll through several "call me back" texts until I see one from Edda saying that she is heading to my house. I run to the door and fumble through the locks before swinging it open.

Edda.

Her eyes well up, and it's obvious it's not the first time she's cried today. Something bad happened. Something awful. I wait for Edda to explain, my heart running a marathon now. I know that look—I've used it far too often in the past ten months.

Not again. I can't lose anyone else.

"Brandon is at the police station," Edda says. A tear falls down her cheek. My body tenses. "He found a note. *The child won't be harmed.*"

I can't move. Can't speak, but my mind is screaming. No. Don't say it. Please, don't say it.

Edda sweeps away the tear, then chokes out, "Sarah is gone."

CHAPTER 10

"We checked the neighborhood? Friends? The school?" I scroll through my phone for anyone who knows Sarah as Edda drives.

"Yes, everything. We woke everyone up, her friend's parents, her teachers, neighbors. Everyone."

"There have been, what? Maybe ten Wolf kidnappings of children throughout the country. Why Sarah?"

Edda bites her lip. "I don't know. Why anybody?"

"And we're sure it was the Wolves? Could it have been anyone else? Or maybe she snuck out?"

"She's not exactly to the 'sneaking out' stage yet," Edda points out. "And Brandon found the same note that was left in the other kidnappings."

I give up on my phone, run my hand through my hair. Anger makes its way to my muscles until my hands are in fists. I swing my arm down and strike the car door. "Damnit!"

Edda gives me a moment, nods. "I know," she says.

Not again. This isn't happening again. The sense of loss overwhelms me, and it's so familiar. It's the feeling I hide from, the one I work so hard not to experience. The last time I felt it was the worst day of my life.

I saw Dad right before the bombing.

"How's my favorite daughter doing?" He walked around to the nurses' station where I sat and gave me a kiss on the head.

"Hi, Dad."

"Dr. Kepler," another voice said. A few nurses, doctors, and techs around me excitedly dropped what they were doing to say hello. Dad always had this effect on people.

"My favorite ER team," Dad says.

"We're so excited about the party tonight, Dr. Kepler."

Dad clapped his hands together. "Oh, good. I hope each of you can make it! Resi volunteered to do face paintings."

"I did *not* volunteer to do face paintings," I said.

"I don't get off until 11:00 PM," a resident lamented. "Otherwise, I'd be there."

"We'll just be getting started," Dad assured her. "The dance contest starts at 11:30. Then we'll open the bouncy-house-waterslide so everyone can cool down afterwards."

A newer nurse leaned over to me. "Is he kidding?"

"Unfortunately, no," I said. "My parents might change the theme and games from party to party, but the dance contest always starts at 11:30. I usually lose about two songs in."

"Not true," Dad replied. "I remember a time when you won!"

"Was I three?"

"Somewhere around there. Anyway, I was heading out to help your mother set up."

"It's 4:15. You're already done for the day?"

"I finished surgery an hour ago, and I decided I would surprise your mom by coming home early. She stayed home today to set up for the party. I'm surprised she could pull herself away from the lab. She heard about this new material called carbon nanographene from a colleague, and she's been utterly fascinated— studying it nonstop ever since."

"Carbo-nano-WHAT-ene? You made that word up."

Dad chuckled. "Carbon-nano-graph-ene," he repeated a little slower. "And I wish I could take credit for the discovery. It's a fascinating and dynamic substance."

He addressed the room again. "Now, I'm off to surprise my lovely wife. I'll see you all at 8:30. Or 11:30 for the dance contest!"

An hour later, my phone began buzzing incessantly in my pocket, but I was with a patient, assisting Dr. Locke in a procedure. I was about to apologize for the distraction, but Locke's phone started buzzing too. We shared a look of concern. When he finished the procedure, I washed my hands and pulled my phone from my pocket, which was still vibrating as it received text messages in the dozens:

Answer your phone.
Are you okay?
Resi, where are you?
Turn on the news. Is everyone okay?
Are you okay?
Is everyone safe?
There was a bombing in Houston.

Bombing in Houston. Bombing in Houston. Bombing in Houston.

I couldn't take my eyes off the words. When the patient's TV switched on, I saw that Dr. Locke had taken the remote and was flipping through the channels. His cell phone was in his other hand. He must have received the same messages.

"We're reporting from the air above the destruction," a news reporter said as a helicopter flew above a barrage of debris. The roofs of houses laid in disarray on the ground, pieces of burned wood were all that was recognizable at first glance. "We can't believe what we're seeing." The reporter's voice hitches. "This is the aftermath of a bombing that took place minutes ago on Harvard Street in the Houston Heights."

Their phones went straight to voicemail over and over as I paced the sidewalk in the ambulance bay. *Dad just left work,* I thought. *He couldn't have made it home before the bomb. Mom probably went out for supplies. They're fine. Just answer your damn phones.* Between the water in my eyes and the tremble in my hands, I couldn't dial any other useful numbers. I pressed the wrong name. Hung up. Another wrong name.

"Damn it!" I threw my phone, not caring where it landed. My knees weakened until they hit concrete. I held my head in my unsteady hands, begged whoever was listening for them not to be dead.

"Your parents' street?" The voice was calm, quiet, and steady.

I lifted my head to find Brandon's partner, Kyle, kneeling right in front of me. His eyes covered me with concern and compassion like a warm blanket. His bulky hand was extended to offer my now-cracked phone.

I took it, then nodded.

"C'mon," he said.

I don't remember the drive. I'm sure we took the

ambulance, but even that I can't recall. All I remember after that is laying on the fallen structures where my childhood home formerly stood. I remember weeping and vomiting and praying that my mom would walk up at any moment and give me a hug. I remember being physically removed from the debris and guided to a tree behind yellow tape.

We were there for hours. Kyle never said a word. He just sat there with me, completely silent.

The sun descended over the scraps of house, and fittingly engulfed every one of my memories into a veil of blackness.

"I have to know what happened here," I whispered.

Kyle looked up, his eyes searching the sky. Then, he nodded. "Okay."

I didn't understand what he meant at the time, but the next day, he was at my house with a flash drive that gave me access to the cameras surrounding my parents' street. "Not many people know I have this skill," he said. And we never spoke about it again.

That was ten months ago: April 17th—the day this all started.

Everyone knows someone who has been affected by the Wolves. But the thing about these attacks is that so few victims are targeted each time that people still believe it won't happen to them. And when it happens to someone close to them, they're sure it can't happen that close again.

Until it does.

"I already called the hospital. They know we're not coming into work today," Edda says. I've been staring through the window, fiddling with the charm on my necklace.

I think of what Edda said earlier—they left a note saying Sarah won't be harmed.

Jack Phillips, the boy who died at the flea market, pops into my mind, and the Wolf's concern when he was on the ground.

"I think I believe them."

Edda turns her head to me, then back to the road.

"Believe who?"

"The Wolves. Maybe they won't harm the kids." I note the confusion on Edda's face and continue, "There was a Wolf that stopped to make sure Jack Phillips was okay before he fled. At the time, I thought he would be. But it seemed like the Wolf was concerned for him."

"So concerned that he broke the kid's neck?"

"That was a different Wolf. Maybe he's the exception. Maybe that Wolf was more aggressive or something. Plus, he threw him, but I don't think he purposefully broke his neck." I'm trying to convince myself as much as Edda.

"Why didn't I have a dream the night that Wolf died at the hospital?" I wonder. "I was with him when he died. If I could see a Wolf's memories, maybe I could find her."

"Any dreams last night?" Edda asks.

"None," I say. "But I don't have them often when I'm at home. Only once."

"I've been thinking through this a lot," Edda says, "and I wonder if it's a proximity thing."

"Proximity?"

"Yeah. You were in the same store when Nico was killed. You must have been close to him because the bullet hit him before it hit you. Then you fell asleep right next to the girl you said was in a play. And you were on the same seating level as the man at the symphony. Someone else had been killed too but they were on another level, further away. Right?"

"Right."

"And the other day, you wanted to tap into Jack's memories, but instead you went into his mom's, who was a few rooms away from where you idiotically put yourself to sleep without any safety measures."

I ignore the last, unnecessary comment and debate the theory. "I thought I received the memories because I was in the same room at the time they died, but being near the body while I'm asleep makes more sense. Except for Roy Maxwell, the state rep. I dreamed about him the night he died. That couldn't have been proximity."

Edda screws up her face curiously.

"What?" I ask.

"Resi, Roy Maxwell lived in the house behind yours. I thought you knew that."

"*He did?*"

"You need to get out more."

I rattle my head back and forth, piecing this together. "So, you're suggesting that when I *don't* have these dreams it's because I'm... out of range?"

"I hadn't put it in those terms, but I guess that's exactly what I'm suggesting."

"That's ridiculous."

She raises an eyebrow. "More ridiculous than having dreams of dead people's memories in the first place?"

"Good point."

We walk into the police station. A long hallway

leads to several offices and other hallways, but an open area to the left is where we are ushered. There are six desks with one police officer on the far side of each, and any number of people dispersed around them. We find Brandon at a desk on the far right and Edda runs to comfort him, but I hesitate. I've seen Brandon get upset and I've seen him overwhelmed, but this is different. He's distraught. Maybe even lost.

Over the past ten months, I've distanced myself from other people who have been affected by the Wolves. They always want to 'relate' to me or tell me that they 'know how I feel'. I would rather not feel anything. Relating requires reliving. Ignoring is much easier.

But Brandon is different. He and Edda are my family now, and he is the last person I'd ever abandon just to keep my own emotions at bay. He has to know that, as much as I'm not alone, he's not either. I don't know what he is going through. I'm not dumb or cliché enough to tell him that. But I admit there is some connection formed when you've been injured on the same battleground.

He catches my eyes while Edda hugs him, and I walk over to do the same. When I pull back from his arms, I reach into my pocket and take out a necklace with a charm that is identical to mine and place it in the palm of his hand.

"Your family emblem?" Brandon asks. His eyes are red and sunken.

"This one was my dad's," I say. "I grabbed it for you before we left the house. It's a compass with an anchor as it's arrow. The anchor is a symbol of hope and love. It's a reminder that no matter where life takes you, or what direction you go, hope and love will always ground you. Your fears, emotions, and expectations will change and sometimes even feel out of control, but hope is always hope, and love is always love. Hold on to those things, and you'll be anchored no matter where you are. Dad made the emblem before I was born. He had no idea how much I would need it one day."

Brandon wraps his fist tightly around the charm. "Thank you."

CHAPTER 11

"Wolf attack on Gessner and Westheimer," a voice announces through the radio on Deputy Roberts' desk as he takes Brandon's report. I'm standing behind Brandon's chair, Edda beside me, when the voice continues, "Three injuries, one fatality. No further backu—". Deputy Roberts rotates a knob on the radio to silence it.

Roberts is a young detective, probably in his mid-twenties, with a lean but muscular build and a pointy nose. He is thorough and attentive but fidgety. It's clear to me he is new and inexperienced, but I'm not going to point that out to Brandon.

"Your report will be filed with the Terrorism Unit. They will assign an investigator to your case and will contact you with updates as anything unfolds," Roberts says.

"But what are you going to do right *now*?" Brandon asks. "And can you find out any details about the Wolf attack they just called in?"

Roberts purses his lips with an understanding stare. "I promise we will do everything we can to find her," he says, warmly.

A loud thud in the hallway causes the room of policemen and report-giving civilians to turn. Two men scurry past the room with a rolling table carrying a human-sized mass in a white bag.

Gasps scatter across the room.

Brandon hops to his feet. "Is that a body bag?"

My heart jumps into my throat as the men hurry to wheel it away.

I didn't get a good look. The body seemed small, but it was gone so quickly. My brain wasn't working fast enough for me to assess whether it was child-sized.

Roberts continues to clack the keys on his computer. "Probably. Sometimes they bring bodies through that entrance if the door to the forensics lab gets jammed."

Before they're out of earshot, I hear one of the body transporters say, "The door didn't hit the kid, did it? I don't want to screw up any evidence."

The kid.

I share a glance with Edda, and I know she wants to keep Brandon as calm as possible until we have more information, but he is already in sheer panic, wide-eyed and pale-faced. He clutches Sarah's backpack, pressing it into his stomach. There is something sad, yet sweet about his large, manly form holding a small brown backpack with yellow trim and teal flowers.

Brandon whips around to Roberts, leans over his desk. "How can you find out whose body that was?"

"I can't," Roberts says. "It's classified."

"What if it was my daughter?"

Roberts' eyes narrow, then look in the direction the body went, then back to Brandon. He sighs. "I don't think that was your daughter, sir. But if it was, you'll be the first to know."

Brandon hit's the desk with a loud thump, turns away. "Coen?" He squints his eyes toward the hallway.

Sure enough, Coen follows briskly in the direction of the body. Brandon says his name a little louder.

He pauses.

Coen is one of the forensic analysts that works with the police department. If there is any reason for him to be at the station, it's to investigate a body in the forensics lab. He will have answers.

His eyes move between the three of us.

"Hi," Coen says. His demeanor changes from walking with a mission, to shock, to a forced happy-to-see-you in a matter of seconds. He kisses Edda's cheek. "What are you doing here, my love?"

Edda eyes him. "I told you. Sarah went missing this morning. We just finished giving the report."

"Of course. Right. Yes. I'm so sorry to hear about this," he says to Brandon, taking his hand in a handshake and sympathetically placing his other hand on top of it. "Children are resilient, Sarah more so than most. She'll be back home soon." His speech makes Brandon's eyes water, but it sounds rehearsed like Edda coached him.

"I'm sorry to cut this gathering short, but I should get to my duties," Coen says.

"Was that a body they just carried in?" I ask. "Was it from a Wolf attack? Do you know who it was?"

Coen locks his hands together in front of him. "Was there a corpse?" he asks, tapping his foot. "I'm unaware of... I, um... I have some paperwork to attend to. That's all."

"Listen, Brandon," Coen says. He stands up straighter, changing his disposition as drastically as he changes the subject. "98.8% of children who go missing return home." Edda's head pops up, and she shakes it quickly. Coen has gone off script. But he doesn't see her protests. "Although, I supposed that hasn't rung true for what we believe are Wolf kidnappings. None of *those* children have returned home. Still, only one in ten thousand kidnappings result in a homicide."

Coen means for the statistics to be comforting. But when someone you love becomes a part of the statistics, the small percentage of children who don't return home safely seems astronomical. They pierce my stomach like a dagger and unveil the possibilities I've refused to consider.

"Okay, well, see you soon," Coen says, holding a hand up to wave goodbye.

"Coen!" Edda says.

"Oh, I'm sorry, my love." He steps toward her and kisses her goodbye. "I will see you at home tonight." He turns and walks away.

"Yeah. It was the kiss I was worried about," Edda says once he rounds the corner and is out of sight.

"Ed, I'm sorry, but your man was full of crap just now. What was that about?" I ask.

"Your guess is as good as mine," she replies. "He usually tells me it's a secure case if he can't talk about work with me. Maybe we caught him off guard. I'll find out later tonight and let you know if I get anything out of him."

Brandon's defeated eyes produce in me an insatiable need to do something. Anything. I just need to act.

If no one tells us who's body that is, I'll find out myself. And even if it isn't Sarah, even if it was a victim from a Wolf attack, maybe I can start using this... *gift* to lead us to the Wolves and find her.

I hate it when my friends are right.

"Or..." I speak slowly and carefully, nudging my friends to walk away from Deputy Roberts' desk. "We could find out now."

"How?" Edda asks.

I survey my surroundings. There are ears everywhere. "Let's go outside."

We finish up with Deputy Roberts and thank him for his time, then meet in the parking lot of the station.

"Well?" Edda asks. Brandon is quiet, but the way his eyebrows furrow tells me he is equally as curious.

I'm still not comfortable speaking so openly. "Car." I gesture with my head toward the parking lot.

"What? Resi, just tell us," Edda says.

"Car!"

We file into Edda's small, silver Toyota Camry, Brandon in the back seat, Edda and I in the drivers and passenger's seats, respectively.

"Resi, what is this about?" Edda asks impatiently.

"Whoever was in that body bag is *dead*." I trust that it will be the only explanation needed, but the blank faces staring back prove me wrong.

Edda eyes me with a slight one-sided curve to her open mouth. "I'm trying to find a more sophisticated word than 'duh,'" she says. "But I'm at a loss."

"*Deeaaad*," I say more emphatically. Simultaneously, they catch on to what I'm implying. Brandon scoots forward and leans in with interest at my unspoken suggestion. Edda's face falls faster than a ton of bricks from a skyscraper. They answer at the same time.

"No."

"Yes."

They gawk at each other and repeat their exclamations.

"NO."

"YES."

Edda holds her hands up disapprovingly. "No. No, no, no, no, no!"

"Edda, you're the one who was saying I should use this *thing* to figure out who the Wolves are. It's even more important for us right now to find Sarah. Why are you against it now?"

"We agreed it's not safe."

"I agreed it wasn't the *safest* thing I've ever done in my life but if you're both here, you can help if anything goes wrong. Which it probably won't," I say. "I still have a good amount of Propofol left, and I'm sure Brandon has plenty of IV start kits in his truck."

"Tons. My truck is Paramedic Heaven." His voice is more upbeat, and it makes me happy to have something to offer, to lift his spirits, give him hope.

"No. I'm sorry, but I won't let you anesthetize yourself just to satisfy your curiosity," Edda says.

That stings. I sit up straighter in my seat, my eyebrows raised.

"Satisfy my curiosity?"

She leans back defensively, knowing how I posture before I'm about to destroy someone verbally. "Okay, wrong choice of words, Resi. You know what I mean."

Fine, but so we're on the same page, I raise my voice, "My friend's kid is missing, Edda. *Your* friend's kid is missing. A kid we both love like she's our own." Edda's hard face softens. "I have this crazy ability to see into dead people's lives," I say more calmly. "You were telling me to use this for good last night. What good is *gooder* than this?"

Edda crosses her arms over her tense posture.

"It could be Sarah," Brandon says to Edda, his voice barely above a whisper.

"It's *not* Sarah," Edda assures him.

"It could be!" Pain is written all over him—in his eyes, his voice, his shoulders.

"Will you be able to sleep without knowing for sure?" I ask her.

She doesn't answer.

I address Brandon. "Look, none of the kidnapped children have been found, which means none of them have turned up dead. It's probably not her, but I can make sure it isn't. And once I confirm that, I'll find out what happened to whoever it is; find out why *this* victim is being assessed by forensics and not others. Maybe something will point to who the Wolves are and put us on the right path to finding Sarah."

Brandon faces Edda. "We'll be with her the whole time. We won't let anything happen to her. You know as well as I do that the police aren't going to find Sarah. They haven't found anyone who's gone missing. We have to do something."

"I'm doing this, Edda," I say. "You can either go home and be mad at me, or you can stay here and be mad at me while you make sure I keep breathing."

Edda releases a harsh exhale. "Do you have headphones with you?"

"I don't think so. Why?"

"You might control the memories better if you listen to some music while you're out."

I smile. "Sarah's iPod should be in her backpack. I went back to my Dad's room the other day to get it for her." Brandon opens the front zipper of the backpack to find it.

"Perfect," Edda says. "But you're not using Propofol. It's too dangerous and we're not in a hospital where we could help if something goes wrong."

I glance at Brandon. We're both confused. "Then how do you suggest we go about the whole 'unconsciousness' thing? I have to be asleep for this to work and I'm not a big napper."

"Brandon's going to have to punch you."

Brandon and I react slack-jawed in revolt at the suggestion. "What?" I say.

"It's the only way this is happening," Edda says. "Propofol isn't safe, Resi."

"Let me get this straight," I say. "You are worried about my breathing and blood pressure with Propofol, I understand that. But you want Brandon to *punch* me at a police station where he could get arrested for assault and possibly cause a concussion?... *Another* concussion? What if I get a head bleed?"

"He won't cause a head bleed," Edda says, waving off the suggestion with a hand. "But I'll do neuro assessments throughout the day to make sure. Either way, losing your ability to breathe will kill you faster than a concussion."

Silence fills the car as I mull over it. A small, airy laugh of disbelief escapes from Brandon. "Okay. You're right," I finally say.

"What? No," Brandon protests. "Don't I get a say here? I can't punch Resi."

"It won't take much," Edda replies. "She's a wimp. You won't have to punch that hard."

"Edda!" Brandon says.

"She's right," I say. "I'm a wimp. So, do it hard enough to knock me out in one hit, but softer than if you were punching Rocky Balboa." I turn to Edda. "Can we get an icepack? I'd rather not have a ton of swelling."

"I don't know if we're close enough." I'm in the back seat with Brandon now and Edda has moved the car to get closer to the body after a quick stop at CVS for an icepack. "Are you *sure* that's where the forensics lab is?"

"I'm sure," Edda says from the front seat. "I've walked through the building several times to visit Coen. That's exactly where I've seen the forensics sign. And we're experimenting with these dreams, so I guess we'll find out if the distance is too far. Still, considering how far you were from Elisa Philips at the hospital when you got her memories, I think we're fine." She scans through Sarah's music library. "What do you want to listen to? You were listening to classical music last time, right?"

"Yeah, but I doubt Sarah has any symphonies in there. Does she have anything other than Taylor Swift?"

"There is nothing wrong with T-Swift!" Edda says.

"Oh, I know," I say. "But this moment doesn't call for songs about ex-boyfriends."

"True." Edda scrolls through the options. "Sarah knows the Spice Girls?"

I'm filled with a bitter warmth, realizing that Sarah must have downloaded the song after we talked about it at the hospital.

"How about Sara Bareilles?" Edda asks.

"Perfect," I say. I accept the earbuds from Edda and place them in my ears. "Make sure these stay in after the punch."

"I never agreed to this," Brandon reminds us. "You two just took action like this is actually happening."

I maneuver myself, so I'm in a spot where the punch will leave room for my head to fall back, and I'll land in a semi-comfortable position.

"Do you know how to get to the correct memories of the victim when it starts?" Edda asks. "If it is Sarah, you'll want to go to a memory of the kidnapper. If not, what memory will you look for?"

Honestly, I'm terrified that it *will be* Sarah. I'm nauseous thinking about finding myself in her memories because it would mean she's dead. If it is her, I don't know if I'll be able to focus long enough to do anything productive. But whether it's her or not, I need to find the Wolves to get to her. "I guess I should try to go to the Wolf attack. Maybe find out why the victim was targeted in the first place and see if I can identify any Wolves."

Edda tilts her head. "You ready?"

"You're right-handed, Brandon?" I use my hands to explain my instructions. "Punch in this direction so I land over here."

"Are you two hearing me?" Brandon raises his voice in frustration. "I'm not punching you!"

"I have one important question," I say to Edda.

"What?"

"Are we about to embark on a high-stakes adventure utilizing my new-found superpower to save an innocent life?"

She hums. "Yep."

"Okay, just checking."

I finally acknowledge Brandon's concern. "B, I know you don't want to, but this is Sarah's life we're trying to save now. She comes before me. She has to."

"She does, Rez," he says. "But I don't know if I can physically force myself to hit you."

I take a deep breath. Getting him to punch me is going to be just as painful as the punch itself. I look at Edda. She nods.

"Brandon," I say, "that body *could* be Sarah's."

Brandon scoffs. "That's not going to work. You already told me that you don't think it's her because none of the kidnapped kids have come up dead."

"She could be lying in that body bag, bloodied and lifeless after a Wolf stabbed her with a—"

There's a flash of light, and my body feels like jelly as I slump down into the back seat. I don't feel pain, but I know he hit me. Music starts to play as the bright light fizzles.

The music is drowned out by my own screaming. A massive wave of pain in my lower abdomen makes it hard for me to breathe. I grit my teeth and groan through my clenched jaw, squeezing a hand next to me. Two other people are holding my legs. My eyes pop open to the fluorescent lights above. A nurse to my right encourages me. "You've got this."

Hospital? Did something go wrong?

The pain shoots through me again. I scream.

"Push!" a man on my left yells. "Push, Jenna."

I'm not the one screaming at all, I realize. It's the victim. Jenna. But I might be screaming with her. This is the worst pain I've ever felt. Jenna peers down over her distended stomach. There's a doctor between her legs.

"I see the head," the doctor says.

Her body contracts again.

"OH. HELL. NO," I shout.

There's a ripping sensation, a tear in the last place I ever want a tear to exist, and I let out another shrill cry. Between the pain and the shock of finding myself in Jenna's labor, I'm having trouble gathering my thoughts to send my dream to another memory.

"Umm, uuhh... Painless memory." I try to no avail. Jenna's stomach hardens as another wave of pain and pressure hits her. "Ohh, please. Anything else. Frolicking in a meadow!"

Still nothing. She pushes, clenching the hand holding hers, throat burning as she screams.

I can't see it, but I know it. I know of a more peaceful memory. I cry out in her body, "You were strolling down the street on a sunny day!"

I'm disoriented when the surroundings change. Confused. There's no weird portal I go through, no *whoosh* or unsteadiness. It just changes, like flipping a television channel. It takes a few seconds for my brain to catch up with the sudden shift. I'm on my feet, or rather, Jenna's feet, walking down a sidewalk. She's taller than me. Her posture is more upright. The sun is shining, and there isn't a single cloud hovering above me.

It worked. Sarah was right about the music.

Sarah. The body isn't Sarah's. Relief washes over me, and I remember my purpose. I take one more moment to recover from the trauma of the previous memory, then decide how to proceed.

"Okay, Jenna. Props to you for no epidural, but I'm officially never giving birth."

Jenna's heels click on the concrete. She reaches into her purse and pulls out a tube of lip balm. It opens with a pop. She glides it over her bottom lip.

"Go to the memory of your Wolf attack," I say.

Nothing.

She rubs her lips together, coating both lips with the balm, then drops the stick back in her purse.

I think of how I got to this memory, and how I ended up in the bathroom in Advik's. I didn't guess. I knew the memory was already there. I directed it once I sensed it.

Focus.

Jenna walks into an office building. She has a goal. I can tell she's burdened with something, carries a heavy weight of responsibility.

But the Wolves. I need information about the Wolves. I think about those bastards, but I sense that she does not feel the same way about them as I do. I don't know what it is she feels. Hatred? Fear? Vengeance? What else is there to feel about them? Maybe this memory took place before the Wolves existed.

No, that's not right. She does know about the Wolves.

Then I find it. I know it. There were faces of people around her, a fight. I can't fully envision it, but I know it's there. "Go to that memory," I tell her. "The one involving the Wolves."

I'm disoriented again, but less so this time. I'm on concrete in the parking lot of a movie theater. Terrified faces stare at me.

I don't recognize the theater. This isn't Gessner and Westheimer. I remember the announcement made on Deputy Roberts' radio. It doesn't make sense. They said the attack was at the intersection of Gessner and Westheimer, then they brought in this body. Right?

As Jenna surveys the terrified audience surrounding her, she raises her arms and adjusts her vision through the scope of a gun. Her arms and hands are clad in gray sleeves and gloves, and I recognize the weapon. It's the type gun that holds the golf ball-sized bullets that hit me in Joey's Market.

"No," I rasp inside her body. Jenna is a Wolf.

I think about my own body outside a police station. I'm not sure what is more disturbing: that the police are hiding a dead Wolf or that Coen is secretly working on it.

A man in a military uniform runs up to Jenna from the crowd and tries to grab her gun away, but Jenna clutches it tightly.

"*Socius*," the military man whispers, training his eyes on hers. Some kind of understanding exists in that one simple word, and Jenna's head nods so subtly that only the man in front of her would notice.

A fake fight ensues between Jenna and the soldier. My mind reels. Is Jenna undercover as a Wolf, but working for the military, or is it the other way around? Is the military working for the Wolves?

"Pass out when I hit your shoulder." Jenna's voice is barely audible. She yanks her gun, giving the illusion that it was a difficult task, but the man readily releases it. She bashes the back of his shoulder with the base of the gun.

Wait, was it his shoulder or his head? Because the man tumbles to the concrete, acting like he is unconscious. Or, at least I assume he's acting based on their conversation, but his performance is convincing.

Jenna dashes forward, her gun poised, and her eyes tracking her surroundings: no other threats from civilians, six other Wolves completing a circle. They all move in the same direction until they reach a safe distance from the crowd, then she and the Wolf to her right sprint toward the building next to the movie theater, a Holiday Inn. She presses a button underneath her mask behind her right ear as they run. The button feels strange, like it's pushing into her skull.

"We're almost there," Jenna says, then releases the button.

A man answers back through her ear. "We have associates ready for you at your conversion point," he says.

"Do you remember what to do when we go through the door?" Jenna asks.

"Putty, then check for cameras," the Wolf running with her answers. It's another girl. She reaches to her belt and unclips a small, cylindrical container.

They burst through a door in the back of the building and enter a storage space. Jenna keeps her gun pointed, moving it between three doors around the room, through which someone could walk in and see them. The other girl closes the back door and points the container at door handle.

"The end of the container clicks like a mechanical pencil. Press it down until you have enough putty to hold the door," Jenna instructs. "If it was a normal handle, you could coat the handle itself, but since this is a bar handle, it's easiest to aim for the edge of the door, between the door and the doorframe."

A man dressed in a suit peeks through a door on the other side of the room. Jenna jerks the gun in his direction.

"*Socius,*" the man says with his arms in the air.

"*Tecum sum.* Come in," Jenna replies and lowers her gun. She sees that the other Wolf has successfully blocked the door with a putty that hardened into concrete.

"Good job," Jenna says. "But if someone had been running after us, they would have reached the door by now. Faster next time." She observes the new Wolf as she evaluates the room.

"There," the new Wolf says. She aims her gun at a surveillance camera. "Now I should disarm the camera."

Jenna sets her hand on top of the girl's gun and lowers it. "Call your training to mind."

"Oh, the bounce," the novice remembers.

"Yes. If you aim straight for the camera, it could hit so hard that it damages something else after the bounce. We never want to do more damage than is necessary. If you start close enough to a sturdy wall and aim perfectly, it should hit the camera with the right amount of force. Watch me this time, and you can do the next one."

Jenna walks to the wall and moves a few boxes, so she has a clear shot for the camera. She eyes it. I have no spatial awareness and almost failed geometry in high school. Yet, in Jenna's mind, I see the angles she needs to hit to shoot the camera. She aims her gun to a point on the wall about seven inches above the ground and pulls the trigger. The gun is powerful and recoils into Jenna's shoulder, but it doesn't move her. Jenna's body is steady and firm. The bullet bounces from the wall to the ground with a sharp metallic ring, then shoots across the room to shatter the camera. It ricochets twice more after that, but with much less force, then it bounces back into Jenna's hand, and she reloads it into her gun. She secures her gun onto her belt and removes her mask and gloves, which she folds and places into a pouch on her belt.

She meets the suited man in the middle of the room. He's a Holiday Inn employee, or he is at least dressed like one. He hands Jenna and her accomplice baggy sweatpants and long-sleeved t-shirts. "Thanks," she says. She hands half the clothes to the other Wolf.

"I'm Matt."

A huff escapes through Jenna's small smile. She's sad as she speaks, but she doesn't let it show. "No offense, Matt, but I'm not in this to make friends. I'll skip the pleasantries. We have work to do."

Matt bobs his head once, then walks out the door he came in. "No sign of them," he says. "The door is cemented, but they're not here."

Jenna turns to the other Wolf. Her mask is off now. She is late-twenties with streaky brown hair that sticks to her sweaty, freckled face.

"It usually goes much faster," Jenna says. She ushers the new Wolf to another door leading to a large meeting room. They pull their new clothes on over their uniforms as they walk. "They gave us the safest escape route so I could train you. You okay so far?"

The girl's hands tremble as she wipes her hair from her face. Her jaw clenches, and she sets her face as if to prove she's tough, but her bugging eyes give her away. "Yeah," she says.

Jenna stops, takes the girl in. She sighs. "It gets easier. You'll become more... numb."

No, Jenna is anything but numb. I sense pride and duty. But more than anything, she's sad, angry. Jenna knows loss.

"Come on," she says. She slings her arm around the girl as they walk through the meeting room to a door leading to the lobby. She doesn't even peek through the window of the door before she opens it.

"Is it safe to come out?" Jenna hollers to no one in particular, her voice suddenly shaky and full of fake emotion. She latches onto the other Wolf. "We heard that the Wolves were coming in, and we hid."

A few bystanders wave them toward a crowd. "They may have gone through a back door," an older man says. "It's safest to stay with us."

"Thank you so much," Jenna says as they scurry toward the crowd in their sweatpants and t-shirts. "We weren't sure what was going on, and we…"

Jenna's voice mixes poorly with the growing sound of music until the crowded lobby fades, and Brandon's face appears as I awake.

"She's back," Brandon says, his voice muffled through the music. I take the earbuds out.

I groan, bringing my hand to my head. It's pulsating—a heavy, dull ache.

"Oh, thank God," Edda breathes. "We did the most impressive deflecting you've ever seen. A policeman came by and questioned us."

"What did you say?" I ask. I rub my cheek, then pull back with a hiss. It's tender. Brandon places the ice-pack on my face, and I hold it in place. My head is killing me.

"Edda was quick," Brandon says. "She said you were so upset about your missing friend that you passed out while you were mourning."

"And they bought that?" I chuckle.

"Yep." Edda leans over to the back seat, and her hands assault my face.

"Watch it, Edda. That hurts."

"Eyes," she says. I open my eyes wide so she can assess them. "Pupils about three millimeters and round." She shines the flashlight of her phone in both eyes. "Both reactive. Name?"

"I'm good, really," I say. "My name is Resi Kepler, birthday is May 2nd, we're at the police station, and Brandon just punched my damn lights out."

"Sorry," Brandon says sheepishly.

Her hands are still on my head as she inspects me. "Nausea? Light sensitivity?" Edda asks.

"No, only a headache and an annoying friend," I answer, swatting her away. "I'm never doing that again. I'll take death by Propofol over Brandon's fist any day. I don't care how much sense you make."

"Well, she's moody and irrational," Edda says, "but given the circumstances, I'd say she's neurologically intact."

"So? What happened? What did you find out?" Brandon asks.

I open my mouth to speak, but close it, realizing that I'm not sure what to say. This is a big one. Edda will feel betrayed by Coen, and I need time to wrap my mind around everything I saw—Wolves, the bouncing metal, military deception, a concierge helping the Wolves.

"Rez?" Brandon urges. "You're scaring me. Say something."

"It's not Sarah," I say quickly, freeing him from his main concern. "It's just a lot, and if I start talking about it, we'll never leave. Let's go back to my place so I can process this. On our way there, I'll tell you about going into labor."

CHAPTER 12

"There is no way. No way! Coen *is not* working for the Wolves," Edda says.

"I don't think he—" I try to interject.

"No! He's not. He's just not. I *know* he's not."

"Okay, but—"

"He's not working for the Wolves, Resi. You're wrong."

"I didn't say he was working *for* them," I explain. I reposition the icepack on my face and lean back on my couch to rest my aching head. "All we know is that he was working *on* one of them."

Edda paces around the coffee table and plops down onto it, facing me. Her eyes are hopeful. "Do you think he doesn't know she's a Wolf?"

I open my mouth to answer.

"You're right. He knows." She throws her head forward into her hands and groans.

"That's not what I'm saying. Give me a second to speak, Ed. I'm saying that Coen's the forensic scientist who works on the bodies at that precinct, and one of them happens to be a Wolf. Whether or not he *knows* it is a different story, but either way, he might have information that can help. Text him and tell him to come over here when he's done with his case," I suggest. "Honestly, Coen is the least of my concerns."

"But what if *Coen's* a Wolf?" Edda asks.

I try not to smirk. "Edda." I place my feet on the floor in front of Edda and lean forward, take the icepack off my face. "I know we've made cracks like this before that we mean as jokes." I glance at Brandon. "Kind of. But I'm serious this time. Coen does not have the social skills to be a Wolf and live a double life with you."

Edda pauses for a moment. "Yeah, you're right," she says.

After resolving that crisis, I explain the rest of my dream. Edda and Brandon listen quietly as I speak, and Brandon starts typing something on his phone.

"The most disturbing thing about it," I say, "is that I didn't get the sense that Jenna felt maniacal or vengeful. I felt a sense of duty in her."

"She was a mother?" Edda's words spill out in disgust as she processes my story.

"Found it," Brandon says, reading something on his phone from a blue chair, caddy-corner to the couch. "*Socius* is Latin, and it means friend or ally."

"So, I guess that's their code word to let each other know that they are all working together," I gather.

"Is all of the military involved?" Brandon asks.

"It makes more sense as to why the Wolves have been so successful," I say, and the notion makes me sick. "The people we thought were defending us are helping the enemy. It's a huge façade."

"But a lot of them have died fighting the Wolves," Edda says. "People join the military to defend this country, why would they turn on us? It can't be all of them."

A knock on the door puts an abrupt stop to our conversation.

"Coen must have gotten my text," Edda says. She stands, but when she doesn't move toward the door, I yell for him to come in.

"Hey! I'm glad you're all here," Coen says jovially as he enters the house and walks to the living room. He seats himself in the chair to my right, across from Brandon. "I drove past a new restaurant on the way here and thought you would all like to join me for lunch."

I look at the clock that hangs above the television. How is it only noon?

"Well, what do you say?" Coen asks.

Everyone is silent. I don't expect Edda to speak up first, but we haven't discussed how this conversation with Coen will go.

Coen scratches his ear as he surveys the room. "I've read that four seconds of silence denotes what some have deemed 'awkward silence', which disrupts the flow of conversation. I think this may be one of those moments."

We don't have time to skirt around the issue. "Um, Coen?" I start. "We know you were working on a Wolf earlier."

"Pardon?" Coen asks with a jolt.

Brandon speaks up. "Resi went to sleep by the forensics lab."

"We think I have to be near the dead person for me to see their memories," I explain.

"She had a dream about the woman in the body bag we saw earlier at the precinct," Brandon continues, his voice pressured. "We know she was a Wolf, and we know that you wouldn't have been at the police station unless you were working on her. Don't give us any BS about paperwork."

Coen studies each of our faces. He seems neither shocked nor guilty. The nervousness I saw at the station is no longer apparent, but I can tell he's determining whether he will divulge the information we want.

"Look, we're not accusing you of anything," I say. "We just want to know if you have any information that will help lead to the Wolves that took Sarah."

He places his fingertips together, so his hands form a triangle, and he touches his middle fingers to his chin. His overgrown hair falls over his eyes. "You've made several wrong assumptions," he lectures. A glimmer of hope forms in Edda's eyes. "The body you saw unprofessionally escorted through the police station had no association with Wolves whatsoever. You're correct that I was called in to assess that body, but it was a teenage boy, not a woman. This boy was found dead in his brother's home, and I verified within minutes that the brother's wife was the perpetrator, as the homicide detectives suspected."

Edda lets out a breath as her eyes seek my approval of her relieved anxieties. I swallow hard. Coen is too awkward to come up with that skilled of a lie on the spot, but I know what I dreamed, and it is not lining up with his story.

"Then why were you so weird and nervous when you saw us at the station?" Brandon asks.

"I was called in from my office, and my superiors were angry that I wasn't more prompt," Coen says. "Plus, I wasn't free to discuss my case with so many people around. Since I had not seen the case yet, I couldn't determine whether it needed to be treated with a certain security level. As it turned out, it was a homicide, so I cannot tell you more than I already have about that particular case."

He's convincing, and I fear that the inconsistencies in this day will make my friends think I'm crazy again. Hell, *I'm* starting to think I'm crazy again. I rest my head in one palm and put the icepack on my face with the other. "But my dream."

"Yes," Coen says, this time failing to meet eyes with anyone. His voice lowers in pitch and volume; he speaks carefully. "That is a more delicate subject that requires a much higher level of security clearance to discuss, and I know only the most basic details." His fingers move from his chin to rest in front of his stomach as he interlocks them. "While I am uncomfortable disclosing this information, you're my friends and I see that you're distressed, so I'll share what I know. But please, understand that I'm putting my job at risk by telling you this."

It's the most affectionate statement I've ever heard from Coen.

"I don't doubt that you had a dream about a Wolf, Resi," he tells me. "But the body in the bag you all witnessed was taken into a vacant office that was sterilized months ago for forensics cases since the actual forensics lab is occupied."

"By who?" Brandon asks.

"Whom," Coen corrects. Brandon closes his eyes and clenches his fists: something he does often to restrain himself when he's around Coen.

"The forensics lab is occupied by Wolves who have died in the attacks. It has served as a morgue, of sorts, for them," Coen says.

I toss the icepack down on the coffee table. "But I thought none had been killed until the one at Hermann

Park the other day."

Edda rises slowly to her feet, as if she's processing the information while her bones straighten out.
"You're *hiding* dead Wolves and letting the rest of the
world believe they're indestructible?"

"I'm not the one hiding them, love," he defends. "I
stumbled upon this information accidentally, and they
forced me to sign a dozen forms declaring that I'll keep
it quiet. I truly do not know anything more than that.
But the Wolves are, in fact, nearly indestructible. Their
uniforms are quite impenetrable. As far as I know, there
are just seven Wolves there. But if there are more locations, I'm unaware."

"How long have you known about this?" Edda
asks, her voice quivering.

Coen's eyes raise to the ceiling as he thinks. "Ap-
proximately six months."

I'm legitimately worried Edda's going to lunge
forward and strangle him. She starts a few words but
doesn't finish any of them. Then she marches through
the house to the back door, slamming it as she steps
into the backyard.

Coen rests thoughtfully in his seat, then flicks his
eyes to me and points a finger in Edda's direction. I nod,
answering the understood question, *I should go after
her, right?*

When he leaves, and a muffled argument com-
mences in my yard, I continue the silent-speaking,
turning to Brandon with a face that says *thank God I'm
not one of them right now*. I expect a similar expression
in return, but it looks like Brandon didn't hear Coen and
Edda's argument at all. He's staring at the floor. I place
an ottoman in front of his chair and sit.

I lean forward with my elbows on my knees and tilt my head to get him to look up. "We're going to find her," I promise when our eyes meet.

"They don't teach you this part in those foster care classes," Brandon says. "They don't tell you what to do when your daughter gets kidnapped."

I think of the day Brandon saved Sarah from the fire, how she wouldn't let anyone touch her except him. He stayed the night with her in the hospital that night, let her fall asleep on his chest, an oxygen mask taped to her face, her little fingers grasping two of his.

"I shouldn't have hit you," Brandon continues. "I put you in danger for my own benefit. I'm sorry."

I hold up a hand to quiet him. "B, I'm fine. I will do it a thousand more times if it means we can find her. And we will." I pause, realizing what I'm saying. "Maybe not a *thousand* more times, but at least once if we are completely out of options. And drunk."

"We can't trust anyone," he says. "The police are harboring Wolves bodies? The military is involved? How are we going to do this? Where do we even start?"

"I know it's complicated. But we can do this together. You, me, our friends."

We've been making eye contact for too long, and I notice that, at some point, my hand made its way to Brandon's forearm, and my thumb is stroking it in soothing circles. It's all too much, so I move my hand and avert my eyes, either dodging the awkwardness or making it worse. I'm not sure which.

My phone buzzes in my back pocket. I pull it out and look at the screen.

Haven't heard from you today. You okay?

In all the commotion, I forgot to tell Cole what

was happening.

I text back, *A lot going on. Sorry I haven't been able to call. I'll explain soon.*

I'm placing the phone back into my pocket when something in Edda's open purse in the corner of the couch catches my attention. The round silver bullet that hit me is loose inside the bag, glaring at me like the lightbulb that switches on in my head. I recall Jenna shooting the bullet against the wall to shatter the camera. I remember handing the bullet back to Edda in the hospital, asking her to hold onto it. *Maybe you can find something in your parents' research*, she suggested at the time.

Studying new or interesting materials was my mom's favorite hobby. But even if she did research it, could it lead us to the Wolves? To Sarah?

Standing, I take the bullet from Edda's purse. It's metal has a strange softness to it. Hard with almost a velvet-like quality. I walk past the carpet to the tile in my kitchen. I hold the bullet at the height of my shoulders, arm outstretched.

The back door opens as the unhappy couple reenters.

"Is that the bullet that hit you?" Edda asks cheeks flushed, arms crossed.

The question must have earned Brandon's attention because he is making his way toward me.

"Yeah, just curious about it," I say. I loosen my fingers and drop the bullet. It hits the floor with a sharp, hard *clang,* then soars a foot above my head, and lands back into my open hand feeling heavier than before. "Wow. It does have a good bounce."

Coen nods. "That would be explained by the

composition of the bullet. I think the manufacturers used a newly discovered substance called carbon nano-graphene, probably mixed with something like chromium or Zectron."

My eyes narrow. *Carbo-nano-WHAT-ene? You made that word up,* I remember saying to my father. "What did you say?" I ask Coen.

He points to the bullet. "I said that the bounce could be explained by the composition of the bullet."

"The first substance you mentioned. What was it called?"

"Oh! It's a newly discovered substance I've only heard of in the past few months. Carbon nano-graphene."

I can hear Dad saying the words with him, telling me that Mom was fascinated by it, studying it non-stop.

"Little is known about it," Coen continues. "No real studies have been published on it, but word has spread amongst scientists about the possibilities for its use. A few of us believe that it is somehow being used to create these bullets."

After my mom died, the FBI suggested that my parents were targeted because of their research. Many of their projects and discoveries were worth a fortune. But security is tight at the lab, and only my parents, Charlie, and I had set foot in there before the bombing. We were all investigated and cleared of any guilt, then the theory was dropped as the attacks continued.

Is it a theory worth revisiting?

"Do you know who is creating it?" Brandon asks Coen. "Who is researching it?"

Coen shakes his head. "I have no idea where it

all originated. This is just speculation amongst colleagues."

Mom might have had connections that could lead us to whoever is using it for the Wolves. She could have run across a Wolf without knowing it during her research. I pinch my eyes shut, force myself not to push the idea away. It isn't much, but it is something. And right now, it's the one lead we have for finding Sarah. As much as I want to avoid the pain of their absence, my parents would have wanted to help.

"My mom studied it."

Everyone turns to me.

"Carbon nanographene," I say.

"But June was a pharmaceutical scientist," Edda says.

I nod. "She also loved metals and materials, new substances. She was fascinated by this carbo-nano-crap. My dad told me about it the day they..." I don't need to finish the sentence. They know what happened. "I know it's a long shot, but maybe we could find some of her research, see who she contacted for the information."

The room stays silent. I look around. "Bad idea?"

"No, not at all," Edda says. "It's just that we would have to go to the lab. That's where their office is, right?"

"I'm aware."

"And you're okay with that?"

No. The thought makes my lungs compress and curl up like a scroll, so I feel like I'm suffocating, but it's all we have right now. "I wouldn't have suggested it if I hadn't come to terms with it."

"The Wolves also have other weapons and uniforms that are more advanced than any retail technology we know of," Edda says. "Astor and June might be our best bet for finding out where they got it."

A shadow crosses my front window. Someone is on my lawn. I peek through the curtain. "You've got to be kidding."

Edda walks up behind me. "What is it?"

"Mischa Linelli."

"The conspiracy theorist? How does she know where you live?"

"I guess it's not a state secret." I turn back to Brandon. "Maybe the lab would also be a more secluded place to work on any other ideas we come up with."

Brandon nods. "Should we use the back door?"

"Our cars are parked in the front. I'll have to deal with Mischa either way."

I take my phone out of my pocket, grab my keys off the coffee table, head for the door. "I'll call Cole on the way, catch him up. He can meet us there."

I'm reaching for the doorknob when Brandon's dark voice fills the room. "No."

I twist around. "No, what?"

"No to Cole meeting us."

My eyebrows raise. "Come again?"

He takes a step forward. "No Cole. You can tell him what's going on, but I don't want him at the lab with us."

My jaw drops. I'm completely thrown. "Why not?"

"Resi, you just saw a memory of a Wolf collaborating with the military and a bell boy at a hotel. There are people out there we thought we could trust, but we can't."

"And one of those people is Cole?"

"I don't know, Rez." His voice is getting harsher. "But, I'm not taking chances when my daughter is involved."

He starts toward the door.

"You can trust him. You don't know him like I do."

"Exactly. I don't know him. He's not coming with us." He opens the door and walks away.

I look to Edda for an explanation.

"Hey, Resi Kepler! It's me, Mischa."

Oh, Lord.

Edda shakes her head sympathetically, speaks quietly so Mischa won't hear. "He lost his daughter, Resi. He needs a sense of control. Let it go for now."

Her psychoanalysis is probably right this time.

I blow out a breath, let it go, and hope my boyfriend will be as forgiving.

Mischa assaults my personal bubble as soon as I step foot on concrete. Edda and Coen walk past me. "I hope this is a better time, Resi," she says.

"What's your latest damage, Linelli?"

"There's a rumor that you were involved in an attack." Her phone is at arm's-length in selfie-mode. I'm impressed by her ability to get both of us in the frame without looking.

I take a beat before giving my usual fake answer. I assumed she would be asking about Sarah, not about an attack that happened four days ago. But I guess it's too soon for Sarah's missing-persons report to have been distributed.

But there shouldn't be rumors about me either. The names of dead victims are released to the public, but not wounded non-targets. Someone from work must have snitched.

"Involved?" I feign ignorance. "You think I attacked someone?"

Edda and Coen approach their respective cars. Edda raises both eyebrows with a thumbs-up, asking if I'm okay. I wave, telling her to leave.

"No, I heard *you* were attacked." Mischa slips one strap of the backpack she's wearing off her shoulder and swings it around, shuffles awkwardly, digging into it while walking with me to the car. Brandon is leaning against the front door. I press a button on my keys to unlock it. He wastes no time getting in.

Mischa pulls out a cord with her microphone attached and plugs it into her phone. She whips her bag onto her shoulders again and holds the mic out to me. "Tell me about the attack."

I stop a few feet away from the car. "If I was attacked, wouldn't I be dead?"

"No, I heard you were *in* an attack, but not the target."

I laugh, slap her on the shoulder, and walk the rest of the way to my car. "You should vet your sources, Mischa," I call back to her. I open my car door and wave goodbye before I get in. "Have a good one."

CHAPTER 13

We walk through a large, white building with walls decorated in ugly floral artwork and an array of achievement plaques. The path to the lab is as ingrained into me as the path from my bedroom to the kitchen. I don't think, I just step as I lead my friends to an elevator in the back of the building and press the button for the basement floor. My nerves grow as the elevator descends, then opens its gates to let us out.

I fidget with the keys in my hand, and I pass an uneasy grimace to my friends.

"This is going to be kind of *Mission Impossible* for a minute," I warn, "but it's not as high tech as it looks. There are just a lot of security measures." For some reason, I'm self-conscious about how technologically advanced everything I'm about to do is.

My friends share glances of intrigue as I usher them toward a door nearby. Next to it, there is a computer screen with a small video camera attached. I insert a key into the door, but instead of opening the lock, it turns the computer on. Red letters flash across the screen that reads, RETINAL SCAN.

I place my eye in front of the camera and a green light scans my eye.

"That's the hottest thing I've ever seen," Brandon gawks, making me chuckle. Maybe it's a good thing Cole didn't come. He might not understand Brandon's humor.

The words on the computer change. WELCOME, RESI KEPLER is displayed at the top and a jumble of gibberish below it. I type, but the screen continues to display nonsensical words.

"It's encrypted as I type," I say. "Nothing that appears on the screen matches what I write. It's effective for privacy because there are other labs down here, and people could walk by, but sucks when you keep typing the wrong letters."

I hold my hand up to the camera. The green light scans across it, displaying all five fingerprints and my palm print on the screen. Everyone faces the door at the sound of bolts unlocking.

I block Edda from walking in with my arm. "Hold on." I continue typing. "It's only expecting me. There's a sensor. If it senses more than one person coming in, it will get pissed and set off alarms." I type for another thirty seconds or so before I'm sure we will all be allowed to enter, then lead my friends into the room.

White walls surround the lab with wooden cabinets and shelves that hold boxes and equipment. There's no ceiling, just an open space where piping, lights, and air conditioning tubes are exposed. Three long tables in the center of the room are littered with goggles, microscopes, cylinders, thermometers, burners, and petri dishes. There's a large silver sink and a matching shower for accidental chemical exposure to the right. Next to it, Hector, my most trusted skeleton friend, stands tall with all 206 bones in perfect anatomical place, dressed in my father's prom jacket and top hat. Hector guards the door to the research office. Past the office, another door leads to Mom's pharmacy and medicine lab.

On our left, there's an incubator and two large television screens that hang above four smaller computers and keyboards. Large glass window panes lead to yet another lab where my father has a few beds, hospital equipment, countless wires and cords that have been attached to many brave heads for harmless tests and experiments. This area also holds a digital projection machine that Dad created and used to research the brain.

"*This* is your parents' lab?" Brandon asks.

I snort in amusement at my friends' underwhelmed faces. "What did you expect?"

Edda surveys the room. "It's always been this mythical illusion. Then the *Mission Impossible* act built up the suspense. I imagined something more... *more.*"

The lab has been a second home to me for as long as I remember. I never thought twice about what other people imagined it to be. It's just a lab. But I see how it might be anti-climactic, given my parents' reputation. When the advanced machinery and technology aren't in use, it could be compared to a lab in a college chemistry class. Only larger. My friends' disappointment amuses me. I love that no matter the amount of exposure, awards, or money, my parents' lifestyle was humble and unimpressive. Nothing about their lives was ostentatious.

My eyes land on two whiteboards on one long wall ahead of us. The left whiteboard was my father's, and it is smaller than my mother's on the right. Mom's board still has an endless flood of color-coded mathematical equations, ingredients for medications, diagrams that show step-by-step metabolic processes of those ingredients, and disease progressions for whatever disease she may have been researching at the time. Dad liked to do his work on paper, so his board contains games of tic-tac-toe and random reminders: work on imaging; call insurance; get chicken, coriander, Shiner Bock, shampoo; tickets to see Wicked. On the middle edge of both boards, which hang about a foot apart, my parents painted one side of a heart to make a whole, like those friendship necklaces you give to your best friend in third grade. The inside of the heart holds their initials: APK and JMK. There is a photo of my parents in my house that shows them standing on their respective sides of the heart, hands behind their backs, bending at the waist to meet in the middle with a kiss.

"Resi?"

I turn to the quiet voice on the other side of the room. "Charlie?" I've seen her from afar at the hospital, but something overwhelms me as I walk toward her now. "What are you doing in the pharmacy?"

She straightens her white coat as I pull her into a tight hug.

"Oh!" Charlie is taken aback by the sudden affection. "No one has been in here in months, so when I heard you, I was startled, and I hid. I didn't know who it could have been and most certainly did not expect..." She decides not to finish her sentence, and instead, melts into my hug.

"It's so good to see you," I say honestly.

Charlie surveys the other guests. "Edda, Brandon," she greets warmly and hugs both.

"Hi, I'm Charlotte," Charlie says to Coen with her hand outstretched.

145

"Coen," he says, accepting her hand. "Pleased to meet you."

"Oh, you have a great handshake," Charlie says.

"Coen and I got married a little over a year ago," Edda says to Charlie. She's smiling, but Edda would have looped her arm through his affectionately had they not just been in an argument. This time, she stands to the side and gestures toward him stiffly like he's a prize on The Price Is Right.

Charlie's eyes dart back and forth between Edda and Coen. "I didn't mean—it was a *firm* handshake. You know, not weak—Strong. A s-strong handshake," she stammers. "Not that I was thinking about his hands. Hand! Just the one."

"Relax, Charlie. She wasn't accusing you of anything," I say. "She was explaining who he was. Coen is Edda's husband."

Her shoulders drop. "Oh. Right. Sorry."

"Charlie was my parents' assistant for several years," I explain to Coen. "She's been working on her Ph.D. and she still uses the lab for her research."

"But Resi and I know each other from college," Charlie says.

"She was my first friend there," I say. "And a fan of my parents, but not in an overbearing way like other science nerds. Mom told me they needed a new assistant right about the time Charlie graduated with her masters, so I suggested she work here while she worked on her PhD."

I've always known Charlotte Clay as "Charlie," so it's strange when she introduces herself by her formal name. Charlie stands several inches taller than me with dark skin and big bright eyes. Her striking beauty is made less intimidating by her perpetual nervousness. I often tease her that she's the most socially awkward hot girl I know.

I came to terms long ago with the fact that I was accepted to Johns Hopkins solely because I'm a direct descendant of medical royalty. Charlie, on the other hand, earned her spot. She is brilliant, graduated first in her class at a competitive private high school in Virginia. Before she turned eighteen, she had already researched electron transfers, the effects of serotonin on the stomach, and something about DNA sequencing. I can never remember all the details.

It wasn't until the moment I hugged Charlie in the lab that I realized how much these connections mean to me, how much history we have. She is more of a sister figure to me than anyone.

"So, um, what are you doing here, Resi?" Charlie asks. "Not that you can't—it's just that you haven't, uh, not since..."

"You remember Sarah?" I ask. "Brandon's daughter."

Charlie's eyes light up. "Of course, I do. How is she?"

I force myself to speak through the painful silence that would undoubtedly follow that question. "She's missing. The Wolves kidnapped her."

The light in Charlie's eyes quenches as soon as the words leave my mouth. She veers her attention over to Brandon, who has chosen a spot on the tile floor into which he drills his eyes. Without hesitation, she asks, "What do you need?"

"You've already helped more than you know," I say, but I'll explain why she sent the Propofol to me later. "We're not sure what we can do yet, but we have a bullet from one of the Wolves guns. I want to go through my parents' research on metals. It's the only place I can think of to find something leading to the Wolves. Do you know anything about my mom's research on carbon nanographene?"

Charlie purses her lips to one side. "I wasn't as involved in June's side projects. Mostly just her infectious disease and pharmacology work. But everything they studied is exactly where they left it." She opens her arm in the direction of the office. "Hector has missed you," she says.

Everyone follows as I walk to the office. I stop at the suited skeleton and straighten his tie. "Looking dapper as ever, Hector. I missed you, too."

I fish my keys from my purse and insert one into the office door. This time, it simply unlocks without any computers asking for retinal scans or fingerprints. I step back to let the others file in. Charlie, being the last one in line, stops in front of me at the doorway. She takes my hand. My chest tightens, and I blow out a breath to force the feeling away.

"It took me a while, too," Charlie says softly. "And it's as 'them' as you're anticipating. Take your time." She squeezes my hand and walks into the office, leaving me with the appreciated warning. I close my eyes and take a deep breath, determined to remain composed in front of my friends. I've managed to keep my emotions at bay so far, but the odds of losing that struggle will increase exponentially once I step into the office. Everything I've avoided for ten months is waiting for me in that room. Every emotion and memory that has been tainted by loss are there, lying in wait like a predator ready to sink its teeth into its prey. Everything that's left of my parents and my home is a few steps away.

I'm here for Sarah, I remind myself.

And with that simple thought, I stand up straight, suit my emotions with protective armor, face forward, and cross the threshold.

My parents spent as much time in their research office as they did in their own home. It's a starkly different environment than the rest of the lab, though almost as large. The walls are painted forest green, and the room is lit by lamps. Two laptops are back-to-back on a large table in the center of the room, and another is on the floor by a beanbag chair in a nook created with book shelves. It's a gigantic space, but the dim ambiance, surplus of bookshelves, and 18 filing cabinets make it look significantly smaller. Warmly colored rugs of different patterns and sizes lay across the beige carpet. The furniture is comfortable: couches and cushioned chairs you would find in a living room.

Photos cover every open space on the walls. I try to ignore them to suck down the sadness that will inevitably creep its way to me from their frames, but I don't need to see them to know what they are. I memorized them long ago: school photos from every year since I was five, a candid moment between my father and grandfather at my parents' wedding, family vacations, birthdays, graduations, award ceremonies, my parents shaking hands with presidents, famous Kepler parties, and many more moments both precious and silly that were captured over time.

I inhale the musty scent of old books mixed with

vanilla-scented candles. It transports me to another time—one that used to be joyful. The sweet nostalgia of my childhood made bitter by a bomb.

"How did the Keplers get anything done?" Edda trails her fingers over the books on one of the many full bookshelves. "Are these books organized in any way?"

"It was their organized chaos," I say, seeing the opened books and files that have been left on the desk, overlapping each other. Handwritten notes are spread over and under and inside each book. "I could never find anything in here without asking one of my parents where it was."

"Studies have shown that people who are less organized are more creative and innovative," Coen says. "Albert Einstein was one of the first to go on record suggesting this. It's no surprise that Astor and June would have a cluttered research space."

"Surprise or not, it doesn't make it easy for us to find what we need," Brandon says.

"I suggest starting with the filing cabinets." Charlie points to the eighteen, large metal cabinets that were each painted like a different hippie's car with flowers, peace signs, hearts, and tie-die-inspired colors. "They're still not in any particular order, but at least all the research is grouped into folders."

All four friends turn to me as if to ask for my blessing. A rush of responsibility floods me. For a split second, I'm overwhelmed with the desire to preserve the room exactly how they left it, my own Kepler Pompeii.

I scoot a book a couple inches to reveal the corner of the wooden desk next to me. Carved into it is the phrase *Resi is the Koolest Kepler,* Dad's attempt to cheer me up one day in second grade after Ashley Sanders told me I was a loser. I admire the carving, dragging my fingers over the indented words. So much of my parents *is* preserved in this room. The last thing they would want to remain stagnant is their research. It's meant to be studied and built upon.

"Let's get to work."

CHAPTER 14

"I don't know what you want from me," Jason Phillips says on the phone. "All I know is that my wife and kid are dead. There was no warning or connection with the Wolves before the attack. How did you even get this number?"

It was easy. I searched Jack's medical records. "I'm sorry, Mr. Phillips. I'm just trying to find out who the Wolves are."

"You and the rest of America. Leave it to the police, and please don't call me again."

The line cuts out. I let out a frustrated groan. We've been searching for three days and have only found contact information for a few victims, none of whom want to investigate separately from the police. It was a long shot, anyway—a desperate attempt to feel productive after failing to uncover anything useful with the remnants of my mother's old contacts.

"You *what*?" Charlie yells when I reenter the office from the main lab. "You used the Propofol to put yourself to sleep?"

"How did you—"

Coen apprehensively raises his hand. "Sorry. It slipped out."

Charlie stands from her bean bag chair, where she was looking through some files, and almost knocks over the lamp next to her. She continues to speak as she catches the lamp and repositions it. "Why would you do that? I thought you were experimenting with it or doing something useful! Who are you? Michael Jackson?"

"That's what I said!" Edda exclaims. She's perched stiffly on a couch next to Coen. The contents of a blue folder are spread all over the table in front of her.

"Can everybody chill?" I sit at the center table, where I have stacks of research piled. "I'm fine. It didn't affect my breathing or blood pressure. And I *was* experimenting with it, technically." I try to find support from Brandon since he's the only other risk-taker in the group, but he's lost in his research. Several folders and books sprawl across the floor around him. His hair is messy and stands up where he's been tugging at it.

"I'm not getting any more for you," Charlie states. "If you can't sleep at night, take melatonin and drink some hot tea like everyone else."

The room is quiet. Everyone looks at me to respond. I haven't told Charlie about my memory-dreams, the reason for taking the Propofol in the first place. I should tell her, especially since she has agreed to help find Sarah, but I'm self-conscious about it all over again. The concept is insane, and I don't want to prove myself to yet another person.

"Well, you won't need to. Now that I'm back in the lab, I have as much access as you do to Mom's pharmacy." The comment receives nothing but a disapproving snarl. "Fine," I say. "I won't use it unless we all agree."

Charlie scoffs. "Why would anyone *ever* agree to that?"

"Did you find anything in that stack of folders, Edda?" I ask, changing the subject. "It seemed promising."

"Nothing," she says. "Anything from Jack's dad?"

"No. He doesn't want to be involved." I rake a hand through my tangled hair. "Coen, any luck with the bullet?"

"I'm hoping to have more information soon, but your college pal and I seem to be at odds on how to go about the separation of the metal alloys."

Charlie clenches her hands in the air. "For the *last time,* you cannot approach the separation of alloys like the separation of water-soluble salts. The systems are fundamentally different. Metals have varying melting points. Since we have no idea what metals are involved, or even whether all the components of the bullet *are* metals, we could end up affecting the purity and quality of the components and render the bullet useless. Why is that so hard to understand?"

I blink. "So, no luck?"

"Not yet," Coen answers. "But we're looking into other options. We're both geniuses, but metals are neither of our specialties."

Edda slaps a folder down on the table in front of her. "Are we sure this is our best chance of finding Sarah?" She gestures toward the folder she discarded.

"Yes, Edda," Brandon snaps. He looks up from his corner. "*You* are the one who said if anyone has information on where the Wolves got their technology, it's the Keplers."

"Okay, okay," Edda says. "Sorry."

The room is thick with tension. Everyone has been on edge. Edda, the ultimate grudge-holder, is still frustrated with Coen for hiding the fact that he knew about the dead Wolves. Brandon hasn't slept in days.

I'm bottling a volcano of emotions. Charlie's mood is surely fed by everyone else's, but the Propofol thing really set her off.

I spot my dad's teal-colored record player next to the smallest bookshelf in the office, which holds all of Dad's vinyl records.

"What are you doing?" Charlie asks, a sharp edge to her voice.

I pull a record out of its cover and place it on the record player. It starts to spin. "A good, old-fashioned, college-style study break."

That earns a half-smile from Charlie.

"We're going to shotgun a beer?" Brandon asks.

"What?" I say. "No. But everyone has to participate."

I let the needle drop on the rotating disc, and David Bowie's "Let's Dance" sounds through the office. My head bobs to the beat. I hold my hand out to Charlie.

Charlie stands still with her arms crossed but can't stifle her amusement as I glide toward her, shoulders rising and falling to the beat, lips mouthing along with the words.

Edda grabs Coen's wrist and stands to join in. She jerks her body and kicks her legs while her thumbs jab outward. Coen sways back and forth in a small, comfortable step-touch.

"Come on..." My hand is still extended to Charlie. "You've never turned down a study break!"

A few seconds of thought later, Charlie's head rolls in perfect sync with her arm as she swings it over her head and into my hand. I pull her in for a twirl. Charlie trips over her own feet, gets caught in my arm, our bodies crash into each other. We double over in laughter before resuming our tradition with the most ridiculous dances we can think of, from the Robot, to an exaggerated Twist, to the elbow-to-knee classic.

Edda tears away from Coen to pull Brandon up from the floor. He grudgingly stands, his shoulders slumped, shaking his head in protest. The rest of us join, dancing around him. Then, without warning, Brandon breaks into The Electric Slide with impressive skill, though not quite in time with the music.

I turn the record player off when the song ends. Everyone plops down into their spots.

"We need a name," Brandon says, leaning against the bookshelf behind him.

"A name?" I ask.

"It does make sense," Coen agrees. "All crime-fighters have names."

"Like a team name?" I crinkle my nose. It's a cheesy idea.

"Think about it," Brandon says. "What group of non-law enforcement crime fighters do you know of that doesn't have a name?"

"What group of non-law enforcement crime fighters do you know of that isn't a part of the Marvel Universe?" I counter.

"Just humor me," Brandon says.

"The Lab Rats?"

Brandon stares at me, unimpressed.

"Science Squad? Hospital Heroes?"

After no deliberation, Brandon decides I'm not allowed to choose the team name.

But I do see what Brandon means. We're taking on an impossible battle alone—a tiny army of intellectuals, five friends with nothing but science, dance breaks, and each other to rely on. We trudge through murky waters of scattered notes, explore books and encyclopedias, exhaust Google's search engine until it practically yells back at us. But the internet doesn't hold what hasn't been publicly discovered. We've spent three sleepless nights in the office pouring over research, trying not to get distracted by interesting topics that have nothing to do with finding Sarah. The only weapon we have is our wit, which we're using to fight an infantry that has outwitted a nation. With the discouraging odds staring at us, we inch forward, determined, and hopeful.

We agree on a plan: go to work as scheduled, spend any spare time at the lab sorting through research, and hit the gym five days a week. I don't want to be caught by a Wolf because I get winded or distracted by a donut. Charlie and I created lab access for Edda, Coen, and Brandon so anyone can get into the research office as needed. I keep Cole's access active for when Brandon changes his mind about including him.

Three weeks later, we're no closer to finding her.

I pour myself a cup of coffee in the breakroom of the ER, thinking about the plethora of research my parents have that we still haven't made a dent in. There are still nine filing cabinets we haven't touched, and notes upon loose notes in books scattered across the office. The longer we search, the angrier I get with my parents for being so disorganized.

Long arms wrap around my waist in a hug from behind.

"Hey," I say sweetly, knowing Cole is the only

one who would do this. At least, if it's not him, someone is about to get a knee to the crotch. I spin around in his arms to hug him back. "What are you doing in the ER? No infectious diseases to treat today?"

"I've missed you, and I wanted to see how the research was going," Cole says.

"I've missed you too." We sit at a table. "We've hardly even cracked the surface of my parents' notes, but we'll get there." I sip my coffee. "We're only a few filing cabinets in. We found some notes of Mom's on carbon nanotubes, but not carbon nanographene. According to Coen, they're very different."

Cole nods, his eyebrows narrow slightly. "I wouldn't discount their similarities. It sounds like they at least both have a carbon component and nano-*something*. It might be the graphene that's different in the new substance. And I'm pretty sure carbon nanotubes are being looked into for use in bullet-proof armor."

Which could be used in the Wolves' uniforms. I retrieve my phone from my pocket and make a note to revisit the research on carbon nanotubes. "That's a good idea, thanks."

"No word from the police?" he asks.

"Nothing."

"I wish you would let me help. I know your parents' lab pretty well from when I studied under your mom in residency."

I reach for his hand on his lap and squeeze it. "I want you to help, but it's Brandon's daughter that we're searching for, and he has to be perfectly comfortable with anyone involved."

"So, he doesn't trust me," Cole concludes.

"He just doesn't know you."

Cole relents with a sigh, but I can tell he's reading into the situation. "Any more dreams?"

"Not since the one at the police station I told you about. The others are mad at me for the Propofol thing," I say, lowering my voice in case someone else walks into the breakroom. "They won't let me go back to the forensics lab to try again. But I think I could get so much more information if I could fall asleep there."

"Charlie's mad too?"

"Yeah, but she is under the impression that I used Propofol because I was having a hard time sleeping at night. I haven't told her about my dreams yet. It's kind of a hard concept to swallow, and I don't exactly love to explain it."

"How have you avoided telling her about it?"

I lean back in my chair, take another sip of coffee. "The Propofol thing only came up once. I guess everyone understood I didn't want to tell her since I didn't explain it then."

I check my watch. "I should get back to work." We stand. I throw my paper cup in the recycling bin.

Cole grabs my free hand as I release the cup. "Can I suggest something?"

"Of course."

"Why don't you go back to the police station at night when you're ready to *actually* fall asleep instead of using Propofol?"

I scrunch my face. "That sounds like the most obvious thing to do, but wouldn't it be suspicious? Some random girl hanging out in the precinct parking lot for the night?"

"You won't know until you try. We could take

turns staying with you overnight. It won't be the most comfortable sleep ever, but worth it, right?"

I note the *we* he slyly threw in. I want him to be involved, but Brandon is so adamant about maintaining a small, trusted group.

Edda walks into the breakroom. "Oh, hey, Cole," she says, then turns to me. "Sorry to bother you on your break, Resi, but we just coded a Wolf victim. They didn't make it, so we're down a nurse while Javier does the post-mortem paperwork. We need you to come back."

"Mind if I join?" Cole asks.

I gesture with my head for him to come along as we walk back to the unit.

"What happened? Where was the attack?" I ask Edda.

"Poison," she says. "She was at work. Her co-workers said she slumped over at her desk, and they couldn't wake her up."

When we enter the victim's room, my breath escapes me. The corpse is a childhood friend. The subtle red streaks in her black hair are perfectly coordinated with her flowy black tunic and red pencil skirt.

"I know her," I breathe out. "Katrina. We grew up on the same street. Her mom, Alice, was in the first attack with my parents. She and my mom were good friends."

"I'm sorry, Resi," Cole offers, placing his hand on my shoulder. "It must be hard to see her like this."

My mind races as I try to piece things together.

"She was sick," I say.

"Katrina?" Edda asks. "You think it wasn't a Wolf attack?"

"No, her mom, Alice," I clarify. "Before the bombing. Alice was sick. Dying, actually. No one knew what it was." My cheeks burn as anger stirs. "My mom was trying to help her. Maybe she could have if she had more time." But the Wolves didn't allow that time.

"I remember that," Cole says. "I wasn't working with your mom anymore at the time, but she consulted the infectious disease team. None of us had heard of the symptoms she was explaining. It seemed to torment her."

I peer outside the room to make sure only Edda and Cole are within earshot. "I have to get into Katrina's memories."

"What do you want to find out from her?" Edda asks.

"I don't know," I say. "But there has to be some connection between Katrina and her mother. Why would the Wolves wait almost a year to kill the daughter of one of their first victims?" I try to find the words to explain my need to get inside Katrina's head, but I can't. I just know there's something important to see.

"How do you plan to do this?" Cole asks. "Do you want to go home and take a nap?"

"No. I need to be nearby," I explain. "If I'm too far away, I don't have the dreams."

"The ER rooms are full right now," Edda says. "There's nowhere for you to fall asleep."

"How long does it take the Terrorism Unit to get here?" Cole asks.

"Hours. They take forever." I watch his eyes as I pick up on what he's suggesting. No one is supposed to touch or move the victim until the Terrorism Unit processes the body and gets whatever it needs. That gives me plenty of time. "We need to tape off the room and close the doors. Edda, can you tell everyone I went home sick?"

Edda worries her lip. "What if you get caught? If they think you're tampering with evidence…"

"I'll be done before they get here."

"Okay," she says hesitantly. "I'll cover for you. We can grab some sheets for you to lay down on. But no Propofol."

"What?" My face scrunches. "I guarantee Cole won't punch me."

"Take some Ativan," she argues.

"It takes longer to work. *And* to wear off. I'll be knocked out for the rest of the shift! You would have to carry me out before the Terrorism Unit gets here."

Edda groans. "Even Ketamine would be safer. And it doesn't last too long."

"It's dissociative. Doesn't always guarantee sleep. Propofol will do exactly what I need it to do.

"You're impossible," Edda gripes.

Maybe, but I'm also right. Propofol will put me to sleep, and it's easy to come out of. It's the best drug for this situation.

"Cole, can you stay with her?" Edda asks.

He answers while typing something into his phone. "Canceling the rest of my appointments now."

CHAPTER 15

A cushioned swivel chair twists under me. Manicured fingers move a computer mouse. The space is cramped with beige cubical walls on three sides.

A long yawn of boredom creeps up to Katrina's throat. Her eyes focus on an Excel spreadsheet.

For the first time since the dreams began, I'm not confused about where I am. I wound up exactly where I expected to wind up, and in the body I anticipated I would inhabit. But it is no less strange. This is someone I knew and grew up with. I feel like I'm invading a friend's privacy, but I know what I need to do.

"I really need you to work with me, Katrina. We can figure this out together."

Katrina types several numbers into a column of the spreadsheet.

"Do you know why you were targeted?" I ask. "Take me to a memory of a Wolf targeting you."

She remains at the computer and sighs.

I try to focus on finding any kind of memory involving the Wolves, but I don't sense anything. "Why did the Wolves attack her so long after they attacked her mom?" I wonder. Then I feel it. "Katrina, take me to a memory of your mom's illness."

The desk disappears, and I'm walking down a hallway—one I recognize. There are pictures of family members and friends, soccer medals, and diplomas hanging on both sides. I ran up and down this hallway as a child. I remember Katrina's younger brother, Danny, chasing me from room to room, trying to spray me with silly string. I was five or six.

Katrina walks into Alice's room with a surgical mask covering her nose and mouth. She holds a bowl of hot soup in her hands, which are covered in blue latex gloves.

She sets the soup on a bedside table, then stations herself on the bed and sighs as she takes in the sight of the woman asleep next to her. I never saw Alice while she was sick. I only heard about the disease from my mom. It was something she had never seen before, nor could she cure it. I knew it was bad, but now that I see her in Katrina's memory, it's not what I expected. Alice's face is gray, a color I associate with patients who have poor cardiac function, but this is a different shade. The color is deeper, more ominous, with red patches spotted all over her face, neck, hands and arms. We call those patches petechiae in medical terms. Alice is in multi-system organ failure.

"Mom," Katrina says. She gently nudges Alice's leg. "Mom, you need to wake up. Try to eat something."

Alice flutters open her yellow, jaundiced eyes to greet her daughter with a weak smile. "Thank you, sweetie. I'll have some in a minute."

I can't audibly hear Katrina's thoughts, but I know them. She thinks her mother is lying; she won't eat it later. I sense a mixture of anger and sadness with Katrina.

"Mom, you haven't eaten in two days," she says. A tear falls down Katrina's face, wetting her cheek. "Please eat something. Just some broth. You need pro-

tein."

"Knock knock!" a familiar voice sings as someone opens the door and taps twice on the doorpost. I'm
confused and anxious at the sound of the voice. Katrina
turns around to greet her.

"Stop!" I panic. Katrina's head stops moving as
her eyes land on the visitor. Every one of my own emotions bombards me and I hear my own labored breathing inside my friend's body as I zero in on the frozen
woman in the doorway, decked from head to toe in protective clothing: mask, gloves, gown, shoe covers. Her
straight, dark brown hair is tied back into a ponytail,
and her green eyes are identical to mine.

"Mom," I whisper. My voice sounds strangled as
it bounces back to me. "Mom!" I shout. I want to run
to her, hug her, tell her I love her, talk to her for days,
for months, forever. But I can't. I can't speak or move or
make Katrina do anything that isn't already in Katrina's
memory.

I soak up her image for what seems like an eter-
nity before I decide to let the memory go on. I need to
see what my mom is there for, and hope that Katrina
will hug her.

"Okay." My heart is heavy with grief, yet full of
hope. "Continue the memory."

"Come in," Katrina says, forcing a smile before
turning her attention back to Alice. "Mom, Dr. Kepler is
here to see you again."

Mom sits on a chair next to the bed, making
sure that her protective gown is all that touches the
fabric. She takes Alice's hand in her own, though hers
are gloved. The joy I'm accustomed to seeing in my
mother's eyes is absent, replaced by sadness and defeat,

maybe some exhaustion.

"I'm so sorry, Alice." Mom's voice shakes like she is barely holding herself together. "I've tried everything. I've studied all your labs, researched every cure. I can't find anything. I'm so, so sorry."

Alice's smile is weak, but confident and assured. There's no fight or struggle. It's the smile of a person who has accepted that they're going to die—a smile that says they are at peace with this fate, and that tries, but always fails, to give their loved ones the same peace.

Katrina flicks away a tear, and her chest heaves as she suppresses a sob.

"It's not your fault, June," Alice says. "Thank you for everything you've done for me. You're a good friend."

"Yeah," Mom says after a long pause.

Alice's head shifts to the side as if studying my mom, then she turns toward Katrina. "Will you give us a minute, Sweetie?"

I start to panic at the thought of leaving, but I sense that Katrina has no intention of going far.

"Sure," Katrina says. She stands and exits the room, shuts the door behind her, and takes one step to the left so that she's leaning against the wall right beside the door. She removes her face mask and cranes her neck to listen to the conversation.

"Alice..." My mom's voice trembles. "I don't know what to—"

"June, please," Alice says. "I couldn't move without pain for a decade, but your medical trial cured my arthritis, remember? I was able to spend more time with my kids and enjoy the last year of my life because of you before I got this illness."

"I know, but…"

"You can't fix *everything,* June."

I sense that Katrina is confused by her mom's claim, but I'm not sure why. Mom was an expert in pharmacology and worked on formulas for a more effective pain killer, so it shouldn't surprise Katrina that she helped with Alice's arthritis.

"But this disease," Mom says. "It's not only you anymore. And I can't cure it. I need to cure it."

Okay. Now I'm confused. I have no recollection of anyone else being sick with this kind of disease.

Mom continues speaking, but her voice sounds muffled. The hallway starts to blur. I'm waking up. *No.*

"Not yet. I need more time!" I protest. But the memory continues to fade.

"No!" I shout. My eyes open. "I need to go back." Cole is sitting on the floor next to me. "Put me to sleep." I sit up, my head spinning. I push through the putridness of food hurdling backward through my bowels, and I grab the Propofol from Cole's hand, which he immediately snatches back.

Edda steps into the room. "Everything okay?"

"What happened?" Cole asks, visibly forcing his calmness, shocked by my intense emotions.

"My mom. She was…"

Mom's voice and her defeated eyes are seared into my memory. Her kind hands holding Alice's, whose skin was grayed and bruised. Alice thanked my mom for curing her pain. Mom and Alice were both killed in the first attack. What if the disease *was* a Wolf attack? A biological weapon.

"Resi?"

Cole rests his hand on my arm, his fingers check my pulse. He lifts his chin toward Edda, indicating that he wants her to check my blood pressure. Edda presses a button on the vital signs machine, and the cuff around my bicep starts to inflate.

"What do you remember about what my mom said when she asked your department about Alice's disease?" I ask Cole.

His eyes look to the ceiling. "I honestly don't remember much," he said. "It was early on in my position as attending physician. I was pretty overwhelmed at the time."

What if my mother did cure the disease and the Wolves found out? What if that's why they killed her *and* Alice? What if the disease is our way to the Wolves?

I glance up at Edda. "Call Brandon. We have to go back through what we've already read and find any research my mom did on diseases before she died."

And it's time for Brandon to get over his beef with Cole.

CHAPTER 16

"What the hell is your problem?" I ask Brandon late that night.

"I don't trust him," Brandon says. "My daughter's life is on the line, and I don't want someone here just because he wants to hang out with his girlfriend."

"You know, I've understood this rule of yours so far, but now you're hindering our progress," I argue. "Cole studied infectious diseases with my mom. He could help us find something."

"You're going on a hunch, Rez. We're not sure if June knew about the Wolves, so his help could be pointless."

"And what if my hunch is right? What if she does have information stashed away somewhere around here, but the one person who could find it and interpret it the fastest is banned from the lab because you don't like him?"

Brandon tugs at his hair with a frustrated groan.

"He's unreasonable, right?" I ask Charlie. She's been watching the argument, but her eyes widen when I face her. She quickly swivels her head to find another focus.

"*Charlie.*"

"Uhh..." Charlie points to herself and stutters. "I-I don't—what? Were you two saying something?"

"Charlie, we know you're listening. You're the

only other person here. You know Cole from when he worked with my mom," I say. "Tell Brandon he's being ridiculous."

"Nuh-uh." She shakes her head. "I'm staying out of it."

"I don't trust him," Brandon reiterates.

"Do you trust *me*?" I ask.

His head falls to the side, leaving the rhetorical question unanswered.

"Okay, then I'm calling it," I say.

"What?" Brandon asks incredulously. "You can't just—"

"You're too emotional and defensive about this. I understand why, but we need Cole. We're adding him to the team."

"And you're *not* emotional?" Brandon asks. "You have one dream about your dead mother, and suddenly you're the dictator of this group?"

My hand stings before I realize that I slapped him across the face. But shocked as I am by my own action, I set my poker face toward him, too pissed to back down.

Brandon burns bright red through his dark cheeks. His hands clench into fists at his sides, his jaw twitches. "Fine," he grunts, then turns to walk out of the office.

"Where are you going?"

"Home. Do whatever you want." His voice carries back, but he's already out of my sight.

I settle down next to Charlie on the couch. "He's infuriating. Why does he hate Cole so much?"

Charlie snorts.

"What?"

She cocks her head to the side. "Are you really

that oblivious?"

"Oblivious to what?"

"He has a thing for you." She reaches for the bag of Goldfish beside her and pulls it open. "Always has."

"*Brandon?* Brandon does *not* have a thing for me."

"Whatever you say." She pops a cracker into her mouth.

"Why would you say that? All we do is fight."

Charlie squints like she is trying to read me. "Nah, I think you know. I don't have to convince you."

I rub my forehead where a headache is developing. "I've had a long day. I should go home."

"Can I ask you something?" Charlie says before I can stand. She sets the bag down, brushes her hands together to get the salt off.

"Sure."

"That thing Brandon said about having a dream about your mom. What did he mean? What exactly is this 'hunch' you have about a disease your mom studied?"

I settle back into the couch. I was so angry with Brandon that I didn't think about what he revealed in front of Charlie. "Do you remember Alice? She was friends with my mom."

She furrows her brow, sucks her bottom lip in between her teeth. "She was also in that first Wolf attack, right?"

I nod. "But she was already dying—before the attack happened."

"I remember. June was working on a cure."

"Do you remember the details? The studies she did about the disease?"

"I remember that June was upset, working on

Alice's case day and night, but it was a personal project of hers. She didn't involve me. She took a lot of it home with her, actually, which your parents rarely did."

I sink further into the couch with a slump. "That's what I was afraid of."

"But that doesn't really answer my question. You had a dream about this?"

I knew I'd eventually have to tell Charlie about my dreams, but I've been putting it off, knowing it will take a lot of convincing to get her to believe something so unbelievable.

"It would be easier to explain this with everyone else here to validate what I'm about to tell you." I take a deep breath. "But I can try." I maneuver myself on the couch to face Charlie better. Her forehead creases, and she follows my lead, turning her body toward me to listen.

"I've been having these dreams," I begin. "But they aren't dreams, they're memories. Well, they *are* dreams, but in the dreams, I'm experiencing their memories. The memories of dead people. Real dead people. Mostly victims of Wolf attacks."

I'm not explaining this well. I gauge Charlie's reaction before proceeding, and brace myself to be mocked or for a speech about how crazy I am. Instead, Charlie contemplates my words, her narrow eyes shifting to the right. I'm not sure how to interpret this behavior, so I continue.

"It first happened when I was attacked in the neighborhood market. I was knocked out next to someone who was killed, and I sort of got sucked into his memory while I was unconscious. It freaked me out at first, but now I have more control over it."

Charlie stands and walks out of the office without saying a word.

After a few dumfounded moments on the couch, I follow. "Charlie?" She's across the lab, climbing onto a countertop. She opens a cabinet. "Charlotte Clay. What is going on?"

"Hold on a second," Charlie answers. She moves a few boxes and cylinders out of the way, then puts her finger through a small hole in the back panel of the cabinet. It loosens and falls toward her, revealing a red folder. It's like the ones stuffed into the filing cabinets we've been rifling through for weeks. It's older, worn. On the front of it, my father's handwriting is scribbled in permanent marker, *The Afterthoughts*.

Charlie hops down from the counter and holds the folder out for me to take.

"Three or four years ago, I was here late at night finishing an inventory for your parents, and the back of the cabinet fell out. I found this. I never told him I found it because he clearly wanted it hidden. I haven't thought about it since, but..." Charlie pauses and beams. "Wow." It comes out in a whisper.

"I don't understand," I say. "What is this?"

"It was Astor's. It's a journal and notes about some attempted experiments, but he didn't seem to get far," she says. "At the time, I just thought it was 'Crazy Astor,' reading too much into his dreams." Amazement glows in Charlie's eyes, and my pulse starts to race as I piece her words together. "Resi," she says, "Astor fell asleep by your grandfather the night he passed away. He talks about inhabiting his body in a memory. He later locked himself in the morgue at the hospital to test his theory, and sure enough, he saw their Afterthoughts. That's what he calls the memories in this journal, 'Afterthoughts.'"

The words on the folder glisten through my wet eyes. I don't know whether to be shocked or relieved.

Laughter bubbles up from my belly.

"What's so funny?" Charlie asks.

"It's just, I had no idea where these dreams came from, but the last thing I ever expected was for it to be genetic."

CHAPTER 17

"A ton happened today, Resi," Cole says. He drives into the parking lot of the police station. "Maybe you should go home and get some restful sleep instead of going into these memories."

"Afterthoughts," I correct, holding Dad's folder up for him to read the title. "Park on the left side of the building. We were on the right last time, so maybe I'll get the Afterthoughts of someone else if we're in a different spot." Cole pulls into a parking spot. "And no, I don't want to go home. The more I do this, the faster we find Sarah."

He turns the ignition off and shoves the keys into his pants pocket. The weather is cool, so it shouldn't get too stuffy.

"I already went through everything my father wrote about this ability. It irked him for a month or so in his late-twenties. After my grandfather died, he slept in the morgue a few times.

Cole shivers. "We see death a lot at the hospital, but that's a bit..."

"Morbid? Yeah, I thought so too, but my dad was weird."

He laughs. "None of the Keplers are normal. That's for sure."

I slap his chest with the back of my hand and flip through the file. "He had Afterthoughts about a construction worker pouring cement, a teenager getting his first kiss, and an old man playing Bingo at his retirement home."

"Did he have any idea what caused this?"

I flip through a couple pages and show Cole a diagram of the brain with notes scribbled under it. "He theorized that he always had the ability, but now could use it because his frontal lobe was complete at age twenty-five. He never understood how he gained the ability to begin with. But it also seems like he didn't try that hard. After those few memories, it's like he gave up. I was born soon after these entries, so I guess I was a distraction."

"I agree with that. You're a *huge* distraction."

I look over and see Cole smiling. "Shut up," I say with a laugh. I close the file and secure it into my bag.

"Alrighty," Cole says, leaning his seat back into a reclining position. He reaches behind him and grabs two pillows from the back seat that he collected for the night and wedges one of them behind my head. "Sounds like you have work to do. Got your music?"

I reach into a pocket of my purse for my headphones and plug them into my phone. "Yep. I came prepared." I lean my own seat back and position the pillow to get comfortable. "I can't believe that's what you changed into to sleep in," I say, eyeing his jeans and button-up shirt. I opted for a t-shirt and plaid pajama pants. "You're like one of those lawyers on TV who goes home and changes into *jeans* to lounge around the house."

"What can I say? I dress to impress," he says.

I chuckle and place the earbuds into my ears.

"Will you be able to sleep?"

"Today, I saw my mother in my childhood friend's memory, had a huge fight with one of my best friends, and found out that my father passed on a trait that enables me to see into dead peoples' thoughts. I'm exhausted."

"Your life is *so* dramatic," he jokes, grinning with that stupid dimple that makes me swoon. I place my hand on top of his and interlock a couple fingers, press Play on the iTunes library and close my eyes.

The sun bakes my skin as children run and climb on a playground at an elementary school. A woman beside me on a bench finishes tying a child's shoe before she turns and speaks to me.

"Anyway, Dina's parents are convinced she's this little angel, so of course the parent-teacher conference was a waste of my time," she says. Her southern accent isn't often heard in Houston; the kind that makes me expect her to 'bless my heart' at any moment. She's not a native Houstonian.

A low rumble falls out of my chest. I'm in a man's body. He chuckles at the woman's anecdote "Aren't they all?" he asks.

He points to her arm. "That bracelet suits you," he notes.

"Aw, thank you, darlin'!" she says. "My mama gave it to me for my birthday not too long ago." She holds her arm out to show off the bracelet. It's nothing special, just a simple silver band if it was silver at all. But I'm straining to observe the bracelet through the man's periphery because his actual focus is on the woman's forearm.

"How sweet of your mom," the man says. "I'm going to go back inside and work on some lesson plans."

"Sure thang, Tyler," she says to him. "I'll see you soon."

Tyler waves to the children as he makes his way across the playground and into the elementary school. He admires the projects and assignments displayed on every wall as he goes. He enters through a door that says "Mr. Meeks" and makes a beeline for his desk in the front of the classroom.

Tyler Meeks. I commit the name to memory, wanting to remember it for later research. I learned this the hard way. Trying to research Jenna without a last name was futile.

He powers on his computer and glances at the door to make sure no one is coming before he opens a secured browser on the dark web. I know about the dark web from the news. It's a part of the internet only accessible through a special kind of software that allows its users to remain anonymous and untraceable. It's used by innocent civilians who are paranoid about the government tracking their searches. But it has also been used by murderers and terrorist groups. It poses a huge challenge to law enforcement agencies around the world.

Tyler clicks an icon within the Dark Web browser that reads WOLF WEB. I wonder if the Wolves were the first to call themselves Wolves or if they decided to play along with the media and adopt the name we gave them. The Wolf Web opens to another page that says AS-SIGNMENTS at the top. Below it are pictures of people with names listed under their faces. Sixteen pictures are shown on the screen, but if Tyler would scroll down,

I'm sure there would be more. He moves the mouse, so the cursor hovers over the picture of the woman he was speaking to outside. The name under her face says JO ANNE HYDE. He clicks her picture, and four options appear on a new page: ASSESSED, CLEAR, IMMUNE, and TARGET. ASSESSED already has a green checkmark over it, and another check pops up when he clicks CLEAR.

"Why?" I ask aloud in his body. "Why is she cleared? How do you decide who you're targeting?"

Tyler goes back to the previous screen and clicks on a young girl's picture. Her name: VERONICA WEST. She can't be more than seven or eight years old. The same options appear when he clicks her name. He chooses CLEAR again.

He follows the same pattern for three other people until he comes to a man named J.R. Pollard. The picture over the name is of a middle-aged man with dark, thin hair and a stubbly face. The word TARGET is already checked, but Tyler clicks it anyway, prompting more options to drop down below it: HIDDEN, STAINED, and BEYOND.

HIDDEN is checked, but he clicks it again, and the check is removed.

He clicks STAINED.

A pop-up message asks a YES or NO question:

SUBMIT FOR TERMINATION?

Tyler hovers over the options, then clicks YES.

I sense Tyler's memory of when he made this decision.

"Go to the moment you decided to target J.R. Pollard," I say.

Instantly, Tyler is knocking on the door of an office. The man in the picture, J.R., answers the door and greets Tyler enthusiastically, pulling him in and slapping his back like men do to make hugging feel manlier.

"Good morning, Tyler. How are you today, son?" J.R. asks, his voice booming.

"I'm doing well, sir," Tyler answers. "I wanted to check in and see how your week has been so far. I haven't seen you in a couple days."

"You know, Tyler," J.R. says. "It's nice to have someone like you in this school. Not many people voluntarily check in with me so often. Most teachers avoid the principal until it's absolutely necessary."

Tyler inspects J.R.'s hands, which are folded together on top of his desk. There's a subtle, but distinct rash under J.R.'s sleeve.

A pang in Tyler's chest rises to his throat. Something about the rash saddens him. But he draws in a breath and pushes it away. "Well, I see no reason for avoiding you, sir," Tyler says. "You're one of the most pleasant men I know."

"Wait," I say. The memory pauses. "Go back to when you saw the rash on J.R.'s arm and stop."

The scene backtracks a few seconds and stops as Tyler's eyes focus on J.R.'s arm. I study it. *Is* it a rash? It could be a birthmark. It's barely pinker than his normal skin tone, and it isn't raised or splotchy. It's more like a splatter like someone spilled a glass of red wine over fabric. It looks like a wine stain.

Stain, I recall. Tyler clicked the word STAINED before signing away J.R.'s death sentence.

"Get down," a voice whispers harshly as my body rocks from side to side. "Resi, wake up. Get down!"

I'm startled awake by Cole, who is shaking me and twisting his body to get lower in his seat.

"What the hell, Cole?" I ask, pulling my earbuds out of my ears. I gesture to my reclined chair. "I *am* down."

He shushes me and points out the front window. I peer outside to find a Wolf pack of seven standing outside the door to the forensics lab, an eighth Wolf lying lifelessly on the ground.

"Oh, shit," I hiss, scurrying to burrow myself below the dashboard. "What are they doing?"

Cole awkwardly bends his knees to make more room for himself to scoot lower in his seat. "They drove into the parking lot in that black SUV. I started waking you up as soon as I saw who was getting out of it."

"Can we roll the windows down so we can listen?"

"Not without turning the car on!" I catch a tone from him that I'm sure is more accusatory than he means it to be. Given the circumstances, I'll let it slide.

I peek over the dashboard, but Cole pushes me back down by the shoulder.

"They're going to see you. Stay down," he says.

"No, they won't." I peer over it again. "Look at them. They're not on guard. They're standing around like this is their regular hangout. They aren't expecting anyone to be watching them."

Cole, who is also crouching beneath the dashboard, props his elbows on the driver's seat to see for himself. "That's so strange," he says. "Are they waiting for something? Did they kill their own man? Coen said this place was where they put dead Wolves, right?"

Someone opens the door to the forensics lab from inside the station, startling us. Cole flinches, and his shoulder hits the car horn. A deafening honk sends a shockwave of fear all the way down to my toes. We throw ourselves back down under the dashboard as far as we can go. I cover my mouth with my trembling hands, stifling the need to scream.

"Drive!" I say.

Cole shoves his hand into his pocket. The keys jingle as his trembling hand misses the ignition several times, his body still halfway under the steering wheel. I try to listen for talking or footsteps or any indication that the Wolves found us, but I hear nothing over my labored breathing and the clacking of metal.

I have that feeling: the one that's full of tension when you can't see them, but you know someone is watching you. The muscles in my shoulders and abdomen tighten. I hug my knees and clench my jaw. The strong urge to glance over my shoulder seizes me, and I twist my head slowly, but the crashing of glass breaking violently into small shards causes me to shield my eyes.

CHAPTER 18

The Wolf reaches into the shattered window and unlocks the door. He opens it, and grabs me by the elbow to pull me out of the car. I yell and try to duck when the other window shatters, but the Wolf holds my arm above my head.

My entire body trembles when I see the Triangle Blade gripped firmly in the Wolf's fist. "We—we were on a road trip and got too tired, so we pulled over to sleep," I lie, my voice vibrating.

This is it. We're about to die.

"We figured the police station would be the safest place," Cole adds. He's pinned against the car by another Wolf with his arms behind his head.

The door to the lab shuts with a metallic thud.

My arms are locked behind my back. A Triangle Blade grazes my neck. I hold my breath and squeeze my eyes shut.

"What did you see?" the Wolf growls into my ear. His voice makes even my bowels cower. "Where did you follow us from?"

"They're not a threat to The Cause." I open my eyes to see the other Wolves walking toward us. Yes, that was a woman's voice. A female Wolf would be more reasonable, right? "And what do you suppose they're going to do? Stab us with their good looks?" She walks up to me and sticks her masked face an inch from my nose. "I think they're shaken up enough to have learned their lesson." She isn't assuming, she's informing, telling me that their mercy isn't automatic and that they could kill me if they felt it necessary.

"How do you know they're not a threat?" The Wolf holding Cole asks. "We should assume that anyone not for us is against us, right? As far as we know, they were spying on us."

"You have a point," the woman says. She points to me. "Does this one look familiar to you?"

"We weren't spying," Cole says. "I swear."

"Let them go," another woman's voice yells. She walks up in her matching uniform to join the crowd. A flashlight she pulls from her belt blinds me, causing my eyes to shut tightly. "It's her."

Fuck.

The other Wolves examine me in the light. The one holding me lowers his blade and loosens his grip on my arms.

"Let's go," he says, sounding annoyed. "Take the keys to make sure they don't follow us."

One of the Wolves grabs Cole's keys from the driver's seat, then they pile into the black SUV outside the forensics lab and drive away.

We've stood in silence for several minutes, gaping at the empty atmosphere into which the Wolves disappeared. I'm still shaking. "Why the hell do they know me, Cole?"

His head shakes. "I don't know."

It's because I'm a target. I must be. My picture must be up on the Wolf Web, but I'm not ready for termination yet. Or did they know my parents? Maybe they wanted their research, and now I'm in the way. I exhale a long breath. I have no idea what's happening.

I hear Cole's shoes crunch on the glass. He's inspecting his car. I shake my head at the ridiculousness of the situation. "Should we report a crime that happened at the police station and might have been committed by people who are working for the police?"

"I don't know," Cole says again. His tone is low and sleepy. "They'll see it on the surveillance cameras, right? But I don't see how we can report it. What would we tell them we were doing here?"

"Same thing we told the Wolves: we got sleepy on a road trip."

"And then they'll ask for our identification and see that we live a few miles away," he points out.

I shiver and fold my arms around myself. Cole draws me into his body, rubbing my arms up and down to warm me up. I burrow into his chest. "Then what do we do?" I ask into his shirt. "I need a drink."

My head moves with his chest as he chuckles. "I guess we should call someone to take us home," he says. "I'll deal with the car later."

It's 2:00 AM, and Edda has a twelve-hour shift in the morning, so I call Charlie to pick us up from the police station, but she doesn't answer the phone. Brandon is the next best option, but I hate to call him. Not because he will feel put-out, but because I'm positive he will come to our rescue without any hesitation. Despite our fight and the fact that I'm with the person we fought about, he will show up. That's just who Brandon is. And as much as we need rescuing, I feel like I'm using him and putting him in an awkward position.

But as I predicted, he comes to the rescue, and fifteen minutes later, I'm riding stiffly between the two men in Brandon's truck. Topics of conversation that the three of us can take part in together dwindle quickly after I give the full explanation of what happened at the police station. The tension in the silence makes me anxious and fidgety.

"Let's get some drinks," I blurt out. I was serious when I said I needed one. Cole and Brandon both turn their heads toward me.

"Right," I say. "That's crazy. It's almost 2:30 in the morning." Their heads turn back to the road. But as I think about it, I find more reasons for why the idea isn't crazy at all. We're all overwhelmed so it would calm us, I need to break the ice with Brandon, and maybe Brandon and Cole could use some liquid encouragement to realize they can be friends.

"Actually, it's not crazy," I say. Cole's head turns to me again, but Brandon stays fixed on the road. His shoulders bob. He's mocking at me. "I need a drink. We could all use one."

"I'm in," Brandon says. "The Dogwood is open twenty-four hours, and it's a block from Resi. We could walk from her house."

"How are you not exhausted?" Cole asks me.

"I am, but I'm also kind of exhilarated after being so shaken up, so I might as well have a couple drinks before I go to bed."

Cole sighs. "Honestly, I want to go home and sleep," he says to both of us. "I'll buy a round the next time we go out."

It may be my imagination, but I'm pretty sure the truck just sped up. We're in front of Cole's apartment building in a matter of minutes.

"Thanks for coming to get us," Cole says to Brandon as he steps out of the truck. Brandon waves a hand to say, 'don't mention it.'

I take the spare key to Cole's apartment off my keychain and hand it to him. He gave it to me last week, and I've never had the chance to use it.

Cole's hand cups my cheek, and right before he kisses me goodnight, his eyes flick to Brandon. Is there a threat in that exchange? Possessiveness? I'm not sure. But after my talk with Charlie, I'm hyper-aware of the silent actions and thick tensions between the two men.

I dismiss the confusion as soon as the door closes and initiate my traditional argument with Brandon over who will buy the first round of drinks. "Driver buys," I state matter-of-factly.

"That is the furthest thing from being a rule I've ever heard," Brandon exclaims.

"I just went through a traumatic event. I need it more!"

"I just rescued you from your distress. You owe me!"

We banter through our reasons for why the other person should pay until we reach my house. I do have *some* social standards, so I run inside to swap my pajama pants for jeans, then I meet Brandon outside to walk to the bar.

"Brandon. Hey, buddy. What are you doing here at this hour?" the bartender asks when we take our seats on the stools in front of him. "And what can I get for you and the beautiful lady?"

"Hey, Doug. Long story," Brandon says. "A vodka tonic for me and a gin martini with a twist for Resi, please."

"First name basis with the bartender?" I ask when Doug walks away.

Brandon lowers his head, rubs the back of his neck. "Since Sarah," he starts, "I haven't been sleeping well, so sometimes I come here, have a couple drinks, and Doug and I talk. And when I say sometimes, I mean, it's probably every other night. Maybe more."

The confession triggers a release of emotion in my gut. I knew Brandon struggled to sleep, but I had no idea it was so bad that he would frequent this bar enough to become friends with the bartender. I'm around Brandon enough to know that it isn't a huge problem, so I'm not necessarily worried, but protective. I pull my credit card out of my purse and hand it to Doug when he returns with our drinks.

"First round is on me," I say.

"Thanks," Brandon says. He pulls his lips between his teeth like he's holding something back. Maybe tears? I can't handle seeing Brandon cry tonight.

"No problem," I say, waving him away with my hand. I sip my drink, the smooth taste warming and relaxing me as soon as it slides across my tongue.

"And I lied," Brandon says, his tone changing drastically. A wry smile sneaks onto his lips. "Doug and I went to high school together. He owns this place. I come here sometimes to say 'hi'. But thanks for buying the first round." His laughter starts timidly in staccatoed breaths, but when he sees my fallen jaw his whole body tightens and he convulses into a turbulent cackle.

I punch his arm. "You're the worst!" My reprimand is ineffective because I can't help snickering with him.

He sips his drink after the surprise of his prank dies down. "So, I think I'm all caught up on what happened tonight, but what's with the Wolves knowing you?"

The reminder is jarring. I feel like my blood is draining from my body. I lean forward with my elbows on the bar top. The solid surface helps me to stay upright. This is the second time a Wolf has recognized me, and I can't come up with a single positive reason that the terrorists might know who I am. I put the martini glass to my lips and throw my head back, finishing the drink in a gulp. "Way to kill the buzz before I even get it," I say.

"Wrong subject to bring up?" Brandon asks.

"No, it's fine." I spin my empty glass in circles along the edge of its base against the wood. "I'm just sort of stumped by that whole thing."

Brandon's hand raises into the air. "Doug," he says, calling to his friend. "Another round."

I eye his vodka tonic, still three-fourths full.

"What?" he says. "You think I'm going to let you out-drink me, Kepler?" He throws the cocktail back like it's water from the Ozarks, then faces me again. "You say you're stumped, but you must have *some* ideas."

I resume the repetitive motion of circling my glass against the wood. Ideas swarm me, but none that I want to admit.

Brandon's hand rests on my back, surprising me. His thumb rubs back and forth over my spine. I take a deep breath. There has never been anything romantic between us, so this gesture shouldn't affect me. But Charlie's voice echoes in my mind, *"he has a thing for you.*" Cole's threatening side-eye as he left the truck makes me wonder if he suspects the same thing.

Just as I find myself leaning into his touch, his hand moves from my back to my face, and his fingertips gently push my chin to turn my head. The events of this long day have rid my face of its makeup. Brandon hasn't seen the bruise he caused, now a strange shade of yellow and brown, without ten pounds of Cover Girl over it.

And there's this tingle in my chest that gets stronger every time he touches me.

"Does it hurt?" he asks.

"Not anymore." I rotate my face back toward him. "It stopped hurting a while ago. Looks worse than it is." I search his eyes. I can't quite pinpoint the emotion I see, but I take a stab at it. "I asked you to hit me, B. Stop feeling guilty."

A joyless huff makes his nostrils flare. "About what?" he asks. "Hitting you to accomplish my own agenda or allowing my daughter to be kidnapped while I was asleep in the next room?"

"You didn't *allow* anyth—"

"I didn't even know she was gone until I got up for work that morning, Rez. How could I not wake up when my daughter is being taken in the middle of the night?"

"The Wolves are professional and skilled. They know what they're doing. This isn't your fault."

My hand lands on his knee. I meant it as a simple, comforting measure, but his hand covers mine, and I can't remember a time he's ever touched me this much. At least, I've never noticed it before.

Doug arrives to deliver our drinks. The shift in focus is welcome, and I remember Brandon's original question about why the Wolves know me. Suddenly, the answer to that question seems much easier than exploring the feelings I apparently have for someone I've always known as a friend and generally find infuriating.

"Do you remember after my parents were attacked, there was a small investigation to see if the bombers were after their research?" I ask.

He sips, swallows. "Yeah, vaguely."

"It's vague because it didn't hold up. No one had been in the lab who wasn't authorized, and the attacks continued elsewhere, so it didn't make sense anymore."

"Okay," Brandon draws the word out, trying to make sense of the story.

"Maybe they did target my family for their research, and they know me because they know I'm their daughter."

"But if that's the case, wouldn't they want to kill you too?" he asks. "It seems more like you have immunity or something. They stopped their attack against you because of whoever they think you are."

"I guess." I rest my cheek against my fist. "I get this sickening feeling that this has something to do with my family. And this girl who died yesterday, Katrina, her mother was in the same attack as my parents. They waited eleven months to kill her. Maybe I'm next. Maybe they're not allowed to kill me because they have a particular time and place that I'm supposed to be targeted."

Brandon presses his lips together, then he scoots the fresh martini closer towards me. "Drink up."

We order another round. Then a shot. Then another round. And Brandon orders yet another in between rounds three and four. It's his "ffffour and a haffff round". *That* round is followed by a list of reasons the Wolves might know me, corresponding with letters of the alphabet. 'A' is because I'm Awesome, 'B' is because I'm Brilliant, 'C' is because Coen did something stupid. The further along in the alphabet, the more intoxicated the answers become: 'M' is because Mariah Carey isn't available, 'N' is because I used Nut-butter on my sandwich last week, and so on. Around six o'clock in the morning, workers getting off their night shift start trickling into the bar.

When I see the time on my phone, I slip off the barstool, grabbing Brandon's shoulder to catch myself as I stumble, and he lifts me back up. I know Brandon is muscular, but his strength still surprises me. I point to the door. "Itthhs innn the daytime! We need to home go." I slur. "Go hooome," I correct.

Brandon checks his watch, tilting his head and moving his wrist close to his face and back again to focus his vision. "Whoa," he says. "Lessss go!"

The chilled wind breezes over us when Brandon opens the door, and I plant my feet on the ground, flexing my entire body as if it will warm me. A cold front blew through in the hours we were drinking. It's painful, the kind of cold that reaches deep in my bones. Brandon grabs my wrist and drags me forward in a power walk.

We skip across the streets and wave to drivers at stoplights, saying, "Good day, sir!" Complete with British accents and fancy bows. We race from mailbox to mailbox and somehow manage to stay off the ground when we trip over our own feet. I open the door when we make it back to my house and step forward, but Brandon stops me and points to the sky. Rays of golden sunlight beam over rooftops into a royal blue sky with wisps of pink clouds scattered in the sunrise. The drunken blur of the sight makes it dance, more in harmony with a painting than reality, and I'm captivated by the radiant colors.

"Beautiful," Brandon says quietly. I agree, but realize Brandon isn't looking at the sunrise anymore. He's standing over me, leaning his arm against the doorpost above my head, staring at me intensely. My instinct is to mention that being told I'm beautiful while staring at a sunrise is a total cliché, but those feelings from hours before in the bar rush back to my chest. His face is inches from mine, but I don't feel my usual need to step back and retreat.

He takes notice of the charm around my neck, then he reaches for his own, pulling it out from behind his black tee-shirt.

"Every new day that Sarah isn't found is another day I..." his voice cracks, and the words fall apart.

I smooth my hand over his chest and trace his charm with my finger, circling the compass and following the outline of the anchor, then I rest my palm over it on his chest. Whereas I've been relieved by the thought of a new day after the crappy one I had the day before, he is miserable by the thought of going another day without Sarah.

"Hope and love, Brandon," I remind him. "They will never fail you."

My back hits the doorpost behind me. A small yelp of surprise leaves my lips and is absorbed by his as Brandon leans his whole body into mine and kisses me. My mind catches up to what's happening, and for a moment, I think I should stop him, but some other part of me I don't recognize takes over. I sink into his kiss, push him into my house, and shut the door behind me.

CHAPTER 19

I'm drying my frozen feet off with a blow dryer in the ER bathroom. It started snowing last night. I don't own snow boots, so I had to suffer through the snow melting through cloth tennis shoes on my way here, the freezing liquid threatening to take my toes.

Each year in Houston, the temperature drops below forty degrees Fahrenheit for a total of about ten days at most. On a particularly cold year, a few of those days might drop below freezing. And two or three times every decade, the clouds align with the frozen air, and fluffy white flakes of snow fall to the ground and melt instantaneously, inducing a city-wide holiday: Snow Day. Schools are shut down, appointments are canceled, businesses are put on hold, and UPS won't deliver Amazon packages.

People who live in the north scoff at this practice, but Houstonians are not equipped to drive on icy roads, so the precautions are necessary. This is evidenced by the plethora of patients who land themselves in the ER due to falls and car accidents these days, which is what I walk into twenty-four hours later. The ER is packed with traumas.

"You feeling better after your hangover?" Edda asks as I place a neck brace on a patient.

"How did you—"

Edda smiles, then helps me finish strapping the

brace on. "I got some drunk texts from you that night, and Charlie said that you didn't show up to the lab yesterday, so I figured you were sleeping it off," she says. "How late were you guys out?"

In truth, I still feel off. I woke up around noon with a pounding headache after the night at the bar. When I went to the kitchen for some water, I saw Brandon passed out on my couch, and our make out session from hours before hit me like a frying pan to the face. I mouthed some expletives before tiptoeing back to bed. He was gone the next time I awoke. We haven't spoken since.

"Late," I answer. "Sorry about the texts." I go to pull medication for my patient.

"Don't be sorry," Edda says as she follows. "Your drunk texts are funny. Plus, you needed to relax. It was probably good for you."

I force what I hope is some semblance of a polite facial expression.

"Hey, it's Cole," Edda announces. My stomach tangles into a knot of guilt at the mention of his name. I think my intestines are laughing at me. And Edda's bubbly voice makes me want to take an elbow to her face, but that would require energy. "Was he with you and Brandon the other night?"

The wound is wide open for you to keep throwing that salt at, Edda.

She must sense my hesitation because her eyebrows arch as far as they can go. Her mouth opens to speak, but I cut her off.

"Later," I hiss. "He's coming in."

I focus on the medication I'm administering to my patient as Cole walks in. "This morphine might make you feel dizzy, so I'm giving you nausea medication with it," I explain to the patient.

"Hey, Dr. Walton," another nurse says. I reluctantly lift my eyes to see his fresh face and perfectly pressed scrubs.

"What are you doing here, Cole?" Edda asks, giving me time to compose myself.

"I got a call from the ER about a prisoner being brought in," he says. "He's suffering from an unknown, rapidly progressing disease, so they needed an infectious disease consult."

"Need a hand?" Edda offers.

"Yes, please."

Another nurse working on the patient I just medicated calls my name, her voice carrying across the room and into my hangover like a gong. "Resi, I've got it from here. You can help out with Cole's patient if you want."

She grins at me like she's doing me a favor.

I let out a long breath, then poise myself to stand up straighter and walk over to Cole. "Need help?"

"I'd never turn down the best nurse in the ER," he says.

Forget salt, just pour some gasoline on the wound.

Cole walks to a cabinet nearby and pulls out protective gear for Edda and me, including N95 Particulate Respirator masks, which filter out microorganisms, gowns, caps, goggles, and gloves. The whole gamut.

"I called the prison clinic," he says, "and they sounded pretty freaked out by this illness. I don't know what to expect, so we should gown up." He does the same for himself, then we set up the room to receive the patient. It has a negative-pressure system, keeping infectious diseases from escaping once they are contained in that room.

"You sure this isn't overkill, Cole?" Edda asks, adjusting her goggles. "I feel like we're preparing for a pandemic."

"Just to be safe," Cole answers.

The patient arrives handcuffed to the stretcher wearing an orange jumpsuit. The paramedics begin reporting the situation as soon as they wheel him in. Their voices fade to murmurs as I zero in on the prisoner: dark gray skin with patches of red petechiae around his face and neck. I've seen it before.

"Resi," Cole nudges me to get my attention. "Oxygen."

I look at the monitor—oxygen saturation 65%. With a start, I reach for the oxygen and place a nonrebreather mask over his face.

"Rez, what did you see?"

Brandon. He's one of the paramedics.

"What did you see?" he repeats, his eyes concerned and knowing.

I use my gloved finger to lift the patient's closed eyelid. The white of his eye is yellow, further confirming my suspicions.

I whip my head back up to Brandon. He is wearing gloves, but no mask, no gown, no goggles. Anxiety strikes through me like an electric current.

"Brandon, get out!" I yell.

Brandon's head jolts back in offense. His eyebrows furrow, and he glares at me in befuddlement.

I turn to Cole. "It's Alice's disease."

Cole's face morphs into recognition. He eyes the

patient. "Are you sure?"

"I'm sure."

He glances at the paramedics and realizes what I'm worried about: they aren't protected.

"Go!" I yell at Brandon again, pointing to the door. But he doesn't move. I look past him. My eyes burn when I see Kyle and Travis. "All of you. Go. *Now.*"

Kyle studies me before looking at Travis. He gestures toward the door with his head. They start to walk away.

"Wait," Cole says, stopping the men in their tracks. His voice is low, solemn. "Don't go."

"*What?*" I'm ready to strangle him.

"They've already been exposed," Cole says. "We have no idea how this disease works or if they're infected now. They're contagious until proven otherwise."

My mind reels. I know he's right, but every instinct in my body wants to get them out of this room.

Cole dials a number on his phone and watches the nursing station from the sliding glass door as Devon, the only nurse visible from the room, answers.

"I need my entire infectious disease team down here," Cole says. Devon trains his eyes on Cole as he listens. "Call the Center for Disease Control and..." He hesitates as he glances at Brandon, then closes his eyes and exhales. "We need security here to make sure none of the paramedics leave this room." Devon's eyes flit around the room to take inventory of each person, and after a long pause, he hangs up the phone.

"We're not going to leave," Brandon says.

"I know," Cole replies. "It's just protocol." He turns to Edda and me. "Draw up every lab you can think of, including blood cultures and arterial blood gases."

Edda starts gathering supplies while I finish connecting the patient to the cardiac monitor.

"Why didn't they bring this guy in sooner?" Cole asks the paramedics.

Brandon points a thumb toward the door. "The prison guard should be outside if you want to talk to him."

As Cole starts toward the door, I notice that nurses, patients, and family members are running throughout the ER, ducking behind doors, and hiding under the desks at the nurses' station.

"What the hell is going on?" Edda asks.

Then I see it: a circle of eight Wolves charging through the ER with their guns and Triangle Blades poised, ready for action. Two of them hold large, black blankets. I stand next to Cole, watching through the door. The others join, forming a line behind the glass, searching for what the Wolves are after.

When they turn a corner and head directly for our room, we take a unified step back.

A sense of dread runs over me like ice, creeping up my spine and numbing my brain. This is it. I'm the sheep ready for the Wolves' next slaughter. My stomach is full of lead. It weighs me down, sinking my feet into the tile below. My mouth opens, but words are frozen inside my throat. I force my hand out to grab Edda's. She wraps it around mine in what she thinks is comfort, but it's just the warmth of another human that I need to melt the icy fear and form words. It works.

"They're coming for me," I finally say. "They have to be. Katrina was first, now me." I stare back at confused faces, except for Brandon, to whom I had explained this fear a couple nights ago. He stands tall, his muscles flex, and his eyes are determined, like he's prepared for battle.

He lifts his hand to the door and thumbs the metal lock to the right, so the flimsy deadbolt might buy us a few more seconds. "They won't get you," he says. "Everybody hide, fight, do whatever you want." The Wolves are a few feet away now. "But Resi might be their target so our priority is to protect her."

It won't work, though. They always finish off their targets. They will kill anyone who gets in the way and tries to protect me.

I'm trying to tell them to stay out of the way and let them kill me, but the closer our assailants get, the more my brain fills with ice again.

When the Wolves reach the door and fail to open it, they stop. They confer with one another for a moment, but their voices are muffled through the door. Three of the Wolves walk around the nurses' station and point their weapons to someone under the desk. Devon comes out with his hands in the air. Even from ten feet away, his body visibly shakes. After some poking and prodding, he hands one of the Wolves a key.

"Why don't they just break the glass?" Edda asks. "They're suddenly polite?"

I know from Jenna's memory that Wolves don't cause more damage than necessary, but again, this new-onset aphasia isn't allowing me to communicate, probably because I'm preoccupied with the fact that I have about thirty seconds to live.

The Wolf unlocks the door and slides it open. Travis leaps forward and tackles him around the waist. The Wolf whacks his head with the base of his gun, causing Travis to fall over.

A Wolf with a Triangle Blade is next to walk through the door. He marches in as three others guard him. Brandon, Edda, and Cole jump in front of me as I shield myself with my arms, but the Wolf walks directly to the prisoner.

A thick black, heavy sheet covers our heads. We yell in confusion and grapple at the sheet to get it off, but before we can do it ourselves, the sheet is removed, and most of the Wolves are walking away. The prisoner's orange jumpsuit is torn at the chest, blood seeping out to stain it where he's been pierced by a downward blow. The Wolf with the bloody murder weapon stands there until he is sure his victim is, indeed, dead. Then he directs his feet to exit, his guards in front of him.

I'm not the target. My brain starts working again —neurons melting from their frozen state to send signals to the right places. I find a sense of courage. They still can't hurt me.

He moves so fast I don't have time to react.

"Brandon, no!" I scream, but he has already snatched the blade out of the Wolf's hand and Brandon impales his side, turning his own weapon against him.

The other Wolves reverse. Two of them charge toward Brandon, but I ram myself through the defensive linemen protecting me to get in front of him.

"You can't hurt me," I yell, my back against Brandon's chest, flinging my arms backward like wings to shield him as they approach. "And retaliation against him won't help The Cause." I remember the strange words the Wolves spoke the night Cole and I were pulled out of the car.

The Wolf closest to me huffs and steps closer. "You think you're somethin' special?"

I remember I'm clothed in protective gear, so they might not recognize me. He rears his arm back as if he is going to backhand me, so I cover my face to guard myself from the blow and try one more time.

"My name is Resi Kepler," I announce.

No slap comes.

The Wolf drops his arm, his eyes squinting to observe me.

I reduce my volume to just above a whisper. "My name is Resi Kepler." I lower my own arms and stand up straighter. "And I don't know why, but you can't hurt me."

The Wolf steps back. Two other Wolves crouch down to pick up their dying friend from the floor.

"Leave him," I order. My voice sounds far calmer and more confident than I actually am. And to my shock, the Wolves obey. After a beat, they run out of the room, leaving their accomplice on the floor.

My entire body slumps in relief.

Slowly, people around the ER peer into our room to see the scene from a distance. Devon pops up from under the nurses' station. He grabs an N95 mask from a nearby bin and shuffles closer to the opened door. The mask trembles in his hand as he attempts to fit it on his face.

"Is everyone okay?" he asks.

The room is silent as we all try to figure out the answer to that question.

"Should I still call the infectious disease team down to the ER?" he asks Cole.

"Dr. Walton?" Devon repeats when there is no

reply.

Cole blinks hard. "Yes," he answers. "Uh…" He composes himself, blinks a few more times. "And the CDC. Tell them to come with the necessary equipment to build an isolation tent. This room is too small for all five exposed patients."

Devon runs to the phone. "They're not answering," he says after a few moments. "I'll go up to the unit myself."

When he is almost out of sight, I run out of the room, ripping my protective gear off, and putting my thoughts together as I go.

"No," I shout when I catch up to Devon. He stops. "Call the CDC and Cole's team, but tell them they'll be setting up an isolation room somewhere else, so prepare it for transfer to another site. Then call transport services to take everyone in that room," I point back to my friends and see Cole approach me, "to Astor and June Kepler's research lab. They will set up for isolation there."

Devon cocks his head to the side quizzically, then his eyes shift to Cole, who is now only a step behind me. I'm about to explain myself to Cole, but he's already speaking. "Do what she says."

CHAPTER 20

The CDC responds rapidly. Legal documents are signed for transfer. Hazmat suits are donned on the paramedics and the two dead bodies until everyone is safely isolated. Layers and layers of protective plastic are used to deliver them to the lab.

We use one of my father's mini-labs for the isolation room, which is separated from the main lab only by glass walls and a door, so extra lengths are taken to seal the edges, close any cracks, and engineer the vents for negative pressure.

It takes six hours, an incredibly efficient process considering all the necessary precautions.

The two deceased are placed in coolers in the corner of the isolation room: the prisoner, Wayne Mueller, who, according to the prison guard, had been incarcerated for nine months for selling drugs; and the Wolf, who we have yet to identify.

With the deceased are the three paramedics: Brandon, Kyle, and Travis.

Kyle is poised on one of the hospital beds that Dad used to do experimental trials. He keeps his head low.

Travis is eager and excited about the prospect of helping find the Wolves, but whiney about everything else: his head hurts, he's bored, the room smells like a hospital, Kyle is breathing too loudly, and so on. He's holding an icepack to his head where the Wolf pounded him with his gun.

Edda, Coen, Cole, Charlie, and I stand on the other side of the glass from the isolation room.

I turn to the four friends on my side of the glass. "Alright, Lab Rats."

"That is *not* our team name," Brandon says. He is pacing behind the glass wall, hands on his hips.

"Edda, find out everything you can about our prisoner, Wayne Mueller," I say. "Charlie, will you dissect the Wolf's mask and figure out what it's made of? Start with carbon nanotubes. Cole thinks they might be a component."

"Sure. The CDC is almost finished sanitizing the uniform. And I am close to finding a way to separate the metal alloys of the bullet. Hopefully, one of these will lead to something."

Both women bounce away to start their assignments.

"Cole, do you know where I can find Mom's work on Alice's disease? Any idea where to start?"

"As far as I remember, June kept her notes on unidentified diseases in the eighth filing cabinet, top drawer," Cole says. "You can start searching there."

We've already been through twelve of the eighteen filing cabinets, including the eighth, but we weren't looking for diseases at the time. A new lead is progress, but it feels like a step back.

"The lab at the hospital is running tests on the prisoner's blood," Cole continues. "They'll call when they're done, but it was drawn post-mortem and could be hemolyzed." He leans to the side and pokes his head around me to address Brandon. "Can you draw up labs on everyone in isolation? Blood from exposed patients would be helpful."

Brandon nods.

"There are supplies in the drawer under the table," I tell Brandon.

"While I wait for that," Cole says to me, taking his phone out of his pocket. "I'll see what I can find on this name you gave me, Tyler Meeks."

"Thank you." I nod toward the research office. "Go ahead and get started. I'll join you in a minute." He goes to a table and gathers the supplies he needs before heading to the office.

I face Coen. "Coen, I don't have a job for you yet, so continue the research you've been doing until someone needs help."

"Aye aye, Captain," he says, saluting me before he retreats.

I shake my head with a smile. Such a nerd.

Kyle is sitting quietly in the isolation room, and Travis is messing with some of Dad's equipment while balancing his icepack on his head. Brandon was the only one listening at the window.

Travis flips a switch on the thought-projector my dad invented, and he jumps back when it powers on. His icepack falls from his head. Kyle punches Travis' arm without a word, giving Travis another reason to whine. "Will you watch him, please?" I ask Brandon. "He's going to break something."

"Yeah, I'll watch him," he says. "Can I help with research?"

"No," I answer shortly, then start to walk away.

"Why not? Those guys made it safe for you to come in here with protective gear."

I spin back around. "We don't know if this disease survives on surfaces like paper." My tone is harsh. "You wouldn't be able to give it back. We don't need you for this. Just go draw up the blood we need."

"Are you mad at me?" he asks.

"What do you think, Brandon?"

He screws up his face like my anger is uncalled for. "Is this about the other night?"

"No!" I scan the room to make sure no one is listening, then face Brandon again pointedly. "This has nothing to do with that," I whisper harshly.

He surrenders with his palms up in a way that says, 'I'm sorry,' but insincerely.

My eyes travel to the coolers in the left corner of the isolation room. "You shouldn't have done it."

He follows my eyes, then draws them back to me, and his eyebrows crease. "It was in defense."

I huff in disbelief. "Sure, in the sense that no one would ever hold you guilty in court for killing a terrorist, but that was not defense, Brandon."

"Yes, it was."

"He was done!" I yell. "He killed his target, and he was walking away. You *knew* he wasn't going to kill anyone else. That wasn't defense, Brandon. It was rage."

He takes a step forward. His face is so close to the glass that his breath creates fog in front of him. When he speaks, his voice is low and forceful. "Of course, it was rage. Those bastards have my daughter."

"Then, by all means, Brandon, *murder* your way to her."

"I will if I have to."

"This isn't what we agreed on. What would Sarah say if she knew you killed someone to find her?"

Brandon's face is stoic. He doesn't hang his head or look away in remorse, he doesn't roll his eyes in frustration, he just glowers at me unapologetically. After a long silence, I fall away from his heavy stare.

"I should get to work," I say, and I start towards the office.

"Can we talk about the other thing?" he asks.

The question makes me want to stop, but I force myself to keep walking.

"No," I answer. Whatever happened between us is the least of my worries right now.

Cole looks up from a computer when I enter the office. "I found some information on Tyler Meeks."

I stand behind him at the center table, looking at the screen over his shoulder.

"He was an elementary school teacher in Beaumont," he states, scrolling through a page that looks like a biography. "This is the school website. Each teacher has their own info page for the parents to see. Meeks is incredibly accomplished. He wrote the third-grade curriculum and conducts a space camp for students during the summer. He went missing a few weeks ago."

"Missing?"

Cole nods. He clicks on another window and brings up his Missing Person's page.

"The Wolf that was brought to the ER by Life Flight, Bert. He was a Missing Person also."

"Do you think these disappearances are Wolf recruits?"

The thought startles me as I think about the

endless number of Missing Person flyers spread across Joey's Market. "I really hope not."

"I found something interesting, Resi," Coen says. He stalks toward me, holding a red folder, thick with paper. "Your parents have studied the possible components of the Damascus Sword rather recently." He hands me a picture of a meticulously crafted ancient sword. It has a rosewood handle with gold accents, and at the base of the metal, there's a vine pattern engraved into it.

"The Damascus Sword?" I ask. "Isn't that a myth?"

"Oh, no," Coen says, rejecting the idea like I'm an ignorant child, then he explains the sword from his own vault of facts. "The Damascus Sword gained its reputation in medieval times when Muslim warriors defeated the Christian crusaders who had invaded their territory. It rose to fame quickly, but the Muslim blacksmiths guarded the secret to its production so well that no European blacksmith has ever been able to reproduce it. But your parents might have come close."

"Coen, what does this have to do with our current situation?"

"Ah, right," Coen says. He licks his middle finger and uses it to flip through some of the pages in the folder. "One second. It's in here somewhere."

I lean onto one leg and cross my arms. Coen is always the one who gets distracted by research he finds interesting, and I do not have time for it today.

"Here."

The illustrations he shoves into my hands assault my conscience. "Coen, what is this? Is this a joke?"

"Joke?" he repeats.

The date written on the page catches my attention, and I snatch the entire folder from Coen's hands. "Cole, how long ago did you finish your residency with mom?"

He turns around with a curious expression. "About eighteen months ago. Why?"

Good. That cuts the people I'm about to yell at in half. I power-walk out of the room to where Charlie is observing the Wolf's mask under a microscope in the lab, picking it apart with small tweezers. I slam the sketch down in front of her. Charlie raises her head up from her microscope slowly, very aware of my intensity.

"Look at these dates," I say, almost yelling. "A year. One. Year. Twelve months, Charlie. These sketches are from twelve months ago. You were *here*. How could you not remember this when you see the Triangle Blade on the news every damn day?"

"Whoa, Resi. Calm down," Edda says behind me. But I persist in my accusatory glare.

Charlie considers my words carefully, hardly moving as she examines the page.

"Resi," she says, "I don't know what this is."

I study her for any evidence that she's lying.

Charlie continues. "I want to help you, but I need more information on what you're showing me."

"I already told you—"

"No," Charlie says. "You showed me this picture of a Triangle Blade and said it was dated a year ago. That means nothing to me. What are you trying to imply?"

"I would like to interject and say that the date is slightly less than one year ago," Coen says, holding his index finger in the air. "It is from eleven months and twelve day—" he shuts up when Edda whacks his arm.

I inspect the page again. The Triangle Blade is perfectly sketched in four different angles. *April 10* is written in my mother's handwriting, a week before the first Wolf attack. A week before her death.

"How could you not know about this if my parents were working on it while you were here assisting them?" I ask Charlie.

"They worked on *this*?" Charlie asks. My anger begins to subside when I see how perplexed Charlie is. "I didn't know," she says, "They didn't include me on everything. Do you think the Wolves stole this from your parents? How would they have known about it?"

"And if the Wolves stole their idea, why would they have left it here in their lab?" Edda asks.

"They couldn't have stolen it," I say. "No one has been in here that we don't know about. It's too heavily monitored."

"Maybe they had copies at home," Brandon suggests from several feet away behind the glass door. "It could be why they blew the house up. They stole it and got rid of the evidence."

I deliberate his theory. "They never really took their work home, but it's the only thing that makes sense."

"Resi," Charlie says. She's sorting through the other papers in the Damascus Sword file. "This might sound strange, but I think the blade and the uniforms are made from some of the same materials. Carbon nanotubes, like Cole suggested."

"Brilliant," Coen says. "I wish had seen it earlier, but Cole was right to direct you back to it. Carbon nanotubes are cylinders made of hexagonally-arranged carbon atoms. They are one of the strongest materials known to man and have incredible elasticity."

"And that's what Cole said is used in bulletproof armor," I say.

"I apologize for misleading you," Coen says. "I was thinking that the nanotubes do not have a graphene component, which is what we were searching for."

"This might." Charlie is looking into the microscope again. "The carbon nanotubes are woven in with another material. It could easily be graphene, but I'll have to test it."

Could we have found what we've been looking for? What my mom was looking for? I glance again at my mother's sketches. She called it a modern Damascus Sword.

I imagine her sitting in the office, a pencil in her hand, dreaming about this powerful material, sketching a weapon she thought was beautiful. But she never would have intended for it to be used. She would be devastated to know all the destruction this sword has caused.

There's pressure behind my eyes now. Damn it. Don't get emotional.

"So, what do we do now?" Charlie asks.

I rub one eye with the heel of my palm. "I don't know," I say, frustrated. "I haven't thought that far ahead."

"Find out who the manufacturer is who makes bulletproof armor from that material," Brandon yells from the isolation room. "Call them and find out if they have any idea how these uniforms were made and who they were made by."

"I'll start calling," I say. "Coen, keep looking through those notes and the research around the area you found it."

"Certainly," he says.

"Sorry, ma'am, we only use Kevlar."

"Do you know any companies that use carbon nanotubes?" I lean forward on the stool, my elbow leaning on the lab table in front of me. Charlie and Cole are also in the lab. They're both in full-on scientist mode— white coats, goggles, gloves—Charlie is burning things and mashing stuff up in a crucible. I have no idea what she's doing, but it's pretty fascinating to watch. Cole is placing blood cultures onto different mediums for testing.

"Try BCU Body Armor," the man on the phone says.

They were the second company on my list, already crossed off.

I sigh. "Thank you for your time." A line through another name.

The sixth number is for a company called Point Blank Safety. I dial.

"This is Archie."

"Hi, Archie, my name is Lisa Burgundy." The only real fun I'm having at this point is coming up with fake names for each call. I also add a hoity-toity professional flair to my voice. "I'm a representative of the Houston Police Department, and I'm looking for the latest technology for bulletproof armor that will keep the men and women in our department safe."

"Uh-huh." Archie sounds either distracted or

disinterested. There's noise in the background: tunneled voices—probably a TV show.

"I'm specifically looking for a product that incorporates carbon nanotubes into their armor. Possibly even graphene. The research we've done shows that these materials could revolutionize bulletproof armor."

There's a pause. I'm not sure if he expects me to continue talking or if he's not listening. "Archie? You there?"

"Yeah."

Should I repeat myself? "I said I'm looking for armor that incorp—"

"I heard you."

"Oh."

The talking in the background stops. "We don't sell that kind of armor anymore," Archie says.

My heart skips a beat. "Anymore?"

"Yeah."

"But you used to?"

Another pause.

"Archie?"

"What did you say your name was?"

Shit. I made it up, and I don't remember what I said. "Martha," I say it firmly, hoping confidence will make up for the fact that I made up a different name. I don't want my real identity to shut any conversations down if they know my parents or they're Wolves and killed them.

"Martha, I'm sorry to disappoint you, but we don't sell the product you're looking for." There's a rumble, like he blew into the speaker of his phone. "And if I were you, I'd stay away from it."

"Why?" I ask. "Is it unsafe?" I know that's not the case, but I need him to tell me more.

"Don't call here again."

"Wait, just—"

He hangs up, my phone goes back to the keypad screen. I dial again.

"This is Archie at Point Blank Safety. Leave a message."

There's a beep. I'm not sure what to say. "Archie, hi. This is... Martha." How do I play this? He knows something, but he seemed uncomfortable, not like he was hiding it because he is Wolf, but because he was scared or sad. A Wolf would have had a story prepared. Archie didn't have much of anything. "Listen," I say. Suddenly I'm empathetic toward Archie like he's been affected by the Wolves too. I drop the professional façade. "I know this is strange, and whatever you've been through, I get it. And it sucks. But I need to know what happened." I pause, swallow. "I really, *really* need to know what happened." My voice cracks that time. I'm screwing this up. "Please. Call me back at this number."

I hang up the call, rub my face. Scribble Archie's name down next to his number, circle and star it a few times, then I save the number on my phone.

Thankfully, we have so much to do that I'll have plenty of things to distract myself while I wait for Archie to call back. If he calls at all.

I make my way into the office and follow Cole's instincts, searching through the top drawer of the eighth filing cabinet. I'm frustrated, having already gone through this drawer looking for anything on metals. All of this work is getting tedious and exhausting. I sort through the first set of files but find nothing on diseases. Why couldn't my parents stick to their own fields of science?

The next several files from the same drawer are just as useless, but the bunch that follows seems promising: files on Ebola Virus and renal failure along with some drug concoctions Mom was experimenting with for both illnesses. I take as much as I can hold and sit down at the table across from Edda.

"Anything from the manufacturers?"

I take a deep breath, let it out. "Yes and no. I think I have a lead, but didn't get much information." I pull my phone out of my back pocket and set it on the table in front of me. "Hoping he'll call back."

She gives a sympathetic smile. "We're making progress, it's just taking time."

I nod, can't even fake an encouraging grin. I open the first file.

CHAPTER 21

I enter a cold, gray room where I'm escorted to a table and bench that are bolted to the floor. I steady myself on the table with my hands close together as I sit. The sound of metal chains clinks as my wrists touch. Anxiety makes me jittery as I wait.

I'm waiting. What am I waiting for?

"Ah, crap," I gripe, but no sound leaves my body. I must be in the Afterthoughts of one of the dead guys in isolation. "I don't have time for this. Listen, whoever you are, I have a lot of work to do, and I didn't mean to fall asleep. So, if you could do something to wake me up that would be super."

I planned on going into their Afterthoughts tonight anyway, but I wanted it to be more controlled. I would position myself to be closer to one over the other, so I'd know whose memories I was experiencing. I was going to fall asleep with purpose, plan to visit certain events or places. This isn't how I wanted to do it.

A heavy door opens to the sound of an ugly buzz. A petite woman marches toward me but refuses to make eye contact. She slaps a stack of stapled papers on the table, followed by a pen.

"I'm done, Wayne," the woman says.

Wayne. The prisoner.

Wayne reads the bold words on the top of the pile: PETITION FOR DIVORCE.

He bows his head, and I see an orange jumpsuit and handcuffs.

"Go to a memory of when you first felt sick," I say.

Nothing happens. But I know it's there. The memory is almost tangible.

Wayne's fists clench. "Please, don't do this," he begs. "Think about the kids."

"You will be doing all of us a favor," the woman says. "The next time you decide to sell your pain pills, it won't be as part of this family."

"Go to a memory of your illness," I try again.

"You cannot take my children away from me," Wayne says to the woman, his voice rising.

I'm not listening to music, I realize. I can't control the Afterthought.

"I can, and I will," the woman says, the intensity of her voice matching Wayne's. "Sign the damn papers."

I need to find out more about his and Alice's disease, but I can't control the memory without music. As the two continue to yell, I start to hum Row Your Boat.

Wayne stands, and a guard holds him back with one arm. "I sold those pills because you wanted a better life. I was getting the money we needed to meet *your* standards."

"And where did all that hard work get us?"

I put words to the tune of Row Your Boat:

Go to a me-mo-ry

Of your i-illness

Before I finish the song, I'm lying on my side on the thin mattress of a bunk bed. Stabbing pain seizes my abdomen. I wheeze at Wayne's rapid pace, never feeling like the air is filling my lungs. I know I'm in his body, not mine. But the misery is so palpable I can't separate myself from him. I try to hum again to get out of the memory, but I'm too weak to sing—my body trembles. The sheets below me are soaked in sweat. I want to curl up tighter into the fetal position to lessen the excruciating pain. No, even the thought of moving my legs is too exhausting. Wayne's trembling hand comes into my view when he wipes sweat from his brow. His arm is gray and bruised with petechiae.

I'm so, *so* cold.

I need help.

Two legs appear on the ladder of the bunk bed, and an older man with a long beard steps down to the floor.

His eyes bug out. "Whoa, Wayne. What the hell happened, man?" He bangs hard on the door of the cell. "We need help. Somebody help!"

I wake with a start to the sound of my phone buzzing against the table. My head flies up from the desk, and a warm soreness on my cheek tells me I've been laying on my hand for quite some time. The papers I was reading stick to my elbow. I must have fallen asleep soon after I sat down because I hadn't read far.

I take a deep breath, fill my lungs with plenty of air, then let it out slowly.

I look at my phone, hoping Archie called back. But the buzzing was a reminder that I have a staff meeting tomorrow at work that I will definitely skip.

"Nice nap?" asks Edda. She's buried in notes on the other side of the table. "I'm the only one left awake."

I scan the room to see Coen sprawled across a

couch with his hair draped over one of his eyes. Charlie is curled into a ball in a beanbag chair, fast asleep. I wonder if she got anywhere with the metals. The clock on the wall above her reads 3:32 AM. I stretch my neck to one side, then the other, trying to free the crick I developed in my neck while sleeping.

"Why are you still awake?" I ask Edda.

She shrugs through a forced smile. "I don't know. I need to sleep, though. My head is killing me." I cock my head and frown, prompting her to explain further. Edda sighs. "We see death all the time in the ER, but it was different yesterday. It's been bothering me, so I haven't wanted to sleep." She pauses, picks at her fingernails. "I can't stop thinking about Brandon stabbing that Wolf."

She reaches down to the floor next to her to get something from her purse. "I'm having a hard time with that too," I say. "But I'm not sure if it's because of the stabbing in general or if it's because Brandon is the one who did it."

"Exactly," Edda agrees. "Maybe both." She sits up straight again with a bottle of Advil and pops the top off to pour two pills into her hand, then throws them into her mouth and swallows. The process takes about three seconds, then something she recalls puts a small smirk on her face. "Speaking of Brandon, what happened between you two the other night when you went to the bar?"

I hear the words, but Wayne's Afterthought boomerangs back to me as Edda places the bottle of Advil back into her bag.

Wayne's wife talked about selling pain pills.

I hold my breath as I remember every single

Afterthought I've had since I first experienced them: two Tylenol pills flash through my mind when Nico emptied his pockets and set the contents on the side table; the girl in the play invades my thoughts next and her voice resonates, saying that her back wasn't hurting anymore; Elisa's searing migraine; and Alice told Mom that she cured her joint pain.

"Pain," I say.

"What?" Edda asks. "Need some Advil?" She lifts the bottle again and offers it across the table.

"No." I wave the medicine off. "She was curing pain. In the last few years of her life, my mom worked on a cure for chronic pain. In every victim's Afterthought, they are in some kind of chronic pain." I rise from my seat. "She tested it on Alice."

"Do you think her cure is what made Alice sick?" Edda asks, standing as I go to the filing cabinets. I frantically flip through and read the tabs of the files before shutting the drawer and opening the next.

I shake my head. "She tested it on multiple people. Alice is the only one before Wayne I've ever heard of getting this disease, and she cured her pain almost a year before she got sick."

"How are the rest of the victims connected to this?"

"I..." Nothing is coming to me, but there's a reason. I know there is. "I haven't figured it out yet."

"Everyone has pain," she says. She's standing right next to me at the cabinet now. "It's not surprising that the victims did too. That's life. That's why we're employed as nurses. How much morphine have you given over the past four years? People have pain."

"Yes," I say, still flipping through files and pages

within the files. "That's also why her cure for pain was dangerous. Think of how many huge pharmaceutical brands would be out of business if someone cured pain, or how rich the person who cures it will be."

"So..." Edda says. "The Wolves have something to do with your mom's cure for pain?"

"It *must* be why she was killed." The words burn in my chest. My fingers work faster. I read through the tabs on the files quickly, but accidentally skip over a few, so I go back and flip through them again. My mind wanders to the thought of some jealous CEO of Tylenol or Motrin finding out about my mother's research and killing her so they can steal the credit. I lose my train of thought and realize I've flipped through tabs without reading them. I go back. The titles on each tab the second time through start to blur, so I stop and rub my eyes.

"Damn it!" I yell when I lose my spot. There's stirring behind me, movement against fabric. I'm sure my outburst woke someone up. I try to estimate where I left off, but I can't remember exactly where I was, and I don't want to miss anything. I groan and start over, flipping through the files until a hand lands on my shoulder. I pause.

"It doesn't make sense." Edda's voice behind me is calm and sympathetic. I turn around and question her. "It would make sense if it was only your mom, but it isn't. The Wolves have killed *hundreds* of people since the first attack. Tons of those people are in other states. Your mom couldn't have been treating all of them."

Edda's eyes are unwavering. She's right. If they wanted my mom's research, they would have killed her and been done. But I'm not ready to stop for tonight now that my adrenaline is pumping.

"I need to do something," I say. "I'm all worked up. Did Cole find anything?"

"Let's go see," Edda says.

We leave the research office and walk into the lab. Cole is slumped over on his stool with his face down on the lab table in front of him. I chuckle at the sight of a Bunsen burner just centimeters away from his hair.

"Guess I wasn't the only one awake," Edda whispers, nodding toward Brandon. He's on the floor in the isolation room tucked into the corner where the wall and glass window meet, opposite the coolers that carry the dead bodies across the room. He stares at them vacantly.

A pang of guilt aches in my stomach. I was so harsh with Brandon, but he's punishing himself enough. I walk over to Cole, unplug the burner, then go to Brandon and kneel on the other side of the glass. He's startled when I tap.

"You didn't see us walk in?"

He rubs his face, then rakes his hands through his hair as if trying to rub the tiredness away. "No, I didn't. What time is it?"

"Early." I'm tempted to tell him to get some sleep, but it would be fruitless. I observe the coolers he's been staring at. When I was asleep in the office, the prisoner was closer to me. From this angle, I'm closer to the Wolf.

"He knows, Resi," Brandon says. "That bastard knows where my daughter is." His pleading, desperate eyes, and the verb tense that he uses tells me that he is thinking the same thing I am. He said "knows" as if the dead man still has something to say. I turn to Edda.

"I'll go get you a couple pillows. Coen is hogging them all right now," Edda says as she walks toward the office. We're all on the same page.

"I'm sure you'll get the Afterthoughts if you fall asleep in the office," Brandon says. "It would probably be more comfortable for you."

"Already did. Dreamed about the prisoner because of how they're positioned."

"I could move them if you want me to," he offers.

"That's okay. Some company might help you sleep, too."

Edda returns with pillows and my headphones. I wobble around on the pillows until I'm comfortable-ish. She switches some lights off in the lab as she makes her way back to the office.

Brandon props his head on his bent arm, laying parallel to me. We're facing each other, and though a thick glass wall separates us, there's something oddly intimate about this situation.

He gives me a sleepy grin, and I can't help but return it.

"You know, this is how I wish we ended up the other night," he says. "Minus the glass."

"Brandon!" I hurl myself up with a crunch and browse the lab for Cole.

Brandon snorts. "He's asleep, Rez. And I'm just messing with you."

I roll my eyes and lay back down.

The humor in his eyes wanes. "I'm sorry 'bout that night. I shouldn't have kissed you."

It's the millionth thing he's blamed himself for, and I wonder why he puts so much pressure on himself. "You weren't the only one there, B. We were drunk, we've both been through a lot." I want to tell him that it shouldn't happen again, but I already note disappointment on his face at my excuses. So, I go a different route. "That whole night was what I needed. I needed to drink, I needed to talk, and I needed my friend. I needed..." Passion? Touch? To be kissed like that? I can't say what I really think, so I settle for, "I don't regret it."

"No?"

I have no idea what to do with this entire conversation, or what it means, but my own honesty surprises me. "No. But we can't..."

"I know," he says, graciously saving me from having to say it.

My eyes grow heavier, and I hold in a yawn. "Get some sleep," I say.

"And you go get some memories."

CHAPTER 22

The smell of bacon fills my nostrils. I find myself standing in front of a stove cooking breakfast. My time might be limited, and I want to get straight to my mission, but the scent is so enticing.

I can spare ten seconds, right? "Go to the memory of when you eat this bacon."

A small table set for three appears in front of me, and the man's hand reaches for a plate of fully-cooked bacon and chomps down.

"A bit salty for my taste," I say as he chews. "Okay. Go to Wolf headquarters."

The next moment, I'm walking down a hallway with a man dressed in army attire and a woman in a pantsuit. Whistles blow, and random yells are in sync with the sound of marching. The building is familiar to me. Familiar, but different. There's something nostalgic and eerie about it. It's an older building, the structure and walls are concrete, and the ceiling above us is slanted. The entire hallway curves like it will eventually make one huge circle if I keep walking. I'm positive I've been here before, but I can't place it.

"She'll be late, but we can debrief the assignment with her when she gets here," says the woman. We stopped to get food at a concession stand called MR. RICKLE'S NACHOS AND CHILI, according to the sign above it. "Are you getting something, Adam?"

"I ate before I left the house." I note the name of the Wolf I'm inhabiting: Adam.

The other two grab their food, and we turn away from the concession and face the center of the building.

"Stop," I say softly, and I take in the sight. "Well, I'll be damned."

I know exactly where I am. The Wolves are hiding in plain sight—right in the middle of the city.

It's the Astrodome. It was abandoned when NRG Stadium was built right next to it nearly two decades ago. Still, my childhood memories of going to Astros games here are fresh and joyful.

I behold a giant open space. Rows of chairs are scattered all around it. It used to be stocked full of chairs, but now it's mostly just descending levels of wood and concrete. There are men and women in groups all around the stadium. They're frozen in the middle of assorted workout routines: some groups are running up and down the stairs, some are on the ground doing pushups, some are sparring with Triangle Blades in their Wolf uniforms, and others are using bars for pullups on the ground level.

"Continue the memory."

"You two go ahead and eat," Adam says to the two he's been walking with. "I'll meet you back at the office."

He walks away from the concessions and the field, trudges up one flight of stairs, and enters an area with several closed doors. Abstract paintings hang on the walls in the hallway. When he reaches for the door-knob of one room, the buzz of a phone in his pocket stops him. I see when he searches his pocket for his phone that he too is in a military uniform. The phone he pulls from his pocket is ancient. It reminds me of my first cell phone. It's small, gray, and has a thick rectangular shape with real buttons rather than a touchscreen. I read the message: *I have papers for you in the schoolroom. Alpha needs them to approve the new recruits. -Judy*

At that, Adam walks to a different room several doors down and knocks. A flustered woman with red-rimmed glasses and straggly, dark hair in a half-pony-tail opens the door. She seems hurried, and she shoves a small stack of papers into Adams hands.

"Nice to see you too, Judy," he says sarcastically.

Judy makes a face that can't really be called a smile because it's so insincere. She shuts the door, but right before it closes, Adam peeks into the room.

"SARAH!"

My voice echoes back to me in Adam's body.

The door shuts, and Adam turns to go back to the room from which he came.

"No!" I yell. "Go back. Go back to talking to Judy."

"Nice to see you too, Judy," Adam says when the memory rewinds.

"Stop!" The world freezes before Judy can shut the door.

I peer into Adam's periphery, and there she is. Sarah is sitting at a desk with her hair in pigtails. She wears clothes I've never seen on her before, black pants and a gray polo. The Wolves are really into this black and gray look. There are other children around her. Sarah is writing and biting her cheek like she does when she's thinking.

"Sarah!" I shout again. It's in vain. I know Sarah won't hear. But I can't help it. Whether it's out of joy that Sarah is alive, or desperation to get her out of that room, I just have to shout.

"Go to a memory of talking to Sarah," I say. But nothing happens.

He doesn't know who Sarah is. But I'm sure he's been around the children before.

"Go to a different memory of those children."

It's similar. Adam knocks on a door, but to a different room. When it opens, he stands for a minute at the doorway and speaks to the man who answers. I watch in his periphery again as he talks.

"Stop." It barely comes out as a strained whisper.

I'm not sure which part of the Afterthought horrifies me the most. The children lounge in tan, leather reclining chairs wearing the same uniform as before. They chat with one another and Sarah leans over to the girl next to her with a folded piece of paper she made into an origami fortune teller. Each child is hooked up to an IV with fluid infusing. Adam isn't close enough for me to see what it is. IVs are placed in their other arms too, where a man is drawing blood: Dr. Locke.

Rage boils as I stare at Dr. Locke frozen in memory. The man who claims I'm like a niece to him took someone so special from me. A man who was supposedly a dear friend of my parents was an accomplice in their demise.

I think of the birthdays he attended, the gifts he brought, the parties he joined, even danced in when he caved to my dad's badgering.

He's a fraud.

"Go to a memory of Dr. Locke," I say.

Nothing happens. I know it's there, I can sense it, but my own memories of Locke are overpowering the

Afterthought.

I take a breath, push my emotions aside, along with my memories. All those months of coping poorly and avoiding my feelings are coming in handy now. I focus on Adam. "A phone call," I sense. "A phone call with Locke. Go to that memory."

That command puts me in the front passenger's seat of a van. Adam wears business clothes. He has his phone up to his ear. Dr. Locke's voice is hushed on the other side.

"It's confirmed," Locke says. "He will be highly contagious, so make sure your uniforms are on correctly. The target will be in room seven. Alpha signed off on immediate termination and states not to leave until you know the job is done."

"Understood," Adam says. "Do you have access instructions?"

"I'll be walking out of the emergency room entrance. Hold me at gunpoint and take my badge from my coat. Your exit plans will be sent to your watches individually in three minutes."

Adam ends the call and places the phone in the cup holder next to him. He reaches for the buttons of his shirt and unclothes himself to reveal his Wolf uniform. He's almost fully dressed in his battle garb when the van approaches the hospital, so he reaches into a pocket and pulls out his mask and gloves. He puts them on, then leans to his left to speak to people behind him. "Room seven," he says for the whole van to hear. "Masks on tight. The target will be contagious. Victoria, when you see Locke, hold him at gunpoint. Marty, you grab his badge." He speaks into the rearview mirror, and in the reflection, I see seven other Wolves in the backseat, already dressed and ready for their assignment.

Adam addresses the driver, an older gentleman with graying hair and a Hawaiian shirt. He's not the type of person I expected to be driving the Wolves to kill their prey. "We will scatter when we're done, and we all have different escape assignments," he says as he reaches for a stick from his belt. "Switch cars when you are clear, and we will all meet back when we can at the safe house to debrief." Adam holds the stick he retrieved from his belt in an open space in front of him. He faces forward as the van approaches the hospital, and his mindset switches focus. He twists the bottom of the stick until it clicks, then pushes the twisted piece up until it clicks again, and blades spring up to form a triangle. We roll up to the ER, and Adam is opening the car door before it has time to stop.

He's gone into a military mindset. He has an order to kill, and he won't stop until it's done.

My mind reels as Adam runs forward, letting some of the other Wolves run in front of him until he is surrounded in a strategically formed circle.

I see Locke, but my view of him starts to blur, and the hospital fades.

"No, I'm not ready," I say. But everything fades more as Victoria holds a gun to Locke's jaw.

"Wait! Go back to Sarah," I beg, but my parents' lab comes into view when I blink.

"Sarah!" I scream, waking up with a thunderbolt of energy.

I glance next to me and see Brandon stir. I hop up to my feet and waste no time running across the lab, past the office, to my mother's pharmacy. I type the code into a computer and press my finger to a designated spot to scan my fingerprint. The computer opens to reveal the names of all the medications in the pharmacy, and I scroll down to Propofol.

"Resi?" Charlie asks. "Are you okay?"

Charlie, Edda, and Cole have followed me into the pharmacy. I must have caused a ruckus when I awoke.

"You have to help me go back to sleep," I say. A small door opens, and a drawer shoots out. A lid inside the drawer flips open, and I take a bottle from it. "I have to find out how to get in."

"Get into what?" Edda asks.

I grab an IV start kit and a needle. "Headquarters." I leave the pharmacy and walk briskly back into the lab. Coen is also awake now, rubbing his eyes as he meets us.

"Resi, calm down for a minute," Edda says. "What headquarters?"

"*Wolf* headquarters." I'm shorter with them than necessary, but this is too important to slow down. I plummet back down in my sleeping spot, then open the kit and start to tie the tourniquet around my arm.

Right after I fail the first time, Edda's hand stops mine, and she kneels in front of me.

"What's going on?" Brandon asks.

"Resi's freaking out," Edda answers. "What did you see?"

"Sarah. I saw Sarah."

Brandon's eyes widen, mouth unhinges.

"She's alive, and I think she's safe," I say. "She's at Wolf headquarters, but you have to give me Propofol so I can go back to sleep and find out how they get in."

"Where is the Wolf headquarters?" Cole asks.

The question makes me pause—my mouth

twitches. "You're not going to believe it."

    "Tell us," Charlie says.

    "The Astrodome."

CHAPTER 23

"*The* Astrodome?" Cole asks. "As in, the original home of the Astros and Oilers *That* Astrodome?"

"The first domed stadium and inauguration place of Astroturf?" Coen asks.

"Where Mickey Mantle hit the world's first indoor homerun?" Cole asks.

"Former Houston Livestock Show and Rodeo location and concert stadium?" Edda asks.

"The one and only," I say. "They're right in the middle of the city."

"I thought that thing wasn't used anymore," Charlie says.

"It hasn't been used since 2005 when it was used as a shelter for victims of Hurricane Katrina, but they built the new stadium next door to it long before that." Coen states. "Now, the parking lot is the only useful structure of the Astrodome."

"Exactly," I say. "When the new stadium was built, the Astrodome was abandoned and basically left in ruins. No one uses it anymore, and no one would think to check on anything in there. Wolf headquarters is literally hiding in plain sight."

"What do you mean by 'headquarters?'" Cole asks.

"What the hell are you guys talking about?" Travis is standing behind Brandon. He and Kyle look lost.

There's no time for me to explain everything. "When I go back to sleep, everyone can catch you guys up."

My friends nod, and I trust Kyle and Travis will be discrete. We don't have much of a choice but to work with them at this point.

"Our Wolf over there is named Adam," I say, pointing to his cooler. "When I got into his After-thoughts, I told him to go to Wolf headquarters, and that's where we ended up. They were training in combat in their uniforms, and there were office workers too. They kept referring to the leader of the Wolves as Alpha."

"You saw Sarah?" Brandon's voice is quiet and deep. It pierces through the room. He kneels, leaning forward so his face is almost touching the glass.

His eyes practically plead with me to repeat the statement. "Yes. Sarah was there with about ten other kids. She was happy, but—" I hesitate to tell him the rest.

"Just say it," Brandon says.

"She's fine," I preface. "But... they are experimenting on these kids. They were drawing blood and infusing fluids into them. Dr. Locke was the one drawing their blood."

Brandon's entire body flexes as he stands like the Hulk is about to rip through his skin. "I'm gonna kill—" he stops himself and glances at the cooler carrying the body of the man he *did* kill.

"It's okay, B," I say. "I feel the same way."

"What were they infusing?" he asks.

"I wasn't close enough to see."

"Our Dr. Locke?" In contrast to the anger-fueled Hulk, Edda seems sullen and betrayed. Her body sulks, and she leans with her hip against a lab table. I understand both sentiments and probably land somewhere in the middle.

"Yes. Our Dr. Locke. And the sooner we figure out how to get into the Astrodome, the sooner we can get Sarah back and expose Locke and the Wolves." I lift the IV kit and needle, offering it to Edda to help me.

"Show me how you get into the Astrodome," I say as soon as I land in Adam's Afterthought.

The command leads me to the streets of downtown Houston. I'm bouncing along the sidewalk toward the stadium. Bouncing, but not walking. Sitting. I'm sitting high above the crowd migrating to the Astrodome. Denim is everywhere—so much denim. Teenage girls in front of me wear high-waisted shorts and tie their Astros jerseys in knots above their midriffs. Boys next to them wear baggy jeans and high-top sneakers. The girls have their hair pulled into side ponytails with scrunchies.

"Daddy, we're almost there." The voice that comes out of me is as tiny as the body I'm occupying. Small hands pat the head in front of me. I'm sitting on someone's shoulders.

It takes me a moment to realize what's happening.

Scrunchies. High tops. Denim. Is that tie-dye?

"Oh no, crimped hair," I say in the young boy's body. "Not from your childhood, Adam. Go to a memory of getting into the Astrodome as Wolf headquarters."

In the next moment, I'm walking on a bridge over a highway. Adam quickly checks the time on his watch. His eyes are alert, aware of his surroundings. He scans the faces of the people around him. The parking lot of the Astrodome is full. Since the stadium is in the middle of Houston, the parking lot is used for people working downtown. It's always full, so no one would question why someone would park here. It makes me wonder how many of these vehicles are the Wolves'.

Adam counts the rows of cars as he passes them. He takes a left down the eighth row from the back and walks to a man leaning against a blue Ford Focus. His military uniform matches Adam's.

"*Socius*," he says, tilting his head up to him as he continues forward.

"*Tecum sum*," the man says. He straightens and joins Adam. "You're late. My arrival time says 0714."

"It's only 0700," Adam says.

"You should be earlier in case we run into any problems."

Annoyed, Adam glares at him. "You new?"

"Finished training a week ago."

"Ah," Adam says. "You're still in the paranoid stage. Don't worry, I've done this a thousand times. Problems are rare. No one questions military personnel, so we don't get followed. Plus, the Astrodome is the last place anyone will suspect. But if there are problems, we have plenty of things in place to take care of them. What Wolf division are you in?"

"Firearms," the man answers.

"Were you a marksman in the army?" Adam asks.

He confirms with a hum. "Sniper. You?"

"Navy SEAL."

They meet two other Wolves on their way through the parking lot, then stand about 50 feet from the Dome, chatting like a clique of co-workers. But as they make small talk, none of the supposed-friends make eye-contact. Each of them takes turns speaking, and the others peer past the person talking to subtly assess their surroundings.

Adam's watch beeps. It reads 07:13.

"Let's go," he says to the others. They move toward a door in the back of the Dome but continue to watch for any passersby. Adam reaches the door, his colleague's backs are to him, keeping watch as Adam approaches a keypad. He pauses and checks his watch. As soon as the numbers flip to 0714, he punches the numbers 7-8-2-4-6. The door unlocks, and he opens it using one hand and holds his other hand up in surrender. When he steps into the Astrodome, four guns are pointed at them by Wolves in their gray and black uniforms.

"*Socius*," Adam says, and the word is repeated by those who walk in behind him.

"Morning, sir," one Wolf says to Adam.

"Morning." Adam points to one of the guards who is holding a tablet. "You have to use your fingerprint," he explains to the new Wolf. "It takes a while to process, sometimes fifteen to twenty minutes, but it's the most reliable way to identify everyone that comes in."

"You don't have to do it?" the new Wolf asks.

Adam lets out an airy laugh. "These guys know me," he says, slapping one of the guards on the back. "I've been here every day since the Wolves were first established. Our code words and the fact that we know how to get into the building are our primary security measures. The fingerprinting is an added measure since we often have new recruits we don't recognize. The system is still being tested, but the more our organization grows, the more necessary it will become. We need to get the right algorithms to make the process quicker." Adam shakes the new Wolf's hand firmly. "Good luck today," he says before turning away.

I hear more conversation take place after Adam walks off, but it's muffled. My vision blurs as Adam walks through the hallway. I think I'm waking up, but something is off. Bile rises to my throat. I open my eyes. The room is spinning. I lean over and spill the contents of my stomach onto the floor. I'm surprised I had anything to throw up. I can't remember the last time I ate.

"She's pale and diaphoretic," someone says.

"I'm fine," I try to say, but nothing comes out. I lay on my back again. Blood to my head—that's what I need. I close my eyes.

"Get some fluids from the pharmacy."

Someone wraps a cuff around my arm. It inflates.

"Grab phenylephrine just in case."

"The half-life of Propofol is short. It should be transient!"

Can everyone stop yelling?

"Sixty-eight over forty-two."

Not good. I open my eyes. The lab is still spinning —another wave of nausea. I'm going to hurl again. Eyes closed. It's better when my eyes are closed.

"Start the fluids."

I take a deep breath as fluids run through my vein, chilling my left arm through the IV Edda pushed Propofol through just minutes ago. I open my eyes again and see everyone around me. The room stops spinning, and Edda stands over me, squeezing a bag of fluids, so it infuses quickly.

"I'm okay," I croak.

Everyone lets out a singular sigh. Cole plops into a chair with his face in his hands. "Shit, Resi. You scared us."

The paramedics in isolation stand at the glass. Brandon squats down, holding his head. "You're not doing this anymore, Rez. It's not safe."

I prop myself up, honestly feeling back to normal. Charlie retakes my blood pressure. "One twelve over seventy-four," she says.

"Which is *higher* than my baseline blood pressure," I say. "I'm fine, you guys. I was probably dehydrated before I went under. I'll make sure to drink more fluids next time."

"No. There is no next time. This isn't happening again," Edda says. "Not with Propofol.

I consider the worried faces of my friends, and I know I won't win this one. "Okay," I say. I want it to be genuine, but I'm lying. "Why don't we take a break? I'll explain the Afterthought to you guys in a few minutes after everyone calms down. I think I got the information we need."

"According to the last Afterthought," I explain, "there is a code to get in: 7-8-2-4-6. Adam, our Wolf, entered it into a keypad on a back door of the Astrodome. Adam parked far away, met three other people on the way to the building, then they waited until exactly 7:14 AM to use the code and go in. 7:14 was their designated arrival time. When they got in, there were guards at the door with their guns pointed. He used the code word *socius*, and they let him in. Now, we obviously don't have designated arrival times, but I think the digital and verbal codes would help overlook that."

I sit on the lab table closest to the isolation room. Charlie stands at the tripod holding a large poster board, writing the information in bullet points.

"We will have to give fingerprints. The system they use takes twenty minutes to run the prints, so we have time to get in and out, but we will have to work quickly. Once we're in," I continue, "we can't stray from what we know about the Wolves. Let's start making a list."

"It sounds like they're trained in specific areas," Brandon says. "Shooting, the Triangle Blade, targeting their victims, taking care of the children, administration."

"They use their uniforms for protection against physical *and* biological forces," Coen says. "Per Resi's dream about an attack against the sick prisoner, the masks seem to act as a barrier against disease in addition to the impenetrable clothing."

"Impenetrable except for the Triangle Blade," Kyle says. He surprises me. It's the first time I've heard him speak since they showed up at the hospital. I'm not sure his mouth even moved. Words just escaped from behind his mustache. It seems that my friends did a thorough job of catching the two new team members up.

"They are working toward 'The Cause'." Cole uses his fingers for air-quotes. "And their leader is called Alpha."

"The targets are separated into the categories Hidden, Stained, and Beyond," Edda says. "Whatever the hell that means."

Charlie stops writing, turns to face Edda, her marker frozen in her hand. Her eyes narrow. "What did you say?"

"Hidden, Stained, and Beyond," Edda repeats. "From one of the Afterthoughts Resi saw. Those were the categories under the Target on the Wolf Web. Right?"

"I didn't hear about this one," Charlie says.

"Oh, I'm sure you did," Coen says. "It was the memory in which the school teacher had a peculiar interest in forearms."

"Yeah, he was talking to that country girl, then to his principal," Brandon says.

"You guys did not tell me about this," Charlie says, her speech growing angry and pressured.

"Okay, well, we're telling you now," I say. "What's the problem, Charlie?"

She sets her marker down and walks over to a lab table where she experimented with the Wolf's uniform earlier. "I don't know," she says. "It sounds familiar."

"Yeah, because we told you about it."

"You did not tell me about it!" Her hand slaps the table. The sound echoes through the lab. The sudden outburst catches everyone by surprise. The room quiets.

"Sorry." Charlie shakes her head. She avoids eye contact as she moves further away. "You guys keep brainstorming. I need to do some research."

I turn back to the team after Charlie retreats through the pharmacy. "We're all tired. She'll cool off,"

I say. "Let's keep working. I think it would be best if Edda, Cole, and I go into the Astrodome together."

"With what plan? What are you going to do if Locke sees you?" Brandon asks.

"I already checked the schedule," Cole says. "He's working at the hospital tomorrow."

"Okay, so you know how to get in," Brandon says, "but what's next? They'll fingerprint you."

"But the prints don't go through right away. There's a fifteen to twenty-minute delay. That gives us time to find Sarah and figure out a way to escape."

"They know your face, Resi," he says. "What if they recognize you?"

"The plan is underdeveloped, yes, but it's what we have. I don't want to wait around and let them pump these kids full of god-knows-what."

Brandon's knuckles decorate his fists in white.

I sigh, hop off the table, and walk to the glass across from him. "You're anxious because you want to go with us," I say, "but you need to trust me right now. You know I won't let anything happen to Sarah. And yes, they might recognize me but they can't hurt me, remember?"

"We don't know how long that will last," Brandon says.

"Well, I'm going to ride it out as long as possible. Plus, I'll be wearing business clothes and I'll do my hair all professionally. Surely no one will recognize me out of my scrubs."

He shakes his head. "It's not enough. The plan is too underdeveloped, and it's dangerous. You have no idea where Sarah will be, and even if you find her, you don't know how to get out."

"Cole said Dr. Locke will be at work tomorrow," Edda says. She looks at her watch. Which is actually today. It's almost 5:00 AM."

"You want to spy on him or something?" Cole asks.

"Resi and I are supposed to go in for a staff meeting in a couple hours. It might be a good opportunity."

"Yeah, a meeting for nursing staff," I remind her. "Not doctors. Locke won't be there."

"Not at the meeting, but he *will* be at work," she says. "One of us can distract him on the unit, and the other can check his office and computer to see if there's something on it about where we can find Sarah and how to get out."

"Tyler Meeks accessed the Wolf Web through the Dark Web," I say. "I bet Locke has something similar."

"You think Locke's computer won't be password protected?" Brandon asks.

Damn it. Passwords. I pace the wall, smoothing my thumb and middle finger over my eyebrows while I think. We need to hack into his computer, somehow. I doubt computer hacking is one of Charlie's specialties, but she's smart enough to figure it out. Surely, she'll be happy to add to her list of skills.

An image of a flash drive crosses my mind. *"Not many people know I have this skill."*

Kyle.

Kyle hacked *something* to get access to those surveillance cameras I've been stalking every night since the bombing.

When I turn to him, he's already looking back at me, as if he is expecting me to come to this conclusion.

But his warning all those months ago makes me pause. He was such a good friend to me, and I don't want to reveal his secret if he doesn't want it revealed. I lock my eyes onto his and raise my eyebrows. Brandon follows my eyes to figure out what I'm looking at.

At my silent request, Kyle nods. "Get me a computer and USB flash drive."

All eyes veer toward the talking mustache.

"What?" Brandon asks.

"I can create a password decoder," he says, casually. When he's met with silence and odd looks, he continues. "Hacking is a hobby."

"And you knew this?" Brandon asks me.

I'll let Kyle explain how he aided in my insanity. For now, I take off toward the office to find a flash drive.

CHAPTER 24

Edda and I leave the conference room after the meeting, in which I paid zero attention. We say goodbye to some coworkers and make excuses about why we're not leaving yet—something about needing to speak to the managers.

When they walk away, Edda leans in close to me. "You head to Locke's office. I'll go find him on the unit and make sure he stays away while you're in there."

"Okay, text me if anything changes." The offices are at least a minute's walk from the ER. I would be crunched, but technically will have enough time to get out if she warns me.

I enter the administrative area. There are a few cubicles, but mostly a bunch of rooms. It's empty right now except for a secretary at a desk to my left.

She looks at me for about three seconds before returning her attention to her computer. "Can I help you?"

"I'm looking for Dr. Locke."

"He's working on the unit today." She clicks the mouse.

"I'll wait for him in his office," I say, walking past her.

"His shift isn't over until—"

"No problem," I interrupt, making my way to his door. "I don't mind waiting."

Murky lights barely brighten the room when I flip the switch in Locke's office. I leave the door cracked open so I can hear what's happening outside. One last glance shows me the secretary is browsing shoes on Amazon. Perfect.

I've been in this office once before because my dad was visiting Locke, but I didn't take it in. It is cozier than I expected, but a little chilly. There's a desk and swivel chair, of course, but on the other side of the desk he has two living-room-style, wingback chairs with thick cushions and blue fabric, a purple throw blanket draped over one of them.

Locke's laptop is open on his desk. I swipe my finger on the touchpad. The screen wakes up to show a picture of Locke and his family: his wife, Caroline; two kids, George and Grace; and his Great Dane, Leonardo (named after DaVinci, not DiCaprio). I ponder how many lies he's told Caroline and his kids about where he goes while working as a Wolf. I wave my middle finger toward him in the photo then point it down to click the screen.

His name pops up, FRANCIS LOCKE, along with a box below it for his password. I reach into my pocket for the USB. It slides into the USB port, and a red WARNING box appears:

THIS COMPUTER IS PASSWORD PROTECTED.
ANY INTRUSION ATTEMPTS WILL BE REPORTED TO THE OWNER.

The warning startles me even though Kyle told me this would happen. It's to scare people out of hacking. There's another spot within the WARNING box for a password, one that Kyle shared with me before I left. I type: YODA+B@LLET&TE@for2

Kyle is weird. And ever-growing on me.

I press *Enter.* The warning disappears, and the

computer unlocks, everything on the desktop available to me.

Tyler Meeks had a secure browser on the Dark Web that he used to access the Wolf Web. I remember it from his Afterthought. I search the desktop for the same icon. It was a gray and green globe titled *Tor Browser.*

I can't seem to find it on his computer, though. I see the icon for our hospital software, Google Chrome, Firefox, Word documents, an icon that looks like a scanner, another that looks like a husky, Solitaire, PowerPoint.

Wait. I backtrack to the husky.

It's a Wolf.

Click.

A software system pops up. WOLF SYSTEM 9000 sprawls across the screen in blue. Under it, the system asks for a password. Again.

Kyle's USB was only good for unlocking the computer, as far as I know. He didn't say anything about hacking passwords once I was in.

I bite my lip, scan the office for clues. What password would Locke use? The name of one of his kids? His wedding anniversary? First address? I rummage through the top drawer of the desk. Pens, highlighters, Post It notes. Nothing helpful. His top side-drawer holds a bunch of files.

A creaking sound.

I whip my head toward the door. It's exactly how I left it, slightly cracked open. No one is there, no voices outside the door.

After a breath, I turn back around, hear the creaking again as the chair swivels. I relax and roll my eyes at myself. It was just me twisting the chair.

I open the bottom drawer of the desk, a junk drawer from the looks of it. Right on the top of the pile of junk is a spiral notebook that says *PASSWORD KEEPER.*

No way.

I flip the notebook open. Passwords abound. AT&T. Bank. Facebook. Gmail. iPhone. It's all there, and in alphabetical order—the very last item on the list: Wolf System.

God bless old people and their technological incompetence.

Username: FTLOCKE

Password: LEONARDO*7625

Leonardo. Locke's beloved Great Dane. I should have known.

Enter.

The software opens to a home screen. I don't know if I'm excited, happy, nervous, or utterly overwhelmed, but my hands are shaking. There are so many tabs that I don't know where to begin.

TARGETS
SURVEILLANCE
HEADQUARTERS
EMPLOYEES
SCHOOL
THOUGHT REFORM
ARTILLERY

My phone buzzes in my pocket before I can finish reading all the options. I take it out, look at the screen.

Point Blank Safety.

Archie.

It's not the best moment to talk. I don't know how much time I have on Locke's computer before the secretary gets suspicious, and I have everything I need now that I have access to this system. But my gut is telling me to answer. I peek outside. The secretary is still on Amazon, but she has moved onto watches. I close the door, twisting the knob so the latch doesn't make a sound.

"Hello?" I answer, my voice hushed.

"Hey, um... I'm looking for Martha. This is Archie from Point Blank Safety."

"Hi, Archie. I'm glad you called back." I sit back down at Locke's desk and continue looking over the Wolf System. I read more tabs.

DEFECTS
NEWS
ADMINISTRATION

"Look, um, sorry I kind of hung up on you yesterday. I just..." Archie pauses. "This isn't easy for me."

"That's okay. I understand." The computer chimes, and a bubble pops up: FRANCIS, YOU HAVE ONE NEW NOTIFICATION.

"Yeah," Archie says, "that's why I... I don't know. Your voicemail sounded like maybe you..." He doesn't finish the sentence, but I can hear it in his voice.

"I've lost people, too." I spin the chair away from the computer, giving Archie my full attention. "The Wolves. They've taken people from me." I tap my finger on the arm of the chair. I wonder if I should read Locke's notification.

"Martha?"

"Yeah?"

"What's your real name?"

My lips bend into a smirk. "That obvious?"

Archie huffs. "Well, you don't sound like you're over fifty."

I'm hesitant, but I think I need to be honest with

him. "My name is Resi."

"Resi," he repeats.

"Yes."

"Okay. Resi, you said in your voicemail that you need to know what happened."

I nod even though he can't see me. "I'd really appreciate it if you're willing to tell me."

"I've never told anyone before. It's..."

"It hurts."

"Yeah."

"I understand."

"Yeah."

He's quiet again. Delaying. He might not have it in him. I shake my head. I don't have time for this.

"That product you're looking for—it does exist." He hits me with this right as I'm about to give up. "We... my dad and me... we sold them. Hundreds of them. Made a fortune." There's a pause, then he sighs into the speaker. "Next thing I know, Dad goes missing, and our product is all over the news... killing everyone."

"The Wolves," I say. This is what I assumed from the start, but I need him to confirm it.

"We created it hoping to sell it to the military or police force. The Wolf design was meant to be intimidating to whoever they were fighting."

"They look like Raccoons."

He laughs. "Well, anyway, we never meant for them to be used... like this. I'm really sorry."

"It isn't your fault." I spin back to the computer. He said his dad went missing. Just like Tyler Meeks and Bert. Both Wolves. I click on the EMPLOYEES tab.

My stomach flips as hundreds of names fill the screen. The cursor hovers over one name, lights it up in blue. It's a link. I move the mouse, each name turning blue as I hover the cursor over it.

"You said your dad went missing?" I ask Archie.

"Yeah. Right after we sold our product."

"What is his name?"

"Elliot Cleary."

I scroll down to the C's and click on CLEARY, ELLIOT. A page for Elliot pops up, his picture to the left, name centered at the top. Under his name is written UNIFORM MANUFACTURER.

He's one of them.

"Why do you need to know all of this, Resi?"

Archie told me yesterday that he doesn't make the product anymore. I wonder if that's true or if he was just eager to get me off the phone. "I'm trying to find the Wolves, find out who they are, take back someone I love." I don't have the heart to tell him his dad is a Wolf. He also has no reason to believe me.

"How are you going to find them?"

"I can't tell you too much, but I already have found them. Now I need to figure out how to get in."

The computer chimes again, the same message is displayed, reminding Dr. Locke that he has a new notification.

"How can I help?" Archie asks.

"Did you really stop making the uniforms after your dad went missing?"

There's shuffling in the background. "Yeah, I stopped making them." He makes a straining sound like he's stretching or lifting something heavy. "But I do have a few left."

"A few uniforms?"

"Yeah, uh..." I hear him whisper to himself.

"There's four here. Different sizes."

"I'll take them. All of them."

"Where should I meet you?"

A door bangs to a close outside Locke's office. "I know you have a lot of work to do, but it would be helpful if you could show me how that patient's chest tube dislodged."

It's Edda. *Shit.* "I have to go, Archie. I'll text you an address." I hang up and see that Edda texted me while I was on the phone. How did I miss that? I go to shut down Locke's computer, but the notification is still on the screen.

"Edda, I don't have time right now." Locke's voice. They're getting closer.

I click on the notification.

FRANCIS, YOUR HEADQUARTERS ARRIVAL TIME TODAY IS 16:22
SOUTH ENTRANCE
CODE 78246

I frantically find a pen in the top drawer and scribble the information on a Post It Note. I wince as the drawer closes too loudly.

"Is someone in my office?"

I hit *Delete* on the notification.

"Yes, some lady said she was waiting for you."

I stuff the Post It and USB into my pocket, then pinch my cheeks while running around the desk. I sit in one of the cozy chairs with my legs pulled up and sink my teeth into my tongue until my eyes water.

The door opens.

"Resi?"

I look up at him and freeze. Everything in me wants to hurt him, pull his teeth out one by one. But I recover quickly, wipe my hand over my cheek, and sniffle. "Hey, Dr. Locke," I say, forcing a quiver in my voice. "Sorry to bother you."

"What's wrong?" His eyes soften and he walks closer to me, kneels.

"I don't know." I buy myself time to come up with something on the spot. It has to be about my parents if I'm going to Locke about an issue. "I was just missing my mom and dad. Wanted to see someone who knew them."

I glance at Edda. Her face is veered away, hand over her mouth. Her eyes tell me she's trying not to laugh.

"Oh, I see," Locke says. He pulls the other chair close to mine and sits, leans forward with his elbows on his knees.

I swipe my fist across my nose and sniff. "It's silly. I'll get out of your hair."

He stops me as I try to stand. "Nonsense," he says with his hand on my shoulder. "It isn't silly. I miss your parents too."

His eyes drift behind me. He leans and reaches over me, then pushes himself back, pulling the purple throw blanket out from behind me.

"Do you know why this blanket is in here?"

I shake my head.

"June bought this several years ago because she hated how cold my office was. When she and your dad would visit me, they would stay for hours." He laughs as he gazes affectionately at the blanket. "You know how they were," he says. "Story-tellers. Especially Astor."

One side of my mouth twitches upward. A "short visit" with Dad was a running joke.

"Anyway," Locke continues, "she bought this blanket so she would have it when she visited. June was the only one who ever used it." He stretches his arm out, hands me the blanket. "Take it."

I glance at Edda again. She's not laughing anymore. Probably because my sadness isn't fake anymore. I shake my head again. "That's okay, Dr. Locke. It's yours. You keep it."

He places it on my lap. "Take it, Resi."

The material is soft against my hands. I grasp it, thinking about how Mom felt as she wrapped herself inside it. I bring it to my nose, inhale.

Musty and stale, not the scent of my mother's perfume as I was hoping. But why would it smell like her? She hasn't touched it in eleven months. Locke and the rest of the Wolves killed her.

Maybe I could strangle him with it.

I swallow, anger accompanying my saliva, and I look up at Locke. "Thank you," I force out. Then, I stand. "I should get going."

Locke pivots his body to watch me as I walk out, holds a hand up to wave. "Have a good day, girls."

Edda and I make it to the parking lot before we say anything.

"What did you find out?" Edda asks.

We reach my car and climb in. I pull my phone out of my pocket. "Archie called—the manufacturer of the Wolf uniforms. He has some left that we can use at the Astrodome." I type an address to Archie's number as I speak. "We'll meet him before we head back to the lab." I send the message, then pull the sticky note out of my pocket. "Locke's arrival time today is 16:22. I deleted his notification about it, so hopefully, he won't show up and we can use it." I check the time on my phone. It's only 11:00 AM. "We have time, but we should get going."

"But the Wolves will be expecting Locke, not us."

"We'll come up with something."

I drive into the mall parking lot. I park the car and read the text Archie sent a few minutes ago, *I'm in the red parking lot next to a big column with an F.*

We're in the yellow lot, passed red on the way up. I point to the stairs as we get out of the car. "He's down one level."

"Are you sure we can trust this guy?" Edda asks as we descend the steps.

"One-hundred-percent sure? No. But I have a good feeling about him. I think he wants to help." We step aside for a family of five to walk past us in the stairwell, then continue down until the stripe on the walls turns red.

I spot the F column and see a young, thin man in skinny jeans, Vans, and a baseball tee that says *Namaste Home With My Cat.*

It makes me chuckle. I really hope this is our guy.

"Archie?" I ask as we approach him.

He stands straighter. "Resi?"

"Hi." I shake his hand. "Thanks for meeting me. This is Edda. We're working on this together."

He nods. "Kind of a weird place to do this." He stuffs his hands into his pockets.

"I watched a YouTube video once about former CIA agents. They said it's best to do things in crowded places because it's less suspicious."

He raises his eyebrows and nods again. "I guess

that makes sense."

We stand awkwardly for a longer time than I care to waste. "So, we're hoping to use the uniforms to-night."

Archie bites his lip. "Yeah, um..." One hand leaves his pocket, and he rubs his forehead.

I don't want to push him too hard, cause him to trust me less than it appears he already does, but the more time we take on this interaction, the less time we have to prepare. I step in a little closer, but not close enough to make him uncomfortable. "I know this is strange for you," I say quietly. "The last time you let someone have your armor, they used it for the opposite of what you intended."

"Yeah," he says again. "And then my dad..." He twists the ring on his left thumb. His eyes watch the motion. "Sorry, I'm a little nervous."

I nod. "The Wolves took my dad from me too."

That catches his attention, and he looks up from his hands.

"Well, sort of," I say. "He's been in a coma for eleven months. They killed my mom. And now they've taken an eight-year-old girl that means the world to Edda and me."

His arms drop down to his sides, then he pushes his hands back into his pockets. "I'm sorry."

"I'm not going to use these uniforms to kill people, Archie. I promise. I just need them to get to the Wolves."

This time, when his hand leaves his pocket, he's holding a set of keys. He unlocks the trunk of his car, opens it. He lifts the flap of a cardboard box, looks around while he shows us a package full of black and gray, then puts it in my arms. "Good luck, Resi. I wish you the best."

CHAPTER 25

I feel tiny as I stare up at the Astrodome, the exterior dirty and old, but sparking nostalgia nonetheless. The entrances aren't labeled, so we're hoping the "south entrance" is literally the entrance on the south side of the building where we are now. I tug on the collar of my green button-up shirt.

All of the reasons we shouldn't do this flood my lungs, making me feel like I'm suffocating.

Breathe—four seconds in, four seconds out. I tug on my collar again.

"Stop doing that, it makes you look nervous," Cole says. He and Edda are also dressed in business clothes.

"Sorry. Wearing scrubs every day is like 20% of why I became a nurse." I check my watch. 4:21 PM. "Shoot. It's already time. Are you two ready?"

"Ready," Cole says as he pops his neck.

Edda closes her eyes and blows out a breath through pursed lips. "Ready."

"Remember to put your hands up and say the code word when we walk in," I whisper. I wait until my watch turns to 4:22, then I punch the code into the keypad: 7-8-2-4-6. The door unlocks with a click.

I twist the handle and open the door, lifting my hands in the air when I step in to see four guns pointing at us by four large Wolves in full uniform. A thousand pounds of anxiety and adrenaline weigh me down as soon as I cross the threshold like the Astrodome's gravity is ten times heavier than the rest of the earth's atmosphere.

"*Socius,*" we say in unison.

I search for the Wolf with the tablet and act like I'm accustomed to the entry process of giving a fingerprint.

"Good morning, ma'am," one Wolf says. I recognize the voice as the Wolf who let Adam in without getting his fingerprint first. Tiny needles stab their way up my stomach and into my throat. He gestures for me to walk forward. I haven't given my fingerprint yet. He must think he recognizes me because I work here. I step forward and let the Wolf believe whatever it is he believes about me, hoping the trembling of my body isn't as noticeable as it feels.

"This is Francis Locke's scheduled entry time," a guard says.

"Yes, I was just consulting with him," I jump in to explain before someone else can. "We have important business with Alpha today. It couldn't wait. He told us to use his time."

"It's about The Cause," Cole adds.

"Scan them in," The Wolf says to another guard.

He holds the tablet in front of Edda, and I pray they don't see how shaky she is as she presses her finger to the screen. Cole follows her lead, then they're free to join me.

It takes a while to process, sometimes fifteen to twenty minutes, I remember Adam saying. We have to work fast.

"Let's change before someone else recognizes

you," Edda mumbles. "Something tells me the next person will know who you are."

We find a bathroom around the corner. I enter a stall and take off my business clothes. A Wolf uniform from Archie is underneath. Edda, Cole, and I took whichever fit us best, but none are perfect. They're meant to be fitted, but the pants are a little big, bunching up at the bottom of my legs. I fold my business clothes and place them in the trashcan of the stall, then retrieve my mask from the pack on the belt. I pull it over my head, then step out of the stall.

I swing the door open. A Wolf stands in front of me.

"I kind of feel like a Power Ranger in this thing," the Wolf says.

I exhale. It's Edda.

We exit the bathroom, and I recognize Cole's tall, thin frame in his uniform. He waves quickly to let us know it's him.

"Trainees up in the nosebleed section," a woman says as she passes us. When we don't move, she turns to face us more directly. "Hey," she says. She waves her finger between the three of us. "Trainees in nosebleed."

I jump. She's talking to us.

"Right. Of course," I say.

"Yeah, we were headed that way," Cole says.

We scramble and find the stairs where SECTION 6 is painted in blue on the concrete wall and start climbing to the highest section.

"So, the people in Wolf uniforms are trainees?" I ask.

"Probably so they can get used to wearing this," Cole says. "It's not the most comfortable thing in the world."

He's right. It's a thicker, stiffer material than the Wolves let on.

A large pack of uniformed Wolves runs past us on our way up the stairs. "What are you guys walking for? Come on with us before you get in trouble," one says.

After sharing an agreeing glance, we file into the pack of trainees. I keep my eyes on Edda and Cole the whole time, afraid that I will lose them in the sea of identical black and grey uniforms. I lose count of how many flights of stairs we climb, but my legs start burning by the third.

"I can barely breathe," I pant. "My workouts have not prepared me for this."

"Right?" Edda says. "This is what I get for avoiding the Stairmaster."

"I think we're almost there," Cole says, and even he is winded by the tenth flight. "There can't possibly be more than three more flights. The entire Dome is only eighteen stories."

Edda and I glance at him.

"I got a trivia lesson from Coen before we left," he says.

We finally reached the top, and as soon as the group scatters, Edda, Cole, and I double over with our hands on our knees.

"I can't feel my legs," Edda says, wheezing as she speaks.

I stand up straight. "Come on. We have to act like we know what we're doing."

We walk through the hallway until we enter into the seating area of the nosebleed section, which faces the open expanse where the field used to be. Edda and

RENE FENNER

Cole stop in their tracks, their eyes are as wide as they can stretch.

"I'm ten years old again," Cole says.

"It's exactly the same," Edda gawks. "Minus the baseball field."

I take a step closer to them and speak quietly. "Hey, guys? I totally understand the sentiment, but I need y'all to act like it hasn't been twenty years since you've been here."

"Right," Cole says, snapping out of it.

Edda leans in. "Okay, sorry. What's the plan?"

"We need to find the offices," I say. "That's where Sarah should be."

"Offices?" Edda asks.

"I think so," I say. "I don't know. Rooms with doors? She was in a room doing schoolwork or something with other kids."

"But everyone in uniform is up here," Edda says. "People will know if we're separated from the group."

"Maybe they're only starting out up here," Cole says. "Let's play along until they split up."

A girl in a Wolf uniform runs up and grabs my arm. "Come on," she says. "Go to your sections. We're about to start, and Alpha is supposed to make an appearance today. Don't want to make a bad impression."

We follow the girl to a group of about fifty Wolves in their black and gray uniforms. Other trainees gather in sections nearby. Two women in military garb and one man in business clothes stand in front. The man is the one speaking. He's on the lowest step of the nosebleed section, next to the rail. The trainees face him, standing on the stairs or in front of what's left of the stadium seats. Edda, Cole, and I stand in the back and try to blend in.

I kick Cole's shin and gesture with my head for him to take note of the group's stance. They each stand with their hands behind their backs and feet shoulder-width apart. He changes his position to match theirs.

"You have all finished Thought Reform and have excelled in your weaponry skills," the man says. "Today, we will sharpen those skills with the Alpha Rifle. Our very own Alpha created this weapon. It is unique and requires specific techniques in its use. The bullet is made from a material that is undeniably metal, but bounces. The first bounce of the bullet is significant and causes the most damage when used correctly. It is a powerful gun and requires a skilled user. You've been working on angles this week. Let's see how much you've learned. And remember, Alpha will be in uniform among you today, so you never know who is watching you." The masked Wolves turn their heads to each other as murmurs spread through the group.

"I'll go first," a man says in the front. The military woman pulls out a case that was hidden behind a row of chairs and hands the volunteer a signature Wolf rifle. Focusing on the ground floor from the nosebleed section makes me woozy. I hadn't considered my fear of heights on the way up here.

Different colored targets are placed on the concrete at the bottom of the stadium.

"Green target," the leader of the trainees says.

The shooter eyes the massive room. He aims for the other side of the stadium with the gun pointed high, nowhere close to the target. A *clang!* resounds when he pulls the trigger and the bullet fires at a metal pole on the far side of the stadium. It bounces to a rail on the second level on the opposite side, and much weaker once more onto the green target on the ground. Three people on the ground run to the target and give an 'okay' sign. The group applauds.

"Well done," the military man says. "Who's next?"

I take a subtle step back. Since everyone else is in front of us and focused on the shooter, I see a perfect opportunity to split from the group. Edda and Cole, who are on either side of me, glance at each other before stepping back to meet me.

"Everyone's distracted," I whisper, taking another step back. "We should go find Sarah now."

"But everyone will tell us to go back to the trainee group," Edda whispers as she and Cole follow.

"Maybe we should put our business clothes back on," I say.

"Someone will recognize you," Edda protests.

Just then, a siren blares.

"We have experienced a security breach," a voice announces through a booming sound system. Mutters and whispers scatter throughout the Dome, and more people appear in the seating areas to see what's happening. "Please identify everyone around you as a verified Wolf. The intruders are displayed on the screen."

"We've never had a security breach," a woman near us says.

The screen in the middle of the stadium lights up. The word INTRUDERS is written in large yellow letters. Below it are pictures of Cole and Edda.

CHAPTER 26

The Dome erupts into a frenzy as everyone scrambles around for the trespassers. The masked Wolves lean over to one another to make sure the people next to them are who they say they are. They take their masks off to be identified.

"Your fingerprints," I say. "They went through."

"What do we do?" Cole asks. "Should we bolt?"

"No," Edda says. "Play it cool. Act like one of them. Bolting would give us away completely."

"You three," a woman says, pointing at us. "Why were you stepping away from the group? Take your masks off and identify yourselves."

"Bolt!" Edda yells.

I didn't know I could run this fast. I hasten through the halls of the Astrodome. My eyesight sharpens, my lungs take in more oxygen, I evade the people I pass. One man grabs my shoulder, but adrenaline propels me past him.

We dodge Wolves and knock things over and snap around corners and run until there are fewer and fewer people behind us.

"We'll never get out. The exits will all be blocked!" Cole yells.

But I'm not concerned about the exits yet. I recognize a concession stand from Adam's Afterthought. The sign above it says MR. RICKLE'S NACHOS AND CHILI.

"This way," I say as I turn into an opening right next to the concession and run up the stairs.

"*More* stairs?" Edda asks. "I thought we were already in the nosebleed section."

We sprint left down a hallway at the top of the stairs and find an empty room with a huge orange lever on the wall outside of it. We duck behind the opened door. The room is blindingly white and completely empty.

"There are hundreds of us and two of them," someone says. "How did they get away?"

"Three. There were three that ran away, and they're in our uniforms, sir. They blend in," another person says.

"That doesn't change my point. Go. Find them. They haven't gone far."

The voices fade into the distance until all we can hear is the alarm blaring.

"I'm not sure how we got away either," Cole says.

I take my mask off and wipe the sweat from my forehead. "We're not out of the woods yet." I push the heavy door.

"Wait." Edda grabs my arm and stops me. "No door handle on this side." She points. "Don't close it all the way." She's right. We'd have no way to get out if we shut the door. Edda and Cole take their masks off. "What the hell is this room?"

"The ceiling," Cole says, pointing upwards, "The whole thing is lighting or heat lamps or something. Do they do performances in here?"

"Yeah, I'm sure the Wolves love to do song and dance numbers in their spare time," Edda quips.

I peek out of the room and down the hall and see

the abstract paintings from Adam's memory. "This is it," I say. "This is the hallway where I saw Sarah."

"Resi, there's no way we're going to sneak Sarah out of here now," Edda says. "Everyone out there is hunting us."

"Yeah, but we blend in," I say. "There are at least one hundred people out there in these exact uniforms. We still have a chance. We need to act like we're not on the run."

"And how do you propose we get out of here after we find her?"

"The locker rooms," Cole says. "When I was a kid, I got to meet the baseball players there after a game," he explains. "One of the doors in the room leads outside. I bet it's not guarded."

"I bet it is," Edda argues. "They probably use every room in this place."

"It's worth a shot," I say. "Do you remember where it is?"

Cole slips his mask back over his head. "If we can get to the seats above the dugout, I can find it from there."

"We should find the locker rooms first to make *sure* there's an exit," Edda says. "It's too dangerous to find Sarah first and just wing it."

I open the door wider and peek out. The coast is clear. "We don't have that kind of time, Ed. Put your masks on and follow me," I say. "Keep your eyes peeled. We won't hear people coming with this obnoxious alarm."

"Resi!" Edda protests. "This is stupid. We need to get out and devise a way to find Sarah later." But I'm slipping out of the room as she says it, not wanting to

waste time arguing. We've already been made. There's
no way we'll be able to get back into the Astrodome
after this once we leave. It's our only chance.

"Are you listening to me?" Edda asks as she follows behind me. Her voice is more muffled now, so I assume her mask is back on. "Finding Sarah right now is
dangerous. We need to get home and try again."

I spin around and face her. I get that she's scared,
but leaving right now isn't an option. "There is no 'trying again,' Edda. This is it. We don't get another shot at
this."

Cole nods. "She's right. We have to do this now."

She doesn't respond, which tells me she doesn't
quite agree, but she also can't disagree.

We sneak down the hall and knocked on the first
door next to the weird white room. When there is no
answer, I opened it to find an empty conference room
with windows that overlook the parking lot.

"Across the hall," I say.

There's no answer when we knock on that door
either, so I open it. It's an office. A messy desk sits next
to a packed bookshelf, and red stadium seats are scattered around the room. It overlooks what used to be
the field, but it's high up enough that no one outside the
window could see in. I move toward the desk, curious
about what paperwork needs to be done for a group of
terrorists, but as soon as I step in, a large machine with
a glass control board and at least twenty glass screens
to the right catches my attention. A beam next to the
control board has an oval-shaped pad on the top. I start
toward the machine, but Edda grabs my hand.

"No time," she says. "Let's go, Resi."

She's right, of course. I turn to walk out, but I

spot another long, wooden desk on the wall next to the door. Scattered papers litter the entire table. Some of the papers are long documents, but others are drawings of weapons or attack strategies. One stack of clipped papers stands out to me.

"Resi, come on," Edda urges.

I don't budge. The weakness in my legs returns, and my face heats. Anger radiates from my fingers to the papers as I lift the stack from the desk.

"Resi?" Edda asks, her tone growing with concern. "What is it?"

"They did raid my parents' house," I say. "Brandon was right. They raided it and blew it up to get rid of the evidence. That must be how they got my mom's research on the Damascus Sword." I spin the stack toward Edda so she can see it. "And they took souvenirs." She and Cole step in closer to see that the papers are held together by my father's engraved money clip: ASTRO KEPLER, PhD, MD.

Edda's eyes widen, then resolve. She takes the stack from my hand and sets it on the desk. Then she grabs me by the shoulders.

"Hey," she says, pleading for my attention. I come out of my blank stare and meet Edda's eyes. "I need you to find that unnatural Resi-state-of-mind that compartmentalizes and bottles everything up, so we can do what we came here to do. Find Sarah."

"Find Sarah," I repeat, knowing that Edda only agrees to find her to placate me. But she's right. I have to think about Sarah right now. "Let's go." I push my burning thoughts to the side, suck them down into the hidden vortex that is so familiar with my suppressed emotions.

A vortex that is starting to feel pretty full these days.

We travel back into the hall where the abstract paintings hang and sneak to the next room. I knock. This time, there's an answer. It's Judy, the flustered woman with red-rimmed glasses and straggly hair in Adam's Afterthought.

"Judy!" I'm so excited to recognize someone that I hug her reflexively.

She shoves me away. "Who the hell are you?"

I search the room behind her. The desks are all there, but the children aren't. "Where are the kids?"

"They're in the presidential suite," Judy says like it's common knowledge. "They're never here at this hour. This alarm is driving me crazy."

"But you're their teacher, right?" I ask.

"Of course, I'm their—"

"You three," a man yells. A large group of people charges toward us. "Remove your masks and identify yourselves."

"Run!" Cole yells.

We take off in the opposite direction and run back down the stairs. We turn into the hallway with the concessions, but as soon as we enter that hall, a group of trainees blocks us off, some with their new Alpha Guns pointing at us.

"We're blocked in," Edda says.

"Go right," I say.

We run into the seating area, getting two steps down before realizing that more Wolves have gathered to capture them. We turn back, but the Wolves that were chasing us originally close us in. We're trapped, circled in by dozens of Wolves.

"Would one of our trainees like to do the honors?" someone asks, but I can't find the source of the voice. "Might be good practice."

An unmasked redheaded woman in a Wolf uniform walks up to me.

"Take your mask off," she demands.

I step forward. "What are you going to do if I don't?"

While I'm blunt and ornery regularly, never in my life did I dream of challenging someone who most likely wanted to kill me. But being in a room with all the people who have caused my friends and me so much pain doesn't scare me anymore, it pisses me off. These Wolves kidnapped an innocent girl with a heart of gold, they killed my parents, and took the time to raid their house for their own office décor. It makes me indignant. My entire body is fueled with rage. So, when the redhead demands that I remove my mask again, I take a swing.

As soon as my fist meets the woman's cheek, the entire crowd swarms us.

I lose Cole and Edda. I hear them yelling my name, but I can't see my friends. There are hits and kicks, but the material of the Wolf uniform absorbs most of the blows. I'm not hurt, or at least I don't think so, but I'm too overwhelmed by the number of people attacking me to fight back. The best defense I can think of is to hold on tightly to my mask. If they find out who I am and stop their assault, I'm afraid they'll kick me out, and I'll never see Sarah again. The crowd pushes me down a few steps until my side hits a pole, and I'm pressed into it.

"Everyone get back!" a man yells above the rabble. The room quiets, and most of the crowd steps back, but two Wolves continue to press me up against the rail, one with a Triangle Blade to my neck. Other Wolves drag Edda and Cole into view, both captured and de-masked. I'm the only one left unidentified.

"These are the two that were on the screen," a woman says of Edda and Cole. "Who is that?"

The man who yelled for everyone to get back grabs my mask at the top of my head and pulls, but I grip the edges so that my fingers are looped into it, making it harder to remove.

"Take it off!" he yells.

"Screw you!"

He grabs at the mask again, pulling my hair through the material, but I refuse to let go. He hits my face in anger, forcing my body to whip to the side, but the uniform protects me again. His hand is probably hurt more than my face. He spins me around and throws me stomach-first into the rail so he can get a better grip on the mask. I wince and squeeze my eyes shut when my ribs are shoved into the metal. I felt the pain that time, but it isn't until I open my eyes that I let out an involuntary scream. We are in the nosebleed section again, and I'm hanging halfway over the rail, which has no landing below it but the ground level, several stories down.

I force my shaking hands back to my mask, realizing that I grabbed the rail in fear. I close my eyes.

"She's afraid of heights," the man says mockingly. "Let's see how long you can hold onto that mask on the other side."

"No!" I hear Edda shout.

As the crowd jeers, the man's strong arms flip my

body over the rail with ease, and my hands fly from my mask to grab hold of anything I can grasp. I slip past the top pole of the rail, and my knee scrapes the concrete floor, pulling my weight down until I latch onto the lowest pole.

There's silence throughout the Dome.

"Vin, what are you doing? I thought you were just going to threaten her," a man asks. *Vin* doesn't answer.

"This is unnecessary," a woman says. "Pull her back up."

"She said to pull her back up!" Edda yells.

"We don't have permission to terminate," another man says. "We need to find out if she's out to destroy The Cause."

I try to control my rapid breathing as I dangle helplessly over the Astrodome. I attempt to swing my legs up to the balcony floor, but I'm not strong enough. My body is trembling so much that I won't have the strength to hold on for long. The gloves of the Wolf uniform have rubber grips that are helping for now, but as soon as my hands weaken, I will fall hundreds of feet to the concrete floor of the world's first domed stadium.

Vin kneels and glances back at the silent crowd. "And now for the reveal," he announces like this is all a performance to him.

My hands slip around the diameter of the pole, the heels of my palms abandoning my fingers to hold my weight by themselves.

Vin effortlessly slips my mask off.

His face drains of its color when he sees me. He whips his head back to the crowd in shock, then lunges forward to grab my hands through the rail.

"Hold on," he says. He moves to get a good grip

on my wrists, but his awkward angle from the opposite side of the rail makes things worse, and I slip. My hands land on the concrete in which the rail is planted. There is nothing left to hold onto after that. If I slip again, I'm dead.

Vin moves again to hold onto me even more awkwardly through the railing. I try to keep breathing rather than scream. I'm afraid that if anything too loud comes out of my chest, it will take away from the strength of my hands or propel me backward and cause me to fall away.

Four seconds in. Four seconds out.

Mutters and whispers scatter throughout the crowd. My name is repeated over and over as people peer over the edge one by one.

"Move!" a woman yells. The crowd above me parts.

A Wolf in uniform jumps over the pole and lands with her feet on the concrete next to my hands.

"Alpha, wait," Vin says. "Be careful."

She grabs onto the rail and squats down, holds her arm out to the man, who grasps it with both hands to hold her up. She grips my left arm, but she will only be able to pull me up if I let go of the concrete and hold her arm in return.

"Swing your arm and grab onto her," Vin says.

"I can't!" Water runs down my cheek.

"You don't have a choice," he says.

The bastard is right. I don't have a choice.

I take one chance. I grip the edge of the concrete with my right hand as much as I can. I don't give myself time to think. I boost my left hand and take an eighth of a second to grab the woman's arm.

"HELP!" I scream as my body drops. I'm not quick enough, but the woman catches my hand before I fall too far. Her grip is strong, but she struggles to pull me up as I dangle.

I'm going to die. My life doesn't flash before my eyes. I don't see a light. All I can think is *I'm going to die.*

"Don't just stand there," Vin says as he holds on to the woman. "Somebody help!"

A man jumps over the rail on the other side. I swing my free arm to him. As more Wolves gather in to help, my body is lifted until I can get my feet on the floor and climb back over. I land safely on the other side, but my legs are trembling.

The loud clap of the female Wolf's open hand hitting Vin's face echoes through the Dome. Then the Wolf pulls me close and hugs me. It's a desperate hug—intimate. The same hand that lifted me up from my impending death and left a red welt on Vin's cheek now softly cradles my head.

When I come to my senses, I shove her away.

"What the hell is going..."

My words trail off when I see the only thing the Wolf uniform exposes. Everything I thought I knew crashes into tiny shards of sharp, piercing glass when I stare into the Wolf's green eyes. I can practically smell them—spearmint.

I stumble back and suck in a breath. My stomach jumps up into my throat as air vacates my lungs. It isn't possible. But it's her.

"Mom?" I gasp.

The Wolf closes her eyes, then reluctantly removes her mask.

It's June Kepler.

CHAPTER 27

I examine my hands, making a fist and releasing it twice. They're mine. My head moves back and forth. This isn't a dream. I'm not in an Afterthought.

But my dead mother is standing in front of me.

"We are gathered here today to say farewell to June Kepler and to commit her into the hands of God." That's what the pastor said as my mother's photo stood on a table next to a bouquet of white lilies and a small urn. They didn't find enough of her body to have a large one, just enough to identify her DNA. *"She was a loving mother, loyal friend, and a pillar of the medical community."*

An office, I note as I survey the room and try to get back to reality. I'm in an office. I've been here before. The large control board below the glass computer screens I saw earlier stands to my right. The beam next to the board has blood on it. It's small, but obvious in contrast to the clean, glassy appearance of the rest of the contraption.

"Francis Locke called as the alarms were going off." My eyes are drawn back to the ghost leaning on the edge of the desk in front of me. "When they told me there was someone with Edda and Cole, I assumed it was Brandon. But Locke told me that his Wolf System had been accessed when you were in his office."

I recall walking away from his desk. I grabbed the

USB but forgot to log out of the system and turn off the computer. Obviously, he'd figure it out—rookie move. "I found you as fast as I could," Mom says. "The guard must have recognized you and let you in without fingerprinting because he thought you worked here. I'll take care of him."

My body feels like it's tilting slightly. I straighten my back, but it keeps tilting, arching to the left while everything else in the room moves to the right at the same, slow speed.

Vertigo? Oxygen. Am I breathing? I take a deep breath. And another.

"So, it was okay if they killed Edda and me," Cole says. "Just not Resi."

"Of course not," June says incredulously. "No one here is allowed to kill anyone without my consent. They had orders to capture, not kill."

"Oh, good. Thanks for clarifying," Edda says. "Very comforting."

"Vin has been reckless before," June says solemnly. "He claimed that it was an accident the first time, but this is unacceptable."

"Forgive us if we're not following," Edda says, "but there's a lot that needs to be explained here, June."

"June." Everyone turns when I speak. "You said June. You see my mom too."

Edda takes my hand, and I noticed that our gloves aren't on anymore. None of the Wolf uniform is on me. I'm in ripped jeans and a black V-neck t-shirt. When did I change? Whose clothes am I wearing?

Edda's voice is gentle. "You've been in shock. We're with your mom at the Astrodome. She's alive."

Mom draws closer to me with cautious steps. "I

279

know this is a lot to take in, Honey," she says. She kneels and places her hand on my knee, but I flinch and pull away, still wondering if this is all fake, if this woman is real.

"You're dead," I say. "I buried your ashes. They found remnants—"

"Of someone's corpse," she says. "A hand with my fingerprints expertly indented, and some DNA that I planted for them to find. It helps that I had a DNA expert working for me."

My heart skips, probably throwing a premature ventricular contraction. Maybe two. Three PVCs in a row is technically considered ventricular tachycardia. I don't think I'm there yet, but it wouldn't surprise me if I am by the end of the night. I hope my mom has some beta-blockers on hand.

Wait. A DNA expert?

"Charlie," I say. "She helped you do this?"

"She didn't know what she was helping me do," June says.

"Fake your death."

"Yes," Mom says. "She already had my DNA for some research, so I asked if she would take some more for my own side-project. I'm so sorry you had to find out this way."

This way? My face contorts into amusement, a smirk taking shape and morphing into a miserable laugh. "How would you have *liked* for me to find out that my mother wasn't dead?" I rediscover the strength in my legs and stand, crossing my arms as I wait for an answer and fight the urge to wince when my arm hits my ribs.

"I guess," Mom starts, then her voice wavers.

"You were never supposed to find out, Resi."

"I planned your funeral," I say. "Dozens of friends, doctors, and researchers came to mourn your death even though there was a terrorist threat in the city. There were too many people for the church to hold."

"I know," she says softly.

"I gave a eulogy. And a damn good one at that."

"It's true," says Cole. "People still talk about that eulogy."

"You have no idea how much I wish things were different, Resi," says Mom.

"But why fake your death? Why would you do this? What the hell is *wrong* with you?"

She holds her palms out in a *tone it down* motion. One of those palms was supposedly found after the bombing. Whose hand was it if not hers? "Maybe you should take some time to calm down before I explain."

"No. Explain now."

"Okay, okay," Mom resigns at my demand. She rubs her hands on her pants, then tucks her hair behind her ears. There's a contrast between a strong leader and my anxious, fidgety mother. She straightens, her body confident, but her eyes find the carpet as she talks. "There's a virus. It's called The Stain. I discovered it one year ago, but the first cases were contracted about two years ago. It is named after one of the stages of the disease progression; the victim gets a subtle rash that looks like—"

"A wine stain," I say, remembering the Afterthought of the principal, J.R., and the subtle discoloration of his arm.

"You've seen it?" Mom asks. "Most people don't

even notice it on themselves."

I meet eyes with my friends. Surely, they don't expect me to tell her about the Afterthoughts right now. "No," I say. "A wild guess."

Mom's eyes narrow. "I see," she says. She walks to the screens above the large control board and taps the screen furthest to the left on the top. She places her hand on the screen, and it scans her palm, then she types something on the board, and familiar words appear:

HIDDEN: 7-12 MONTHS
STAINED: 14 DAYS
BEYOND: 8 DAYS

Hidden, Stained, Beyond. I meet my friends' eyes again, knowingly.

"These are the stages of the disease," says Mom. "I'm going to let Grady explain."

She taps the screen again, and a video of a young man begins to play. His hair is dark and wavy, sporting a neatly trimmed beard. His dark-rimmed glasses have been a popular accessory for a few years, and he wears a plaid shirt underneath his gray sweater.

"My name is Grady Lowe," he says to the camera. "I've been infected with a virus called The Stain. I have chosen to record a series of videos with the help of my colleagues so that we can monitor the progression of the virus."

Grady rolls up his right sleeve and holds his forearm in view of the camera to show a small bump. "This is where the Stain Test was injected," he says. "It could be mistaken for a bug bite, but it's a reaction to the test that confirms I'm infected." He drops his arm and fixes his sleeve. "Right now, I feel incredible. The Stain is still in the latent stage, or what we call the Hidden stage, which will last anywhere between seven and twelve months. My vital signs are stable, and I'm training for a marathon with no difficulty. Those who don't know I'm infected may think I'm the healthiest man alive."

Mom taps a section of the screen, and the video moves faster. "I'm skipping ahead to nine months later." The video speeds through Grady's progress in the Hidden stage. I see footage of his marathon and vlog-like footage of the man speaking to the camera, probably giving updates. He is smiling in some but seems sad in others. Grady must have gone through every emotion possible, knowing he had a year or less to live: gratefulness for life, fear of death, anger, love, anxiety, adventure, grief, acceptance.

Grady appears in front of the camera again when the video continues to play. He's in a small room with a hospital bed and is attached to a cardiac monitor. "It's been nine months and twelve days since I was exposed to the virus, and today I've moved into the Stained stage," says Grady solemnly. He lifts his arms up to the camera. "The Stain appeared today at 3:37 PM." His arms have the markings I saw in the Afterthought with the principal, JR. If I met him on the street and he told me that someone spilled red wine on his arms, I'd believe him. "My rash is more prominent than I've seen in other people," he says. I agree. "But it is generally more noticeable on the first and last days of the Stained stage. From our prior research on this virus, I know that I have exactly two weeks before I go into the Beyond. Four-teen days. I am still feeling healthy, my vitals are still stable, and I am not contagious yet, but for the sake of our research I'll be staying here in isolation for the remainder of my time." he says. He bows his head and shifts in his seat. "The remainder of my life."

My mom skips ahead in the video again.

"Today is the fourteenth day since The Stain appeared," Grady says. He assesses his arms. "The rash subsided to a faint discoloration during the last two weeks, but it is back in full today, and I will go into the last stage, The Beyond. So far, everything we've suspected to be true about The Stain has been confirmed during this process, so the transition should happen at any mo —"

Grady stops suddenly to let out a breath that makes his chest sink in. His eyes blink slowly. I feel weak. I sit back down in my seat, and Edda gasps next to me as we watch the frightening footage of the pink hues in Grady's cheeks fading into gray in a matter of seconds. The time on the video reads 3:37 PM; fourteen days to the minute since The Stain appeared. The heart rate on the monitor rises as Grady lays himself down on the bed. He curls into the fetal position and clenches his fists.

"No. No. I can't do this," Grady repeats several times over. "I can't do this," he says weakly. "Alpha, please. I change my mind. Terminate me. Let me die. Please!" My eyes sting, listening to him beg for his life to end.

Mom stops the video. I notice that she's been facing away from the screen. She couldn't watch.

"The Beyond lasts for eight awful days." Her eyes are low. I can't tell if she's avoiding eye contact, or if she's just sad. "Many of the mechanisms are unknown, but as soon as the virus activates into the Beyond, it binds to and destroys hemoglobin on red blood cells, depleting oxygen availability. That's why the victim's skin color changes so rapidly. Soon, it attacks the liver and kidneys, which eventually fail. The victim will become altered due to lack of oxygen to the brain." Mom swipes down on the screen, and the video disappears. "Exactly eight days after this video, at 3:37 PM, Grady's heart stopped. He begged for us to end his life until he was too weak to speak." She presses her hand to a screen again, and it shuts down completely. She walks back to the desk. "The Beyond is not only excruciating but extremely contagious. Simply being in the same room without the proper protective gear will spread the virus. But when the victim dies, The Stain dies with them, and it is no longer contagious. Once Grady was gone, we could go in and retrieve his body without fear of contracting it."

"That's why a sheet was thrown over us in the hospital when the Wolves attacked the prisoner," Edda realizes.

"Yes," Mom says. "He was in The Beyond. Some of you were in the appropriate protective gear, but we needed to shield you from any blood that might have splattered, so we used a shield made from the same material as our uniforms. But once he was dead, past the Beyond, you were safe.

"During the Beyond, however," Mom continues, "the virus is a violent predator. It seeks out any and every victim it encounters and infects every unprotected human it meets. It is vicious and unstoppable. And there is no cure."

She leans in as if to tell us a crucial secret.

"If the virus is killed *before* it enters the Beyond, it cannot infect another person. However, if it does go into the Beyond, it will infect every victim it can latch onto. It is so contagious and deadly that without being controlled, this virus could wipe out civilization in five to ten years."

Mom sits back and lets her explanation settle.

Her laid back demeanor makes my stomach tighten. *"What?"* I make no attempt to conceal the disgust in my voice. "I asked you to explain why you faked your death and you gave me a biology lesson on a virus."

I squint my eyes a little as I scrutinize my mother. Her straight brown hair falls to her shoulders as it always has, but her face is different. Her content, strong, youthful glow is missing. The lines around her eyes and lips are more defined. Her uniform is loose like she has lost weight since she was fitted for it.

My head shakes at the notion that I don't know this woman at all. Not anymore. "Why would a virus cause you to fake…"

"Alpha is in uniform among you today, so you never know who is watching you," I remember the man saying as he taught the Rifle session.

"Alpha, wait!" Vin said when she hopped the rail to save me.

I recall the sketch of the Triangle Blade that Coen found along with research on the Damascus Sword, the sketch I yelled at Charlie over.

"Alpha," I start, speaking as I think. "The Damascus Sword. The carbon nanographene for bulletproof uniforms." I think about Grady's gray face. "Alice's disease."

"Resi?" Edda questions.

I hold up my hand to quiet her. "Hold on," I say, standing. I pace to the back of the stadium seats we've been sitting in. "I just found out that my dead mother is alive, and now I'm figuring out that she's also bat-shit crazy. I need a second to process this."

Mom shifts, tucking her hair behind her ears again. "Maybe I should explain better."

"No, I get it now," I say. "But let me see if I have it all straight." I point to the screen that played the video. "There's a virus that could wipe out civilization, so instead of telling the public what is going on, you track the victims down and kill them before they become contagious." I remember the sketches of attack strategies on the back desk. I march over to it, and grab one of them into my fist, wave it in the air. "And you built an army to do it for you."

"The army was given to me," Mom says. "It became a problem of national security. I've been working with the government from the beginning. The best of the army is involved. 1,400 of them. They have been crucial in keeping the peace. They choreograph fights, make the public think they're keeping them safe. And technically, they are, just... in an unconventional way."

"But some of them have died," Cole says. He rubs his forehead. "We've seen it. This doesn't make sense."

"Yes," Mom says. "A few from our team were infected and knew they were going to die, so they chose to do so during an attack. It helps us maintain our cover. Others weren't Wolves at all, just military men and women who were not chosen for The Cause. Unfortunately, there has been some collateral damage. But it's a small price to pay considering the outcome if we did nothing.

"And if the public knew," she continues, "there would be no way to control it. They would run and hide as soon as they found out they were infected, and the virus would spread in ways we wouldn't be able to predict. There would be widespread panic, and the nation would erupt into chaos."

"Oh no, we wouldn't want chaos," I say. "Much better to keep everyone guessing as to when the unidentified terrorists will target and kill them for no apparent reason."

"You might not see it now," Mom says, "but it's better this way." Her voice is nostalgic, reminding me of my childhood. *You'll understand when you're older.* Who does she think she is to use that tone at this moment? She doesn't get to be maternal. Not right now. "We have eyes everywhere, and we test everyone regularly."

"How do you know who has been infected?" Cole asks. He looks like he has a headache, leaning forward in his chair, his head leaning with his fingers against his right temple.

"We started with the people who were first exposed to the disease and tested them and their families," Mom says. "We have a device." She walks around her desk and opens a drawer, pulls something out, holds it out for us to see in her palm. I step in closer, leaning in. I don't see anything. She brings it closer to us, but I take an instinctive step back. Distance is apparently important to me at the moment. "There's a clear band that fits around the finger like a ring. A cartridge is attached, which rests on the inside of the finger so it's hidden when you wear it." She slips it onto her left middle finger and holds her hand up. It is barely noticeable. I wouldn't see it if it wasn't pointed out. "The cartridge holds a small needle with a fraction of a mock virus in it. It works like a Tuberculosis test. All I need to do is tap your arm, and the needle injects the test. It feels like static shock or something equally as innocent. If you have been exposed, that area of your arm will react like it would to a spider bite but will subside in a couple days. If the person has not been exposed, nothing will happen. We monitor those who show that they are exposed and terminate them when The Stain appears. That way, they've been given seven to twelve months to live, but we stop the spread of the virus before it gets to the Beyond."

I try to think back to a specific time that I was shocked by static or felt a sting when someone touched me. I know it has happened over the past eleven months, but nothing stands out. Those are such common, harmless things. They aren't memorable.

I feel sick, realizing how brilliant the Wolves are. How brilliant my mom is.

"Resi, that means Brandon isn't contagious," Edda says. "At least not for seven to twelve months. They can all come out of isolation."

Brandon. My heart pounds, and my brain automatically replaces Grady with Brandon in that video. I want to vomit at the thought of him enduring that pain.

"He and the paramedics do have some time, yes," Mom says.

Some time? Seven to twelve months. That's not nearly enough. Mom is watching me when I look at her, concern etched in her forehead. I hate that I want her to comfort me. I hate that I want to allow her stupid green eyes to give me the hope I've been missing for almost a year.

I hate her for making me need her.

I hate her more for making me hate her.

I miss Brandon.

"You know about the paramedics?" Cole asks.

"Of course," Mom says. "I know all that goes on with The Stain. Plus, Brandon killed one of my men."

I feel numb. Stuck. Brandon just received his death sentence. I want to see him now. Spend as much time as possible with him. I don't care what has happened in the past, who he killed, our fights, our kiss. I need to see him.

Cole shakes his head. "But how? Not just the paramedics, but everyone. How do you keep tabs on everyone?"

"I have people everywhere," Mom says. "Wolves who are trained for The Cause. And we have incredible technology—drones the size of mosquitos. It's imperative to have a close eye on the infected because The Stain is very subtle. Like I said before, sometimes the victim doesn't even know it's there. It is only prominent on the first and last days of the Stained stage. If we wait until the last day, they might go into the Beyond and infect everyone around them."

She never answered my original question, the one that matters most. She may have built a terrorist organization, left friends behind, but I need to know why she left *me*. "Why did you fake your death?" My voice is so low I can barely hear my own question.

Mom's eyes dart to Edda and Cole, then back to me. She clears her throat, walks behind her desk. "Too much of my own research is involved, and this is a full-time job." She straightens a stack of papers on her desk that didn't need straightening. She's avoiding eye contact, anxious. "There was no way I could lead the task force and keep it under the radar with my notability. I had to disappear." She places the pens on her desk into a small penholder, rearranges them in no order. "The first people infected with The Stain lived on our street."

Our street. More and more weight settles on my chest.

"So, unfortunately, they were the first to be terminated. It made sense to throw myself in the mix." Mom stops fidgeting and leans with her hands against the desk. Her chin quivers before she hangs her head low. "It was the hardest thing I've ever had to do." She lifts her head and locks her eyes onto mine. "Please believe that, Resi."

I close my eyes, unable to think objectively when she looks at me like that. "Alice. She got our neighbors sick? And you..." I can't breathe. "You planted the bombs to kill them?"

"Our friends were going to die anyway," she says. "This is exactly what The Cause stands for. We kept them from killing others by stopping The Stain before it became contagious."

"How many have died at your hands thus far?" Cole asks.

Mom looks at him. "Too many."

"How many?" I insist, stepping toward her.

She takes a breath, exhales sharply. "To date, 1,721."

My eyes stay fastened onto her. "And how many are left who are awaiting the same fate?"

"Our estimates predict that we can eradicate The Stain in two years. Many more will need to die, but it's better than the 300 million in the United States who would die if we didn't control it this way."

"No," I say. "No. There has to be a better way. You're an expert in pharmacology and infectious diseases. You can find a cure!"

Mom snaps her eyes open, charges toward me. "You think I've been letting this happen without searching for one?" I'm not fearful that my mom will hurt me, but I feel my entire face widen at her outburst. She registers my surprise and composes herself, steps back. "We *are* looking for a cure," she says, her voice calm, but eyes sharp. "There are a few people that have been tested who show exposure but never develop symptoms. They're the immune—all of whom are children. We're working with them to find out what makes them immune so we can find a cure."

"Sarah." All three of us say her name in unison.

"*You* kidnapped Sarah," I realize it for the first time. My anger propels me toward her, but I stop before I'm close enough to grab her.

"Yes," she says. "And I'm sorry. But she's vital to The Cause."

"How was she even exposed?" Edda asks.

"It doesn't matter."

I rattle my head. "*What?* It doesn't matter?"

"What matters is that I know she was exposed. We've tested her at school and on the playground several times, and she has never reacted. Sarah is immune. She and nine other children. She will be returned to Brandon eventually. But for now, she's committed to helping us with The Cause."

"Stop saying 'The Cause'! This isn't a *cause*. A cause is something that people work toward for the greater good. You're committing murder."

"Resi," Mom pleads. "Please think about—"

"And why is it that you have taken it upon yourself to fix this problem?" I ask. "What makes you responsible for this virus? Why did it start with people on our street?"

Mom sucks in a breath. Her eyes fall. She's hiding something. Her face is downcast in a way that screams of guilt.

"Mom." My voice is soft but firm. "What is it?"

"Dr. Kepler?" a deep voice interrupts us as it knocks politely on the door. A large man in full Wolf-garb appears in the doorway. The uniform is small on him. It's short at the ankles and hugs him more tightly than it's made to. If he lifts his arms up, his top will show midriff.

"What?" Mom replies. But before she can turn her head to see who it is, the man aims an Alpha Rifle at Edda and pulls the trigger.

CHAPTER 28

The bullet hits the metal leg of Edda's seat, knocking the group of chairs back. It bounces to the office ceiling, and finally to the back of Mom's head. Shocked, Edda, Cole, and I gape at my mother as she sinks to the floor, unconscious. We simultaneously turn to the shooter.

"Whoa," the shooter says. "I wasn't sure how that was going to pan out. Lucky shot."

Cole moves to the floor, places two fingers to Mom's pulse. "She's okay."

The Wolf's arm rotates in a half-circle. "Come on!"

We stand in place, bewildered.

"Oh, right." He reaches for his too-small mask, but when he tries to get under the edge of it, it snaps back into place. He digs his thumb under the edge again but fumbles. "Hold on." He sets the Alpha Rifle down and uses both hands to work on the mask, struggling to lift it because of the tight fit, but finally, he pulls it up.

"Brandon!" I run to him, throw myself into his arms, so he has to pick me up. My hands find his face when I pull back. I've never been so happy to see him.

"I planned for that to be a much cooler de-masking moment," Brandon says. "But the only uniform we had left doesn't fit well."

It's when he sets me down that I realize what just happened.

"You shot my mom!" I start toward her, but I'm torn between wanting to help my mother and not wanting to touch the woman who betrayed me.

"I'm sorry, Resi," Brandon says. "Once she started talking about Sarah..."

"She should be fine," Edda says. "It hit her on the third bounce."

The reassuring looks I'm getting from Edda and Cole help to refocus me. "Brandon," I say. "We found out that you're not contagious for at least seven months."

"I know."

"You know? How?"

"I'll explain everything once we get to a safe place. But we need to get going for now."

"But my mom." Seconds ago, I was infuriated. Hell, I'm *still* infuriated, shocked, and angry, but suddenly the idea of leaving my mother again is unthinkable. June Kepler is everything I've wanted for the past eleven months. Angry or not, I have my mom back.

Cole places his hand on my shoulder. "She'll be okay."

I shake my head. "I can't lose her again."

Edda gently turns my face with her hand, so she's in my direct line of sight. "Resi, listen to me," she says. "Your mom is who we've been fighting against this whole time. We need to go right now. When you're ready, you'll know where to find her."

I have a thousand more questions I need my mom to answer, but Edda is right.

"Okay," I say, apprehensively. "Let's go."

Brandon peeks around the corner into the hallway. "Rez," he says as he turns back to us, "they'll recognize you, so you stay in the back, and we'll cover you."

"They're going to recognize all of us," I explain. "These two caused a bit of drama earlier." Cole and Edda grin innocently. "Plus, we're all in normal clothes now. Everyone out there is either in a Wolf uniform, military uniform, or work clothes. We'll stand out no matter what."

Brandon nods. "That changes my plan, but we can improvise. We're not going far, just downstairs."

Brandon grabs Cole by the neck and pushes him into the hallway.

"Dude, that hurts. Let go!'

"Suck it up and play along," Brandon says, stifling a smirk. "You two walk behind us." He marches forward squeezing Cole's neck.

I follow closely. "What is your plan, Brandon?"

"Excuse me." A man stops us before he can answer, right as we reach the stairs. "Aren't these the intruders?"

"Yes," Brandon says. "I have orders from Alpha to take them to the holding room."

Holding room?

"I see," the man says. He sighs. "How disappointing. Did Alpha already put them through Thought Reform?"

Brandon nods. "Yes sir, but it didn't take."

Thought Reform. I remember seeing the phrase on the Wolf System in Locke's office.

"That's a shame. What unit are you in, young man?"

"Poison Brigade."

The man pulls his phone out of his pocket. "What is your ID number, sir? I hope you don't mind me double-checking after the security breach."

I start to panic, scanning the area to figure out where we will run next.

"Not at all. 1-5-3-1-7-4," Brandon says.

The hell? Either Brandon is secretly a professional improviser, or he's really frickin' prepared.

The man types the numbers into his phone. I nudge Edda and tilt my head toward the office next to us. Inside, there's a baseball bat encased on the wall. We could use it as a weapon when this guy doesn't find the ID number in the system.

"Here you are," the man says. I shield the surprise on my face as the man proceeds to commend Brandon for being in the Poison Brigade as if it's something to be proud of. "Do you need help getting them to holding?"

Brandon has a Wolf ID number. He just aimed an Alpha Rifle perfectly to hit my mom's head on the third bounce. He knows the set-up of the headquarters. He's taking us to a holding room.

Is Brandon a Wolf?

After everything I've been through today, it wouldn't be the most unimaginable thing. I don't know what to think anymore.

"Nah," Brandon says. Cole groans as Brandon squeezes his neck more firmly. "This guy is the only one giving me trouble. I'll be fine."

"Well then, carry on," the man says.

We walk into the stairwell, out of the man's sight, when I take Brandon's arm and yank it hard, pulling it off Cole's neck. I plant myself on the concrete. "Stop."

Everyone turns to me.

"What was that, Brandon? How the hell do you have an ID number?"

"We don't have time right now, Resi." He takes

another step down the stairs. "I'll explain when—"

"Are you a Wolf?"

Slowly, he turns, faces me. His mouth agape, but his eyes sharp. When Brandon is angry, the dark brown of his irises blends in with the blackness of his pupils. "Are you seriously asking me that?"

I stand firmly in my place. "Yes."

"Bullshit, Resi. We don't have time for this. Let's go."

He starts walking again, but I'm not moving. "Not until you explain."

This time, he plows toward me like a raging bull, his jaw twitching before he growls out, "You know, it's pretty shitty that after four years of friendship you don't trust me."

"Four years?" I fling my arm back and point in the direction of my mom's office. "The woman I've known my entire life faked her death and started a terrorist organization, but you want to talk four years?"

Brandon's eyes relax, the brown starts to stand out against the black. He sighs. "Charlie and Kyle hacked the Wolf Web and added me. I'm not a Wolf."

"How did they hack into it?"

He cranes his neck to make sure there is no one nearby. "She used your mom's information, but she thought the Wolves had stolen it. She didn't realize June was..."

"Yeah," I say. Alive. A liar. A Wolf. Alpha. I don't know which word he was going to use, so I save him from having to use any of them.

"I'll explain more when we get out." He takes my shoulders in his hands. "Can you trust me? Please?"

Maybe I shouldn't. Hell, I shouldn't trust *anyone*

at this point. But I do.

"Okay," I say. Then, he grabs Cole by the neck again and leads us down the stairs.

We receive several strange looks from Wolves as we land on the ground floor and head toward a dark hall. We are stopped one more time, and Brandon is asked for his ID again. It seems the Wolves are on high alert since our intrusion. We move down the dark hallway where no other Wolves are heading. Finally, the end of the hall comes into view, where a woman fiddles with her phone at a desk. Behind the desk is a glass door that opens to the outside, and at the end of the hall are two ominous metal doors that look like they lead to a dungeon.

Do dungeons still exist?

When we get close, Brandon slips his mask back on.

"I have some new Defects," Brandon says to the woman at the desk. "Thought Reform didn't work."

Seriously, what the hell is Thought Reform?

The woman screws up her face when she sees Brandon. She swings her head to swish her auburn hair out of her face and chews her gum between sentences. "By yourself?" she scoffs. "They usually bring like ten combat Wolves just to put one person in holding. You have three, and you're alone?"

"Julia?"

The woman's eyes brighten. It's her. Julia was a co-worker who went missing a month ago.

"Resi, Edda!" Julia gets up from her seat and skips around the desk to hug us. "Wow, I'm so glad you guys are here. I haven't met many Wolves that I knew previously. How were you recruited? I knew they would get to you. When I was first recruited and went through Thought Reform, they kept showing your picture, saying, 'Resi Kepler is never to be harmed'. I kept thinking how great a Wolf you would be if we could recruit you too." She taps her hand to her chest. "I chose to be here full time, but I'm sure you could choose to stay undercover at the hospital." She frames her face in her hands. "Oh my stars, I'm so glad they got both of you."

Brandon clears his throat to get her attention again.

Julia's face falls. "Oh." Her eyes flit between Brandon and me. "They're here for holding?"

He nods.

Julia's shoulders slump. "Maybe they should try Thought Reform again." She speaks to me. "I promise, once it turns green, you'll understand that The Cause is more important than anything else."

What?

"Holding orders are directly from Alpha," Brandon says. "Open the doors. Now."

"Directly from Alpha?" Julia's pitch increases. "Did you get to meet Alpha? I've heard such wonderful things. And she takes such good care of us full-time Wolves. She's so dedicated to The Cause."

"JULIA," Brandon shouts.

"Ugh. Fine." Julia uses a key tied around her wrist to open a drawer, which holds three other keys. She removes one and gestures for Brandon to follow her with the intruders as she walks toward the metal doors. She inserts the key, and a computer next to the door turns on to a screen that reads, RETINAL SCAN, just like the security at my parents' lab. As she stands in front of the camera for the scan, Brandon releases Cole, reaches for the belt around his uniform, opens a pocket, and pulls out a bottle and rag. The bottle is labeled *Chloroform*.

The retinal scan starts. "Isn't this technology wonderful? Alpha's security system is so advanced."

"Brandon, what—" I don't have time to process what is happening before Brandon pours the chloroform onto a rag and shoves it toward Julia's face. But before he can muffle the sound, Julia's piercing scream echoes down the hall. Seconds later, her body goes limp, and Brandon carefully lays her on the floor.

He grabs the keys from her wrist and tosses it to Edda. "Grab those other keys from the desk. One of them should open the back door."

Edda runs to the desk and grabs the keys from the drawer. She tries the first one. It doesn't work.

I kneel down over Julia, press my fingers to her neck. She still has a pulse and is breathing evenly. I look up at Brandon. "Chloroform?"

"Your mom's pharmacy comes in handy," he says. "Charlie's idea."

"She doesn't like that I used Propofol, but she's fine with you knocking some girl out with Chloroform?"

"Got it," Edda says as a key turns the lock. She pushes the door open carefully. We all pause, waiting for an alarm to go off. It doesn't, so she pushes it open further. "Now what?"

Brandon points as he runs ahead of us. "Ticket booth. Run!"

CHAPTER 29

Brandon holds the door of the ticket booth open. "Go. Get in!"

Edda runs in first, and I check to see how far behind Cole is. I crash into Edda.

"OW. Geez," She says under me. I'd been running so fast I didn't realize there was little room to stop myself.

"Ouch!" I yell as Cole completes the train wreck, running into me.

"Get down!"

Charlie is cramped into a corner of the ticket booth on her computer. Coen, Kyle, and Travis are with her. There are two other computers and boxes scattered around the floor of the booth. It's a wide, hall-like room. The space from the window to the back door is about two large steps, but from side to side, you could parallel-park three cars.

"I said, get down," Charlie says, pulling at my jeans. I duck, and the others follow. Brandon shuts the door and crouches down with us.

"Don't get me wrong," I say, "I'm happy to see all of you, but what the hell is going on?"

"I was trying to explain it earlier." Brandon tucks his legs underneath him, but his small uniform is constricting his movement. He shifts, settles for his legs bent in front of him, and he continues. "Charlie figured everything out and helped Kyle hack the Wolves' system, the Wolf Web. It's a private network on the Dark Web, and it connects to the software you accessed on Locke's computer. We found all the information you described in your Afterthoughts, and it explains everything about the Wolves."

"It was that Afterthought I hadn't heard about yet," Charlie explains. "Edda said something about 'hidden, stained, and beyond.' I knew I had heard those terms before. And I was right." She pulls her phone out of her pocket and opens it to a photo.

It's a ripped piece of paper, my mom's handwriting all over it. Charlie zooms in. In the messy writing of disease processes, pharmacologic agents, their properties, and formulas, there was written in small, black letters in the right corner:

Hidden: 7-12 months
Stained: 14 days
Beyond: 8 days

It's exactly what my mom showed us on the control board in her office.

"It took me a few hours, but I remembered that I had seen those words. I found this page in her pharmacy a few days after the bombing. It was a loose piece of paper, so I thought it was trash, but I never want to mess with June's work, so I stuffed it in a cabinet. I found it right after you guys left for this mission." Charlie closes her phone, slides it into her back pocket. "After I saw it, everything came back to me," she says. "Before June died, she was working on curing Alice's disease. You already knew that."

"Charlie," Brandon says. "There's something we should clarify."

"These sequences—hidden, stained, and beyond —were the words she used for the disease progression," Charlie continues. "It stuck out to me back then because people don't usually make up code words for the stages of a disease."

"Charlie, June's not—" Edda tries to interrupt.

"She was anxious in those last days," Charlie says. "She must have gone several days without sleep. She was so determined to find a cure."

I hear her voice, but it's hard to listen to her speak about my mother in the past tense. I move farther and farther away from the conversation like I'm disconnected from my own body, witnessing the conversation from above. It's still impossible to me that I was speaking to my mother just minutes ago. And that the woman who tucked me in at night as a child, sang nursery rhymes, and created forts out of bedsheets is the mastermind behind a nationwide terror.

"Everything the Wolves do revolves around this disease," Charlie says. "Since June had all the research on it, they must have killed her for it and stolen all this other stuff that she created. Once I understood that I had everything I needed. The idiots even use June's passwords and fingerprints. All of which I have. So, I found out how to hack into most of the system with Kyle's help." Kyle bows his head as if he's tipping his invisible hat. "The Wolves have been using June's information to create an entire Web system. And now that I have access, not only can we find Sarah, but we can also take down the Wolves and avenge June's death."

"Charlie!" Edda says.

Charlie jumps and whacks Travis. "What?"

Travis scowls at her and rubs his eye.

"June is alive," Edda says. "No one stole her ideas or her software or whatever it is you hacked. It was June this whole time. She's the leader of the Wolves. You're able to use June's information because it's *her* system. June Kepler is Alpha."

Charlie blinks a few times before disbelief takes shape on her face. She shakes her head. "No. June is dead. That's not possible."

Brandon pulls one leg under the other. "It's true," he says. "June is alive. We saw her." He bobs his head toward Cole and me. "They talked to her."

Charlie's muscles grow tense. Her shoulders raise and jaw drops. She turns to me. "They're serious?"

"Do you honestly think we'd be throwing jokes around right now?" Cole asks. "We're camped outside the headquarters of terrorists."

"*What*?" Charlie stands up, and her arm swats Travis again before she holds her head in both hands.

"Seriously?" Travis gripes.

"What do you mean she's alive? She did all of this? June is the one killing the people infected with this virus?"

"Charlie, get down," Brandon says.

"How is this possible? They found her DNA at the scene."

Hearing it again without my mom right in front of me is somehow making the situation more real. Everything in me is deflating, growing weak, sad, confused—all the emotions I work hard not to feel.

"DNA," Charlie repeats quietly, her eyes softening. "They found her DNA." She sinks back down to the floor, stepping on Travis' hand in the process. She ignores his disapproving exclamation. "She had me take several DNA samples for some project she was working on. She used it to fake her death?" Charlie's eyes dart back and forth as her mind catches up. "The virus. June. After everything I worked..." Her words disappear into her thoughts as the truth pours acid onto whatever memories Charlie has of my mom. "It all makes sense now."

"What does?" Cole asks.

She looks up at his voice, but her stare is still vacant. "Everything."

She's in shock. I can relate. I keep my eyes on the ground, wondering if everyone expects a response from me, but I'm as clueless as they are. I've been more fooled and betrayed than anyone.

"Can someone explain why we're on the floor of the ticket booth?" Cole asks abruptly, his tall frame working hard to stay below window-level.

Coen speaks up for Charlie, who is still in a blank stare. "Well, per the system that Kyle hacked and Charlie commandeered called the Wolf Web, the cameras that the Wolves have installed show that this is the spot they are least likely to walk by. So, we took video footage of this spot from another day and made it so they see *that* instead of what is happening in real-time. If we stay lower than the windows, we shouldn't be seen. Plus, the Wolves are protective of their hideout. The last place they would want to attack someone is right outside their headquarters. They would need time to strategize a way to do it first."

"We have access to every camera," Kyle says in his monotone voice. "Including these tiny drones that fly around and watch people all over the nation. We had to figure out how to narrow it down to Houston and the

Astrodome. It was pretty overwhelming at first, which is why it took us so long to get here." Kyle opens another computer, shows us the screen.

"There must be 200 cameras in that place," Cole says.

"Close," Kyle says. "There are 230 cameras. But thanks to Charlie's knowledge of Dr. Kepler, Coen's knowledge of everything, and my hacking expertise, we have control of them. The entire place is covered with surveillance except for Alpha's office, and we have access to all of them. In addition to that, we can control the locks on secure doors in the Dome, and we can add and delete member information."

"Is that Julia?" Edda asks, pointing to a part of the screen that shows a woman at a desk. "She's already awake and working again?"

Kyle reaches for the computer Charlie was using.

"That's what the security footage shows on the Wolf Web because we paused it on that loop," he says. "Here's what is happening in real-time." He hands Charlie's computer to Edda and points to where two people are checking on Julia, who lies on the floor.

"What's that flashing light?" Cole asks as he points to a red light in the corner of the screen.

"That means an attack is taking place," Kyle says. He clicks the light, and a larger image of the scene pops up. "They monitor the attacks with those mosquito drones."

"I can't believe mosquito-sized drones exist, but we still don't have real hoverboards," Brandon gripes.

Charlie crawls back to the computer to see what's happening. She reads the right side of the screen. "They're in Boston," she points out. "The Museum of settings from me. It all makes sense now."

Fine Arts."

"Can we stop them?" Cole asks.

"No," Charlie says. "We can see the cameras, operate them, control some of the doors, and hack into the Wolf Web to mess with the Wolves' identification, but only Alpha... June... can approve and cancel Wolf attacks. It's done straight from her office."

"There was an operating system in her office," Cole says.

"That's what I figured," Charlie says. "And she got the privacy settings from me. It all makes sense now."

"What are you talking about?" I ask.

"You know I specialize in DNA," Charlie says. "A few years ago, I was approached by the NSA about how to increase privacy and security in their line of work. The plan uses DNA in white blood cells as a strong measure of security for top-secret operating systems. I shared my plan with June. When we tried to hack into the control system for the Wolf Web, I expected the usual retinal scan and fingerprint, but it was a fingerstick blood sample. June is the only one who can approve or cancel 'terminations' by using blood DNA."

"That must have been why there was blood on the beam next to the control board," Edda says.

I lean my head back against the wall and close my eyes. "So, my mom has NSA-level security commanding the Wolf attacks."

The ticket booth silences as we all come to the same conclusion, but it's Brandon who verbalizes it for us. "Which means we can't hack into the most important parts of the Wolf Web and take them down."

"Hey, guys?" Edda asks as she peers onto Charlie's computer. She turns it around for everyone to see. One section of the screen is on the real-time footage of the ticket booth. Julia and at least fifteen other Wolves are headed towards us. "Your brilliant hide-out plan is about to fail massively."

A surge of adrenaline fires through me, and I peek over the wall of the ticket booth. This is it. It's all over.

Kyle takes two of the computers and powers them down, but Charlie snatches hers from Edda, types furiously, and clicks the touchpad for a few more seconds.

"What are you doing?" I press. "They're coming!"

"I'll tell you in a minute." Charlie finishes typing and closes the computer. Brandon yanks on a piece of loose wood on the wall of the booth. They shove the computers into the space, then replace the wood so everything is hidden.

"The plan isn't failing at all," Brandon says. The door swings open, and Wolves fly in, seizing each of us. Brandon whispers to me before I'm swept out of the booth. "We're just getting started."

CHAPTER 30

The dungeon-door to the holding room slams shut. Dozens of people are scattered around. It looks like we're in a warehouse with concrete walls on every side. Boxes are stacked up on metal shelves that are lined up in rows in the back of the room, but several shelves have been removed to make it into a type of living quarters. Cots litter the center of the room with assorted bed sheets and comforters. A nook on the right has microwaves and heating plates set up as a makeshift kitchen, and there's a space closed off by ugly brown curtains to the left where I hear water trickling.

We're trapped in a warehouse prison, and so far, I'm not impressed by my friends' brilliant scheme. "This is your plan?"

"Yep. This is the plan," Brandon says. "We were caught sooner than we expected, so we didn't get a chance to show you everything on the Wolf Web. There are 86 people here in this holding room."

"So?" Cole asks.

"So, from what we gather, the people placed in holding are called Defects, which, we assume, means they defected. These people were recruited and worked for the Wolves but turned against them. They know the inner workings and how the Wolves operate. They can help form an army and infiltrate from the inside."

"Sorry to interrupt, but we don't *all* know the inner workings of this place. Only some of us." The man speaking to us holds his dark, muscular arm out for me to shake his hand. His tee-shirt is dirty and stained but tucked neatly into his camouflage pants so that it hugs his brawny chest. "There's no question whose daughter you are," he says. "It's your eyes. Not everyone has met Alpha, but I was one of the first army generals recruited for The Cause, so I worked with her directly. General Oliver Rosales. You can call me Olly."

"Hi, Olly," I say, surprised by my own nerves. I'm rarely intimidated or nervous around handsome men, but something about his physique and confidence makes me blush.

"Nice to meet you, Olly," Brandon says. "Can you explain what you mean? Why wouldn't you all know the inner workings? I thought you were here because you defected from the Wolves."

"Not exactly," Olly says. "We are Defects, as in, we didn't work properly, or we didn't work the way they intended. We didn't 'defect' in the military sense that we betrayed our country." He ushers us over to a few cots. "Have a seat."

"Whoa, eight Defects at once?" A young man says as we get comfortable. He runs his fingers through his hair and puffs out his naked chest. His sweatpants hang low on his hips. He appraises Charlie. "Hey babe, I'm Patrick."

Charlie blushes, eyes him warily.

"Pat, what have I said about hitting on the new Defects?" Olly's presence is demanding like he blocks the man's access to Charlie without moving from his spot.

Patrick waves Olly off. "Whatever he tells you, add the fact that General Olly doesn't tolerate any fun around here."

"Go put a shirt on, Pat," says Olly.

"See?" Patrick says. He bends to retrieve a shirt from a cardboard box, then starts toward the kitchen. "Welcome to the land of misfit toys."

"We're actually not Defects, per se," I explain to Olly. "We broke in. I think they're keeping us here until they know what to do with us."

"Broke in?" Olly raises his eyebrows. "Impressive. I thought I'd never see the day. Wolves are careful. But I'm sorry to tell you, they are probably not concerned about what to do with you." He holds his arms out wide, showcasing the warehouse. "This is it. Once you're in holding, you don't get out."

"What can you tell us about the makeup of the Wolves?" Brandon asks. "Are they all military?"

"Many are military, but not all. Everything the Wolves do is strategic," says Olly. "They choose the strongest, most stealthy military men and women to fight, but also recruit non-military personnel who can be trained in the areas of need. They consider athletes, people who are clever in disguise, CIA agents, but also people who have wide areas of influence in their communities.

"For instance, that woman over there." Olly points to a woman on the other side of the room. She leans against a wall reading a book. "Her name is Maya. She was a college professor, but she also volunteered with the homeless, started an intramural Ultimate Frisbee league, and was involved in her church. She had a large sphere of influence. She wasn't chosen for combat, she was chosen to test the people around her for The Stain. These Wolves keep tabs on those who test positive, and report to the Wolves when the Stain appears so they can be terminated before they enter the Beyond. They choose top-of-the-line warriors and the most influential men and women in the infected communities so they can be successful with the fewest number of Wolves possible."

"We were told they have 1,400 Wolves," Cole says. "That's not a few."

"1,400 Wolves from the *military*," Olly corrects. "Overall, there are at least 6,000. But by war standards, that number is still low."

"How is it possible that out of 6,000 people, only 86 disagree with The Cause?" Cole asks.

"Thought Reform, right?" Brandon asks. "We read something about it on the Wolf Web."

"Right. It's not about disagreement," Olly says. "People are sent here because they failed Thought Reform. You see, once Wolves are 'recruited,' whether it's an order through the military or through a kidnapping, the first thing they do is inject an implant behind the ear." Olly turns his head to show us a small, flesh-colored device that protrudes out behind his right ear. "The implant is connected to the auditory canal, so it is also used for communication, but ours are turned off."

I recall Jenna's Afterthought when she pressed a button behind her ear to communicate with the person she would be meeting inside the Holiday Inn after the Wolf attack.

"The main purpose of the implant, however," Olly says, "is to manipulate us into believing in The Cause. The 'moral compass' of the brain lies behind the right ear."

"Ah, yes," Coen says, "the right temporal-parietal junction is indeed the moral compass. There has been research on the use of magnets to disrupt the area to make people temporarily less moral. But the researcher reported that this information should not be used because it could carry horrible consequences."

That's because it was my dad's research. I remember he was so excited about the discovery, but the implications terrified him.

Dad.

Was he in on this? Did he plant those bombs and detonate them before he could get away? Did he create these implants? So many questions cross my mind as I think about his body lying in a coma on a hospital bed at Parkhill. He couldn't have known about this. Right?

"Yes, that part of the brain is moved around by magnets. The implants they use are subtle enough that each person's main beliefs and personality are still intact," Olly says. "If the implant is successful, the person will be moral enough that they are saddened by the need to kill someone, but they will do it because they believe it is for the greater good. Between the magnets and a little coaching, Thought Reform is almost always effective."

"Coaching?" Edda asks.

"When the implants are injected," Olly says, "someone sits at Alpha's control board. The implants are individually connected to that system. One screen on the control system shows an image of our brains. The magnets are adjusted through the control board. Our original moral state shows up as yellow. The operator adjusts the magnets until the right temporal-parietal junction goes from a yellow color to light green. That's when they know that they can convince the Wolf that The Cause is necessary and that they must kill people with The Stain to save the rest of the world. They sit in a room for three days repeating the goal of The Cause, saying that it's worthy of sacrifice and that it is a sad reality, but a necessary one. They go into more specifics than that, but that's the gist."

My mom is brainwashing the most respected men and women in the country. I want to vomit, but I don't think I can. When is the last time I ate?

"And they also show your picture, Miss Kepler."

My eyebrows pop up at my name.

"All throughout Thought Reform, they tell the Wolves that you are never to be harmed."

"That's why the Wolves have recognized me."

Olly nods.

My empty stomach churns again, sickened by the idea that I'm the only person immune to the Wolves because my mother is their leader. I take a breath, rub my stomach like it will soothe the nausea. "And Thought Reform didn't work on you?"

"For some reason, our implants are defects. Hence, the name. Mine worked at first. It turned green like it was supposed to. I operated the Wolves with Alpha at that time. But three months later, I started to see how wrong everything was that we were doing and opposed Alpha and the other army generals. They opened my information on the Wolf System and saw that my brain had turned yellow again, back to my original moral state. They tried to fix my implant, but they couldn't change it back to green without going too far and turning it black, which would shut off the moral compass completely, so they put me here. That was about eight months ago. I was the first Defect. For some, that section of the brain never turned green at all. There are people here who even believe in The Cause, to begin with, but since their brains couldn't be manipulated, the Wolves wouldn't take a chance on them."

"But they are still 'moral' enough that they didn't kill you, so they put you all in this warehouse," Cole says.

"Exactly," says Olly. "Our implants are just turned off. The Wolves only kill if they must. There have been Wolves, however, whose implants went too far in the opposite direction. Instead of light green, that area turned black. It deactivated their moral compass altogether. They were too aggressive to stay here with us, so they were done away with in a special way for Wolves that have gone bad."

"What do you mean?" Brandon asks.

"They are killed in a way that destroys evidence that the person ever existed. They will never be found or traced to the Wolves." His expression alters with his tone from the retelling of facts to something softer, more personal.

"How?"

"The Incinerator," Charlie says. "It was on the Wolf Web."

"You really know a lot about the Wolf Web for the short amount of time you hacked into it," I say.

She shakes her head. "It was the first thing that caught my attention because of the name. I looked at it briefly before we all strategized how to get in here."

"I'm regrettably a culprit in the creation of this

machine," Olly says with a slight wince. "I was a leading scientist in the military, which is why I was put on the team with your mother. The Incinerator is a large box built inside one of the Astrodome offices. Inside is empty, and the ceiling is made of the most powerful lasers in existence."

"The white room," Edda says. I nod, remembering the strange room we stumbled into earlier that day. A shiver runs down my neck thinking we could have closed ourselves in.

"Yes," Olly says. "The offender is locked in and incinerated at about ninety-six thousand degrees Fahrenheit."

I'm dizzy at the thought.

"The worst part is the ten-second time-lapse after flipping the lever to power the machine. It's the longest ten seconds you can imagine. And once it is on, only Alpha can cancel it using her DNA. After the ten second power-up, the lasers take less than a second to incinerate the body, and nothing is left of them. Not even ashes. It's an awful invention."

And it's approved by my mother. I feel like the lasers are actively heating my chest. The woman I knew wouldn't do this.

"The hottest laser actually goes up to 2 million degrees," Coen says.

"It doesn't add up," Edda says. "I know June. She and Astor were always cautious about research that could potentially be dangerous. I don't see how she could manipulate everyone like that. It's just not her."

A weight lifts. A small one, like a three-pound dumbbell. I'm not the only one trying to reconcile what I'm hearing with who I know June Kepler to be.

Olly rubs the stubble on his jaw. "You might understand more if you saw the Wolves whose implants malfunctioned. They were uncontrollable. Lethal with no restraint. That doesn't justify the incinerator, but we would all be dead if the Malfunctioned were kept here."

"The children," Brandon says. "Do they put the implants in the children?"

Olly furrows his eyebrows. "I'm sorry. I wasn't aware that there were children who were recruited."

"They're kidnapped," I say. "The children are immune to The Stain, so the Wolves study them in hopes of developing a cure."

"Are you sure?" Olly asks. "Alpha must be getting desperate if she is kidnapping children. She said from the beginning, she would always work to protect them."

"We're sure," I say.

"So, that must be why you're here. You were trying to rescue a child." Olly's taps his chin, then excitedly points. "And you broke in, so you've at least partially succeeded, which means the Wolves are slipping up."

"Not exactly. We just have more... *insight*... into the situation than others," I say, hoping I won't have to explain the Afterthoughts to a complete stranger.

"We could use your help, Olly," Brandon says. "It seems like you know everything about the Wolves."

"I *did*. But I'm not so sure I will be of much use to you now. I was a high-ranking military officer and one of the first recruits. More information was divulged to me at the time than anyone else you will meet down here," Olly says. "But I also knew the Wolves of a year ago, when it only consisted of an anxious scientist and some government officials planning a bombing. It was the beginning stages, not what it is today. The Wolves have grown immensely."

"Mom recruited you before the bombing?"

He cocks his head to the side. "Actually, I was recruited by President Hayden."

I feel the air drying my eyes as they bug out. No wonder the Wolves recruited so many high-ranking military personnel. They're working with the president of the friggin' United States.

"Development of the weapons wasn't finished at that point, so we used bombs before anyone else went into the Beyond. Once those victims were dead, we could control the spread of the Stain from there."

The same images of the bombing I've been assaulted with for eleven months flash into my memory. The news replaying it like a broken record, debris scraping my knees as I knelt at the site of my childhood home and wept. But those flashbacks I'm so familiar with include the death of my mother in that explosion. Now I know that she didn't die in it, she created it. I shake the images away, along with the question of how bad my PTSD will be after this. "How did you know who was infected?"

Olly's shoulders raise. "Alpha somehow knew who was directly exposed. She was able to track it, so we started with those individuals and their families. She never shared how she knew."

My head is pounding now. I don't know how much more of this I can listen to.

"General, the Wolf Web said the weapons are in the basement," Brandon says.

"That's where they made them back then, yes," Olly says. "But I don't know if they are still there now."

"They are," Brandon says. "This is Charlie, and this is Coen." He gestures to them as he speaks. "They are both certified geniuses. And this is Kyle. He's a dude I work with who happens to be a skilled hacker. With their combined skills, we hacked into the Wolf Web and took control of the surveillance cameras in the Astrodome. Most everything else has to be done from the control board and requires Alpha's DNA, but the cameras were fair game from our computers. The cameras, and some of the doors."

"That's why we wanted to get caught by the Wolves," Charlie says. "We knew from the Wolf Web that they would most likely throw us in here. This room has a secured door that I set to open at midnight so everyone can escape, and we have 86 people to fight with us to get Sarah and get out. There are 33 Wolves that stay here overnight, including Alpha, the guards, and the children's caretakers."

"You'll need a better plan than unlocking the doors to the holding room," Olly says. "There are over twenty Defects who believe in The Cause, so only 60 will fight with you. And the last time we tried, they withheld our food for a week."

"You've attempted to escape before?" Cole asks.

Olly gives an airy laugh. "Of course. The last attempt was a few months ago. We had wooden baseball bats in some of those boxes back there." His eyes drift to the shelves in the back of the warehouse. "But the Damascus Swords slice right through them, and the Alpha rifles crushes them with one shot."

"She *was* trying to replicate the Damascus

Sword," Coen says.

"She did," Olly says. "Possibly a stronger and more deadly version of it."

"You were talking about baseball bats," I remind him.

"Right," Olly continues. "There are only a few remaining at this point. We waited until the Wolves came to replenish our food supply and deliver clean sheets and clothing. As soon as the door opened, we attacked. We were defeated within minutes, didn't eat for a week, and three Defects died in the fight. So, if you have a plan, it better be convincing."

"This is only part of the plan," Kyle says. "We also located the armory in the basement. Charlie used the Wolf Web and programmed the armory to be locked at midnight tonight. At the same time, the door to this room will be unlocked. The Wolves that don't already have weapons out at that time will not be able to get one. Weapons locked. Defect door open."

Olly strokes his chin. "The Wolves will be outnumbered and fewer will have access to weapons."

"Exactly," Brandon says.

"Surely someone will figure out that the Wolf Web was hacked and see these discrepancies," says Olly.

Charlie shrugs. "It's possible, but hopefully it won't cross their minds to look for it. We'll have to wait and see."

Olly considers it for a second before he shakes his head. "I don't know. The guards will still have their weapons, and their uniforms make it impossible to hurt them."

"Their own weapons break through the uniforms," Edda says. "We discovered this recently. Our strategy should be to disarm them and take their weapons. If we're two against one, our odds are favorable."

"Favorable?" Olly huffs. "These are top-trained military personnel."

"So are you," Edda replies.

"But *you* aren't," he argues.

Brandon hangs his head low, rubbing the back of his head before he takes a few deep breaths. Then he draws his eyes back to Olly, pleading. "One of those children they're experimenting on is my daughter."

Olly leans forward, elbows on his knees, and sighs. He checks his watch. "It's 7:00 PM," he says. "I'll rally as many Defects as I can by 8:00. That will give you four hours to midnight to explain the plan and get ready."

7:00? Our arrival time was 4:22. It feels like it's been a week since we got here, but it's been two and a half hours.

"We can work with that," Brandon says. "Thank you."

"Meet here at 8:00." Olly walks toward a crowd of Defects playing cards at the only table in the holding room.

I close my eyes and allow my body to flop onto the cot. I can't begin to process everything that has happened. "Mischa Linelli is going to have a field day with this," I say.

Cole leans over, kisses my forehead. "I'll go find some food for you." I grab his hand and squeeze it before he leaves.

"I'll go with you," Travis says as Cole walks away. "I'm starving."

Edda sits on the edge of my cot. "How are you

holding up?"

I tilt my head to see her better. "Me? Better than ever."

Brandon lies down on the cot next to me. "Just another day, huh?"

Edda smiles half-heartedly. "You don't always need to have it together," she says. "You're a tough chick, but it's okay to be hurting."

I roll my eyes. Edda, the therapist, is here. "I know. I'm being sarcastic, Ed."

"You don't need to bottle everything up."

I fling my arm over my eyes with a groan. "I don't need to hear it right now."

"Will you shut up for a minute? Maybe *I* need to say it," Edda says. I look up at the unexpected outburst. "Not everything is about you. Let me talk."

I sit up in the cot, taken aback. There's no anger in Edda's stare, though. She's overwhelmed. I let go of a breath. I'm being selfish. Edda was close to my mom, too. She's processing everything just like I am.

"You're right," I say, and I wrap my arms around my knees. "I'm sorry. Go ahead."

"You feel like you need to be so strong all the time, Resi, and you are, but I know that you feel things deeply and bottle them away. And you're not always okay." She shakes her head. "Today, your mom had the same hardness you sometimes have when you push away the pain and choose to ignore it because it hurts. I see her and—"

"Whoa. Stop." Is she really comparing me to my mother right now? "I might avoid stuff that sucks, but I'm not going to end up murdering thousands of people."

"Do you think she thought she was going to?" Edda stands and her voice rises. "Come on, Resi. I know her. *You* know her. Sweet June Kepler! Do you think she saw this coming? But she's hiding all this pain over a façade of strength and forcing herself to believe that this 'Cause' is good." She lowers her volume when she sees that I'm taken aback. "Look, part of what makes you a good friend and leader is your strength and cynicism and freakish ability to compartmentalize. I don't expect you to become some Hallmark Channel fanatic, but you are never stronger than when you let us in and allow us to help you protect those broken places. Protecting them on your own leads to this insane anxiety and destruction. June is a prime example of that. Even Olly said that a year ago, she was just an anxious scientist. She did this with people she knew she could manipulate. Not with people she loved and trusted with her pain."

Even now, I'm blocking my grief—refusing to give in to the ache. I can't delve too deeply into the matter because a grenade of pain is waiting for me there. But Edda is right. My mother excluded everyone she loved from this plan. My dad and I could have helped her come up with another way, but she didn't let us in. She did it all on her own.

"Resi," Edda continues. She sits beside me on the cot. "You're strong. Everyone knows that. You're strong enough to brave going into the minds of the dead and strong enough to rescue Sarah. I believe that. But if you're not vulnerable enough to feel the pain of the struggle along the way, you won't feel the full joy of the victory when it comes." Edda takes my hand and interlocks our fingers. "You don't give your trust out freely.

Which is why I have never been prouder to be your friend than when you've allowed me into your most vulnerable places. I love those pieces of you more than anything else."

"Me too," Brandon says from the cot next to us.

I swallow the emotions weighing heavily against my throat. If I open my mouth and tell her how I'm feeling, tears will flow, and I won't be able to stop them. I'm not ready for that. So, I settle on a simpler truth. "I'm ready for this to be over. I'm ready to get Sarah, go home, and down a bottle of wine while watching a Law and Order: SVU marathon."

"We all are," Edda says. She hops onto the cot next to my feet and lays down. "Maybe we can get a quick nap in before the meeting."

I sputter at the thought. How anyone could sleep after everything we've learned today is beyond me. And I'm feeling vulnerable after her little speech, so I'm compelled to remedy it. "Hey, Edda?"

"Hmm?"

"I need to tell you something."

Edda props herself up on her elbows. "Anything. Go ahead."

"My boyfriend in fifth grade broke up with me because he liked Amanda Nunez and said she was prettier than me and it made me so angry that I stole Amanda's pencil and never gave it back."

"Oh, Lord." Edda falls back down on the cot.

I blow out an exaggerated sigh like I just lightened a massive load of emotional baggage. "I've been holding onto that for years."

"Couldn't last one minute without cracking a joke," she says.

"I'm serious, you don't know what you're asking," I say. "I've got *a lot* to get off my chest."

Edda chuckles. "I know what I'm asking."

"I'll send you to therapy," Brandon says.

I give him a lazy smile. "After this, I'm going to need it."

I stare at the ceiling of the warehouse, exhaustion taking over my body, but my brain too stimulated to sleep, all synapses firing at once. I think about how Dad would explain that my neurons are making new connections with each other as I learn new information. I imagine them sparking when they meet, like the tips of electrical wires. He would tell me that with stress and trauma, the amygdala sends a distress signal to the hypothalamus and pituitary gland, which will signal my adrenals to secrete epinephrine, norepinephrine, and cortisol.

I bet my blood pressure is higher than ever.

I hope I don't have a stroke.

I think about how prolonged stimulation of the sympathetic nervous system will cause a deterioration in health.

I think about how ridiculous it is that I'm thinking about this right now.

I hope my dad knew nothing about the Wolves.

I keep staring at the ceiling. Metal upon metal comes together to form all sorts of geometric shapes that work together to hold the roof over my head. One metal beam is broken in a corner, separated from where it was once bolted into the wall. But even with one broken beam, there's no threat of the roof caving in. It would take several broken beams to cause the roof to fall.

It makes me wonder how many beams I have left to hold me up, and at this rate, which one will inevitably cause my collapse.

CHAPTER 31

"You're not joining this meeting until you put a shirt on, Pat," Olly says. He stands on a stool in the middle of a huge group of Defects, possibly the entire group, but I can't see if anyone chose to sit the meeting out because I'm right in the middle of the mosh pit. The Defects are young, mostly late twenties to mid-thirties, and a few pushing the middle-ages.

"Everyone quiet!" Olly's voice booms over the crowd. The chatter around me ceases. "There are some here who oppose this idea." He steps off the stool, addresses my friends and me. "Defects who believe in The Cause. For the record, I'm with you, but they asked for a chance to explain their views."

"Let's hear it," Brandon says.

A short girl who looks like an ad for a CrossFit gym steps forward.

"This is Cloe," Olly says. "She was recruited four months ago. She's a West Point graduate. Top of her class. She believes in The Cause, but her implant never worked, so she was put here with the Defects."

I try to remain positive and listen to their side, but if Charlie's hack works, we only have a few more hours until the doors open. We need to strategize, not argue. And if the opposing Defects all look like Cloe, we could get our asses kicked.

"I've been asked to speak on behalf of everyone

here who believes in The Cause," Cloe says. "We hope you won't consider us malicious or sociopathic, but we see the reality that there is a dangerous virus out there that is currently under control. There is a minimal spread of the virus because it isn't allowed to get to the contagious stage. The Cause chooses to do something unthinkable to save the majority. If you stop the Wolves, the disease will break loose, and even more people will die, including you, your friends, and your families. That would be on you."

"It's wrong." I can't help myself. I have to say something. "Yes, more people might get infected, but there are other ways to contain a disease."

"People will hide or refuse to quarantine at the right time," says Cloe. "As it is, the public is unaware. The Wolves have extreme surveillance on anyone who tests positive, so when they show The Stain, they act —"

"Kill," I correct.

"—without fear that the Stained person will also notice and run away. But without the Wolves, when people find out they are infected, they will hide so they won't have to end their days in isolation, and they will spread the virus uncontrollably."

"I don't see that happening," I say. "Once people realize how serious this disease is, they will make sure everyone around them complies with the rules. We could set up isolation tents all around the most heavily infected cities and have the people who are 'Stained' come to the tents where we can treat them while we work on a cure."

"Not everyone pays attention," Cloe says. "The Stain lasts exactly fourteen days before it goes into the Beyond. It is most prominent on the first and four-teen days, but it is otherwise extremely subtle. You could tell the public to go to the tents when they are Stained, but if they don't see it until day fourteen, they could go into the Beyond and infect everyone on their way there."

"If it's so subtle, how have the Wolves caught every case?" Brandon asks.

"No one knows how," Olly says. "But Alpha knows exactly who has been directly infected, and the Wolves have trained eyes for the rash. Mosquito drones follow them every day, and when they can't get access through those, they send an undercover Wolf in person."

I still can't comprehend how my mom knows. What is she hiding?

"And without those things in place," Cloe says, "the Stain will be too widespread to control."

Without the Wolves, how many people will die horrible deaths? Are the Wolves saving the nation? Are they technically performing tons of mercy killings?

I should have developed an opinion about eu-thanasia before now.

But for or against, euthanasia is the choice of the dying person. It's a way to go peacefully. The Wolves are violently attacking people who have no idea that they're sick.

"Everyone will die!" I hear over an increasingly chatty crowd.

"That's life!" I yell. The noise in the circle hushes. "Sometimes you catch a cold. Sometimes it's a world war. Sometimes a disease strikes, and you have an Ebola crisis. People die. It sucks, but it's life. We can try to control the spread in different ways. What you're allowing the Wolves to do is dishonest. You're playing God—and an awful one at that." I step toward Cloe. "Who the hell are you to choose who lives and who dies?"

"I won't pretend like I don't see Cloe's point," says Cole. "This virus could get out of control."

I face him sharply. "There better be a 'but' that follows that statement."

"*But,* Resi is right."

Smart man.

"You can't go around committing murder so fewer people die."

"And they're kidnapping children and using them as experiments to find a cure," Edda says. "If murder isn't immoral enough for you, is child-experimentation?"

"I can help with that," a quiet voice says from the back of the crowd. The Defects part for a chubby young man to walk to the center of the circle. "I'm Tristan. My implant defected a couple months ago. The Wolves recruited me when they discovered that some children were immune to the Stain. I was in Atlanta working with the CDC on a new flu vaccine when I woke up one day in the Astrodome. I, uh," Tristan titters, and his freckled cheeks blush. "I'm actually a fan, Dr. Walton," he says to Cole. Cole stands straighter, his face beams with pride and surprise. "I followed your blog when you were in Paraguay studying Chagas disease and Dengue fever. It was quite enlightening."

"Ah, well. Very nice to meet a fan!" Cole says.

"Probably your only fan, dude. Calm down," Brandon says.

"The children get their blood drawn each week

and are given portions of the live virus to study how their bodies defend it," Tristan says. "But the infusions are mostly maintenance: fluids and electrolytes."

"They *give* kids the virus?" Brandon stalks toward him, probably more reactive than intentional.

"Yes, but they're immune!" Tristan cowers, leans back with his hands in front of his face like he expects Brandon to hit him. "The virus will not harm them."

"They don't know that!" Brandon yells.

Cloe steps in front of Tristan, and Edda pulls on Brandon's arm. His bicep is flexed, his stance strong, but he steps back when Edda's hand lands on him, and he realizes how intimidated Tristan is.

"We get that the Wolves have hurt you and your families," Cloe says, "but if they hadn't, *you'd* be dead too."

Brandon takes a deep breath, shakes his head. "I just want to stop them long enough to get my daughter back."

The way Cloe gnaws the inside of her cheek reminds me of Sarah. She studies Brandon, looks him up and down. "How old is she?"

"Eight. But I've only had her since she was four."

"Adopted?"

"Yes." He takes a step closer to Cloe, his tall stature a contrast to her short one, but his demeanor is soft this time, much less intimidating. Although, I doubt someone like Cloe is intimidated by anything. "And she's the most incredible kid you'll ever meet."

"Cloe was adopted when she was six," Olly whispers to me. I feel my eyebrows raise and I watch the stare-down with heightened interest.

Cloe nods slowly. "We won't stop you."

"But, Cloe, the—" Cloe raises a hand and silences the girl next to her.

"We won't *help* you. But we won't stop you." She extends her hand to Brandon and shakes it. "Your daughter is lucky to have a father who loves her." She turns to me. "I also hope you know what you're doing."

"Thank you," says Brandon.

"Anyone on Cloe's side can leave now," Olly instructs.

The number of people who fall away from the circle shocks me, about twenty-five, leaving around fifty Defects willing to fight with us. "Seriously? They would all rather people be murdered?"

"They haven't been Stained," Maya says. She still has her book in hand. Her index finger holds her place. "Some people need different perspectives to see what's right. If they were infected, I'm sure they would see the justice in being allowed to die naturally, but as it is, they just want to stay virus-free, and the Wolves have been successfully ensuring that for almost a year."

"Brandon," Olly says. "Would you like to explain your plan?"

The group focuses its attention on Brandon. He's still wearing the Wolf pants, but Olly gave him a green t-shirt to wear since the uniform top was too tight. Even in his strange outfit, the way he carries himself with confidence and humility makes everyone gravitate toward him. He's a natural leader.

His eyes scan the warehouse. "Are there cameras in here?"

"Six and three o'clock," Olly says, his eyes fixed on Brandon. "We have Defects here who worked security before their implants stopped working. They say there is no audio, only video. They can't hear us."

"Good," Brandon says. "It's not much, but here's what we have: The goal is to find the children and disable the Wolf Web operating system long enough to get the hell out of this place. Charlie used the Wolf Web to set a timer that will unlock the door to this room at midnight tonight. At the same time, the door to the armory will be locked, leaving the few Wolves that stay here overnight unarmed. The children and the control board are on the top floor, but we want to attack the Wolves on the first floor. The Wolves will be alerted that we've escaped and will hopefully rush to the armory. We will wait for them to come back unarmed to attack them."

"But we're not killing," Edda says. "We're *incapacitating*."

"Yes," Brandon says. "Knock them out, lock them in a room, do what needs to be done on the first floor so that we have the fewest possible problems on our way up. If we do run into armed Wolves, the goal is to disarm them. The Triangle Blade and Alpha Rifle cause damage to the Wolf uniform, so use their own weapons against them if you can. *If*," he emphasizes the word to reassure Edda, "and *only if* the Wolves are armed and the only way to rescue the children is to kill them, so be it. We are, in a sense, going to battle here."

A screeching sound pierces through the room, bouncing off the concrete walls and disrupts the conversation.

"Resi Kepler?" Julia's voice asks over a speaker. "You have a visitor. Please come to the exit with your back facing the door and your hands in the air."

"It must be my mom," I say. "What time is it?"

"8:40," Olly says.

I'm not sure what to do. How will I help the Defects if I'm gone?

"Go, Resi," Cole says. "We will still move forward with the plan. If you go to June's office, maybe you can find a way to shut down the control board."

"I don't know what to say to her," I confess. "I'm not ready to see her again." I need some time to figure this out.

"Resi Kepler," Julia's voice projects once more. "Please come to the front with your back to the door and your hands in the air."

"I don't think you have a choice, Rez," Brandon says. "You should go."

"When something needs to be said, you'll know," Edda says.

I stand and follow Julia's instructions to leave the holding room. When the door opens, a Wolf pulls my arms down and locks them behind my back. He extends his Triangle Blade out in front of me. Then we walk into the dark hallway, where we met Julia earlier today. When the door closes, I see six other Wolves poised with their weapons. Behind them is Dr. Francis Locke.

"Locke?" My blood starts to heat my skin, anger consuming me at the sight of him. "What the hell are you doing here?" Now that I'm not in his office trying to fool anyone, I have an insatiable need to hit him.

"Thank you, team," Dr. Locke says to the Wolves. "You can go now. You too, Julia. Give us a minute."

The Wolf drops my arms. As soon as everyone is out of sight, I rear back and swing my fist toward Locke's face. He blocks it, wrapping my fist in his hand with more strength than I expected. He holds my other wrist down when I try again.

"You bastard! Where is Sarah? Take me to her!" I demand, pulling to get my arms away from him.

"Resi, stop." His voice is soft and steady. It's maddening.

"Stop?" I struggle against his hold, anger fueling me as images of Locke taking blood from Sarah flash through my head. "I can't believe I've trusted you for so long just to find out that you're—"

"It's your dad."

My heart pounds in my ears, beating so hard I feel the pulse in my fingertips.

"What *about* my dad?" I already know the answer, but I need to hear it.

He releases my wrists. "I just came from the hospital." His eyes are tired, sunken. He reaches into his pocket, then hands me the keys to my car and my cell phone. The Wolves must have confiscated them while I was in shock. "You need to go see him."

Since seeing the Afterthought of Dr. Locke as a Wolf, I've vilified him in my mind. His face would be sneering, his eyes would be dark and pointed, he would do and say vile things that would make me hate him. But what I see right now isn't evil. It's someone who cares about me. I hate that I understand the moral dilemma: These are good people who have been manipulated into believing in something that is hurting others. This gesture of Locke's is surely not something that has been approved, but he's risking getting into trouble to allow me to see my father.

"Mom?" I ask.

"She doesn't know yet," Locke says. "I've been trying to get a hold of her, but she won't see anyone.

You need to go now."

He opens the back door. This is literally my Get Out of Jail Free card and I know I have to take it. I hesitate, though, unsure of what to say. Strangely, I want to throw my arms around Dr. Locke and hug him before I go. I hate him, and yet I long for the simple comfort of human touch—comfort from my dad's friend.

"Go!" he says.

That one word cures me, fills with contempt once more at the audacity he has to command anything of me. I scowl, turning away from him with a hateful chuff.

I run out the door and duck into the ticket booth to grab Charlie's computer. I pull at the loose piece of wood hiding the device, but it doesn't fall forward like it should. I wedge my hand behind it, but my fingers barely graze the edge of the laptop. I try to pry the wood away again. It's stuck.

None of this is right. This isn't how it's supposed to be. I shouldn't be clawing for a laptop before heading to say goodbye to my father while everyone else I love is in danger. It shouldn't be my own mother who put me in this position.

I squeeze my eyes shut, and every muscle in my body tenses, pushing back against the pain threatening to overwhelm me. I take the piece of wood in both hands, and with a shout, break it off the wall completely, then slam it on the ground with all my might. Again. And again. And the wood splinters and breaks until it's in pieces before me.

I gasp for air, realizing I'd been holding my breath. With all the energy I just used, I feel like the whole booth should be in shambles, but it's one tiny slat of broken wood. My lungs are spastic as I laugh through uneven breaths, and I push the heels of my palms against my eyes, so tears don't find their way to my face. I shake my head and steady my breathing. The pain can wait. There's too much at stake tonight.

I grab the laptop and bolt toward my car. It's a fifteen-minute drive to the hospital, but I need to stop at the lab first for a few essential supplies.

He kept himself alive for eleven months, breathing on his own. When the breathing center of the brain is intact, the person stays alive even in a coma because they can oxygenate their own body. If it shuts down, they need the help of a ventilator to breathe, sometimes referred to as "Life Support". Once they're on Life Support, the family gets a call. The call says "your loved one is no longer breathing on his own. You should prepare yourself to say goodbye."

Dr. Locke was my call.

I arrive at the hospital and walk up the stairs to his floor. My heart is still hammering. I glance at my phone. 9:10. I don't have much time to spend with my dad before I go back to help, but I need to do this. Every nurse I pass in the hallway gives me a sad, knowing look. I hate sympathy. It's negative attention for a negative event in which no one knows how to act. It's an awkward, unpleasant exchange and I never know what to do with it.

I walk into Dad's room where a doctor and two nurses wait. The cardiac monitor is the first thing that strikes me: normal sinus rhythm. It's inconceivable to me that the simple flip of a switch on the ventilator will stop such a perfect heartbeat. I take in my father, detesting the sight of him with a tube down his throat. His face, as it has been since the explosion, is pale and lackluster.

"Would you all give me some time with him?"

"Of course," one of the nurses says. They file out. "We'll be right outside. Come and get us when you're ready."

I dig in my purse when the door closes to find Sarah's iPod and place the buds in Dad's ears, then press Play. I watch for any change in his state or even his heart rate.

"Dad? Can you hear me?"

Nothing.

I throw off my jacket and move a chair against the door, then I get the IV supplies from my purse. It's the last time I'll do this, I swear to myself. I retrieve the Propofol from my purse after placing the IV and I draw it up in a syringe.

The last time I did this, my blood pressure dropped.

An unused liter of Normal Saline hangs next to my dad's bed. I get up and scour through cabinets and drawers until I find tubing. I prepare the saline, then attach it to my IV.

Once the saline starts, I grab my own headphones, place them into my ears, and press Play. I lay down on the poorly cushioned couch by my father's hospital bed, push the Propofol into my vein, and fall asleep.

CHAPTER 32

Dad hums to himself as he drives, even though the radio is off. No matter the day or circumstance, he's always upbeat. Music is everywhere. His incessant humming used to annoy me. Now, I savor each sound and the vibrations of his chest as the notes resonate through his body.

I notice the sleeves of his white coat as he grips the steering wheel. He's driving home from the hospital.

It worked. I wasn't sure I could get into the Afterthoughts of someone who is braindead since he's technically still alive, but it worked. I did it.

He pulls into the driveway of his house, but when he reaches for his keys to turn the ignition off, he pauses. After a beat, he reverses and drives away from the house to park down the street. I laugh to myself in his body, knowing that Dad always did this so other people could park in the driveway when they come to the party later.

Party, I realize. This is the day of the party. I sense it. It's April 17th: the day of the bombing.

He walks toward the house and steps up on the curb of the walkway.

"STOP!!!"

My scream is so loud that if it had been any other moment, I'm positive my voice would have echoed through Dad's body. But I can't hear my own scream over the booming explosion that is now frozen in front of me. I'm making sounds, but I'm not sure what they are. They aren't words or cries or whimpers, just sounds. But I can't speak.

In a heartbeat, my childhood home disappears into furious flames of gold, red, yellow, orange, and black. The colors violently soar in majestic, round patterns. Debris hovers, frozen in the air, thrown in all directions. Every object in sight, no matter how strong and sturdy—trees, lampposts, cars—lean away from the source, repulsed by shockwaves, bowing to its power. I'm paralyzed by the wonder of how something so glorious is so deeply devastating.

The blow of the explosion pushes my father's body backward. His feet hover just above the ground. His head is thrown forcefully toward whatever is behind him. I feel the searing heat burn against Dad's skin. His lungs compress in the pressure of the blast. Debris stabs his leg. Fear. Whether it's his fear or my own doesn't matter. If this moment continues, not a second will pass before my father's head is hit so hard that it will put him in a coma and eventually lead to his death.

In every previous Afterthought, I could scream or speak inside the body, but no outward expression was made. The people I inhabited were completely unaware of my presence. I could pause a moment or find a certain memory to explore. Still, when I've wanted to cry or lash out or move a different direction, the action was stifled by the person's own outward expression.

But in this frozen moment, my own tears soothe my father's burning cheeks as they fall from his eyes. I know they're mine because they're the only things that aren't paused in the memory.

I close my eyes and Dad's close with them.

"Anything else," I beg. "Please, Dad. Anywhere but here."

I open my eyes. There's nothing.

I try to get an idea of where I am. My head turns where I direct it. I'm not confined by someone else's body. I lift my hands to my face. They're mine. I find my feet. I'm standing, but everything around me is dark. I'm not sure what I'm standing on, if anything at all.

"My gorgeous girl."

I spin around to the sound of my father's voice. He stands five feet away, maybe ten. It's hard to tell in the dark chasm. He's the man I remember. Not the one in a coma, but the one eager to tell stories and share discoveries. He's full of color, his hair is combed, his face shaved, he wears a royal purple dress shirt and gray slacks. His eyes are bright. He's Dad.

He smiles. I miss his smile.

"Dad?" I rasp. I want to run to him, but I'm afraid to move in case I disrupt whatever anomaly is happening to allow this moment. "What is this? Where are we?"

Dad surveys our environment and glances down at his own body. "I don't know," he says. "This is new for me too."

"The Afterthoughts... I was in your Afterthought, then I appeared here."

Dad cocks his head. "You see Afterthoughts? How do you know that's what I called them?"

"Charlie found your file."

"Clever girl, that Charlie."

"Why didn't you study them more?" I ask. "You

could have figured out why we have this ability and what it's for."

Dad grins even brighter. He loves when I question things. I have the mind of a researcher. "Some things aren't meant to be understood until the Afterthoughts are yours," he says. "I spent my life studying the world and discovering explanations for its phenomena, finding cures for its diseases, fixing brains that are minimally understood."

"Fixing all but your own," I murmur.

He chuckles. "Poetic, don't you think?"

I roll my eyes at the implications, a half-smile on my lips.

"There it is! It wouldn't be a proper reunion without a proper eye roll," Dad jokes.

"I tried to research the Afterthoughts, sweetheart," he says. "But it quickly became clear to me that they were a gift that wouldn't have an explanation in this life." He studies me for a moment, then examines his arms, touches his chest. "Does this mean I'm…"

"Not yet," I say. "But you're on a vent. Your heart is beating, but you're not breathing on your own anymore. You've been in a persistent vegetative state for almost a year."

"Has it really been that long?"

I tilt my head to the side. "You know you've been in a coma?"

"Oh yes, I know. But I don't recall anything specific." He stops for a beat and squints his eyes. "The Afterthoughts reach the braindead as well. Amazing." Then I see his scientist face—one that is constantly in awe of the world. He has a child-like wonder about him whenever he discovers something new.

"I learned to control them, too." I love to make him proud. "If I listen to music while I sleep, I'm able to go to a certain memory or pause the memory if I need to. You're listening to music right now too."

"That's marvelous," he says, fascinated by my cleverness. "Activating the entire brain to control your gift. You're brilliant, my girl. Tell me, how did you first discover the Afterthoughts? Who died?"

My face falls. Names and faces pass through my mind. It's hard to remember which one came first, but they all circle back to the Wolves. Not only does Dad not know why he is in a coma, much less does he know the state of the nation—that his wife has killed over a thousand people in the year since he was attacked.

Then, I realize it for the first time.

Mom killed *him*.

"What's wrong, Resi?" he asks.

I'm not sure if I should tell him everything. Or anything at all. "Dad," I start. "So much has happened. We're at war with these terrorists who are killing everyone who has a certain virus. We call them Wolves. You are in a coma because you were in the first attack."

His face contorts and his eyes lower in thought. "Your mother?"

I panic silently. I want to let him rest peacefully. Maybe he should think she's dead rather than die knowing that she's the mastermind behind such horror. It was better when that's what I thought. I shake my head solemnly.

He observes me skeptically. I think he's going to say something else, but he stops, rubs his head. "The explosion," he says. "It's the last thing I remember."

There's a long, quiet moment of grief. It's something I think I've needed for eleven months.

Dad inspects his feet and taps his toe in front of him, cautiously, testing the new environment. When his foot hits the ground, and he sees that we're still here, he takes three more strides before gathering me into his arms. I crumble into him, hug him with all my strength. He's warm and familiar. I feel like a child in his embrace—cherished and protected.

"You're so strong," Dad says. "But don't be so strong that you don't let others in. There is strength in numbers. The hardest times in life are the times you need your friends the most. Your mother and I have left you more money than you'll know what to do with. You will never be without."

The idea hits me as he says it. "Dad, I can use the money to keep you on Life Support. I don't know how I got here, but I'll figure it out and talk to you this way. Maybe this is possible because you're still technically alive."

He takes my face in his hands and dips down, so his eyes are even with mine. "I'm not there anymore, Resi. You know that. A machine is pushing oxygen through my lungs, and my heart is beating, but I'm not there. It's time for me to move on, find out what comes next. Take me off the vent."

But I'm scared. "What if what's next is nothing?"

His eyes crinkle. "How can you say that? You dream the memories of the dead. Don't you see? Their bodies are asleep, but their souls are still wide awake. If their memories live on, so must they. Life just takes another form, and I, for one, cannot wait any longer to find out what form it will be."

I scrunch my nose. "You mean like heaven or reincarnation?"

"All I know," Dad says as he sweeps a strand of hair back and tucks it behind my ear, "is that whatever is next, it involves completion—wholeness. I will finally see what I've studied my whole life: the workings of the universe. Maybe to fully understand it, you have to be taken out of it."

My father's bright eyes begin to blur. I hold on tighter and tuck my head back onto his chest. "I'm waking up," I choke out.

"Listen to me, Resi," Dad says with urgency. "When I'm gone, go to my memory of your mother on April 8th in the research office."

I glance up at his blurry face. "What?"

"It might explain some things you need to know. I love you, Resi."

"Dad, wait!"

I fall off the couch and wake up on the floor of Dad's hospital room.

CHAPTER 33

"Time of death: 22:15," the doctor says. He pats my shoulder. "I'm sorry for your loss, Resi. Astor was one of the most brilliant and vibrant men I knew. I'll give you some time with your father again."

I've known for months that this day would come. Hell, there were even days that I hoped it would come sooner, that he would be freed from this limbo. I've said goodbye to him several times in the months leading to this moment, but now that it's here, I'm confused, lost. Every single one of my friends is holed up in a prison preparing for battle, and I'm standing in a hospital room hardly able to move.

April 8ᵗʰ, I recall Dad telling me.

I force myself out of my daze, and put the earbuds back in dad's ears.

"Okay, *this* is the last time," I tell myself, laying back down on the hospital couch. I hook myself back up to the fluids, draw up the Propofol once more and put myself to sleep.

"I just have to tell you," June says. "Please don't hate me, Astor. Please. Please don't hate me."

"June, calm down," I find myself saying through Dad's body on April 8ᵗʰ. I've never seen my mother so frantic. Her eyes are bloodshot, and her hair is a mess, sticking out from her ponytail as she paces the research office. "What is that machine you're building out in the lab?"

"It's not only Alice." Mom's speech is rapid and pressured, as if she's been mustering up the will to say it for ages. "It's everyone that got my trial drug. Every single one."

"What about them, Honey?" Dad approaches her, his steps soft and voice low. "Our friends who were trying your drug were loving it. I need you to explain the problem."

Mom leans her hands against the table. "Alice's disease," she says.

"It's horrible, I know. But because of you, she has lived without pain for the last year. At least she got to have that experience before this illness hit her."

"No, Astor," Mom says. "Everyone who tried my drug is getting sick."

"What?"

"They take the drug and their pain is completely gone. Several months later, they get the same exact disease Alice has with the same exact progression she experienced. It's violent and contagious, and... I can't cure it."

I can tell my father is starting to panic, but he remains composed. "Okay. It's okay," he says. I'm not sure if he's comforting my mom or himself. "How did this happen? What is in the drug that caused a virus?"

Mom slumps into a chair and throws her head into her hands. "I don't know," she cries. "I'm an expert in two areas: pharmacology and infectious diseases. A disease I was researching must have gotten into the mix while I was creating the drug. But nothing I have in my lab resembles this disease. I have no idea how this happened."

"Okay, okay." Dad walks over to her, rubs her back with one hand. "We can do something about this," he says. "There must be ten or eleven people with the virus then, right? You just gave it to our neighbors with chronic pain to try it out."

"Astor," Mom sobs. "I only *started* it with our neighbors. The FDA wouldn't push my trial through, and you know how strongly I believed in this new pain relief. So, Francis Locke introduced me to some high-profile pharmaceutical reps he knew would be on board with my drug. I made deals with the largest pain-relief names in the nation. Illegally. Tylenol, Advil, and Motrin."

What? Those medications are so common and widespread. I'm surprised everyone in the world isn't infected.

"We tracked the bottles that we mixed my drug into so we could keep track of whether it helped their pain better than those brand-names. It did. But now they're all infected."

Dad's mind is reeling. I can feel his shock. In that one speech, he found out that his wife lied to test her drug illegally, and she accidentally infected dozens of people with a deadly virus.

"How many people did your drug go out to?" he asks.

Mom sucks in a breath. Her voice trembles. "Over two million people."

Holy shit, I think.

"Holy shit," Dad says.

Mom abruptly straightens up and brushes Dad

away. She stands. "It's going to be fine. I'll fix this."

Dad clenches his fists, then releases them. He makes a conscious effort to keep his voice calm. "Honey, you need to report this. Just own up to it. We'll pay the consequences, but it's better than trying to cover it up."

Her face scrunches up as more tears wet her face. "I've tried," she sobs. "But I can't. I can't fail. These are the two things I'm best at, the things people know and love me for, and I screwed both up completely. My two areas of expertise merged to potentially kill thousands of people. The only things I'm good at have failed, Astor. I'll be a joke." She pauses and keeps her head low as she speaks. "No one can know. You can't tell anyone. Especially Resi. She'll never forgive me."

"Shh. Shh." Dad tries to console her. "June, this is your anxiety talking. You know how it can make you do crazy things sometimes."

"No." Tears stream from her eyes as she locks onto his. "I already have a plan to contain the virus, but this part can never get out, okay? Please help me with this. You can't let anyone know this is my doing."

Dad gawks, caught between his morals and his love for his hurting wife. "June, maybe we should talk about this when you're less—"

"You can either help me or stay out of it. I've already contacted the CDC and have been in touch with the president." Her tears begin to subside as she speaks more factually than emotionally. I watch as she shoves her feelings to the side.

A familiar skill.

"The President… of the United States?" Dad asks.

Mom flicks the tears from her face. "Yes. All they

know is that I've discovered a disease that needs to be contained. So, we're coming up with a plan to contain it. They're sending me some of the best military personnel, and I'm building a system that will fix everything. But as far as they know, we have no idea how the disease broke out."

"Is that what the computer system is out in the lab?"

"Yes," she says. "I told Charlie to take a few days off so I could work all of this out. I knew you wouldn't approve, but I needed to tell you. Now that I have, I need you to promise that you will at least keep all of it quiet. Please."

After a beat, Dad nods, still stunned by all the information Mom has just impaled him with.

"I'm so sorry, Astor," she says, a glimmer of emotion poking back through her hard exterior. "I want to be stopped." The pitch in her voice rises. "That's why I'm telling you. My perfectionism and self-preservation instincts... They are too intense." Her chin quivers. "I don't know how because you would never intentionally hurt me, but someone else has to pull the trigger. I can't do it myself."

She leaves as Dad stands in the office with his jaw unhinged.

I awake to a chiming sound coming from Charlie's computer, which I had hidden in my bag of supplies. I rub my eyes and groggily roll over to open it. The Wolf Web is still open on the desktop, and messages are rolling in.

JS: I NEED TO HEAR THIS STRAIGHT FROM ALPHA BEFORE WE ACT.

PW: IF WE WAIT TO ACT, OTHERS WILL BE INFECTED. THIS IS NO DIF-FERENT FROM ANY OTHER ASSIGNMENT.
ML: IT'S VITAL TO THE CAUSE. ANYONE WITH THE STAIN MUST BE TERMINATED. JUDY GAVE THEM THE ENTIRE 14 DAYS. I ADMIRE THAT, BUT NOW WE TERMINATE.
CZ: I BELIEVE IN THE CAUSE, BUT WE WERE TAUGHT EARLY ON NEVER TO HARM CHILDREN. WHAT CHANGED?

My heart skips and I sit up straight, ignoring the bit of nausea that wraps around my gut. "What children?" I whisper. I search the Wolf Web for the page that lists the targets. I click through maps that show where the infected are located, the IDs of the Wolves, camera surveillance of people in their homes, at work, at bars. Messages keep coming through.

LL: THAT WAS WHEN WE THOUGHT THEY WERE IMMUNE. IF THEY SHOW THE STAIN, THEN WE CAN'T USE THEM TO FIND THE CURE ANYMORE. I'M WITH ML ON THIS.
PW: I'M IN AS WELL. THOSE WHO ARE TRUE BELIEVERS IN THE CAUSE WILL INITIATE TERMINATION.
ML: ALPHA'S APPROVAL IS IN. TERMINATION IS APPROVED.

WHAT?

Finally, I find the page that lists everyone the Wolves are keeping tabs on. But the names are listed in the thousands. I go to a search engine at the top of the page and type SARAH DURAN. I click on her name and the options I saw in Tyler's Afterthought pop up: ASSESSED, CEAR, IMMUNE, TARGET. *Immune* was checked but now has a large, red X over the green check. Another check is over the word *Target*.

"No no no no no no!" I click the word *Target* to see if I can change it, but another list pops up: HIDDEN, STAINED, BEYOND. *Stained* is checked and it won't let me take the check off. Below the word is a note:

WOLVES,
ONE OF OUR EXPERIMENTS TO FIND A CURE HAS GONE WRONG. EACH OF THE CHILDREN SHOWED THE STAIN AT MIDNIGHT EXACTLY 14 DAYS AGO. I WANTED TO GIVE THEM THE FULL TWO WEEKS OF LIFE BEFORE THEY WERE TERMINATED, SO I WAITED UNTIL TODAY TO ANNOUNCE IT. BY MIDNIGHT TONIGHT, ALL TEN CHILDREN WILL GO INTO THE BEYOND.

WE MUST TERMINATE THE CHILDREN BY MIDNIGHT TONIGHT.
METHOD: INCINERATE.

-JUDY

I scramble around the Wolf Web to find the surveillance of the Astrodome. I don't see a countdown to any doors being opened or the armory being locked. The only countdown is to the termination of the children. It's 11:15 PM. I have forty-five minutes. I don't know how to set a countdown like Charlie did, and I don't know if the Defects are ready, but I see the *Unlock* button to the holding room. I press the button to free the Defects, then shut down every camera in the Astrodome.

I throw myself over my dad's chest. "I love you so much, Dad," I say, my voice vibrating. He's right. This lifeless body isn't him. It hasn't been him since the bombing.

The bombing arranged by my mother.

With a fire consuming my chest, I leave to face my father's murderer.

CHAPTER 34

I drive to the Astrodome in a fury. No games this time. I don't park far away or time my entrance. I pull my car up right next to the door, run straight to it, and punch in the code: 7-8-2-4-6. The door unlocks. I push it open.

To my surprise, no one is guarding the door.

I find the stairs by Section 6 to start working my way up to the top floor, but a large hand covers my mouth and pulls me into a corner. I'm about to scream, but he spins me around.

Brandon.

He holds a finger to his lips to tell me to be quiet. Olly and Charlie are with him. Olly's eyes are alert, paying attention to his surroundings. Charlie is also alert, but in a petrified way.

"The doors opened early," Brandon says. "Julia is knocked out, but she'll be fine, and we've all scattered to hide. We can't find the Wolves anywhere, but we assume they're trying to get into the armory in the basement. When they realize it's locked, they'll come back empty-handed, and that's when we'll attack. We gave some of the other Defects the bats since Olly and I can fight without weapons."

I shake my head as I process his information. "Brandon, I'm the one who unlocked the door. Someone changed Charlie's plan. There was no countdown to unlock the door to the holding room or to lock the armory. The only countdown was for the children to be incinerated at midnight."

Even in the shadows of the dark corner, I can see the color drain from Brandon's face. "Where is she?" he asks, the volume of his voice no longer discrete.

"I don't know," I answer. "But we know the incinerator is by the offices." I check my watch. "We only have fifteen minutes."

Brandon runs out of the corner and yells as loudly as possible, "ABORT THE PLAN. WOLVES ARE ARMED. DEFECTS TO THE TOP FLOOR!"

We sprint up the stairs. Brandon hurdles several steps at a time. I don't feel the burn in my legs, or the wind leave my lungs. I'm full of energy and purpose. We watch for Wolves along the way, but we see none. We reach the top and take the second entrance on the right, past Mr. Rickles Nachos and Chili concession, then up the next flight of stairs and down the hallway with the abstract paintings.

We come to an abrupt halt. At least thirty Wolves guard the incinerator, fully dressed in their uniforms, armed with their guns and blades poised. Other Defects trickle in and freeze at the same sight. I estimate around forty Defects. We have more manpower, but our fists and bats are nothing compared to the Wolves' weapons and protective uniforms.

I spot my mother standing in uniform, sans mask, in the doorway of her office across from the incinerator. She stares at me, her eyes sad and defeated. My entire body bubbles with anger as she lowers her head and walks into her office.

"Where's my daughter?" Brandon yells.

The Wolves don't move or speak. They stay in

position.

"Where are the kids?" he yells again. They don't respond.

I step toward my mother's office. It's clear to me that she's the best place to start, but before I take a second step, Brandon lets out a thunderous battle cry and charges toward a Wolf, prompting the rest of the Defects to fight. I'm sure he started the battle more out of emotion than strategy, which can't be a good way to begin.

I scream when a Wolf lifts his Triangle Blade above Brandon's head and jabs it down toward his chest. Brandon stops it with his own hands on the Wolf's wrist to keep the blade away from his skin. I start toward Mom's office again.

"Duck!" someone yells as they push me to the ground. I hit the floor and tumble into someone's legs right as a blade slices cleanly through a wooden base-ball bat where my head would have been. The sliced half of the bat falls and hits my shin, and the legs I tumbled into fall over me. A woman in camo pants lands on her back.

"Are you okay?" she asks me.

"Yeah, thanks," I say in a breath. But my hope starts to dwindle when I see four Defects on the ground. We're losing quickly. I scramble to my feet and find Charlie in a corner. "I don't know what to do without a weapon," I say. "I need to get to my mom, but this whole thing is happening right in front of her door."

Charlie doesn't answer. Maybe she's in shock.

I search the mob for Brandon again. He's still struggling against the Triangle Blade. The Wolf knees him in the gut, and Brandon lands on the ground at a disadvantage with the blade coming down from above him.

A shot fires. Maya flies back, doubling over at the waist. She hits the wall and slumps over. A direct hit to the abdomen like that will damage her organs and cause a bleed. She won't survive. As several people stare at Maya, Coen snatches the rifle from the shooter's hands and whacks him over the head with it.

The whimpers of children sound through the room, and a new group of yet another twenty Wolves marches in. They carry the ten children through the chaos to the Incinerator. We're outnumbered now.

I spot Sarah and my heart leaps as quickly as it sinks. She clings to her pillow in a silky blue nightgown. One Wolf carries her while another guards them. She struggles and wiggles but the Wolf's hold on her is strong.

"Daddy?" Sarah notices Brandon on the ground, eyes him as the Wolf continues to carry her through the battle. "DADDY!" she screams. She frees an arm from the Wolf and reaches her hand out towards him even though he's several yards away. "Daddy, help!"

"Sarah!" Brandon shouts. His strength multiplies at the sight of her. He pushes back, advancing the Triangle Blade towards his opponent, but he can't get off the ground for better leverage.

The incinerator door opens, and the children are thrown in one by one. Sarah wails, reaching for Brandon.

"I'm coming, Sarah!" he yells as she moves closer to the blaring whiteness of the room. The Wolves struggle to keep the kids inside the door as they push more in.

I see my mother moving around her office out of the corner of my eye. I'm reminded of Dad's Afterthought, Mom pacing back and forth with anxiety consuming her. How she let her fear of disapproval lead to murder. How she would rather have people think she's dead than to think she's a bad scientist.

Unable to wait on the sidelines anymore, I dash toward Brandon and grip the handle of the blade with him. I press forward and up with all my might until it comes loose and ends up in my hand. With a single thrust, I pierce through the Wolf's leg and pull the blade back, leaving him debilitated.

I offer the blade to Brandon.

"You take it," he says, then he runs forward to the line of Wolves.

"Resi, what do you need?" Cole yells from several feet away. Edda is next to him, fighting with a Wolf for a rifle, blood soaking her shirt at the shoulder.

"Get me to the office."

A blade swings toward me and I block it with mine. The Wolf draws his blade back and tries again, but I block him again. He pulls back once more and jabs the blade like a dagger toward my stomach. I try to block him, but I can't angle my own blade well enough. Right as the blade nicks my shirt, the blunt end of a rifle pounds into his head, and he collapses to the ground. It's Cole.

"Go," Cole says. "Brandon is holding his own on the right, Olly is guarding you to the left. You're clear."

He's right. The path to the office is open. The Defects took our advice and have used the Wolves' own weapons against them. There are far more Defects on the ground than Wolves, but the Defects left standing are all armed.

I sprint into the office and stop at the entrance. My mother faces away from the rampage happening just feet away from her.

"You killed him."

The office door closes behind me. The chaos outside, and the noise in my head become still. My thoughts are clear, my mind is sharp, and for once, my heart is open. Too open. Anger, sadness, resentment, and betrayal have been packed so tightly into me that I'm sure it will be safer if I explode than if my emotions do.

Mom turns from the bookshelf to face me. Her eyebrows crease in confusion at the statement. She opens her mouth to speak, but before she does, her face falls, and her eyes well up.

"Astor..." she whispers weakly.

"You killed him," I repeat. I step forward.

"Resi, you have to understand. I didn't know that he—"

"I know," I say. "You didn't know he was going home. He left work early that day to surprise you. I would have told you that a long time ago if I hadn't thought you were *dead*. But your selfishness and petty, weak inability to get out of your own head when you were anxious made you a monster.

"You killed my dad. You killed your husband. You left me without a family!"

Tension builds inside me until I can't hold it anymore. I try to keep them back, but my tears fight through to my cheeks. "I have missed you every single day for eleven months." My voice hitches, and my chest heaves as I let out a sob. I hate the tightness in my throat and the pit in my stomach. I glower at my mother, squarely. "I have been so, *so* lonely and hurt, and not a day has gone by that I haven't prayed to see you again," I say. "And this is the answered prayer? I finally see you just to find out that you're responsible for leaving thousands of people motherless, fatherless, childless? I find you, and you approve of the murder of ten children right outside your door?"

"I didn't expect this to happen," she says. "You have no idea how much I hate this."

"You abandoned me and terrified an entire nation all because you screwed up," I say. "You created this disease."

Mom's fallen face jolts up. "How do you know about that?"

"And when you realized that your big plan to cure pain failed, you couldn't stand the thought of your name being tarnished. So, you covered it up by murdering every person you infected. You started this. Now end it. Stop them from killing those kids."

"We have to kill them to protect everyone else," she says.

"You don't seriously believe that. If you did, you wouldn't have to brainwash your own army."

She shifts. Her eyes dart around the room. She tightens her face as she sucks in through her teeth. There's a dissonance inside of her that's tearing her apart.

"It's not brainwashing," she says. "It's—"

"Stop it!" I yell. "Just stop. It's over!"

"I can't, Resi. I can't stop it!" she cries. She bangs her fist on her desk. "This is for The Cause. Those children were marked as Stained by a warrior I trust.

They're going to die anyway. They were given the full 14 days, but if they're not dead before midnight, all of your friends out there will be infected too!"

I grab a hold of my mother and slam her back against the wall, pressing the Triangle Blade to the skin of her neck and extending to her jaw. "Then infect us!" I scream. I push into her more, not caring that the tip of the blade is starting to break the skin of its creator. "There is no Cause! Your Wolves aren't warriors. They're machines. Your *Cause* is murder! Just tell them to stop! They take their orders directly from you!"

Tears drip from my mother's cheeks and off her chin. "I want to, Resi," she whimpers. "I can't do it." She tightens her eyes again, grits her teeth. "I swear, I want to. You have to stop me. I can't do it."

The same words she told my father.

The door swings open with a bang. "Alpha," a man says. He lifts his gun to aim at me.

Mom whips her head toward him and holds her arm out. "Do not touch her!" Her hand quakes as she holds it in a stopping gesture. The children's cries echo through the office.

She winces in pain and fresh blood trickles from the metal in my hand. The Triangle Blade put a gash in her jaw when she turned against it.

Then I see it. As she faces the Wolf, I see the small, flesh-colored button behind my mom's ear.

I pull back. "You're being controlled too."

Mom shakes her head. "Not controlled. Adjusted. This was too hard for me in the beginning, so they gave me an implant."

"Who?"

"I can't stop myself from believing in The Cause,"

Mom says. "I'm fully aware of it all, but my moral compass is adjusted. I hate The Cause, Resi. But I can't help but fight for it above anything else."

My eyes land on the silver chain around her neck, the charm of our family emblem rests at her chest—a compass with an anchor for the arrow. I know what I need to do to stop my mom.

"Except for me," I say.

"What?"

"Some magnetic device in your brain isn't the arrow of your compass, Mom. Hope and love are. You can choose love over your Cause."

"Resi, I—where are you going?"

I hurry past the Wolf at the door and back into the chaos. The Wolves push the last child into the Incinerator and are trying to keep them in to shut the door as I plow through the weakening battle. I step over Kyle, willing myself not to look at him. I can't deal with a dead friend right now. Edda is doubled over against a wall to the left, breathing heavily, her hands are up in surrender as a Wolf holds a gun to her head. Travis and Olly are going strong, skillfully Blade-fighting against Wolves all around them. Cole holds Brandon up, and both men fight with one arm. Brandon is bleeding from his side but keeps fighting while Cole shoots carefully, using every angle he can see so as not to kill, but incapacitate by the bullet's bounce.

"Resi! Stop!" Mom yells from behind me.

There's a line of Wolves guarding the door of the Incinerator like pawns on a Chess board blocking everything valuable. The lever to turn it on is right behind them, next to the door. I run straight for the Wolves, disregarding any threats along the way, desperate to get there before the door closes. The Wolves posture themselves when they see me charging them. I find the best opening between two Wolves armed with Triangle Blades. I'll get sliced one way or another, but I have to risk it. One Wolf's eyes widen as I get closer. He recognizes me. The other doesn't.

I lunge forward and duck low to slide between the two Wolves from below waist level, where they have less control over their weapons. I cover my head. Pressure slices through my forearm. The wall catches me, and my foot barely makes it inside the door of the Incinerator to stop it from closing. As I stand, a Triangle Blade speeds toward my heart, but it stops when metal juts out through the Wolf's gut, followed by a river of blood. He crashes to the floor, and Olly appears in his place, pulling the blade back into his possession, his chest heaving.

I recall his words from earlier: Only Alpha's DNA in those ten seconds can stop the Incinerator. He moves his eyes from mine to the lever, and back to me, and I see understanding.

He nods. "Go!" And as I step into the Incinerator, he grips the lever and pushes it up.

The door closes with a dull thud, and the entire room fills with a deep hum that starts soft and builds slowly as the lasers power on. I turn away from the door.

Ten children huddle in a corner. I shiver as their terrified eyes stare back at me. *What did I just do?*

"No! Sarah! Resi! Let them out!" Brandon bangs on the door.

I acted on an impulse—one I'm now doubting. "Come on, Mom," I whisper.

"Resi?" Sarah's head pops up above the group.

The sound of the lasers powering on grows, and a voice projects overhead when Sarah runs to me.

"Ten. Nine."

Brandon's desperate pleas fade into the growing hum of the machine.

"Eight."

I take Sarah into my arms. Tears blur my vision as I hold her tightly. "I missed you so much, kid."

"Seven."

"I'm scared, Resi," she cries. The other children make their way over to me, grasping for any part of me they can hold onto.

"Six."

"Me too, Sarah. I'm scared too." Twenty arms hold onto me. I observe each of them.

"Five."

I don't see the wine-stain rash. All I've heard today is that The Stain is most prominent on the first and fourteenth days. But not one of these children has any semblance of a rash on their arms.

"Four."

I hold Sarah out in front of me and inspect her arms more closely. Nothing. "You don't have a rash. You're not infected."

"Three."

"No. We're the Immune," Sarah says. The lasers above us begin to brighten. A clicking sound indicates that they're opening, preparing to fire.

"Two."

Heat emits from above. I instinctively drape my arms around every kid that huddles around me, wishing I could spread myself over them to shield them from the rays. My body tenses.

"Please, Mom."

"One."

The room is swallowed up into pitch-black darkness.

CHAPTER 35

"What's happening?" a child cries.

"Am I dead?" another says.

I'm not sure I can answer either question. Twenty small hands cling to me for safety, but I'm just as scared and unsure as they are.

Lights above us flicker back to life. A dull, metallic thud turns our attention to the door, followed by the heavy clangs of several deadbolts as the door unlocks. It creeps open slowly. There's no squeak in the door hinges; no sweeping of the base across the floor. It's a dreadful silence.

It opens. The fighting outside the room has stopped, and a strange mix of people stare into the Incinerator: Wolves in gray and black uniforms; Defects in sweatpants, jeans, t-shirts, and military outfits; my friends; my mom. They peer in, maintaining tired, but defensive stances. It's a frozen battle scene. Edda is sitting against the wall, still held at gunpoint. Olly has a Wolf captured in his hold. Brandon is on his knees, his breathing labored. A Wolf tilts Brandon's head up with the flat part of a Triangle Blade under his chin. But there's no movement.

Mom holds a Wolf mask to her face like it's a hospital mask protecting her from a contagious disease. Blood drips from her other hand. She stopped the lasers with her DNA.

I exhale the release of the most colossal amount of tension.

"Get out of there, Resi," Mom begs. "They're going to go into the Beyond at any moment. You might already be infected!"

"But we're not—" Sarah starts. I nudge her and cut her off.

"No," I say. "You proved my point that you can still choose love over The Cause regardless of whatever is going on in your brain. You love me more than The Cause."

"Of course, I do," Mom says. "Now, please get out of there before you're infected."

"You told both Dad and me to make you stop. I'm not coming out of this room until you destroy the entire Wolf Web. Shut down the site and tear down the control center."

"Your dad? He told you that..." Her words falter. She cocks her head, scrutinizing me. "No. You saw," she says. "You have his Afterthoughts." She shifts, then lifts her injured hand to her eyes as if she is just realizing it's wounded. "Did he know that I've become..." She looks disgusted. The thought of the man she loved knowing who she had become kills her.

Now, it's clear.

June hates Alpha.

"No," I say with a soft firmness. "But I think he suspected."

After another beat of silence, Mom meets my eyes again. "Resi, without the operating system, I can't give orders, and without the Wolf Web I won't be able to track the infected. Everything revolves around it. We won't be able to stop people from going into the

Beyond."

"Then keep it, but you'll have to incinerate me with the kids."

"Resi!" Sarah protests.

I tug her close, and whisper, "Trust me."

"Resi, don't make me force you out," Mom says.

"This isn't you, Mom. I know you want this to end. So, end it."

She sets her face and clenches her jaw. She gestures at the Wolves to her left. "Get her out."

"No!" Brandon yells. He lunges toward my mom, but a Wolf stops him.

This isn't working.

The Wolf ordered to retrieve me gathers a few others, and they walk into the Incinerator. The kids scurry behind me as I move in front of them. "They're not Stained!"

"What?" Mom questions.

Two Wolves grab me, one on either side, holding my arms to walk me out. "None of these kids are Stained," I say again.

A third Wolf moves to the kids, grabs, and inspects a few of their forearms. "She's right. No Stains."

"That's impossible. Judy targeted them as Stained. She loves the children. She would never terminate them unless she absolutely had to."

"You said The Stain is most prominent on the first and fourteenth days. Even if it wasn't one of those days, I should at least see a subtle rash." I yank myself out of the Wolves' hold, march to Sarah and hold her arms out. "But today is day fourteen, and not one of these kids has any discoloration. They're perfect. And you were about to kill them because someone lied to you."

Mom's breath becomes ragged as her eyes frantically search the children from afar. She drops her mask. "How is this possible? Where is Judy? Why would she do this?"

"I haven't seen her since this morning," a Wolf says nearby. "She usually stays in her office after the children are done with school."

"Get everyone out of the Incinerator," Mom commands.

There's a soft sigh of relief as the children start to relax.

A wild scream causes them to grab onto me again. It's primal. Feral.

People outside the incinerator forget their current opponents and run toward the source. I unlatch myself from the kids and follow.

"Pat, Stop! What are you doing?" It's Olly's voice.

A man screams again—a long, unrestrained note.

I step outside the Incinerator. A chill runs through me, fills my lungs with ice. There's a tug on my arm. "Resi, what's happening?"

Sarah's voice brings me out of my stunned state. I twist her around, push her back into the Incinerator. "Don't look, Sarah. Stay here, and don't let this door close."

Olly has Pat in a chokehold while Brandon attempts to pry a Triangle Blade out of Pat's hand. There's a Defect on the ground, unrecognizable—blood spewing out of at least ten stab wounds. Pat's screaming continues as he shakes his head back and forth like an animal. If he was foaming at the mouth, I'd think he was rabid.

Brandon finally frees the Blade from Pat's grip.

Olly throws Pat to the ground to subdue him, but Pat bucks wildly. "Stop fighting, Pat. What has gotten into you?"

"Ahh, shit!" A Wolf bends over and holds his head like he is struck with a migraine. He moans in pain.

"Mitch, you okay?" a Wolf next to him asks with a hand on Mitch's shoulder.

"My head!" Mitch answers. Then his groaning dies off, and he drops his arms, the migraine seeming to cease. Mitch straightens his back. He turns to the friend trying to help him. He snatches his friend's rifle, presses it to his stomach, and shoots, propelling him across the room, blood draining from his mouth by the time he hits the ground. Mitch follows him, continues to shoot mercilessly into the already-dead man's body. Everyone else takes cover as the bullets bounce.

"Mitch, stop! That's an order!" Mom yells.

Mitch aims for the next person in his line of sight. Shoots. A Defect is hit in the head at point-blank range. It will kill him instantly.

What the hell is going on?

Wolves and Defects join to swarm the rogue man. They disarm and hold him back as he joins Pat in a wild fight, screaming like a madman.

"Their implants!" Olly yells. His knee is in the center of Pat's back on the floor, his arms barely controlling Pat's on either side of his body. He uses his full weight to keep him restrained. "The implants are malfunctioning. They have no moral compass."

I find my mom by the group restraining Mitch. "Did you mess something up when you turned off the

Incinerator?"

She looks down at the drying blood on her hand. "No, that's all I did." Then, her gasp is sharp. "But I left the system logged on."

Together, we sprint to the office. I turn the handle. It's locked.

"Who is in there?" There's a long, thin window in the door, but I can't see past a part of the wall to the operating system.

"No idea," Mom says.

Another deafening scream. I look back to see a woman clutching her head in pain.

"Restrain her before she kills someone!" I shout to anyone who isn't having their brains hijacked. When I return my attention to the door, Mom has a rifle above her head. She swings it into the window as hard as she can and shatters it, then reaches through the broken glass to turn the lock.

Mom poises to shoot as she makes her way into the office. She leans with her back against the wall, then pivots, spins and points. I'm charging in after her when I see her forehead crease in confusion.

Mom has her rifle pointed at Charlotte Clay, who is armed and aiming a rifle right back at my mother. Behind Charlie, the profile of a woman is pulled up on the operating system—a picture of a brain to the right. The temporal-parietal junction, where her implant is placed, is black.

"Charlie?" My head spins. This doesn't make sense. "What the hell are you doing?"

The barrel of Charlie's rifle drifts from my mother to me. I go numb. Charlie demands, "June, incinerate the children, or Resi dies next."

CHAPTER 36

My hands fly into the air of their own accord, surrendering before my brain has the chance to comprehend what's happening, caught between fear and utter confusion. Something is motivating her to do this. She must be afraid. "Charlie, it's okay. The kids aren't contagious," I say.

Charlie rolls her eyes. "I know, they're *immune*." Her voice is mocking. "I've heard everything you've heard today. And I'll be damned if some idiot grade-schoolers ruin this for me. I worked too hard." I've never seen her like this. She's different. Not herself.

"You worked too hard? For what?"

"Resi, what—"

I face one palm toward Brandon in the doorway. Shake my head. *Don't let anyone come in.* Charlie has lost it, and I don't know what she will do if she feels attacked.

"Why didn't I figure this out sooner?" Fury and frustration punctuate Charlie's words. "You've been alive this entire time?"

I remember Charlie in the ticket booth, her disbelief when she found out that Mom was alive. She was processing something different, realizing something no one else understood.

There's movement in the doorway again. Brandon has stepped into the room, hiding behind the wall with a rifle. He's mouthing something to Cole beside him.

"Drop the gun, June," Charlie says, the barrel of her rifle still staring me down. Mom's rifle starts to lower.

"No," I say.

Mom turns her head toward me, lifts the rifle again. "Resi..."

"She won't shoot me."

Charlie scoffs. "Like hell I won't."

There were no timers to open the Defects' door like Charlie claimed to have set. No plan to secure the weapons room. There was only one plan on the Wolf Web tonight—to incinerate the children. She hacked Judy's account.

"*You* want the kids dead?" I ask.

"Put the gun down, June!" she yells again, louder. The more irritated she becomes, the less confident I am about her not shooting me, but I don't let that show.

I swallow. "*Why*, Charlie?" My voice grows stronger. "Why do you want the kids dead?"

Spit sprays in front of her face when she yells at my mom again. "Put the damn gun down and turn the Incinerator back on!"

"Why, Charlie?"

"Put it down!"

"*Why?*"

"Because *no one* should be immune to my virus!"

"Your virus?"

"*Your* virus?" Mom echoes.

"Charlie, what the hell are you saying?" I ask.

"I've wasted eight years. Eight!" says Charlie. She jabs the rifle toward me in her fit. My breath shutters, but I don't allow myself to flinch. "Four years befriending you and planting ideas in your head about working with your parents. Two years perfecting this damn disease to contaminate it in your mothers' pain killers. A year waiting for the virus to kick in. God, I never expected it to be latent for so long. One person finally got sick. One! Alice. Then these *mysterious* terrorists arise and start killing everyone, but no one else was getting sick. No one needed my cure. I thought I had failed."

"You have a cure? *You* infected my mom's medicine?" I think back to our days at Johns Hopkins, Charlie's fascination with my parents, the DNA samples she took when she worked with Mom, all the time she spent in the lab working on her Ph.D.

Is she working on her Ph.D.? Was she ever?

"Of course, I have a cure," Charlie snaps.

All I can think about now is getting it to Brandon. I already feel lighter, even with a gun pointing at my head. I know he's there in the doorway. I refrain from looking at him, but I hope he heard. *You get to live, B. There's a cure.*

"I'm a genius, remember?" Charlie says. "I was floored when I figured out the Wolves had something to do with my virus. Your stupid little code words for Alice's disease progression gave it away, but I thought they stole it and killed you. I can't *believe* you're alive." She stomps her foot like a five-year-old having a tantrum. "Taking the Wolves down and getting rid of the children is the perfect way to set my plan back in motion, infect more people." She takes one hand off her gun and points to my mom. "You made me think I failed! You took away my fame. The fortune I would have made by now! So, if you don't put the gun down and turn the Incinerator back on, I swear I will crack Resi's head open with one shot." She takes hold of the rifle again with both hands, aims.

How did I not see this? How foolish am I? All the drinks we shared. The study sessions. The dance breaks. "I thought we were friends." My voice comes out scratchy.

Charlie's eyes dart between Mom and me. "And we could have stayed friends if *your mother* hadn't interfered." She lets out a frustrated growl. "I worked my ass off for you," she says to mom. "And you go AWOL and fake your own death?"

"Did you send Judy's message? Where is she?" Mom asks.

"You're worried about *Judy* right now? She's fine. I locked the door to her office and turned off all of her electricity so she couldn't call anyone."

"And why mess with the implants?"

Charlie shrugs a shoulder. "I tried to turn the Incinerator back on, but you had already stopped it." She smiles. I've seen the smile before, but it has never been so sickening, evil. "Figured if I can't incinerate the children, I'll have everyone go ape-shit on each other. It was working great until you barged in."

I watch my Mom. Her eyes move past me. Brandon is behind me in the doorway, but I can't look back at him without being obvious. There's no way for me to know what they're planning, but I have a feeling it involves me getting the hell out of the way.

"I'm not kidding, June. I'll shoot her!" Charlie yells.

Mom whips her head back to Charlie, then to me, then to Brandon, back to me.

I need to distract Charlie while they figure this out.

"You won't shoot me, Charlie," I say. "I'm your friend."

She sneers. "Yeah, you were my only real friend, Resi. And all it took was a couple dead parents for you to abandon me."

She's right. I avoided her for ten months. "I'm sorry. I should have stayed in touch. I was too upset, and I didn't deal with any of it well. I was selfish."

Charlie sees that my mom isn't paying attention to her, so she swipes the controller, exits the woman's profile, and opens another. The brain beside it is yellow at the temporal-parietal junction. If it were a Wolf it would be green. It's a Defect. She's about to cause another malfunction.

I'm right. She won't shoot me. But she will kill everyone else.

I don't know what my mom and Brandon are planning, but they're going to have to put it into action before another implant goes black.

"Now!"

As soon as I shout, I duck and roll through the doorway, and the blast of a gun tells me someone starts shooting. Brandon stays against the wall but whips his arm around the corner with his gun and shoots. Metal bangs and shatters, crashes and falls. They're destroying the operating system.

I start toward the Incinerator to make sure the kids are still okay, that the door hasn't shut. I know I was trying to save her from a murderous, Malfunctioned Defect, but what was I thinking pushing Sarah back into the Incinerator?

In the hallway, though, the Wolves have taken over again. There's no struggle, but the Defects are all in small groups behind armed Wolves.

"Seriously?" I say.

"Olly knocked the Malfunctioned out and we locked them in separate rooms," Cole says. "We let our guards down for a second and the Wolves turned on us."

A bulky hand lands on my shoulder and grips my shirt. I spin around, flinging his arm back. I shove at a Wolf's chest. "Touch me again and I'll see to it that my mother incinerates *you* next."

He glances in the direction of my mom's office. The crashing sounds begin to subside. He steps back, an arm up in surrender.

I get to the Incinerator. One small foot sticks out of the door to keep it from closing. I open it. Sarah sits with her eyes shut tight, her hands covering her ears, one leg tucked into her chest, the other wedged in front of the door.

"No!" Charlie cries. "You ruined everything!" She grunts and struggles as two Wolves escort her out of the office. She limps when she steps on her right leg. She must have been hit.

"Get her out of here," Mom instructs. "Keep her in holding until we know what to do with her."

Brandon walks up behind Mom. "You took cover in time?"

She nods. "I was under the desk before my first shot could bounce back at me. Thank you."

Several Wolves approach Mom. One snatches Brandon's rifle away when he's not expecting it and holds his arms behind his back.

"The hell, man?" Brandon says.

The Wolf at the front of the group speaks. "Alpha, we will help you rebuild. What will you have us do with the Defects?"

Mom doesn't seem surprised to see that her team has taken over. But everyone else is surprised by her answer.

"Drop your weapons."

The Wolves eyes flit to each other, and back to my mom.

"Ma'am?"

"Was my command unclear?" Mom says. "Drop your weapons."

Some of the Wolves slowly lower their rifles and Blades.

"But, Alpha," the Wolf says, "they will continue to threaten The Cause."

Mom steps forward, her stance set. "And will you continue to disobey orders?"

After a beat, the lead Wolf turns to his comrades with a nod. Each weapon lowers and the Wolves back away from the Defects.

I kneel in front of Sarah, and gently pull her hands away from her head.

She opens her eyes. "Is everybody still fighting?"

I can't help but lean in and kiss her forehead, then I shake my head. "It's over, Sarah. You're safe now."

I shift to allow her a view outside the door and I point to Brandon.

She darts out of the Incinerator. "Daddy!" Brandon drops his rifle and lands on his knees with his arms open. Sarah knocks him over in a tackle-hug. He holds onto her, moving his hand from her head to his eyes as he weeps into her hair.

The rest of the children follow me out of the Incinerator. I stop in front of my mom.

"The damage from the implants is already done," she says, reaching behind her ear. "Unless it stops working on its own, the Wolves moral compasses will always be aimed toward The Cause. I can track the virus with the Wolf Web, but without the operating system, I can't order any terminations." She lets out a long breath of air. "I'm going to try my damnedest to remedy this, Resi. But I'll need your help."

Mom rubs her neck, avoids my eyes. "I hope you'll be able to forgive me one day."

I see the vulnerable, loving woman I grew up with for the first time in eleven months. But there was more to her than I knew back then. The parts of her she didn't let me see as a kid are the exact parts of her that drove her to become Alpha.

"Mom, even before the Wolves existed, you lied to the government to save your own reputation and let them manipulate you into all of this. And we still have to deal with them, including President Hayden."

She bites her lip. "You're right. They might disagree with disarming the Wolves, but they will be happy to hear about the cure. And without my technology and tracking system, they have no idea how to control it. They can't do much without me."

I sigh and soften toward her slightly. "We'll figure it out."

She smiles sadly, turns to walk away. But something tugs at me to stop her.

"Mom?"

She backtracks. "Yeah?"

I lunge forward and hurl my arms around her

neck. "Thank you for not being dead."

Her arms tighten around my waist and she sinks into my embrace. Her weight is heavy against my tired body. She pulls back and observes me proudly. Her fingers run through my tangled hair, and she places a kiss to my head.

"The woman you've become," she says. "You're remarkable."

The invisible hand gripping my chest releases, and she kisses my head once more before stepping away to join a group of Wolves.

Edda drapes her arm around my shoulders. "Not a superhero, huh?" she says. "You did it, Resi."

I nudge her with my elbow. "No, not a superhero. I just used my mother's love for me against her to stop her from killing some kids." I look at her, feigning a calm, cool attitude. "No big deal."

"Uh huh," she says. "Tell that to those bags under your eyes."

I don't doubt that. Is it bedtime yet?

She tilts her chin over to Cole and Brandon. Cole is handing water bottles from a concession to Brandon and Sarah. "What are you going to do about those two?"

The two men shake hands. Cole plants himself next to Brandon, and they cheer as Cole gives Sarah a high-five. I eye Edda helplessly. "I have no idea."

"Oh, thank God you're okay, Kyle," I say as he and Travis walk over. "I saw you on the ground earlier, but I couldn't tell if you were dead or not."

"Thanks for stopping to check up on me," he jokes. "It seems I got knocked out for a minute. But I'm fine now."

Wolves leave a group where Mom is talking and

they gather behind Kyle and Travis. The Defects gather with Olly. Soon, a circle forms around me—my friends, the Immune, the Defects, and the Wolves.

Mom finds the front of the Wolf pack. "There are two people set to go into the Beyond tomorrow," she says. "We planned on terminating them today, both at 9:00 AM. It's 2:00 AM now. I have contacted both teams and ordered them to stand down. Resi, what would you like us to do next?"

My mother is handing over her control. In just a few words, I've become the leader of this pack. I take in the eyes focused on me. Some of them have been murdering innocent people for months. Most of them have implants that are ripe for mind control if the right technology gets into the wrong hands. Dead Defects and Wolves lie on the floor behind them. We ended the Wolf attacks, but now there's a deadly virus that will spread at any moment if we don't contain it.

Nine children need their parents.

My friends are injured.

My mom is alive.

Dad…

It's all too much, too soon.

Sleep would be so good right about now.

I don't know where to start. But all these people are looking to me to start somewhere.

"I…" Words. I need words.

"I'll start with the CDC," Cole says.

I find his face in the crowd. Of course. He works with infectious diseases.

"I'll explain that there's a novel virus and we will work with them to come up with a plan for quarantine and distributing the cure," he says.

"Thank you," I say. I hope he knows how much I mean it. He gave me a starting point. The cure. A To-Do list begins to form in my head.

"Olly," I say, searching through the herd until I see him. "When we finish here, you and I will go to the holding room to talk to Charlie. We may need to make a deal with her before she will agree to hand over the cure."

"Do you think she will?" he asks.

Fame and fortune—that's what Charlie said she was robbed of. The fame will be instantaneous once news of the virus gets out, though not quite in the way she expected. And a cure for a terminal virus shouldn't be difficult to fund. "With the right incentives, yes, I think she will."

"Done." He points to a woman I don't recognize. "Morgan," he says, "we'll need the advice of an attorney. Come with us?"

"Sure," Morgan says.

"Mom, keep the Wolves who were going to attack on standby," I say. "They will be taking the targets to the lab instead."

"The lab?" Mom asks. "The Kepler lab?"

I nod. "We engineered a section for isolation. We will also need to contact local and federal government leaders."

"I can help with that." One of the Wolves takes his mask off, then continues. "I work in the state capitol and I'm in contact with many federal officials."

"Thank you." I turn to Edda. "Will you start looking for the kids' families?"

"Of course," she says.

"I need a few volunteers to cover up our fallen

friends and someone to call a coroner to pick up the bodies."

"I'll do it."

"Me too."

I don't even know who said it, but I'll take it.

"What about the Malfunctioned?" someone asks.

Right. Mitch and Pat. They might tear their own heads off if they're left alone too long. "We will have to sedate them until we can get them to a safe place. The rest of you—find a group to help. When you can't find anything to do, go home. See your families. Let's get moving."

The group disperses with a buzz of new energy. It's a little disconcerting, and I'm not sure what I just did or said. We'll see how long it takes everyone to figure out that I don't know what I'm doing.

When enough people are out of the way, Sarah comes into view. I crouch down in front of her, so we're face to face. "Hey, you."

"Hey!" Sarah beams, her smile drawing out a joy inside me that I haven't felt since she disappeared.

"Do you have any idea how loved you are?" I ask.

She flings herself around my neck. "I love you, too, Resi."

I savor it, clutching her snuggly. "No more kidnappings. Promise?"

She giggles, then pulls back. "Promise. What happens now?"

"Well," I say, "remember how much everyone panicked and went crazy when the Wolves first started attacking?"

"Yeah..." Sarah says, drawing the word out.

"Soon we'll get to see how everyone reacts to a brand new, deadly virus."

Sarah slaps her forehead with her palm. "Oh, great."

"Mhm. Things are about to get pretty interesting."

We make our way through the Astrodome, lifting our wounded, leaning on one another for support, beginning new projects, and preparing to further disrupt society with our news.

Fallen Wolves and Defects are covered with blankets. I wonder what memories live on in them. I'll never quite get used to it, but I have a feeling that my adventures with the dead have only begun.

EPILOGUE

I wake with a start after another night sleeping by my mother's grave. It sounds strange, I know. One idiot at school found out about it in third grade and called me the Grave Sleeper, but I don't care. It helps me know her better. I didn't have enough time to know her while she was still here. Her legacy is one thing, but her Afterthoughts show me who she really was. They show me a family that made mistakes and forgave and fought for what was right. They show me a woman who learned to be strong enough to feel. I run my fingers over the emblem carved into the gravestone, a compass with an anchor for the arrow. My sister says it's a reminder that no matter where life takes us, hope and love will always be our anchor. Below the emblem is an inscription:

RESI KEPLER
BELOVED MOTHER, DAUGHTER, FRIEND
REBUILDER OF A BROKEN NATION

"Deka, did you sleep outside again? Mom would hate it if she knew you did this all the time," my sister, Sarah, calls from the house. She's twenty-two, ten years older than me, and has been taking care of me since Mom died.

I roll my eyes, a trait I'm told I get from Mom. "You love hearing my stories." I trudge back to the house, sleepy and stiff from a night on the ground. "And I'm just getting to the good parts."

"Yeah, okay," Sarah says, throwing her arm over

my shoulder when I stalk up to the porch. "I do like to hear about Mom's Afterthoughts. But I was there for a lot of them, you know. I have some stories of my own."

"How about you tell me a good one about Dad during breakfast?"

"Sure," she says. She crosses to the small table below a picture of Grandma and Grandpa kissing in front of a heart drawn on their whiteboards in the Kepler Research Lab. She reaches for an old record under the table and sets it on the record player. "But first," Sarah says, "we need a dance break."

THE END.

ACKNOWLEDGEMENT

To Mom and Dad: I can't tell you how happy I am that neither of you is in a coma, or a sociopath on a murderous rampage. Rather, you have fueled and supported my passions for writing, medicine, and music, and you have raised me to rest in love and hope, no matter what happens or where life takes me. The truths you've taught me from my childhood have grounded me and saved me. I love you and I am eternally grateful.

To my sisters, Rachel and Regina: You two were my very first readers, greatest supporters, and even better suggestion givers. It's also cool that we share DNA. Thanks for your ideas, edits, laughs, and drinks. Also, shout out to my bro-in-law, Rich, who hopes this somehow gets onto Audible. And to my nephews Gabe and Nate—I love you two the most.

To the FBI, who, as far as I know, has not flagged me, and has definitely not arrested me yet for all the weird shit I Googled while doing research for this book.

To Google for helping me with said research. I also blame you for any inaccuracies.

To my earliest readers: Lauren, Callie, and Laura. You were the first people to like this book who were not biologically obligated, and I'm forever grateful for your encouragement years ago when I started this. Each of you is so unique and I am beyond blessed to call you my friends. You have given me so much wisdom and help in this and many other journeys.

To my coworkers in the emergency room at LBJ General Hospital: You technically had nothing to do with this book, but you keep me on my toes and supply me with endless entertainment and inspiration. 2020 was a hard year for us, but I wouldn't have wanted to spend it anywhere else. And to my managers, thank you for not firing me for my eccentric emails and for always encouraging my writing. It means the world to me.

To every foster child everywhere: You are loved and wanted, and your worth is far greater than anything you could imagine. Keep going even when you feel down. Do good and seek the company of people who are peaceful and bright. You inspire me every day. Also, listen to music. It makes you happy and it is yoga for your mind.

Finally, to anyone reading this: I am grateful, amazed, floored, flabbergasted, and a thousand other words I could look up but my thesaurus gave up on me around chapter 3, that you would pick up this book and actually read it. Thank you for your time and your love of adventure. Resi and I hope to meet you again someday very soon.

ABOUT THE AUTHOR

Rene Fenner

Rene Fenner is an ER nurse in Houston. Sometimes Rene eats gluten when she's not supposed to and feels most anxious and alive while watching TV shows about serial killers. She lives in a house with a confused Roomba named Kevin. This is Rene's debut novel.

THE AFTERTHOUGHTS

www.ingramcontent.com/pod-product-compliance
Lightning Source LLC
Chambersburg PA
CBHW060342260626
47160CB00006B/2188